>>>>>

THE
TRANSFORMATIONS OF LUCIUS

OTHERWISE KNOWN AS

THE
GOLDEN ASS

BY
LUCIUS APULEIUS

TRANSLATED
BY ROBERT GRAVES

REVISED WITH
A NEW INTRODUCTION
BY MICHAEL GRANT

PENGUIN BOOKS

PENGUIN BOOKS

Published by the Penguin Group
Penguin Books Ltd, 27 Wrights Lane, London W8 5TZ, England
Penguin Books USA Inc., 375 Hudson Street, New York, New York 10014, USA
Penguin Books Australia Ltd, Ringwood, Victoria, Australia
Penguin Books Canada Ltd, 10 Alcorn Avenue, Toronto, Ontario, Canada M4V 3B2
Penguin Books (NZ) Ltd, 182–190 Wairau Road, Auckland 10, New Zealand

Penguin Books Ltd, Registered Offices: Harmondsworth, Middlesex, England

This translation first published 1950
Revised translation with a new Introduction 1990
5 7 9 10 8 6 4

Printed in England by Clays Ltd, St Ives plc
Filmset in Monophoto Bembo

PENGUIN  CLASSICS

THE GOLDEN ASS

ADVISORY EDITOR: BETTY RADICE

APULEIUS was born *c.* AD 123–5 at Madaurus, a Roman colony in Numidia. On the death of his father, a provincial magistrate, he was left a substantial amount of money. He went to the university at Carthage and afterwards to Athens, where he studied Platonic philosophy, among other subjects. After his initiation into the mysteries of Isis he studied Latin oratory in Rome and made a success at the Bar. Later he travelled widely in Asia Minor and Egypt, studying philosophy and religion. He wrote the *Apologia* (*A Discourse on Magic*) after being accused of gaining the affections and fortune of the widow he married by magic. His other works included *On the God of Socrates*, *Florida*, *On Plato and his Doctrine* and (perhaps) *On the Universe*. He died sometime after AD 180.

ROBERT GRAVES was born in 1895 at Wimbledon, son of Alfred Perceval Graves, the Irish writer, and Amalia von Ranke. He went from school to the First World War, where he became a captain in the Royal Welch Fusiliers. His principal calling was poetry, and his *Selected Poems* and *Collected Poems* have been published in Penguin. Apart from a year as Professor of English Literature at Cairo University in 1926, he earned his living by writing – mostly historical novels, which include: *I, Claudius*; *Claudius the God*; *Sergeant Lamb of the Ninth*; *Wife to Mr Milton*; *Proceed, Sergeant Lamb*; *The Golden Fleece*; *They Hanged My Saintly Billy*; and *The Isles of Unwisdom*. He wrote his autobiography, *Goodbye to All That*, in 1929. His two most discussed non-fiction books are *The White Goddess*, which presents a new view of the poetic impulse, and *The Nazarene Gospel Restored* (with Joshua Podro), a re-examination of primitive Christianity. He translated Lucan and Suetonius for Penguin Classics and compiled the first modern collection of the stories from Greek mythology, *The Greek Myths*. He was elected Professor of Poetry at Oxford in 1961 and made an Honorary Fellow of St John's College, Oxford, in 1971. Robert Graves died on 7 December 1985 in Majorca, his home since 1929. On his death *The Times* wrote of him, 'He will be remembered for his achievements as a prose stylist, historical novelist and memoirist, but above all as the paradigm of the dedicated poet, "the greatest love poet in English since Donne", as his biographer described him.'

MICHAEL GRANT has been successively Chancellor's medallist and Fellow of Trinity College, Cambridge, Professor of Humanity at Edinburgh

University, first Vice-Chancellor of Khartoum University, and President and Vice-Chancellor of the Queen's University of Belfast. He was President of the Classical Association in 1977–8. He also translated Cicero's *Selected Works*, *Selected Political Speeches* and *Murder Trials*, and Tacitus' *Annals of Imperial Rome* for Penguin Classics; his other books include *Roman Literature* (1958, Penguin), *The Civilizations of Europe* (1965), *Gladiators* (1967), *Cleopatra* (1972), *The Jews of the Roman World* (1973), *The Army of the Caesars* (1974), *The Twelve Caesars* (1975), *The Fall of the Roman Empire* (1976), *Cities of Vesuvius* (1976, Penguin), *Saint Paul* (1976), *Jesus* (1977), *Latin Literature* and *Greek Literature* (both 1977 and both anthologies in Penguin Classics), *History of Rome* (1978), *The Etruscans* (1980), *Greek and Latin Authors 800 BC–AD 1000* (1980), *From Alexander to Cleopatra* (1982), *History of Ancient Israel* (1984), *The Roman Emperors* (1985), *Guide to the Ancient World* (1987) *The Rise of the Greeks* (1987), *The Classical Greeks* (1989) and *The Visible Past* (1990).

>>>>><<<<<

CONTENTS

>>>>><<<<<

INTRODUCTION

1. The Career and Works of Apuleius

Apuleius was born in *c.* AD 123–5 at Madaurus (now Mdaourouch), a Roman colony in Numidia (eastern Algeria), which belonged to the province of Africa. His father was a leading citizen of the town and had held office as one of its *duoviri*, the principal annually elected officials; he left Apuleius and his other son a considerable sum of money. Apuleius was presumably given his elementary education at Madaurus, but thereafter was taught grammar and rhetoric at the large metropolitan city of Carthage, of which he subsequently wrote with great devotion. Then, at about the age of eighteen, he proceeded to Athens for further studies – no doubt including courses in philosophy – and stayed there for five or even seven years, finding time however to make several journeys, notably to Samos and Hierapolis in Phrygia (now Pamukkale). Subsequently he went to Rome, where he received further training and pleaded in the lawcourts. After these and other travels he returned to North Africa, and while on his way to Alexandria in Egypt fell ill at Oea (Tripoli) in *c.* AD 155. This was the home of Sicinius Pontianus, an old friend of his from his Athenian days, who proceeded to call on him. Pontianus had been studying in Rome but had returned to Oea because his rich widowed mother, Pudentilla, was proposing to remarry, taking her brother-in-law Sicinius Clarus as her second husband. Pontianus was, justifiably, afraid that this would mean that he and his brother would not inherit his mother's money, and he proposed that Apuleius should marry her instead, hoping, presumably, that this would keep the funds under his control. Despite some opposition within the family, this was arranged. Pontianus died soon after, but Clarus' brother Sicinius Aemilianus – no doubt also anxious about the money – arranged that Apuleius should be accused, first, of having Pontianus murdered, and, secondly, of having won Pudentilla's affections by magic. The first charge was dropped, but the second was tried at Sabratha before the proconsul Claudius Maximus in *c.* AD 158–9. Apuleius defended himself and was evidently acquitted, but he then left Oea for the more congenial surroundings of Carthage. There he enjoyed renown as poet, philosopher, rhetorician (sophist), public lecturer and valedictory speaker, making speeches in honour of departing Roman governors. He was appointed chief priest of the province, and his statues were erected at Carthage, Madaurus and elsewhere.

The speech that Apuleius gave in his defence at his trial, the *Apologia* (*A Discourse on Magic*), has survived. It is brilliant, learned, surprising and outrageous, and deserves to be much better known than it is. The *Florida* (literally 'flowers', but meaning 'anthology'), which has likewise come down to us, comprises excerpts from his declamations on various themes, which vary in style from the trivial, extravagant and amusing to, occasionally, the beautiful. *De Deo Socratis* (*On the God of Socrates*) is the best known of his philosophical works. It deals with a very interesting and still controversial subject, the 'spirit' (*daimonion*) by which Socrates claimed to be moved, but Apuleius takes the opportunity to develop the ancient doctrine of spirits (*daimones*) intermediary between gods and men, whose intervention permitted divinities to influence human beings. Two books entitled *De Platone et eius dogmate* (*On Plato and his Doctrine*), of which the second is dedicated to Apuleius' 'son Faustinus', but may or may not be by his own hand, are brief, popular summaries setting forth what were presented as Plato's views on nature and morals. A third book, on formal logic (Aristotelian rather than Platonic), is certainly by someone else, like a number of other writings that have been attributed to Apuleius. So, perhaps, is *De Mundo* (*On the Universe*), a translation of a pseudo-Aristotelian treatise of the same name. The original Greek work was dedicated to a certain Alexander (whose identity is disputed), but the translator (Apuleius) has again named Faustinus as the addressee.

Among the lost works of Apuleius were a Latin translation of Plato's *Phaedo*, a treatise entitled *De Republica* (*On the State*), a historical epitome, various poems, an alleged novel entitled *Herm-*

agoras (a tantalizing loss to posterity) and a mass of essay
tions and handbooks – in Greek as well as Latin – o
subjects (*Quaestiones Naturales* [*Investigations of Nature*] inc
zoological themes in particular). He also wrote on
astronomy and music. In a word, Apuleius was startlingly versatile.

2. *The Story of the* Metamorphoses (the Golden Ass)

The original title of the work translated here was *Metamorphoses*,
'changes of shape' (*The Transformations of Lucius*). This had always
been a favourite theme of classical mythology – witness the numerous
transformations of Jupiter – and became a fashionable topic among
Hellenistic authors, who sometimes gave this name to their works.[1]
Then, in Latin, Ovid's *Metamorphoses* gained eternal fame. Apuleius'
work, about the transformation of a man into an ass, also became
known as *The Golden Ass*, not later than the time of Saint Augustine
(AD 354–430), who uses the title. 'Golden' was the adjective that
street-corner story-tellers applied to their tales, and the epithet
seems to imply 'the ass *par excellence*', or 'the best of all stories
about an ass'.[2] At what stage in Apuleius' life the work was written is disputed. Some have argued for an early period in his own
career, but on the whole it seems probable that all the numerous
jokes and parodies relating to legal proceedings[3] indicate a date
subsequent to his traumatic trial for magic in AD 158 – and there
is evidence to suggest that the work might even be a good deal
later still.

After a riddling introduction in which Apuleius drops a good
many learned, mock-modest and misleading hints about his inten-
tions, the *Metamorphoses* is told in the first person by its principal
character, a young man called Lucius. Riding through the mountains
in Thessaly, Lucius meets two other travellers and is told the story of
a murder committed by a witch at Hypata, the Thessalian town to
which he is going. Once there he receives hospitality from Milo,
whose wife, Pamphile, proves to be a witch. At a party given by his
relative Byrrhaena, Lucius hears a further macabre tale of a man
mutilated by witches, and on his journey back to Milo's house he
kills three robbers who, however, after his mock-trial at the Festival
of Laughter, turn out merely to have been animated wine-skins. He
makes love to Pamphile's maid, Fotis, who allows him to see her

mistress transform herself into an owl. He, too, wishes to experience a magical metamorphosis, but owing to a technical error finds himself transformed into an ass (though retaining his human faculties, with the exception of his voice). To recover his human shape he needs to eat roses, but, before Fotis can bring any, robbers attack the house and take him away. In the robbers' den he listens to stories telling of the deaths of three of their number and sees them bring in a beautiful girl, Charite, who had been kidnapped for ransom on her wedding night.

To comfort her, the old woman who cooks for the robbers tells her the story of Cupid and Psyche. She recounts how a certain king had three daughters, the youngest of whom, Psyche, was so lovely that she was as greatly adored as the goddess Venus herself. As a result the goddess became jealous and sent her son Cupid to make Psyche fall in love with some ugly wretch. But instead Cupid fell in love with her himself and dispatched Zephyrus, the West Wind, to transfer her to a fairy palace, where he visited her as her unknown husband – always in the dark so that she would not recognize him. After a time she begged that her two sisters should be allowed to visit her, and he very reluctantly agreed. But, on learning that Psyche had never seen her husband, and suspecting him to be a god, the sisters became madly jealous. Persuading Psyche that her husband was in fact a fearsome monster, they gave her a lamp and a knife to kill him. As he slept, Psyche saw Cupid revealed in all his beauty by the light of the lamp. But a drop of oil falling on his body woke him up, and he rebuked her for her disobedience and left her.

Psyche then set out to look for him and, after bringing her sisters to a bad end for their jealousy, came to the house of Venus, who received her harshly and set her three tasks. Impossible though they were, she accomplished two of them, with the help of ants and an eagle. But, after Venus had instructed her to go down to the Underworld and fetch a casket full of beauty from Proserpine, curiosity moved her to open the casket. It contained, however, not beauty but a deathly sleep, which overcame her. But now Cupid intervened to save her, having at last gained the consent of Jupiter to their Olympic wedding, the celebration of which brings the story to a close.

After listening to this story, Charite is rescued by her lover, disguised as a robber, but he is subsequently assassinated by a rival, and his death is violently avenged by Charite. In his ass's form Lucius then passes into the hands of three further owners or sets of owners. During this period he beholds the indecent, effeminate orgies of priests of the Syrian Goddess; listens to three sex-orientated anecdotes, which may be entitled 'The Tale of the Tub', 'The Lost Slippers' and 'The Laundryman's Wife'; and witnesses a fourth, 'The Baker's Wife'. Next comes the tale of a wealthy young man and his savage treatment of his neighbours; the story of an amorous stepmother who tries to poison her unresponsive stepson; and the account of a brutal woman who commits five murders. As part of her punishment it is proposed that she should be publicly displayed having sexual relations with the ass Lucius, who finds the prospect so appalling, however, that he runs away from Corinth to Cenchreae, where he falls asleep, exhausted, on the sea-shore.

Then the work takes an altogether new turn. As Lucius sleeps, the Goddess Isis, in all her splendour, appears to him and promises her help. At the ceremonious spring festival for the launching of her sacred ship her priest offers him a wreath of roses, and he is restored to human shape. Resolved to dedicate the rest of his life to the service of his divine saviour, he undertakes the exacting preparations for initiation, during the course of which further visions are vouchsafed to him, and finally, alone in the shrine of the goddess at night, he is granted the experience of death, rebirth and revelation which only the elect are permitted to attain. Lucius then goes to Rome in order to devote himself to the service of Isis, and at her direction is twice initiated into the mysteries of her partner, Osiris, finally attaining a respected place in the hierarchy of the cult. And so the *Metamorphoses* ends.

3. The Background and Character of the Metamorphoses

Like most of the greatest 'original' literary achievements of all time, the *Metamorphoses* is not entirely original, in the sense that its author drew quite heavily on earlier writings.[4] We have a shorter Greek version, *Onos* (*Lucius, or the Ass*), of unknown authorship – not, probably, by the brilliant Lucian of Samosata (born *c*. AD 120), to whom it has been attributed – which contains much of the material on which Apuleius drew[5] (but not his concluding chapters, relating to Isis, and 'Cupid and Psyche'). To cut an enormously lengthy controversy short, it seems that both Apuleius' *Metamorphoses* and the Greek *Ass* were derived, separately, from a lost Greek *Metamorphoses* about a certain Lucius of Patrae,[6] which could, indeed, have been by Lucian, but this is not certain[7] (once again, it appears that Apuleius' Isis sections and his Cupid and Psyche story, like many other features, did not figure in this work).

Apuleius' story of Cupid and Psyche derives its form from a very widespread type of folk-tale.[8] No classical author had presented the tale of the two lovers in this form before, although the pains of their love had become a common theme of Hellenistic writers and artists. In his introduction to the *Metamorphoses* Apuleius refers obliquely to a further debt to the 'Milesian tales', which were sexy short stories that had enjoyed a considerable vogue since the first century BC.[9] But he had, of course, changed and amplified this genre beyond all recognition, and the same applies to his debt to the Greek novel, several of whose most distinguished practitioners were his contemporaries.[10] These Greek romances were mostly starry-eyed affairs figuring boys and girls who were separated by various vicissitudes and eventually enjoyed a happy reunion. Apuleius' *Metamorphoses*, on the other hand – although it has a happy ending of quite a different kind – is emphatically *not* starry-eyed; it echoes the Greek romances chiefly in order to guy them.

An earlier Latin novel in a similar vein was Petronius' *Satyricon*, written, probably, by a minister of Nero (*c.* AD 65).[11] Its surviving portions depict wittily and satirically an extremely sordid low life quite alien to the sentimentalities of the Greek romances, and it has often been supposed that Apuleius – although his work is quite different – must have known about the work and been influenced by it. Indeed, this is not impossible, though during the last few years it has become a slightly less tempting conclusion than before, since finds of papyrus fragments have revealed small portions of previously unknown Greek novels that are far closer to the seedy, macabre low life portrayed by Petronius and Apuleius than to the sugary type of morality depicted in the Greek romances that were hitherto known.[12] Here, then, was a whole genre, of which we now have three Greek fragments, together with (in Latin) the incomplete *Satyricon* of Petronius and the complete *Metamorphoses* of Apuleius. But Apuleius was very well versed in a whole range of earlier classical writings – and liked to parade his learning, moreover – so that those who are interested may trace influences, echoes and parodies of many other forms of literature, notably the epic (especially Homer's *Odyssey*),[13] Platonic dialogue, tragedy, comedy, the pastoral, mime and adventure stories of various kinds. The Isis climax in the *Metamorphoses* reminds us that Apuleius was also very knowledgeable about Egypt, and in his introduction he himself refers to the extent of his Egyptian literary debts, which may be wider than we can now recognize.[14] With the literature of more easterly origins he could scarcely have been directly acquainted, but it is interesting to note that a number of his themes had appeared on Mesopotamian inscriptions thousands of years earlier.[15]

In his introduction Apuleius announces his desire to entertain the reader – and he succeeds. All the same, the statement is somewhat disingenuous, since he achieves a great deal else besides. The view that the whole work is a gigantic moral allegory is now somewhat discredited, but nearly all the proper names that he introduces have a self-descriptive significance, as frequently occurs in ancient writings. The story of Cupid and Psyche, at least, surely has some link with the progress of the soul ('psyche'), via various hazards, towards happiness,[16] further illustrated by Lucius' heartfelt conversion to the religion of Isis at the end of the work.

Many other features in Apuleius' earlier works point in the same direction, and one of the most arresting features of the *Metamorphoses* is its progress from the squalid, brutal miseries of the earlier scenes to the sublimity of the Isiac initiations. Of the religion of Isis – except to point out that this was the only pagan cult that might have become universal – nothing more need be said here; Apuleius' narrative is the best description in existence of its glory and its appeal.[17] On the other hand, he seems to have hated at least one other pagan deity, the Syrian Goddess (Atargatis), whose debased devotees receive very severe treatment in the book. Apart from Isis, Apuleius' strongest religious belief – and here he is very much a child of his time – is in Luck (Tyche), the blind Fortune that strikes random blows but is superseded in the end by the happy Fortune, which (like so many other deities) is incorporated in Isis herself.[18]

As for philosophy, Apuleius, although his mind did not run very deeply in that direction, firmly believed himself to be a Platonist, as his other writings showed. That is to say, he subscribed to the Middle Platonism of his epoch, that somewhat indeterminate stage between the Platonism of the old school and the Neo-Platonism of the future.[19] He was also a pretty typical example of a 'sophist' (of the Second Sophistic), one of those rhetoricians and lecturers who travelled around during the second century AD giving public lectures and popularizing philosophy, earning themselves large fees and reputations to match.

All of this emerges in the *Metamorphoses*, and much more besides. There is a lot of fairly lecherous sex in the book – based on the assumption that no woman's virtue is unassailable – and indeed this has substantially contributed to the renown, or notoriety, of the work throughout the centuries. It is a type of sex that very easily takes a nasty and sadistic turn, to which Isis provides a welcome change and relief. There is also a great deal of magic in the book. As we have seen, magic constituted the burden of the charge against Apuleius at Sabratha; indeed, Saint Augustine, among others, was quite prepared to see him as a magician.[20] From this miasma, too, Isis rescues him: or does she, for wasn't she believed to be a magician herself? Augustine condemns Apuleius for his interest in magic, and this damaging, unsatisfied, lethal curiosity about the unknown runs right through the *Metamorphoses*. What happens to Lucius and Psyche are but two conspicuous examples. Once again, this obsession reflects the spirit of the age;[21] indeed nobody could have been more restlessly inquisitive than the Emperor Hadrian (AD 117–38). But Apuleius is at pains to show in the book that indulging this trait can lead one along perilous paths and bring evil results.

There has been a great deal of discussion as to whether the *Metamorphoses*, for all its discursive appearance, is a unity, and to what extent:[22] whether, for example, the Isis episode was part of the original conception. In my opinion it was, but it is difficult to be absolutely certain because Apuleius is determined to confuse us. For one thing, he leaves loose ends and does not appear to mind. More of a problem, though, is that nothing is quite what it seems. It is not always clear, or indeed meant to be clear, what has really happened in the book. For example, there is a dual point of view, that of human beings and that of animals, and both perspectives are treated with sympathy. Nor is it clear to what extent Lucius is to be identified with the author: towards the end, for instance, Madaurus, and no longer Greece, is named as his home, from which we might suppose that the vision of Isis and what follows actually happened to Apuleius himself. But as to what takes place before, how should we make our way in this atmosphere pervaded by magic, where illusions abound? It has become fashionable to see *aporia* ('puzzlement') as the principal characteristic, and intention, of some of Plato's earliest dialogues. Apuleius' *Metamorphoses* are riddled with *aporia*. And it is precisely this prevalence of ambiguous fantasy and confusing contrasts of subject and tone; this original, experimental synthesis of the comic, romantic, macabre, tragic and edifying; this dream-land atmosphere of mystery, unreality and inconsistency, that intrigues us and keeps us thinking.

4. The Subsequent Destiny of the Metamorphoses

As I have indicated, Saint Augustine was most unfavourably impressed by Apuleius' interest in magic and was quite prepared to believe that he had actually been a magician himself.[23] From Augustine's time onwards, throughout the Middle Ages, other Christian writers accepted him as a magical worker of miracles, using the aid of the demons whom he invoked. By comparison, any evidence for his recognition as a novelist during this period is slight. But this all changed when Giovanni Boccaccio (1313–75) transcribed the *Metamorphoses*, with his own hand, from a fourteenth-century manuscript. Frankly desirous, as he was, to justify the carnal life, he was soon retelling these stories, in his Latin *De genealogiis deorum gentilium* (allegorizing the story of Cupid and Psyche) and Italian *Decameron*. Gian Francesco Poggio Bracciolini (1380–1459) translated the shorter Greek *Lucius, or the Ass* into Latin. The surviving writings of Apuleius were among the earliest classical books ever to be printed, appearing in Rome in an *editio princeps* (1469). During the sixteenth century translations appeared in Italy, Germany, England (William Adlington, 1566), France and Spain, where Apuleius was adopted as the enthralling and enlivening entertainer of the Renaissance world, and his *Metamorphoses* became a great favourite, decisively influencing the development of the picaresque novel.[24] In all these countries his tale of Cupid and Psyche enjoyed special success:[25]

Don Pedro Calderón de la Barca retold the story no less than three times, first in a three-act comedy, *Ni Amor se libra de Amor* (1640), and then twice in his allegorical plays, the *Autos Sacramentales*. In France La Fontaine rewrote one of Apuleius' stories in his poem *Le cuvier*, and in 1669 he published *Les amours de Psyché et Cupidon*. *Psyché, tragédie lyrique* (1673), with music by Lully, was at first attributed to Pierre Corneille and then claimed by Bernard Fontanelle. In Germany, in 1767, Christoph Martin Wieland began, but never finished, an allegorical treatment of the Cupid and Psyche theme in the form of a huge narrative poem about the progress of the soul. In England John Keats echoed the story in his *Poems* (1817), and published an *Ode to Psyche* three years later; and in 1885 Walter Pater incorporated the tale of Cupid and Psyche, and other Apuleian stories, into his brilliantly effective, rhythmically subtle *Marius the Epicurean*.

5. Style and Translation

Apuleius' prose style in the *Metamorphoses* is extremely florid and extravagant, poetical and bizarre, crammed full of archaisms, neologisms, Graecisms, colloquialisms and hybridisms, and constructed with an incantatory, rhythmical complexity and subtlety.[26] His apology for his Latin in the introduction is a typical piece of self-depreciation.[27] His was a style that must have appeared at its best when the work, or excerpts from it, were recited aloud (as they were to the Romans, apparently, since there are recondite allusions to Roman topography and legal processes). Obviously a good many of these features are lost in translation. This we must accept philosophically and translate as well as we can. Incidentally, it is – as might be expected – very difficult Latin, which only a restricted number of people have been trained to understand (far fewer, in these days of diminished Latinity, than could understand it fifty or a hundred years ago, though even then the number was limited, since people were brought up on the immensely different Ciceronian language).

'In my translation,' writes Robert Graves, 'I have made no attempt to bring out the oddness of the Latin by writing in a style, say, somewhere between Lyly's *Euphues* and Amanda Ros's *Irene Iddesleigh*: paradoxically, the effect of oddness is best achieved in convulsed times like the present by writing in as easy and sedate an English as possible.'[28] Whether the 'convulsed times' are relevant or not, I agree with this. ' "Sedate",' as I have remarked, 'is surely not an ambitious enough epithet for a good rendering of Apuleius or Tacitus [or for Graves's own excellent style]; but his reminder that twentieth-century English has to be plain is still relevant. No amount of colourful or fanciful language will make the strange personality of Tacitus [or, even more, I might have added, of Apuleius] understandable to contemporary readers, who find rhetoric and grand style unnatural and unreadable.'[29] Simplicity, therefore, is the only hope. 'Certainly,' as I commented later, 'by aiming at "natural" English something is lost. But it still seems to me that any alternative philosophy of Latin prose translation is likely to involve even larger losses. However, perhaps someone will give a practical demonstration to the contrary, and show I am wrong. At least I very much hope they will try.'[30] But now I am not quite sure that this last observation was entirely honest. Let them try, perhaps, but I do not really think it can be done.[31] English *must* be readable, and readable *today*, whereas no English version faithfully endeavouring to reproduce Apuleius' fantasies *can* be readable. Adlington's translation (1566) was eminently readable in its day, and in 1915 Sir Stephen Gaselee cleverly brought it more or less up to date, though, even with his adaptation, after the passage of three and a half centuries it could scarcely still be expected to be a readable work. Graves's version (1950) remains, in consequence, thoroughly enjoyable, and this is the rendering, therefore, that I have adapted.

But I am afraid 'adapted' has to be the word with regard to the original text too. Graves points out, and all translators know, that if you stick too closely to the exact text the effect of authenticity is lost, and so he has 'sometimes felt obliged to alter the order not only of phrases but of sentences, where English prose logic differs from Latin'. This is perfectly justifiable – up to a point. 'And to avoid the nuisance of footnotes I have brought their substance up into the story itself whenever it reads obscurely. Adlington often did the same.'[32] This is *not* such good practice; in fact, in a modern translation it will not do. Moreover, Graves's insertions are not always justified and are sometimes merely expressions of personal opinion. Mistakes, too, occur, not surprisingly when the Latin is so impenetrable.

Having said this, however, I would repeat that in general his version is a splendid one, and in inserting suggested corrections I sincerely hope I have not damaged his extremely skilful and attractive style.

In conclusion, I should like to thank Paul Keegan, editor of the Penguin Classics, Kate Parker and their colleagues for their help.

MICHAEL GRANT, 1990

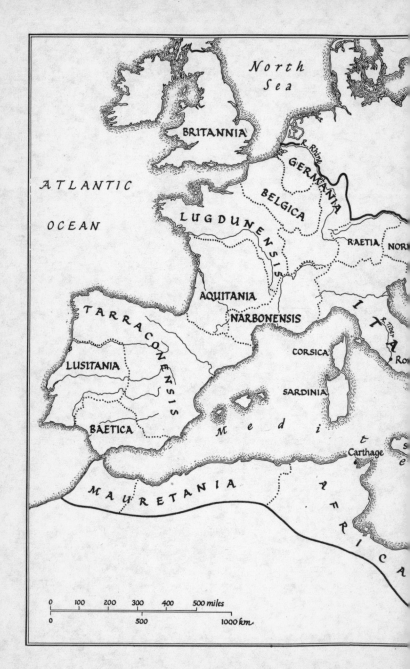

PROVINCES of the ROMAN EMPIRE
at the death of Antoninus Pius (AD 161)

DACIA

Black Sea

R. Danube

MOESIA

THRACIA

ILLYRICUM

MACEDONIA

EPIRUS

Aegean Sea

ASIA

BITHYNIA–PONTUS

GALATIA

CAPPADOCIA

PAMPHYLIA

CILICIA

LYCIA

•Antioch

R. Euphrates

SYRIA

ACHAEA

Athens

CYPRUS

CRETE

SYRIA-
PALAESTINA

Mediterranean Sea

IA

Alexandria

ARABIA

CYRENAICA

EGYPT

R. Nile

Red Sea

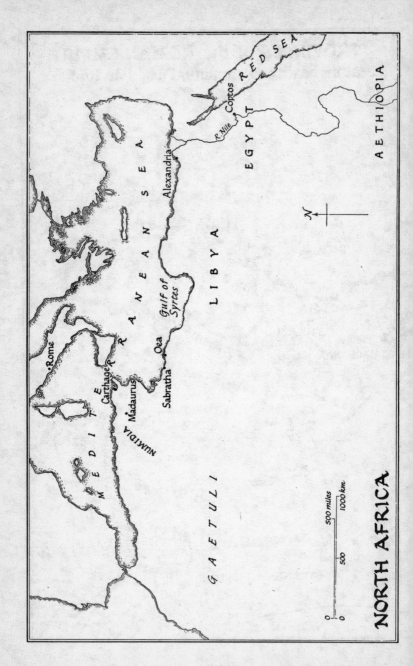

NORTH AFRICA

RED SEA

AETHIOPIA

Coptos

R. Nile

EGYPT

Alexandria

MEDITERRANEAN SEA

Gulf of Syrtes

LIBYA

Oea

Sabratha

Rome

Carthage

Madaurus

NUMIDIA

GAETULI

500 miles
0   500
0   1000 km.

GREECE

N

MACEDONIA

Thessalonica

PIERIA

Mt Olympus ▲   Dium

Larissa

THESSALY   Iolcus

AEGEAN

Bay of
Actium

Hypata

EUBOEA

AETOLIA

Calydon   Delphi   Chaeronea

BOEOTIA   Aulis

SEA

Aegium   Thebes

Patrae   Plataea   Rhamnus

Mt Cyllene ▲   ▲ Mt Cithaeron

Corinth   Eleusis   Athens

ARCADIA   Cenchreae   ▲ Mt Hymettus

ZACYNTHUS   Olympia   Argos

IONIAN   PELOPONNESE

SEA

LACONIA   PAROS

Taenarus

CYTHERA

MEDITERRANEAN

CRETE

Mt Ida ▲   Mt Dicte ▲

SEA

0   50   100 miles
0   50   100   150 km

ASIA MINOR

BLACK SEA

THRACE

Hellespont
Propontis

Aegean Sea

TROAD

Troy
·Mt Ida
Methymna
·Mytilene
LESBOS

MYSIA

GALATIA

·Pessinus

CAPPADOCIA

LYDIA

PHRYGIA

SAMOS ·Ephesus
·Hierapolis
·Aphrodisias
Miletus
CARIA

·Cnidus

R. EUPHRATES

CYPRUS

Paphos·

MEDITERRANEAN   SEA

EGYPT

N

0		100		200 miles
0	100	200	300 km	

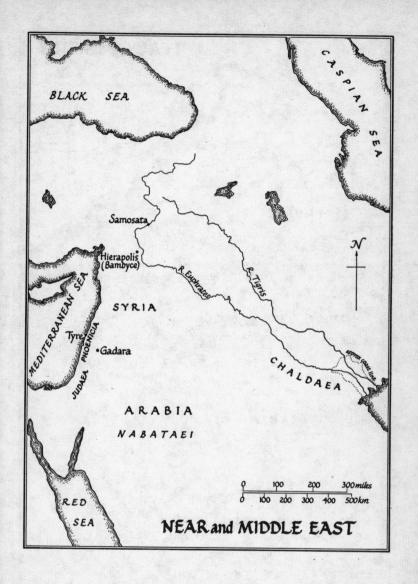

BLACK SEA

CASPIAN SEA

Samosata

Hierapolis
(Bambyce)

R. Euphrates

R. Tigris

N

SYRIA

MEDITERRANEAN SEA

Tyre

PHOENICIA

•Gadara

JUDAEA

approx. coast line

CHALDAEA

ARABIA

NABATAEI

RED SEA

0   100   200   300 miles
0   100 200 300 400 500 km

NEAR and MIDDLE EAST

ITALY and SICILY

0   50   100 miles
0   100   200 km

N

ADRIATIC SEA

ETRURIA

I T A L Y

R. Tiber

Rome

Ostia

Gulf of Cumae   CAMPANIA
Cumae   Neapolis
L. Avernus

TYRRHENIAN
SEA

Croton

MEDITERRANEAN SEA

SICILY
Henna

THE
TRANSFORMATIONS OF LUCIUS

OTHERWISE KNOWN AS

THE GOLDEN ASS

>>>>><<<<<

APULEIUS' ADDRESS TO THE READER

IN this Milesian story[1] I shall weave together a variety of tales to make you wonder and charm your friendly ears with a pleasant whispering, if you are not put off by the Egyptian, Nilotic story-telling convention[2] which allows humans to be changed into animals and later restored to their proper shapes: to make you wonder. And so I begin.

Who is the author? I'll give you a brief account. Various ancestors of mine lived on Mount Hymettus in Attica, on the Ephyraean (Corinthian) isthmus, and at Taenarus, in Spartan territory – all famous names immortalized by more famous writers than myself: there when I was a child I learnt the Attic Greek speech. Later I went to the Latin city of Rome where I carefully studied the native tongue of the Quirites[3] – a painful task, since I had no schoolmaster to guide me. You will, I hope, forgive me if I cause offence by my crude utterance of this exotic language of the Forum. After all, such a change from one language to another corresponds with the subject I am proposing to handle, in the manner of a rider vaulting from one horse to another.[4] For it is a story adapted from the Greek that I am going to tell you. Listen to it, reader, and you are sure to enjoy yourself.

CHAPTER I

>>>>><<<<<

THE STORY OF ARISTOMENES

BUSINESS once took me to Thessaly, where my mother's family originated; I have the distinction of being descended through her from the famous Plutarch and his nephew, the philosopher Sextus.[1] One morning after I had ridden over a high range of hills, down a slippery track into the valley beyond, across dewy pastures and lumpy ploughland, my horse, a white Thessalian, began to puff and slacken his pace. Feeling tired myself from sitting so long cramped in the saddle, I jumped off, carefully wiped his sweating forehead with a handful of leaves, stroked his ears, gave him the rein and walked slowly beside him, letting him relax and recover his wind. While he breakfasted, snatching a mouthful of grass from this side or that of the track which wound through the meadows, I saw two men trudging along together a short distance ahead of me, deep in conversation. I walked a little faster, curious to know what they were talking about, and just as I drew abreast one of them burst into a loud laugh and said to the other: 'Stop, Stop! Not another word! I can't bear to hear any more of your absurd and monstrous lies.'

This made me thirst to hear more. I said to the story-teller: 'Please don't think me impertinent or inquisitive, sir, but I'm always anxious to improve my education, and few subjects fail to interest me. If you would kindly go back to the beginning of your story and tell me the whole of it I should be most grateful. It sounds as if it would help me pleasantly up this next steep hill.'

The man who had laughed went on: 'This lying tale is no more true than if you said that magic can make rivers run backwards, freeze the ocean and paralyse the winds. Or that the sun can be stopped by magic in mid-course, the moon made to drop a poisonous dew and the stars charmed from their proper spheres. Why, you might as well say that day can be magically annihilated and replaced by perpetual night.'

But I persisted: 'No, sir, don't be put off. Please finish the story you were telling; unless this is asking too much of you.' Then turning to the other, I said: 'As for you, sir, are you sure that it isn't either natural dullness or cultivated obstinacy that prevents you from recognizing the truth of what your friend has been trying to tell you? People always make the mistake of dismissing as untrue anything that happens only very seldom, or anything that their minds cannot readily grasp; yet when these things are carefully inquired into they are often found not only possible but probable. Tell me, for instance, what you make of this. Last night at supper I was engaged in an eating race with some fellow diners and tried to swallow too large a mouthful of polenta cheese. It was so doughy and soft that it stuck half-way down my throat, blocking my windpipe, and I nearly choked to death. Yet only a few days before, at the Painted Porch in Athens,[2] I had watched a juggler actually swallow a sharp cavalry sabre, point downwards too; after which, he collected a few coins from us bystanders and swallowed a hunting spear in the same astonishing way. We watched him tilt his head backwards with the handle sticking out from his throat into the air; and presently, believe it or not, a beautiful boy began to wriggle up that handle with such slippery movements that you might have mistaken him for the royal serpent coiled on the roughly-trimmed olive club carried by the God of Medicine;[3] he seemed to have neither bone nor sinew in his whole body.' Then I turned once more to the other man: 'Come, sir, out with your story! I undertake not only to believe it, even though your friend will not, but to show my gratitude for your kindness by standing you a meal at the next inn.'

'Many thanks for a most generous offer,' he said, 'but I need no reward for telling you my experiences, every word of which – I swear to you by the Sun who sees everything – is absolutely true. And this afternoon when we reach the next town in Thessaly, you will no longer need to make the least mental reservation about its truth, because everyone there knows the story of what happened to me. It was by no means a private affair, you see. I must begin with some particulars about myself – where I come from and my business. I am from Aegium, in the wholesale provision trade, and I travel regularly through Thessaly, Aetolia and Boeotia buying honey, cheese and goods of that sort. Well, news reached me one day from Hypata, which is the principal city of all Thessaly, that a large stock of prime cheeses was being offered there at a very tempting price. I hurried off at once but, as happens only too often in the trade, my trip was ill-timed. I found as soon as I arrived that a fellow named Lupus, a merchant in a big way, had cornered the market only the day before and so I was disappointed of my profit. Tired out by having travelled so fast and to so little purpose, I went along early that evening to the public baths; and there whom should I meet but my old friend Socrates. I hardly recognized him, he looked so miserably pale and thin, sitting on the ground half-covered with a filthy, tattered old cloak, just like a street beggar. Though we had once been on the most intimate terms I hesitated a little before greeting him.

'"Why, dear Socrates," I said at last, "what in the world is the meaning of this? Why are you sitting here in such a frightful state? Have you committed some crime? Don't you know that there is weeping and lamentation for your death and your home, and that your family have gone into mourning and paid you their last devotions? Your children are now wards of the provincial court, and your poor wife, who has ruined her looks by crying herself nearly blind for you, is being worried by her parents to remarry and put the family on its feet again. And here you turn up like a ghost! Really, it is humiliating for us."

'"Oh, but Aristomenes," he replied, "if only you knew what extraordinarily unkind tricks Fortune can play on a man, you would never speak to me like that." He blushed and pulled his rags over his face, which had the effect of uncovering the lower part of his body from the navel downwards.

'I could bear the sight of his wretched misery no longer. Catching hold of him, I tried to pull him up from the ground but he with his head still covered up, just groaned: "Leave me alone, leave me alone! Let Fortune have her way and enjoy her triumph over me and finish what she has begun." However, in the end he promised to come along, so I pulled off one of the two garments I was wearing and put it on him. Then I hurried him into a bath, where I gave him a good scrubbing and took off a huge quantity of filth. Finally, though exhausted myself, I managed to drag him along to my inn, where I made him lie down on a mattress and gave him plenty of food and plenty of wine, and entertained him with conversation. After a time he brightened up and we began to laugh and joke together and got very noisy – until all of a sudden he heaved a passionate sigh, beat his forehead with his fists and cried: "Oh, how miserable I am! It all started with my wanting to watch that much advertised gladiatorial display near Larissa. I had gone to Macedonia on business, as you probably know, and I was coming home after ten months with a tidy sum of money when, just before reaching Larissa, I was waylaid by bandits in a wild and pathless valley and robbed of practically everything but life. Well, I managed to get away from them in the end and, almost at my last gasp, reached this town. Here I went to an inn run by a woman named Meroe. She was no longer young but extraordinarily attractive, and when I told her my sad story and explained how anxious I was to return home after my long absence she was very kind to me, cooked me a grand supper for which she charged me nothing, and afterwards, feeling lascivious, pressed me to sleep with her. But from the moment that I first climbed into her bed my mind began to sicken and my will-power to fail. While I was still well enough to work for a living I gave her what little money I picked up by carrying bags while I still had my strength, and I even presented her with the clothes that the kind robbers had left me to cover my nakedness. And now you see the condition into which bad luck and a charming woman have brought me."

"Good God," I said, "you deserve all this and more, if possible, for having deserted your home and children and made yourself a slave to an old bitch like that!"

"Hush, hush," he cried, a forefinger to his lips, looking wildly round in case we were overheard. "Say nothing against that marvellous woman, or your tongue may be your ruin."

"Really!" I said. "Then what sort of inn-keeper can she be? From the way you talk, anyone would think that she was an absolute empress possessed of supernatural powers."

"I tell you," he answered "she is a magician of god-like powers, able, if she pleases, to pull down the heavens or uplift the earth; to petrify the running stream or dissolve the rocky mountain; to raise the spectral dead or hurl the gods from their thrones; to quench the stars or illuminate the dark Land of Shadows."

"Come, come, Socrates, this is the language of melodrama! Ring down the curtain for Heaven's sake and let me have the story in plain words."

'He answered: "Will a single instance of her powers convince you? Or must you have two, or more? Her ability to make men fall passionately in love with her – not only local people but Indians and both sorts of Ethiopians and even the mythical Antichthones [4] – this is only a slight sample of her powers. If you want to hear of the greater feats that she has performed in the presence of reliable witnesses, I will mention a few. Well, first of all, one of her lovers dared have an affair with another woman. She only needed to pronounce a single word and he was transformed into a beaver; because the beaver, when alarmed by the hunt, bites off its own genitals and leaves them lying by the river bank to put the hounds off the scent – and Meroe hoped that this would happen to him just because he fancied another woman. Then there was the old inn-keeper, her neighbour and rival, whom she transformed into a frog; and now the poor fellow swims around in one of his own wine casks, or buries himself in the lees, croaking hoarse greetings to his old customers. And the barrister who had once been briefed to prosecute her: his punishment was ram's horns, and now you can see him any day in court bleating his case. Finally, when the wife of another of her lovers spoke nastily about her, Meroe condemned her to perpetual pregnancy by putting a charm on her womb that prevented the child from being born. This, by general agreement, was about eight years ago; and now the poor woman swells bigger and bigger every month until you would believe her to be on the point of giving birth to an elephant."

'"And when all these things came to be generally known there was public indignation, and it was decided to stone her cruelly to death the next day. This single day's grace was enough for Meroe, just as it was for Medea when King Creon ordered her to quit Corinth.[5] Medea, you remember, set fire to her supplanter's bridal head-dress; soon the whole palace was alight, and the new bride and Creon himself were both burned to death. But Meroe, as she confided to me the next morning when drunk, dug a trench and performed certain rites over it, and by the dark power of the spirits that she invoked, she shut the whole people up in their houses by her secret magical power, so that they could not break open their gates and doors or even tunnel through the walls. In the end the whole town had to appeal to her, promising if she freed them never to molest her again but, on the contrary, always to defend her against harm; then she relented and released all the town from the spell. But she took her revenge on the principal instigator of the meetings directed against her by spiriting away his house at midnight – walls, floor, foundations and all, with himself inside – to a town a hundred miles off. This place stood on the top of a waterless hill – the towns-people had to rely on rain-water for all purposes – and the buildings were so closely crowded together that there was no space to fit the house in; so she ordered it to be flung down outside the town gate."

'"My dear Socrates," I said, "these are certainly very wonderful and terrible stories and I am beginning to feel a little scared myself; in fact, really frightened. Suppose that your old woman were informed by some familiar spirit of all that we have been saying? So let us go to sleep at once. The night is still young and when we have slept our weariness away we could make an early start tomorrow morning, getting as far away from here as our legs will take us."

'While I was speaking, poor Socrates suddenly fell asleep, and began snoring loudly: the natural effect of a good meal and plenty of wine on a man in his exhausted condition. I locked and barred the bedroom door, pushed the head of my bed against the hinge, fixed it firmly and lay down. For a time I could not sleep, because I was so frightened, but about midnight I dozed off for a little. I had just begun to sleep when I was awakened by a sudden crash, and the door burst open with greater force than if a pack of bandits had broken in, falling to the ground with its hinges shattered, and my old camp-bed, a bit short for me and with one leg damaged and rotten, was tossed into the air and fell upside down, pinning me underneath it.

'Emotions are contradictory things. You know how sometimes one weeps for joy: well now, after this terrible awakening, I found myself joking to myself: "Why, Aristomenes, you have been transformed into a tortoise!" Though knocked flat, I felt safe under the bed and poked my head out sideways to watch what would happen next. Presently in came two old women: one of them carried a lighted torch in her hand, the other a sponge and a drawn sword. In this get-up they stood over Socrates, who was still asleep, and the one with the sword said to the other: "Look, sister Panthia, here is the man whom I chose to be my sweet Endymion, my Ganymede,[6] who took advantage of my girlish years day and night and took little account of my love for him. And now he has been not only spreading scandal about me but actually planning to run off! He will abandon me like the cunning Ulysses, will he, and expects me to howl and sob like Calypso when she awoke and found herself alone on her island [7] for ever?" Then she pointed at me and said: "And this creature peeping at us from under the bed, down on the ground on the point of death and watching everything that goes on, is his adviser Aristomenes, who put him up to abandoning me and expects to be able to get safely away from me. I'll see that he repents at this very moment (though it's too late) of all the nasty insulting things he said about me earlier tonight and of this new impertinent prying."

'When I heard this I broke into a cold sweat and began to tremble so violently that my spasms made the bed rattle and dance over me. But good Panthia said: "Sister, so shall we tear him to pieces at once, or shall we first tie strong twine around his private parts and cut them off?"

'But then Meroe (for by now I had learnt that she was the woman Socrates had been referring to in his story) replied: "No, let him live at least long enough to bury the corpse of this poor wretch in a bit of earth," and then she turned Socrates' head to the other side and drove the sword up to the hilt through the left side of his neck. Blood spurted out, but she had a small bladder ready and caught every drop as it fell. I saw this with my own eyes. Socrates' windpipe had been sliced through, but he uttered a sort of cry, or indistinct gurgle, and then was silent. To complete the sacrificial rite in what, I suppose, was her usual manner, Meroe thrust her hand through the wound, deep into my poor friend's body, groped inside and at length pulled out the heart. But Panthia took the sponge from her and stopped the gaping wound with it, muttering as she did so:

> Sponge, sponge, from salt sea took,
> Pass not over the running brook!

Then they came across the room to me, lifted away the bed, squatted over me and urinated disgustingly until I was completely wet.

'After this they left me; and no sooner had they crossed the threshold than the door rose up by itself and bar, lock and hinges miraculously refixed themselves in their original positions. I lay lifeless on the floor, naked, cold and drenched with urine, like a new-born child rather than someone who was half-dead, yet still surviving in some sort of posthumous fashion, like a criminal on his way to the cross. "For what," I asked myself, "will become of me, when they find Socrates' corpse with his throat cut? Who will believe I am telling the truth, though it is the truth I will be telling. 'You ought at least to have cried out for help if you were no match for the women,' they will tell me. 'A big, strong man like you, allowing a man's throat to be cut before your eyes and not uttering a word!' And: 'How do you explain being left alive yourself? Why didn't these fierce, cruel people kill you, as a witness to the crime, to destroy all evidence against them? Your punishment for being alive to tell the tale must be death.'" My mind circled around these arguments. But the night was now nearly over and at last I made up my mind to steal out of the inn before daylight and start with trepidation on my journey. I took up my bundle of belongings, drew the bolts of the door and put the key in its lock, but the honest and faithful door, which during the night had opened of its own accord, now refused to let me out until I had turned the key this way and that a score of times. Once outside in the courtyard I called out: "Hey door-keeper, where are you? Open the gate, I want to be off before daybreak."

'He was lying on the bare ground beside the gate and answered, still half-asleep: "What is it? Don't you know that the roads are swarming with bandits? You may be tired of life, or you may have some crime on your conscience, but don't think that I'm such a pumpkin-headed idiot as to risk my life for yours."

'I protested: "But it's almost morning. And anyhow, what can bandits take from a traveller who hasn't anything to take? Don't you realize, idiot, that ten professional wrestlers couldn't take anything worth having from a man as naked as you are?"

'But the door-keeper, drowsy and half-asleep as he was, turned over on his other side and asked: "How do I know that you haven't murdered the man you brought in yesterday afternoon and are running off to save yourself?" At that moment I remember how I had a vision of the earth opening wide and Hell gaping and the dog Cerberus hungry for me. I was convinced that Meroe had refrained from cutting my throat only because of her vicious intention to get me crucified. I went back to my room, determined to kill myself in my own way. But the only way was to get my bed to help me. So I began talking to it. I said coaxingly: "Now listen, my dearest little bed, which has endured so many hardships with me, observer and judge of what has happened during the night, the only witness I can call to my innocence, give me some wholesome instrument to help me on the way to the lower world that I am hastening to make." And then at once I began to tug out a length of the rope with which its frame was corded, made one end fast to a rafter which stuck out above the window, and knotted the other into a running noose. I climbed on the bed, ready to cast myself from aloft to destruction, put my neck into the noose and kicked the bed away with one foot, so that the noose when it received my weight might throttle me. But the rope was old and rotten and suddenly broke under my weight. Down I tumbled and fell upon the body of Socrates which lay not far off, and we rolled together on to the floor. At that instant in came the porter and shouted: "Hey you, you who a moment ago were raring to get off in such frantic haste, what are you doing here, wallowing around and snoring down there?"

'Before I could answer, Socrates sprang up, as if suddenly awakened – whether by my fall or the porter's hoarse voice was not clear – and said: "I have often heard travellers cursing at porters and their surly ways, and upon my word they have every right to do so. I was tired out, and now this busybody bursts into the room and shouts at us – I am sure with the notion of stealing something – and wakes me out of a very sound sleep."

'At the sound of Socrates' voice I jumped up in an ecstasy of relief and cried: "No, no, you are the most honest of door-keepers, my friend and my father and my brother. But look, look, here's the man whom in your drunken daze just now you accused me of murdering." I hugged and kissed Socrates, but he, smelling the stink with which those Lamiae[8] had infected me, pushed me away violently, saying: "Go away, you stink like the bottom of a lavatory!" and began to inquire, considerately enough, how I came to smell so dreadfully. In my confusion I made him some sort of lame excuse – I forget what – and turned the conversation as soon as possible. Catching hold of his hand, I cried: "What are we waiting for? Why not start at once and enjoy the freshness of the early morning air?"

'So I shouldered my bundle once more, paid for my stay at the inn, and soon Socrates and I were out on the road.

'When we had gone some little distance from the town and the whole countryside stood out clear in the rising sun, I took a long careful look at Socrates' throat to see where the sword had gone in. But nothing showed, and I thought: "Here's Socrates as well as he ever was and without a scratch on him. No wound, no sponge, not even a scar to show where the sword went burrowing in such a short time ago. What a vivid and fantastic dream! I was mad to drink so much." And I said aloud: "The doctors are right. If you stuff your stomach with food the last thing at night and then flood it with drink you are bound to have nightmares. That was why, after drinking too much yesterday evening, I have such frightful and savage dreams that I still feel as though I were spattered with human blood."

'Socrates laughed. "Blood indeed! The plain truth is that you soaked your bed and still stink of it. But it is true that last night I dreamed that my throat was cut and I had all the sensations of agony from the wound, and then someone pulled my heart out, which it frightens me so much to remember that my knees are trembling and I am staggering about, and would like to eat something to revive me."

'"Here is breakfast ready for you," I replied, taking my haversack off my shoulder and hastening to give him some bread and cheese. "Let us sit down under that large plane-tree."

'I had some too, but I noticed that his healthy looks had faded and that, though he ate ravenously, his face was turning the colour of boxwood. I must have looked almost as pale myself because the vision of that terrible pair of Furies had repossessed my mind. I took a small bite of bread, but it stuck in my gullet and I could neither swallow it nor cough it up. I grew more and more anxious. By this time a number of people were about, and when two men are travelling together and one dies mysteriously by the roadside suspicion naturally falls upon the other. He ate a huge meal, a great deal of bread and nearly a whole cheese, and then complained of thirst. A few yards off, out of sight of the road, a brook ran gently past the roots of the tree. It was bright as silver, clear as crystal, placid as a pond. "Come here, Socrates," I said. "This is as good as milk. Take a long draught of it." He got up, walked along the shelving bank until he found a place that suited him, knelt down, bent his head forward and began to drink greedily. But hardly had his lips touched the water when the wound in his throat opened wide and the sponge dropped out into the water, followed by a small trickle of blood. He would have fallen in after it, if I had not caught at one leg and lugged him up to the top of the bank.

'After I had mourned my wretched companion for a good long while I buried him in the sandy soil as his eternal resting place, there by the brookside. Then, trembling with great fear, I fled away through the wildest and most desolate country.

'With a conscience as bad as any murderer's, I abandoned my home and voluntarily exiled myself to Aetolia. There I married again.'

*

That was the end of Aristomenes' story. His friend, who from the first had obstinately refused to believe a word of it, turned to me and declared: 'Well now, I have never in all my life heard such a fabulous and nonsensical falsehood. You are an educated man, to judge by your dress and general appearance; did you believe a word?'

I answered: 'I think nothing is impossible; for whatever the Fates have decreed, that is what I believe will happen, in its entirety. And, in practice, things do occasionally happen to you and me, as to everybody else, which are so marvellous and almost unheard-of that we can hardly believe in them ourselves, and which any ordinary person would certainly reject as mere fiction. As a matter of fact, I do believe Aristomenes' tale and I'm most grateful to him for having entertained me so well by the pleasant telling of this fine story; I hardly noticed the roughness and steepness of the hill. And I believe that this horse of mine enjoyed it too. For without getting tired at all he has brought me to this city gate, not so much on horseback as towed along by my ears.'

That was the end of our talk and our journey; for the two of them turned off towards a little house to the left of the road.

>>>>><<<<<

AT MILO'S HOUSE

I RODE up to the first inn I saw and asked the old woman who was the inn-keeper: 'Is this the town of Hypata?'

She nodded.

'You know a man named Milo, one of the first citizens of the place?'

'Well, you might call him that, I suppose,' she answered, 'because his house is one of the first that you come to. It's outside the city walls.'

'Joking apart, good Mother, would you mind letting me know what sort of a man he is and telling me how to reach his house?'

'Do you see that last row of windows facing the city, with the gate on the other side opening on an alley? That's where Milo lives – a very rich old man and a disgrace to the whole district – the meanest, most miserly, dirtiest fellow. He's a money-lender – devotes all his time to making loans on pledges of silver and gold – and lives shut up there in that little house, gloating all day over his stacks of coin. Nobody lives with him except his unfortunate wife and one slave-girl; and when he does go out, he dresses like a beggar.'

When I heard this I laughed and said to myself: 'My friend Demeas has certainly given me a valuable letter of introduction. While I'm staying with Milo I need not at least be afraid of smoky fires or pervasive kitchen smells.'

With these mild reflections I came up to the door and found it stoutly barred. I banged at it and shouted. After a time a girl came out and asked: 'You, who are banging at the door so noisily, what terms do you hope to borrow on? Are you the only man who doesn't know we only accept gold and silver as pledges?'

'Speak more politely,' I replied, 'and tell me if I would find your master in the house.'

'Of course he is. But what's your business?'

'I have come with a letter of introduction to him from Demeas the Corinthian.'

'Wait here,' she said, 'while I give him your message.' She barred the gate again and went back into the house. Presently she reappeared and opened the doors and said: 'My master asks you to come in.'

I went in and found Milo in his dining-room, stretched out on a very narrow couch and just beginning his dinner. His wife sat at his feet.

He waved a hand at the bare table and said: 'Just in time for a meal.'

'Right,' I said, and handed him the letter, which he hurriedly read. 'I'm grateful to my friend Demeas,' he said, 'for giving me an opportunity to have such a fine guest.' Then he sent his wife away and asked me to sit down in her place. Naturally I hesitated, but he caught hold of my tunic and steered me to the seat. 'Sit there,' he said, 'for there isn't any other stool or enough furniture. It's a necessary precaution against burglary.'

I sat down.

'I guessed at once,' he said, 'from your attractive physical appearance and your truly maidenly modesty, that you must be a man of good family, and from Demeas' letter I now see that I was right; but please don't despise our little cottage. The decent spare bedroom which adjoins this room is at your disposal; if you can manage to content yourself with this humble lodging you will be doing us an honour, and at the same time earning credit such as the famous Theseus earned – I noticed that your father's name is Theseus too – when he condescended to accept the hospitality of poor old Hecale.'[1]

Then he called the girl: 'Fotis, take this gentleman's bag into the spare bedroom and put it down carefully. Then quickly fetch a towel from the cupboard, and a flask of toilet-oil, and take him along to the nearest public baths. He must be hot and tired after his long and tiresome journey.'

When I heard this I saw at once how extraordinarily mean Milo was, but decided to humour him. I said: 'Please don't trouble about the oil or the towel. I always carry that sort of thing in my bags, and I can easily find my way to the baths. My only anxiety at the moment is for my horse. He deserves a reward for having carried me here so willingly. Please, Fotis, would you mind buying him a good feed of hay and oats? Here's the money.'

When this had been done and Fotis had arranged my things in the bedroom, I walked towards the baths, first visiting the provision market to buy something for my supper. There was plenty of fish for sale, and though I was first asked two hundred *drachmae*[2] a basket, eventually I beat a fishmonger down to twenty, paid him and walked off with my purchase. As I left the market, a man named Pythias, who had been one of my fellow-students at Athens, happened to pass by. After looking at me for a considerable time he recognized me and gave me a most friendly embrace.

'My dear Lucius! Heavens, what a long time it is since we last saw each other – not since we finished studying under Clytius. Tell me, what brings you here?'

'I will tell you tomorrow,' I said. 'But what's this I see? A magistrate's robe and a posse of constables armed with truncheons marching behind you? My heartiest congratulations!'

He explained: 'I am now the aedile[3] in charge of markets, so if you want anything for your supper, please call on me.'

'How kind of you! But I have just bought myself enough fish for my meal.' But when he saw my basket, he shook the fish about so that he could inspect them more closely and then asked: 'Do you mind telling me what you paid for this refuse?'

'It took me a long time to beat the fishmonger down to twenty *drachmae*.'

On hearing this he took me by the hand and led me back into the delicatessen market: 'Which fishmonger? Point him out to me.'

I pointed back at a little old man seated in a corner. Pythias at once began abusing him in his severest official tones: 'Hey, you, is this the way to treat the Inspector-General's friends, or for that matter any visitor at all who comes to buy in the market? Asking such a huge price for these absurd little tiddlers! Hypata is the most prosperous town in all Thessaly, but with fellows like you forcing up food prices to such a preposterous height we might as well be living in the rocky wilderness. And don't think that you're going to escape without punishment. By Heaven, I intend to keep you rogues in check, so long as I hold my present appointment.'

He emptied the basket on the ground, ordering one of his constables to jump on the fish and squash them underfoot on the pavement.[4] Contented with his own severity, Pythias advised me to go home, declaring his satisfaction that the old wretch had been sufficiently humiliated.

My knowledgeable old fellow-student! Flabbergasted at having lost both my supper and my money as the result of his kind intervention, I went on to the baths. After bathing I returned to Milo's hospitality and had not been long in my bedroom before Fotis came in. 'The master is expecting you at the supper-table,' she said.

Remembering Milo's frugal habits I sent him a polite message, begging to be excused: 'Explain to him, please, that I'm so tired after my ride that I need sleep more than food.'

Fotis took my message in and presently Milo himself appeared, grabbed hold of my wrist and politely tried to drag me off with him to the supper room. I held back and modestly tried to excuse myself. But: 'I won't stir from here until you consent to come with me,' he swore. So I had to give in to his insistence, and he led me again to the same old couch, where he sat me down.

'Now tell me,' he said. 'How is our mutual friend Demeas? All's well with him, I hope? And how is his wife? Are his children in good health? Any trouble with the servants?'

I answered him in detail. Next, he demanded an exact account of the business affairs that I had come to settle in Hypata, and again I satisfied his curiosity. Then he wanted to know all about conditions in my native province, asking for full biographical details of all our leading citizens and, finally, of the Governor himself. I began to nod – the journey had been wearisome enough without all this boring talk – and kept stopping short in the middle of sentences, or getting my words mixed up. He saw that I was dead tired and at last allowed me to go to bed.

And so I finally escaped from this smelly old man's meagre talkative supper and returned to my room heavy with sleep (not with food, since I had only dined on conversation) and gave myself up to peaceful and welcome slumber.

*

The next morning I awoke early and rose at once. I have an almost morbid interest in everything queer and out of the way, and I remembered that here I was in the heart of Thessaly, a province notorious as the native home of magic and sorcery; and in the very city, too, which had been the scene of Aristomenes' story. So I looked around me with excitement, carefully examining everything within view. How could I be sure that anything in the whole city was what it seemed to be, rather than transformed into quite other shapes by deadly spells? Thus I wondered whether the stones I kicked against were really, perhaps, petrified men and whether the birds I heard singing were people in feathered disguise,[5] and I began to entertain similar doubts about the trees around the house and even about the faucets through which the fountains played. I was quite prepared to see the statues and the images of gods step from their pedestals, or hear the walls speak, have strange news told me by oxen and other cattle; or even to be granted an oracle from Heaven and the sun in the sky.

In this stupid, overwrought and dissatisfied mood, though nowhere finding the least justification for my suspicions, I wandered all round the town from door to door and at last found myself once again in the market. A woman came by with a crowd of servants in attendance, her long jewelled ear-rings and the jewel-studded embroidery on her dress showing her to be of high rank. At her side walked an old man who cried out as soon as he saw me: 'Bless my soul! Here's Lucius.' He came forward and embraced me, and then going back to the lady whispered something in her ear, after which he came up to me again and said: 'Come, come, Lucius, why don't you go along and give your relation an affectionate kiss?'

'I could never take such a liberty with a lady to whom I have not the honour of being introduced,' I quickly answered, with a blush, staying where I was and looking down at my feet. She was staring attentively at me. 'Really,' she exclaimed, 'he shows just the same dignified behaviour as his saintly mother, Salvia. She had exactly the same slenderness and upright carriage, the same rosy cheeks and delicate skin, the same yellow hair neatly dressed, the same alert, shining grey eyes that used to remind me of an eagle's, the same graceful way of walking.' Then she said: 'I nursed you with my own hands as a baby, Lucius. But there's nothing so strange about that, because your dear mother and I were not only maternal cousins (the celebrated Plutarch was our ancestor) but foster-sisters, brought up together in the same house. In fact, the only difference in rank between us is that she married a nobleman, I married a commoner.

Byrrhaena is my name – your mother must often have mentioned it when telling you about your early childhood. You must come to stay with me at once and treat my house as your home.'

By this time I had recovered from my embarrassment. 'God forbid, my kinswoman,' I replied, 'that I should forsake Milo's hospitality without having anything against him. But I shall be most happy to see as much of you as my obligations to him permit: whenever I come this way I shall call on you without fail.'

While we were engaged in this sort of chat, a very few steps brought us to her house. Its courtyard with ornamental pillars at the four corners, surmounted by winged Victories, was very beautiful. The figures were extraordinarily life-like, each hovering, palm-branch in hand on outspread wings, her dewy feet so lightly poised on a motionless globe that you would never have guessed that they were carved from the same block of stone – they really looked as if they could be in motion and were on the point of soaring off again. But a sculptured group of Parian marble that stood in the very centre of the court put everything else into proper perspective. It was a Diana with Hounds; wonderful work. The goddess seemed to be striding towards you as you entered, her tunic blown back by the wind and awing you by the majesty of her presence. The brace of hounds on either side of her were balanced on their hind legs, ready to bound off in a flash. They looked so menacing with their fierce eyes, pricked ears, dilated nostrils and snarling jaws, that if any other dog near by had barked you would have thought for the moment that the sound came from their marble throats. Behind the goddess was a rock formation in the form of a cavern, its entrance carpeted in moss, grass, fallen leaves and brushwood, with shrubs and creepers growing here and there; the back was a highly polished slab which marvellously mirrored her shoulders; and under the lip hung apples and grapes, ripe for eating, so exquisitely carved that you fancied yourself in the wine season of autumn. And when you looked down at the rivulet which seemed to spring and ripple from the goddess's footprints, you could see the sculptured grapes that hung down and seemed almost to move like real clusters of fruit. But this was not all: from the tangle of branches appeared the face of Actaeon peeping eagerly out, already half-transformed into a stag – as also showed in the reflection of the scene carved on the surface of the water – for spying on the goddess when she was about to bathe.[6]

As I was examining the group with delighted curiosity, Byrrhaena said: 'This is all for you.' Then she sent off the servants so that we could talk privately. And then, when they had gone, she said: 'In the name of this goddess, Diana, dear Lucius, I beg you to be on your guard. I find it difficult to express my anxiety for you in your present situation; but please understand that my feelings for you are almost as tender as if you were my own son. I must give you a warning, a very solemn warning, against Milo's wife, Pamphile, who, I fear, will try to fascinate you by magic. She is a well-known witch and said to be a past mistress of every sort of necromancy; so much so, that merely by breathing on twigs, stones and so on, she can transfer the light, the starry sky, to the dark depths of Hell and thus restore the reign of primal Chaos ... She falls in love with every handsome young man she sets eyes on, and at once fixes her eyes and affections upon him. She begins her campaign with flattering advances and subdues his will, after which she binds him to her with the unbreakable fetters of boundless eroticism; but whenever she meets with resistance, her rage and hatred are so violent that she petrifies her victim on the spot, or transforms him into a ram or a bull or a wild beast, or kills him out of hand. You can imagine my concern on your behalf, because Pamphile is a nymphomaniac and you're exactly the type of good-looking young man that would most attract her.'

This was the warning that Byrrhaena anxiously gave me. But as soon as Byrrhaena mentioned the magical art, which has always aroused my curiosity, so far from feeling inclined to be on my guard against Pamphile I had an irresistible impulse to study magic under her, however much money it might cost me, and take a running leap into the dark abyss against which I had been warned. I was madly excited; I disengaged my hand from Byrrhaena's, almost as though I were snapping a chain, and left her with an abrupt goodbye. I set out at a run for Milo's house, and as I raced madly through the streets I was saying to myself: 'Now, take care, Lucius! Have your wits about you, because here at last you have a chance: your secret ambition has always been to study magical marvels. Forget your childish terrors. Face this new undertaking boldly and practically – though of course you must avoid any entanglement with Pamphile so as to avoid going to bed with your worthy host Milo's wife. On the other hand, there's no reason why you shouldn't try to seduce

Fotis; the girl is beautiful, lively and amusing. And last night when you went to bed, she led you tenderly to your room, lovingly covered you up, and gave you a charming kiss on the head and showed quite plainly how sorry she was to leave you; indeed, she kept stopping on her way to the door and looking back at you. The very best of luck to you, then, Lucius; but, whatever may come of it, good or bad, my advice is: go for Fotis.' As I thought all this over, my mind was now made up, and when I reached Milo's house I walked in as determinedly as if I were marching into the division lobby.

I did not find Milo or his wife at home but there was my charming Fotis, preparing a dish of pork rissoles for her master and mistress, while the appetizing smell of haggis-stew drifted to my nostrils. She wore a neat white house-dress, gathered in below the breasts with a red silk band, and as she alternately stirred the casserole and shaped the rissoles with her pretty hands, the twisting and turning made her loins and thighs quiver seductively.

The sight had so powerful an effect on me that for a while I stood rooted in admiration; and my penis, hitherto recumbent, stood up as well. At last I found my voice. 'Dear Fotis,' I said, 'how daintily, how charmingly you stir that casserole: I love watching you wriggle your hips. And what a wonderful dish you have there! The man whom you allow to poke his finger into your little casserole is the luckiest fellow alive.'

'Go away, you scoundrel,' the sharp-witted girl replied. 'Keep clear of my little cooking stove! If you come too near, even when the fire is low, a spark may fly out and set you on fire; and when that happens nobody but myself will be capable of putting the flames out. Because I know how to keep things spiced and on the move – between the sheets as well as on a kitchen-stove.'

She turned and laughed at me. I did not leave the kitchen until I had taken a careful look at her from head to foot. But for the moment I need only write about her head; the truth is that I have an obsession about heads and hair. Whenever I meet a pretty woman, the first thing that catches my eye is her hair; I make a careful mental picture of it to carry home and brood over in private. This habit of mine I justify on a sound logical principle: that the hair is the most important and conspicuous feature of the body, and that its natural brilliance does for the head what gaily coloured clothes do for the body. In fact, it does a great deal more. You know how women, when they want to display their beauty to the full, shed their embroidered wraps and step out of their dresses, and proudly reveal themselves with nothing on at all, since even the brightest gold tissue has less effect than the delicate tints of a woman's naked body. But – and here you must excuse a horrible idea which I hope nobody will ever put into practice – if you shaved the head of even the most beautiful woman alive and so deprived her face of its natural setting, then I don't care whether she originally floated down from Heaven and was reborn from sea-foam. [7] I don't even care whether she were Venus herself, with every one of the Graces and Cupids in attendance, Venus dripping with precious balsam and fragrant as cinnamon, and with the famous girdle of love clasped around her waist – the fact is, that her baldness would leave her completely without attraction even for her own husband. [8]

What joy it is to see hair of a beautiful colour caught in the full rays of the sun, or shining with a milder lustre and constantly varying its shade as the light shifts. Golden at one moment, at the next honey-coloured; or black as a raven's wing, but suddenly taking on the pale bluish tints of a dove's neck-feathers. Give it a gloss with Arabian lotion, part it neatly with a finely toothed comb, catch it up with a ribbon behind – and the lover will make it a sort of mirror to reflect his own delighted looks. And oh, when hair is bunched up in a thick luxurious mass on a woman's head or allowed to flow rippling down her neck in profuse curls! Such is the glory of a woman's hair that though she may be wearing the most exquisite clothes and gold and every kind of jewellery, she cannot look well got up unless she has done her hair in proper style.

Fotis, I grant, needed no expert knowledge of hairdressing: she could even indulge an apparent neglect of the art. Her way was to let her long, thick hair hang loosely down her neck, braiding the ends together and catching them up again with a broad ribbon to the top of her head; which was the exact spot where, unable to restrain myself a moment longer, I now printed a long passionate kiss.

She glanced back at me over her shoulder, and rolled her eyes sidelong at me. 'Oh, you schoolboy!' she said. 'Always greedy for anything sweet, without a thought for the bitter aftertaste.'

'What do I care, you beautiful thing? I give you leave to lay me at full length on this fire and grill me, so long as you just give me a single kiss first.' I threw my arms around her and began to kiss her. Then she returned my embraces with answering passion. Her breath smelled as sweet as cinnamon, and the darting of her tongue was like nectar in Heaven. I gasped out: 'Oh, Fotis, this is killing me! Unless you take pity on me I'm as good as dead.'

After I had said this, she kissed me again and said: 'Cheer up; I feel just the same as you do and am utterly yours, and we shan't have to put off our pleasure any longer, because as soon as the torches are lit tonight I'll come to your bedroom. Now go away, and keep in good condition, for I'm going to fight you all night long with vigorous courage.'

After a good deal more in the same strain, we parted; and about noon a complimentary present arrived from Byrrhaena. It consisted of a fat pig, a brace and a half of chickens and a jar of expensive vintage wine. I called Fotis. 'Look, darling,' I said. 'We didn't remember to invoke the God of Wine,[9] did we? But he always aids and abets the Goddess of Love, so he's come of his own accord. Let's drink up the whole of this wine tonight. It will rid us of all embarrassment and supply us with the energy we need for our work. In provisioning the ship of Venus for a night's cruise, one needs to make certain of two things only; that there's enough oil for the lamp and wine for the cup.'

I spent the rest of the day at the baths and on my return found that my two slaves, who had been following me on foot from Corinth, had just arrived and that the worthy Milo was expecting me to join him and Pamphile at their neatly arranged little supper table. Fotis had put part of my gift to immediate use and forced Milo to be generous for once. With Byrrhaena's warning fresh in my mind I kept as far as possible out of Pamphile's view. But every now and then I stole a frightened glance in her direction, as if she were the Lake of Avernus[10] itself; but Fotis was waiting on us, so most of the time I looked behind me and gazed at her and felt completely at my ease.

It was now growing dark and the table lamp was lighted. Pamphile studied the wick and pronounced: 'Tomorrow it will rain heavily.'

'How do you know that?' Milo asked.

'Why, by the lamp.'

Milo laughed: 'We are evidently entertaining a famous Sibyl:[11]

from the watch-tower of her lamp-stand she surveys the universe and foretells what sort of a trip the sun is going to enjoy the next day.'

I broke in: 'But is it really to be wondered at that this flame, though small and artificially lighted, should retain some memory of its father the sun, the prime source of fire, and so be able to foretell, by divine instinct, what is about to happen in the skies? At Corinth recently we saw an Assyrian astrologer[12] who had put the whole city in a flutter by his accurate answers to questions he was asked. For a fee he would tell people exactly on what day to marry, or on what day to build if they wanted a building to stand for ever, or on what day to conclude a business deal, or on what day to set out on a journey by land or sea. When I questioned him about this expedition of mine, his answers were strange and rather contradictory: he told me, for instance, that it would make me very famous and that I should write a long book about it which nobody, however, would take seriously.'

Milo laughed again: 'What did this Chaldaean of yours look like, and what did he call himself?'

'He was tall and rather dark. His name was Diophanes.'

'The very man who once came here to Hypata and made the same sort of predictions! He earned a lot of money, a small fortune, in fact, but in the end fate proved unpropitious, or downright vicious, for the unfortunate man. It happened like this. One day Diophanes stood in the middle of a crowd of people, all wanting to hear their own peculiar fates. A business man named Cerdo had just asked him to name a lucky day for travelling. Diophanes gave him the answer and Cerdo opened his purse and began counting out the fee of a hundred *drachmae*. At that moment a young nobleman came up from behind and tugged at Diophanes' robe. He turned round and they embraced affectionately. "Sit down beside me!" said Diophanes, and, astonished by suddenly seeing him, he forgot all about the business he was engaged upon and said: " What a pleasure this is! I have hoped to see you for so long. When did you arrive?"

'"Only last night," he answered; "but, brother, you must explain your sudden departure from Euboea and tell me what sort of a sea and land journey you had." Then this notable Chaldaean Diophanes, thoroughly off his guard, cried out: "If only all my enemies and ill-wishers could meet with as much bad luck as I did on my way here.

The ten-year wanderings of Ulysses on his return from Troy were nothing to it. To begin with, our ship was struck by a sudden gale as soon as she put to sea and tossed about from whirlpool to whirlpool, then both her rudders snapped and, finally, just as we made the opposite coast she sank like a stone. Some of us managed to swim ashore, but with the loss of all our belongings, and we had to beg or borrow money to help us on the next stage of our journey. And, as though all this had not been enough, we were attacked by bandits, and my brother Arignotus, who showed fight, was murdered before my very eyes."

'While Diophanes was still telling his sad story, the merchant Cerdo picked up his money again and slipped off, and it was only then that he came to himself and realized that he'd given away the whole show; for we were all shouting with laughter. Nevertheless, Lord Lucius, I sincerely hope that what this celebrated Chaldaean told you was the truth, though you may be the only man to whom he ever told it, and that you will continue to have a pleasant and prosperous journey.'

I groaned silently as Milo went maundering on. I was vexed with myself for having started him on a train of anecdotes at a time like this: I saw that I was in danger of losing the best part of the night and all the pleasures that it promised me. At last I yawned shamelessly and said: 'It's all the same to me what misfortunes happen to Diophanes and I don't care whether land or sea get the bigger share of his earnings the next time he's forced to disgorge. The fact is that I'm still suffering from the effects of my ride and feel quite worn out. Please forgive me if I say good night at once and go straight to sleep.'

I rose and went to my bedroom. On the way I noticed that the palliasse that my two slaves shared in the inner courtyard had been moved as far as possible away from my door – evidently Fotis had taken this precaution against their overhearing our love talk that night – and, inside, I found a feast waiting for me. My bedside table was covered with little dishes of tasty food saved from supper and generous cups of wine, with only just enough room left at the top for the necessary tempering with water, and there was a bell-mouthed decanter, handy for pouring out more wine – everything set for erotic gladiatorial combat.

By the time that I was in bed, Fotis, who had succeeded in getting her mistress off to sleep quickly, appeared in the doorway with a bunch of roses. A rose in full bloom was tucked between her breasts. She glided towards me, kissed me firmly, wove some of the roses into a garland for my head and sprinkled the bed with the petals of the rest. Then she took a cup of wine, diluted it with hot water and put it to my lips; but before I could drain it she gently pulled it away and, gazing fixedly at me, took sweet little sips at it, until it was empty. This performance she repeated two or three times.

The wine went to my head; but it also went to my body and made me lascivious. Lechery was striking at the top of my groin, and pushing aside my clothes I gave my Fotis visible proof of my impatience. 'Have pity on me,' I said, 'and come quickly to my rescue. As you see I'm well armed and ready for the merciless battle to which you challenged me, without official permission.[13] Since the first of Cupid's sharp arrows lodged in my heart this morning, I have been standing to arms all day, and now my bow is strung so tight that I'm afraid something will snap since it's so stiff. However, if you want me to show even greater enthusiasm, let your hair down so that it ripples all over your neck and shoulders, and give me a lovely kiss.'

Without delay she snatched away the plates and dishes, pulled off every stitch of clothing, untied her hair and tossed it into happy disorder with a shake of her head. There she stood. The gesture with which her pink hand screened her hairless crotch was deliberate and had nothing to do with modesty.

'Now fight,' she challenged me. 'And you must fight hard, because I shall not retreat one inch, nor turn my back on you. Come on face to face if you're a man, strike home, do your very best. Kill me, and perish yourself! There's no time-limit for today's fight.'

With these words she climbed into bed, sat on top of me and jogged up and down, with amorous wrigglings of her supple hips, a straddling Venus whose fruitfulness gorged me completely; and at last with overpowered senses and dripping limbs Fotis and I fell into a simultaneous clinch, gasping out our lives.

However, after dosing ourselves with more wine, we presently recovered from our weariness and renewed our sexual energies and pleasures. This was the first of many nights which we spent in the same way.

>>>>><<<<<

THE STORY OF THELYPHRON

ONE day Byrrhaena sent me a pressing invitation to a supper party, and though I made various excuses she refused to accept any of them. There was nothing for it but to go to Fotis, as one might consult the auspices, and ask her advice. She now resented my straying a yard from her company, but I was generously excused my amorous military duties that evening and granted a short leave of absence. However, she warned me: 'Listen! Don't stay too long at the party. Come back as soon as you can, for in the early hours Hypata is terrorized by a gang of aristocratic young men who murder whoever happens to be passing by and leave the streets strewn with corpses. The Governor's troops are a long way away, so nothing can be done to end the nuisance. You are in particular danger of being attacked, because you look prosperous, and because these youths have no respect for foreigners.'

'You needn't worry, dearest Fotis,' I told her. 'That supper party has far less attraction for me than our pleasures here; so I promise to shorten your anxiety by coming home as soon as I can. Besides, I shall not go without company, because I shall wear this sword, which I know very well how to handle in self-defence.'

The supper party proved to be a large one. Byrrhaena was the leading woman of Hypata and everybody was there who was anybody. The tables shone richly with citrus wood and ivory; the couches were upholstered in cloth of gold; each of the large wine-cups, though all were of different workmanship, was equally valuable – whether of glass engraved with fine designs, or unblemished crystal, or brilliant silver, or glittering gold, or beautifully carved amber, or precious stones made into drinking receptacles. In short, think of anything impossible in the way of cups, and there you had it.

A swarm of splendidly liveried waiters kept the tables deftly supplied with food, while curly-headed pages in handsome clothes ran up and down replenishing those jewels of cups with vintage wines of great age.

The lights were brought in, and the conversation began to get lively, amid rising laughter and abundant jokes and merriment. Byrrhaena turned to me and asked: 'Well, what do you think of our beloved Thessaly? So far as I know we are a long way in advance of all other countries in the world, if you judge by temples, baths and other public buildings, and our private houses are incomparably better furnished. Besides, anyone who has the time can do just what he likes: if he is on business he can enjoy all the bustle of Rome, and if he wants a thorough rest there are houses here as peaceful as any country manor. Hypata, in fact, has come to be the chief holiday centre of the province.'

I agreed with her warmly. 'Nowhere in all my travels have I ever felt freer than I do here – though I do have to admit my terror of the mysterious arts of your local witches, against which there seems to be no known means of protecting oneself. I am told that not even the tombs of the dead are safe – that they rifle graves and pyres to dig up remains and pieces of corpses in order to blast the lives of the living. And that these old sorceresses, the moment they hear of death anywhere about, run off at top speed and mutilate the corpse before it is buried.'

'There's no doubt at all about that,' said a man at my table, 'and, what's more, they don't even spare the living. Not long ago a certain man got dreadfully damaged all over his face.'

An uncontrolled burst of laughter greeted this remark, and everyone turned round to look at a guest reclining in a corner. The man, thoroughly embarrassed at the way they went on gazing at him and muttering to himself, was on the point of walking out when Byrrhaena spoke to him.

'No, no, my dear Thelyphron,' she protested. 'Sit where you are for a bit. Show your usual good humour and tell us that adventure of yours once again; I am anxious that this son of mine, Lucius, should have the pleasure of hearing it from your own lips. It is a wonderful story.'

He answered: 'My Lady Byrrhaena, you are always the perfect hostess and your goodness of heart never fails; but the insolence of my fellow-guests is past endurance.'

He was still very angry, but Byrrhaena told him firmly that he would be doing her a great disservice if he went against her wishes, however disagreeable he might find the task that she had set him. So he made a little heap of the coverings of his couch and propped himself up on it with his elbow; then with his right hand he signalled for attention in oratorical style, protruding the forefinger and middle finger, pointing the thumb upward and folding down the two remaining fingers.

This was the story he told:

'While I was still young I came over from Miletus to attend the Olympian Games. Afterwards, feeling a strong desire to visit this famous province,[1] I travelled throughout Thessaly. One unlucky day I arrived at Larissa, having run through nearly all the money I had brought with me, and while I was wandering up and down the streets, wondering how to refill my purse, I saw a tall old man standing on a stone block in the middle of the market place. He was making a public announcement at the top his voice, offering a large reward to anyone who would stand guard over a corpse that night.

'I asked a bystander: "What is the meaning of this? Are the corpses of Larissa in the habit of running away?"

'"Hush," he answered. "You are only a boy and very much of a stranger here, else you would realize that you are in Thessaly where witches are in the habit of gnawing bits of flesh off dead men's faces for use in their magical concoctions."

'"Then would you mind telling me," I said, "what this guardian-ship of the dead involves?"

'"First of all," he replied, "it means watching attentively the whole night, one's eyes wide open and fixed on the corpse without a single sideways glance. You see, these abominable women have the power of changing their shape at pleasure: they turn into birds or dogs or mice, or even flies – disguises that would pass scrutiny even in a Court of Law, and by daylight too – and then charm the guardians asleep. I won't try to tell you all the extraordinarily ingenious tricks that they use when they want to indulge their beastly appetites; at any rate, the usual reward is no more than four or six pieces of gold. Oh – I was almost forgetting to tell you that if next morning the guardian fails to hand over the corpse in exactly the same condition as he found it, he is obliged to have bits cut from his own face to supply whatever is missing."

'That did not frighten me. I boldly told the crier that he need not repeat the announcement. "I'm ready to undertake the job," I said. "What fee do they offer?"

'"A thousand *nummi*. But take care, young man, that you defend the corpse vigilantly against those terrible harpies: the deceased was the son of one of our first citizens."

'"You are telling me silly nonsense," I said. "You see before you a man of iron; I never trouble to go to sleep, and I have sharper eyesight than Lynceus or Argus[2] – all eyes, that's what I am."

'I had hardly finished before the old man hurried me along to a house with its gates barred. He took me through a small side door and along corridors until I reached a dark room with closed shutters, where a woman in deep mourning sat wailing.

'The crier went up to her and said: "This man has been hired to guard your husband's body faithfully tonight."

'She pushed back the hair that hung over her beautiful grief-stricken face and implored me to be vigilant at my post.

'"You need have no anxiety, Madam, if you make it worth my while afterwards."

'Contented with this, she got up quickly and led me into another room, where the corpse lay wrapped in pure white linen sheets. Then she called in seven witnesses and after a further fit of weeping showed them every single part of the body, desiring them to testify to what they had seen. Then she uttered those words which she had deliberately composed, and one of those present noted down on tablets: "See, the nose is untouched, the eyes are intact, the ears are still there, the lips are undamaged, the chin is sound. Good Quirites, bear witness that this is so." And, after this speech, the tablets sealed, she withdrew.

'I asked her: "Will you be good enough, Madam, to see that I have everything I need for my vigil tonight?"

'"What sort of things?"

'"A good large lamp with enough oil in it to last until daybreak; jars of wine; warm water for diluting it; a cup; and a nice dish left over from your supper."

'She shook her head: "Get away with you, you idiot. Dinners and plates of food indeed in this house of mourning, where no fire has been lighted for days! Do you imagine that you have come here for a jolly supper party? You are expected to mourn and weep like the

32

rest of us." Then, turning to her maid: "Myrrhina, give him the lamp and the oil straight away, shut the door and leave the guardian to his task."

'All alone with the corpse, I fortified my eyes for their vigil by rubbing them hard and kept up my spirits by singing. Twilight shaded into night, and night grew deeper and deeper, blacker and blacker, until my usual bed-time had passed and it was close on midnight. I was beginning to feel thoroughly frightened when all of a sudden a weasel squeezed in through a hole in the door, stopped close by me and fixed her eyes intently on mine. The boldness of the little creature was most disconcerting, but I managed to shout out: "Get away from here, little beast; run off to the little mice who're like yourself, before I do you violence. Get away!"

'She turned tail and immediately scuttled out of the room, but as she did so a sudden deep sleep stole over me and dragged me down with it into its bottomless gulfs. I fell on the floor and lay there so dead asleep that not even Delphic Apollo could have really decided which of us two who lay there was the corpse. For I too lay lifeless and in need of someone to watch over me – I might as well not have been there.

'At length the crested band of cocks began to crow declaring that night had called a truce, whereupon I awoke and ran in terror to the corpse. Moving the lamp close to it and uncovering its face I examined every feature carefully, and found it unmutilated. Almost at once the poor widow came running in, still weeping, with her witnesses. She at once threw herself on the corpse and after kissing it again and again had the lamp brought close to make sure that all was well. Then she turned and called: "Philodespotus, come here!"

'Her steward appeared. "Philodespotus, pay this young man his fee at once. He has kept watch very well."

As he counted me out the money she said: "Many thanks, young man, for your diligent services; they have earned you the freedom of this house."

'Delighted with my unexpected good luck, I tossed the bright gold coins up and down in my hand and answered: "I am much obliged to you, Madam. I shall be only too pleased to help you out again, whenever you may need my services."

'These words were scarcely out of my mouth when the whole household rushed at me with blows, cursing the dreadful ominousness of my words. One punched me in the face with his fists, another dug his elbows into my shoulder, someone else kicked me; my ribs were pummelled, my hair pulled, my clothes torn and before they finally threw me out of the house I felt like the proud young Aonian or the Muse's poet of Pimpleia.[3]

'When I paused in the next street to collect my senses and realized what I had said – it had certainly been a most tactless remark – I decided that I had deserved an even worse beating than I had got.

'By and by, after the last farewells and lamentations, the dead man was brought out of the house; and since he had been a man of such importance he was honoured with a public procession. As the cortège turned into the market-place, an old man in black came running up, the tears streaming down his face. In a frenzy of grief he tore out tufts of his fine white hair, grabbed hold of the coffin with both hands, and screamed and sobbed incessantly. "Gentlemen," he cried, "I appeal to your honour, I appeal to your sense of justice and public duty! Stand by your fellow-citizen; see that his death is avenged in full on that evil and criminal woman his widow. She, and she alone, is the murderess. To cover up a secret love affair and to get possession of her husband's estate she killed him – she poisoned the poor young man, my sister's son." The old man continued to sob and scream, until the crowd was stirred to indignant sympathy, thinking that he probably had good grounds for his accusations. Some shouted: "Burn her! Burn her!" and some: "Stone her!" and a gang of boys was encouraged to lynch her.

'However, she denied her guilt with artful tears, and devout appeals to all the gods to witness that she was utterly incapable of doing anything so wicked.

'"So let us refer the case," the old man said, "to a divine arbitration. And here is Zatchlas the Egyptian, a leading soothsayer, who has undertaken, for a large fee, to recall my nephew's soul from the Underworld and revive his body from beyond the threshold of death for a few brief moments."

'The person whom he introduced to the crowd was dressed in white linen, with palm-leaf sandals on his feet and a tonsured head. The old man kissed his hands repeatedly and clasped his knees. "O Priest," he cried, "take pity on me. I implore you by the stars of Heaven, by the gods of the Underworld, by the elements of nature, by the silence of night, by the temples of Coptos, by the flooding of the Nile, by the mysteries of Memphis and by the sacred rattle of Pharos[4] – I implore you by these holy things to grant my nephew's soul a brief return to the warmth of the sun and so re-illumine his eyes, which are closed for ever, that they may open and momentarily regain their sight. I do not seek to resist. I do not deny the grave what is her due; my plea is only for a brief spell of life, during which the dead man may assist me in avenging his own murder – the only possible consolation I can have."

'The soothsayer, yielding to his entreaties, touched the corpse's mouth three times with a certain small herb and laid another on its breast. Then he turned to the east, with a silent prayer to the sacred disk of the rising sun. At the sight of these solemn preparations the whole crowd stood prepared for a miracle. I pushed in among them and climbed up on a stone just behind the coffin, from which I watched the whole scene with rising curiosity.

'Presently the chest of the corpse began to heave, blood began to pour again through its veins, breath returned to its body. And now the young man arose and broke into speech. "Why do you call me back to the obligations of this transitory life, when I have already drunk of the stream of Lethe and floated on the marshy waters of the Styx? Leave me alone, I beg you, leave me alone! Let me sleep undisturbed."

'When he heard the body uttering these words, the soothsayer raised his voice excitedly: "What? You refuse to address your fellow-citizens here and clear up the mystery of your death? Don't you realize that my spells can call up the dreadful Furies and have your weary limbs tortured?"

'At this the dead man, answering from his bier, groaned out to the crowd: "I was poisoned and destroyed by the evil arts of my newly married wife and gave up my bed, while it was still warm, to her adulterous lover."

'His illustrious widow showed remarkable courage in the circumstances. She denied everything with sacrilegious oaths and began contradicting and arguing with her late husband. The crowd were in a turmoil and took different sides. Some were for burying the wicked woman alive in the same grave as her victim; but others refused to admit the evidence of a senseless corpse – it was quite untrustworthy, they said.

'The corpse soon settled the dispute. With another hollow groan it said: "I will give you incontrovertible proof that what I say is true, by disclosing something that is known to nobody but myself." Then he pointed up at me and said: "While that intelligent gentleman was keeping careful watch over my corpse, the ghoulish witches who were hovering near, waiting for a chance to rob it, did their best to deceive him by continuously changing shape, but he saw through all their tricks. Finally they threw a cloud of sleep over him and when he was buried in the depths of slumber called me by name over and over again, until the slack limbs and chilly members of my body began, by strenuous efforts, to obey their magic arts. He however, who was alive, though for the time dead with sleep, happened to have the same name as I. So when they called his name he rose up like a senseless ghost and walked forward, and they, although the door of the room had been carefully closed, made their way in through the hole and cut off first his nose and then his ears, inflicting on him the injuries that were intended for me. But to divert attention from what they had done, they fitted him with a wax nose exactly like his own, and a pair of wax ears. And now what the poor fellow has earned is not a reward for his diligence, but mutilation."

'Terrified by this story, I clapped my hand to my face to see if there were any truth in it, and my nose fell off; then I touched my ears, and they fell off too. A hundred fingers pointed at me from the crowd and a great roar of laughter went up. I burst into a cold sweat, leaped down from the stone and slipped away between their legs. Disfigured and ridiculous, I have never since cared to return home; and now I disguise the loss of my ears by growing my hair long and glue this linen nose on my face for decency's sake.'

The drunken diners laughed as heartily as before when Thelyphron had finished his story, and called for the usual toast to the God of Laughter. Byrrhaena explained: 'At Hypata, ever since the city was founded, we have celebrated a unique festival: the happy celebration of Laughter Day.[5] I do trust you will be present at the ceremony tomorrow and especially that you will be able to think out some joke of your own as a contribution to the proceedings; so that our offering to the great deity may be that much more substantial.'

'Certainly I will do as you ask,' I answered. 'And I only hope that I'll be able to invent something really good, something funny enough to clothe the mighty god himself with distinction.'

By this time I had drunk as much as I wanted, and when my slave came up to my table and told me that the night was late, I took a hearty leave of Byrrhaena and unsteadily made for home. The slave was carrying a lantern, but a sudden gust of wind extinguished it halfway down the first street and we had a difficult time finding our way out of this sightless nocturnal obscurity to our lodging, exhausted by catching our toes on the cobbles. And when at last we had both practically arrived, there were three strapping men heaving with all their strength at Milo's gate, trying to force their way in. They seemed not in the least alarmed by our arrival, but redoubled their assaults with greater violence than before. I had no doubt that they were house-breakers, desperate ones too, and neither had the slave. Drawing my sword from under my cloak where I was holding it ready for just such an emergency as this, I rushed straight at them, and as they turned to close with me I drove the blade into each one's body up to the hilt. They fell, and I thrust at them repeatedly as they attempted to rise, until all three, riddled with wounds, gasped out their lives at my feet.

The noise of this fighting woke Fotis, who opened the gate for me. I crawled into the house, panting for breath and dripping with sweat, and flung myself on my bed. There I fell asleep in a moment, as exhausted by my fight as if I had been battling like Hercules with Geryon.[6]

>>>>>><<<<<

CHAPTER IV

THE FESTIVAL OF LAUGHTER

DAWN with rosy arm uplifted had just begun to urge her gleaming steeds through the morning sky, when I woke from a tranquil sleep: night had handed me over to the custody of day, and I remembered the acts of violence I had committed while it was still dark; my mind was in a ferment. I sat hunched up in bed with my feet crossed and my fingers nervously clasping and unclasping themselves as I hugged my knees. I wept bitterly, picturing to myself the scene in court, my trial and condemnation, my executioner. 'How can I hope to find a judge,' I asked myself, 'so mild and understanding as to find me not guilty of deliberately murdering those three men? I suppose that this was what Diophanes the Assyrian had in mind when he persistently predicted that my journey was to make me famous!'

I was still brooding on these matters and lamenting my unfortunate situation when I heard a violent knocking and shouting at the gate. As soon as it was opened, in rushed a great mass of people, headed by the magistrates and town lictors,[1] and occupied every room in the house. Two constables were ordered to arrest me and, though I offered no resistance, I was dragged violently off. When we reached the end of the lane I was astonished to see an enormous crowd waiting for my appearance: the entire population of Hypata seemed to be present. But as I walked miserably along, staring at the ground and into the very jaws of death, I was astonished, as I glanced up for a moment, to see that among all those many thousands there was not a single person who was not bursting with laughter.

They took me along a circuitous processional route, turning corner after corner. It was as though I were the sacrificial victim which is led in procession when an offering is needed to placate the local deities. Eventually I was put into the dock, and the magistrates took their seats on the bench. But when the herald bawled for silence, protests were heard from every side. 'There are so many people here that we're being crushed to death! Try him in the theatre instead!'

The crowd emptied itself into the theatre with remarkable speed. Every single seat was occupied, every entrance blocked; even the roof was alive with people. Some balanced on the top of columns, some clung to statues, some squeezed themselves in at the windows or straddled the rafters; nobody seemed to pay the least attention to his own safety in the general desire to witness my trial. The constables led me across the stage and placed me right in front, close to the orchestra, like some sacrificial victim.

The herald began bawling again, this time summoning the chief witness for the prosecution to appear. Up stepped an old man. He was invited to speak for as long as there was water in the clock;[2] this was a hollow globe into which water was poured through a funnel in the neck, and from it gradually escaped through fine perforations at the base.

He spoke as follows:

'We are dealing today, your Honours, with a matter which I regard as of no small importance, because it affects the peace of the whole town; and I trust that your Honours' sentence will be an exemplary one – that your sense of civic dignity will not allow you to condone this bloody multiple murder of your fellow-citizens committed by this homicidal villain. You must not suspect that I am motivated by any private grudge or feud in bringing this accusation. The fact is that I am the Captain of the Town Watch, and I doubt whether there is a man alive who can charge me with any irregularity in the performance of my duties. So let me report in detail exactly what happened last night. About midnight when I was completing my rounds, having visited every street from door to door and made sure that all was in order, my attention was directed to this brutal young man who was running amuck with his sword; three men had just fallen dying at his feet, with blood spurting from their wounds. The murderer at once ran off, well aware of the enormity of his crime, and though it was dark we saw him slip into a house close by, where he lay low all night. However, by the mercy of the gods, who never allow crimes to go unpunished, we were able to pick him up early this morning before he had managed to escape by a back passage. Now I have fetched him here before your Honours for the sentence that he deserves. He is a murderer in the first degree, caught red-handed, and though he is not a native of Thessaly, I trust that the sentence will be as severe as if he were one of your own citizens.'

The cruel accuser had hardly finished his terrible story before the herald spoke out and ordered me to begin my defence at once if I had one to make. At first I could do nothing but weep, not so much because of the ruthlessness of the accusation, as because of my own guilty conscience; but at last I found myself divinely inspired with enough boldness to plead.

'I know very well,' I said, 'how hard it is for someone accused of slaying three persons to persuade a large crowd that he is innocent, even if he tells and voluntarily confesses the truth.

'However, if you are kind enough to grant me a hearing, I undertake to prove that I now stand on trial for my life not because of anything I have deserved, but as the accidental result of having given way to righteous anger. I returned from a supper party last night somewhat later than usual, and rather the worse for drink – I admit that – and just as I reached the house of your worthy fellow-citizen Milo, whose guest I am, I saw a gang of ruffians trying to break their way in by wrenching the gate off its hinges. They had already smashed the bars and were now openly threatening to murder every soul in the house. Their leader, a larger man than the others who was doing most of the work, shouted out: "Come on, lads, show what stuff you're made of! Let's attack them as they sleep. There's no timid holding back now. Draw your sword and let's spread death and destruction all over the house. Anyone we find asleep and anyone who tries to resist has got to be killed. That's how we'll get out safe – by leaving no one alive in the house." At that, your Honours, I admit I drew my sword, which I carry as a protection against dangers of this very sort. I thought it my duty to frighten off these bloodthirsty scoundrels. However, instead of running away when they saw that I was armed, they audaciously stood their ground and prepared to fight it out. The battle began; their captain and standard-bearer rushed straight at me, grasped my hair with both hands and began forcing my head back. He wanted to hit me with a stone, but while he was groping for it, I got in a shrewd blow myself and he fell dead on the ground. Another tackled me by the ankles and tried to bite my feet, but I ran him through with a

40

well-aimed thrust through the shoulder. Then I struck the third full in the stomach and killed him.

'The fight was over, and I began congratulating myself on having preserved the household of my host and hostess and safeguarded the peace of the town. In fact, I expected not merely to be pardoned for what I had done, but to be given some public reward for my services. After all, I am a man of high standing in my own country, where I have never been accused of the smallest crime, and value my reputation above all the treasures of this world, and cannot see how my just punishment of these abominable bandits could be regarded as criminal: since nobody can prove that before last night I had the slightest quarrel with them, or that I was even acquainted with any of them, or, finally, that this was a shameful deed committed for personal profit.'

After delivering this speech I burst into tears again and, stretching out my hands in a gesture of supplication, appealed to the humanity of the audience. I begged them by all that they held most dear to show me mercy. When I thought that my tears and misery must have impressed their merciful human feelings, I called upon the eyes of Justice and the Sun himself to be my witnesses, entrusting my situation to the divine providence. At last I dared raise my head a little. To my consternation the whole audience was dissolved in laughter – and most of all Milo, my good host and relative, who was laughing quite unrestrainedly.

'Here's loyalty for you!' I thought. 'Here's conscience! I save my host's life, yet when I stand here in the dock on a capital charge, he won't raise a finger to save me. He just cackles with brutal laughter at the prospect of my death!'

Meanwhile a weeping woman, with a baby at her breast, came into the middle of the theatre, followed by an old hag dressed in filthy rags, who was likewise lamenting. Both were carrying olive-branches. Walking round the bier on which the three corpses lay covered up, they beat their breasts and howled dismally. The hag screeched: 'Your Honours, I appeal to you in the name of the pity and rights that are due to all. Have compassion for these young men who have been so undeservedly slain and give vengeance to comfort our bereavement and loneliness. And above all come to the aid of this little child who has been orphaned at so tender an age, and make atonement to your laws and public order with the blood of this bandit.'

When they had spoken these words, the eldest of the magistrates rose and addressed the people: 'Since no one, not even the malefactor himself, can deny that this is a crime calling for the severest punishment, it only remains for us to perform the secondary duty of finding out who were his accomplices in this foul deed. It seems most unlikely that he could have murdered three such powerfully built men as these single-handed. But the slave who escorted the prisoner fled secretly away, so we shall have to extract the names of his companions by torture, so that our fears of this sinister gang may be entirely relieved.'

The instruments of torture regularly used in Greece were produced at once: the brazier and wheel and all the other torments. It accentuated and doubled my misery to realize that I would not be allowed to die at least unmutilated. But the old hag who had spoiled everything by her howling appealed to the magistrates: 'Before you crucify this bandit who has murdered my poor darlings, will your Honours please allow their corpses to be uncovered so that everyone here may see how young and beautiful they were? That will make you all angrier than ever; you will insist on a revenge as cruel as the crime itself.'

Great applause. The magistrates immediately ordered me to go over to the bier and uncover the corpses myself. I refused to do anything of the sort, not wanting to act out my deed once again in front of everybody. The lictors, acting on the magistrates' orders, brought forcible compulsion to bear, managing to wrench my hand from my side and stretch it, catastrophically for myself, over the bodies. There was no help for it: I had to yield. With fearful reluctance, I grasped the shroud and uncovered the bodies.

But good God! what was this? this most extraordinary sight, this sudden complete change of my whole situation? A moment before I was reckoning myself already a slave of Queen Proserpine's, in the household of Orcus, but now, nothing of the kind! I stood goggling dumbly like an idiot; I find it difficult to convey adequately the stupefying effect that the sight produced on me. The three corpses were nothing more than three inflated wine-skins, punctured in several places! And so far as I could recall the details of my fight with the house-breakers, the holes corresponded exactly with my sword-thrusts.

Then the laughter, which had until now been slyly repressed, burst out uproariously from the crowd. Part of the audience cheered me exuberantly, but, so great was their amusement, many could do no more than press their hands to their stomachs to relieve the ache. Now everyone was drowned in floods of mirth, and in this way they poured out of the theatre, looking back at me.

From the moment that I uncovered the bodies I had been standing there as stiff and cold as stone, exactly as if I had been one of the statues or columns in the theatre; and my soul had not yet floated back from the shadows of death, when my host Milo came up and with gentle insistence drew me away with him. Then my tears burst out once more, and I could not restrain my convulsive sobbing; however, he took me home by side-streets and narrow passages so that I should not be seen on the way. He tried to calm my misery and fright with various conversational efforts, but I was now burning with such indignation at the insulting way in which I had been treated that he could do nothing with me.

Presently the magistrates arrived at our house with their emblems of office and did their utmost to appease me. 'Lord Lucius,' they said, 'we are well aware of your rank and distinguished lineage, for the nobility of your great family encompasses the whole of this province; so you must not think that it was in wanton insult that we subjected you to the proceedings which you have taken so much to heart. We beg you to forget your present anguish. The fact is that today we annually hold a solemn festival in honour of Laughter, the most pleasing of all gods, which must always be celebrated with some new practical joke. The gracious god always lovingly accompanies his central figure and will now never allow you to be glum, diligently making your countenance glad with serene beauty. Moreover, the town of Hypata has unanimously conferred on you, for the favour you have done it, the highest dignity that it can bestow: it has inscribed you as its patron and decreed that a bronze statue of you should be erected.'

I replied: 'Convey to the citizens of this splendid and unique town how deeply sensible I am of the honour that has been done me; but I suggest that they should reserve their public statuary for older and more worthy persons than myself.' I assumed a cheerful expression for the moment as I uttered these modest words, forcing a happier appearance as far as I could, and so took courteous leave of them.

As soon as they had gone a servant ran in. 'Your kinswoman

Byrrhaena reminds you of her invitation to supper, which you accepted last night; it will shortly be ready.'

Shuddering with terror at the very mention of her house, I answered: 'I should have been delighted to obey my relative's request if I could have done so without disloyalty. My host Milo has charged me, in the name of the god who presides over today's festivities, to dine with him tonight and will neither allow me to leave the house nor come out with me himself. I regret that I must postpone my acceptance to another occasion.'

While I was speaking these words Milo took me firmly by the hand and led me to the nearest bath, ordering the washing materials to be prepared; but I avoided everyone's gaze, huddling as close as I could to Milo, to escape the mirth of the passers-by. How I managed to wash, anoint and wipe myself clean at the baths, and how I ever got home again, I really cannot remember; I was so mortified and confused at being stared at, nudged at and pointed at by the whole town.

I swallowed a wretched little meal at Milo's and then told him that so much weeping had given me a severe headache and that I must go to bed at once. I went along to my room and flung myself on the bed, where I brooded painfully on the events of the day.

Presently my dear Fotis, having got her mistress safely to bed, came stealing in. She was not at all her usual gay, lively self, but frowning and anxious. After a long silence she faltered: 'I have something to confess, Lucius: I am to blame for all your misfortunes of today.' Then she pulled a whip from under her apron and handed it to me. 'Here, take this. Revenge yourself with it on the girl who has betrayed you; yes, punish me as hard as you like. Only don't think for a moment that I purposely caused you so much misery. I call all the gods to witness that I would willingly shed my own blood rather than let you suffer the slightest harm on my account, or sustain any injury whatever. But bad luck dogged me; so something that I was ordered to do for quite another reason had the effect of hurting you horribly.'

My curiosity had not been damped and I was longing to get to the bottom of the mysterious incident. I cried indignantly: 'You bring me this wicked, horrible whip and invite me to beat you with it? Before it ever touches your delicate and creamy skin, I'll chop and tear it into little bits. But, tell me faithfully just what you did that has so ill-fatedly caused my ruin. I swear to you, I swear by your face which I love so much, that nobody, not even yourself, could make me believe that you ever hurt me deliberately; and no innocent intention must ever be viewed as criminal because it accidentally happens to result in bad luck.'

By the time I had finished this speech, her half-closed eyes were moist and tremulous and languid with desire. I began to drink love from them with thirsty kisses; which revived her spirits a little. She said: 'First, I must carefully shut the door in case anyone overhears what I am going to tell you – something very private – and we both get into frightful trouble.' She locked and bolted the door, then came back to me and holding my head close to hers, with her hands locked behind it, said in a soft whisper: 'I should be absolutely terrified to let you into the secrets of this house, and the mysterious doings of my mistress, if I didn't have complete trust in your discretion. You come of a noble family, and you are a very intelligent man, already initiated into various religious mysteries. So I know that you will never reveal to a soul what I am now going to tell you; my deep love for you forces it out of me, and you will be the only person in the world whom I have taken into my confidence. It may seem a trivial story, but you must repay me by keeping it forever tightly locked in the darkest corner of your mind; because it concerns the whole situation in our household and the magic arts by which my mistress exacts obedience from ghosts, puts pressure on the stars, blackmails the gods and keeps the elements well under her thumb.

'She works at these arts with the most frantic fervour whenever she falls in love with a good-looking young man; which is pretty often. At present she's desperately in love with a young Boeotian, who really is wonderfully handsome, and is using all her best sorceries and enchantments. Yesterday evening I heard her threatening the Sun that if he didn't hurry up and set, so that the night could come and give her more time for her spells, she'd throw a cloud of darkness around him and consign the earth to perpetual night. That was after she had seen the Boeotian having a hair-trim at the barber's and privately ordered me to go into the shop and pick up some of the hair lying about the floor and bring it home. Though I took care to attract a little attention as possible, the barber saw me and, as our house has a bad reputation for black magic, he grabbed me and shouted: 'Now really, this is going too far. When are you going to stop stealing good-looking men's hair? Unless you end this nonsense pretty soon, I warn you that I'll complain about you to the magistrates.' Then he felt between my breasts and pulled out the ends of hair already hidden there; he was in a towering rage. I felt very badly about it because I knew my mistress only too well: whenever she gets crossed like this she flies into a vile temper and gives me a savage beating. I wondered: 'Shall I run away?' But as soon as I thought of you, I decided to do nothing of the sort. As I walked gloomily home I saw a man with a pair of shears trimming the hair off some goat-skins. They were hanging in front of his shop, tightly tied at the necks and well blown up, and it happened that the colour of their hair was yellowish and of exactly the same shade as the young Boeotian's. I picked up several strands and brought them back to my mistress, without telling her whose hair it really was.

'When it grew dark, she climbed in a great state of excitement up to the loft at the top of the house, which she finds a convenient place for practising her art in secret; it's open to all the four winds, with a particularly wide view of the eastern sky. She had everything ready there for her deadly rites: all sorts of aromatic incense, metal plaques engraved with secret signs, remnants of ships lost at sea, various bits of corpse-flesh brought out from their tombs – in one place she had arranged the noses and fingers of crucified men, in another the nails that had been driven through their palms and ankles, with bits of flesh still sticking to them – also blood saved from murdered men and skulls snatched from the fangs of wild animals. She began to repeat certain charms over the still warm and quivering entrails of some animal or other, dipping them in turn into jars of spring-water, cow's milk, mountain honey and mead. Then she plaited the hair I had given her, tied it into knots and threw it onto a blazing fire. The power of this charm is irresistible – backed, you must understand, by the blind violence of the gods who have been coerced; the smell of the hair smoking and crackling on the fire endowed its owners, the goat-skins, with human breath and senses and understanding, so that, drawn by the smell of their own hair, they came rapping for admittance at our door, instead of the Boeotian youth. Then you arrived too, pretty drunk, and in pitch darkness. You drew your sword courageously, like Ajax,[3] and cut to pieces not, as he did, entire herds of living beasts but three blown-up goat-skins – which was much braver – so that now here you are safely back in my arms, after your attack of homicidal – I mean wine-skinicidal – mania.'

Such was Fotis' pleasant speech; and I joked back: 'Yes, I'm a regular Hercules. This first glorious deed of mine compares well with his slaying of the three-bodied King Geryon, or his capture of the three-headed dog Cerberus;[4] for I have slain the same number of wine-skins. But if you want me to forgive you wholeheartedly for causing me so much anguish, I insist on your doing one thing for me. It is this: I want to be secretly present when next your mistress makes use of her supernatural powers and invokes the gods, and especially when she changes her shape. I'm determined to know everything possible about the science of magic. And, by the way, *you* seem to be pretty well grounded in it. Of one thing I'm quite certain: that though I have always shied away from love affairs even with ladies of the highest rank, I'm now a complete slave to your sparkling eyes, your rosy cheeks, your shining hair, your fragrant breasts and those kisses you give me with your parted lips. It is a willing slavery too. I don't miss my home or plan to go back there, and I'd give the whole world not to forfeit the joy in store for me tonight.'

'I should love to do as you ask, Lucius,' she said, 'but Pamphile has a suspicious character, and when she starts working on spells it's always in a lonely spot where she can be certain not to be disturbed. All the same, I would risk anything to please you, so I'll keep a careful watch on her movements and let you know when she gets busy again. But remember what I told you: you must promise to keep the most faithful silence about all this.'

Before we had quite finished discussing my plan, a sudden wave of longing swept over our hearts and bodies. We pulled off our clothes and rushed naked together in amorous Bacchic fury; and when I was nearly worn out by the natural consummation of my desire she tempted me to make love to her as though she were a boy; so that when, exhausted, we finally dropped off to sleep, it was broad daylight before we felt like getting up again.

>>>>><<<<<

LUCIUS IS TRANSFORMED

WE spent the next few nights in the same amorous way, and then one morning Fotis ran into my room, trembling with excitement, and told me that her mistress, having made no headway by ordinary means in her affair with the Boeotian, intended that night to become a bird and fly in to the object of her desire, and that I must make careful preparations if I wished to watch the performance.

At twilight, she led me on tip-toe, very quietly up to the loft, where she signed to me to peep through a chink in the door. I obeyed, and watched Pamphile first undress completely and then open a small cabinet containing several little boxes, one of which she opened. It contained an ointment which she worked about with her fingers and then smeared all over her body from the soles of her feet to the crown of her head. After this she muttered a long charm to her lamp, and shook herself; her limbs vibrated gently and became gradually fledged with feathers, her arms changed into sturdy wings, her nose grew crooked and horny, her nails turned into talons, and Pamphile had become an owl. She gave a querulous hoot and made a few little hopping flights until she was sure enough of her wings to glide off, away over the roof-tops.

Not having been put under any spell myself, I was utterly astonished and stood frozen to the spot. I rubbed my eyes to make sure that I was really Lucius and that this was no waking dream. Was I perhaps going mad? I recovered my senses after a time, took hold of Fotis' hand and laid it across my eyes. 'I beg you,' I said, 'to grant me a tremendous favour – one which I can never hope to repay – in proof of your perfect love for me. If you do this, honey, I promise, by these sweet breasts of yours, to be your slave for evermore. I want to be able to fly. I want to hover around you like a winged Cupid in attendance on my Venus.'

'So that's your game, is it?' she said. 'You want to play me a foxy trick: handing me an axe and persuading me to chop off my own feet? That's all very well, but it hasn't been so easy for me all this time to keep you safe from the she-wolves of Thessaly, from whom you would have been defenceless. Now if you become a bird, how shall I be able to keep track of you? And when will I ever see you again?'

I protested: 'All the gods in Heaven forbid that I'm such a scoundrel as you make out. Listen: if I became an eagle and soared across the wide sky as Jupiter's sure courier or joyful armour-bearer do you really suppose that even such winged glory as that would keep me from flying back every night to my love-nest in your arms? By that enchanting knot of hair on your head in which my soul lies helplessly entangled, I swear that I love no other woman in the whole world but my dearest Fotis. And anyhow, when I come to think of it, if that ointment really does turn me into a bird, I'll have to steer clear of all houses; for imagine the pleasant and amusing way ladies would treat their lovers if they were owls! When one of these night birds blunders indoors, everyone does his best to catch it and nail it with outspread wings to the doorpost, because it is believed that they bring bad luck to houses by their ill-omened flight. But that reminds me: once I'm an owl, what is the spell or antidote for turning me back into myself?'

'You need not worry about that,' she said. 'My mistress has taught me all the magical formulas, by which people who have been transformed into other shapes can be turned back into human form. Not, of course, because she has a kindly feeling for me, but because when she arrives home I have to prepare the necessary antidote for her to use. It really is extraordinary with what diminutive and insignificant herbs one can produce such a great result: tonight, for instance, she will need only a little dill and laurel leaves steeped in spring-water. She will drink some of the water and wash herself with the rest.'

She reassured me on this point several times before she went, twitching with fear, into the loft and brought me out one of the boxes from the casket. Hugging and kissing it I muttered a little prayer for a successful flight. Then I quickly pulled off my clothes, greedily stuck my fingers into the box and took out a large lump of ointment which I rubbed all over my body.

I stood flapping my arms, one after the other, as I had seen

Pamphile do, but no little feathers appeared on them and they showed no sign of turning into wings. All that happened was that the hair on them grew coarser and coarser and the skin toughened into hide. Next, my fingers bunched together into a hard lump so that the five fingers of my hands became single hooves, the same change came over my feet and a long tail sprouted from the base of my spine. Then my face swelled, my mouth widened, my nostrils dilated, my lips hung down and my ears bristled long and hairy. The only consoling part of this miserable transformation was the enormous increase in the size of my member; because I was by this time finding it increasingly difficult to meet all Fotis' demands upon it. At last, hopelessly surveying myself all over, I realized that I had been transformed not into a bird but into an ass.

I wanted to curse Fotis for what had happened, but found that I could no longer speak or even gesticulate; so I silently expostulated with her by sagging my lower lip and gazing sideways at her with my watery eyes.

When Fotis saw what had happened she beat her own face with both hands in a frenzy of self-condemnation. 'Oh, this is enough to kill me!' she wailed. 'In my flurry and fear I must have mistaken the box; two of them look exactly alike. Still, things are not nearly so bad as they seem, because in this case the antidote is one of the easiest to get hold of; all that you need do is to chew roses, which will at once turn you back into my Lucius. If only I had made my usual rose-garlands this evening! Then you would have been spared the inconvenience of being an ass for even a single night. At the first signs of dawn I will go out instantly and fetch what you need.' Over and over again she lamented, but though I was no longer Lucius, and to all appearances a complete ass, a mere beast of burden, I still retained my mental faculties. I had a long furious debate with myself as to whether or not I ought to bite and kick Fotis to death. She was a witch, wasn't she? And a very evil one, too. But in the end I decided that Fotis' death would only mean that I would lose all hope of saving myself. Drooping and shaking my head, I swallowed my rage for the time being and submitted to my cruel fate. I trotted off to the stable to my own good horse that had once carried me.

He was there with another ass, the property of my former host, Milo, and really I did expect that, if dumb beasts have any natural feelings of loyalty, my horse would know me and take pity on my plight, providing me with a comfortable lodging. But – O Hospitable Jupiter[1] and the secret Divinity of Faith! – my splendid horse and Milo's horrible ass put their heads together, suspecting that I had designs on their food. The moment I approached their manger they laid their ears back and started kicking me with their heels. Here was I, driven right away from the very barley which only a few hours before I had measured out for that most grateful horse of mine with my own hands.

Thus treated and banished to a lonely corner of the stable and deciding on a bitter revenge on them next morning as soon as I had eaten my roses and become Lucius again, I noticed a little shrine of the Goddess Epona,[2] standing in a niche of the post that supported the main beam of the stable. It was neatly wreathed with freshly gathered roses, the very antidote that I needed. I hopefully pushed my forelegs as far up the post as they would go, stretched my neck to its fullest extent and shot out my lips. But by a piece of really bad luck my slave who was acting as groom happened to catch me at work. He sprang up angrily and shouted: 'I've had quite enough trouble from this donkey. First he tries to rob his stablemates of their food, and now he assaults the images of the gods! If I don't flog the sacrilegious brute until he's too lame to stir a hoof . . .' He groped about for a weapon until he found a bundle of faggots, picked out one with its leaves still on it, the biggest of the lot, and began to whack me unmercifully.

A sudden loud pounding and banging on the outer gate. Distant cries of 'Thieves! Thieves!' The groom ran off in terror. The next moment, the courtyard gate burst open and armed bandits rushed in. Neighbours hurried to Milo's assistance but the bandits beat them off. Their swords gleamed like the rays of the rising sun in the bright light of the torches that they carried. They had axes with them, too, which they used to break open the heavily barred door of the strong-room in the central part of the house. It was stuffed with Milo's valuables, all of which they hauled out and hastily divided into a number of separate packages. However, there were more packages to carry than robbers to carry them, so they had to use their wits. They came into our stable, led out us two asses and my horse, loaded us with as many of the heavier packages as they could pile on our backs and drove us out of the now ransacked house, threatening us with sticks. Then they hurried forward into trackless hill-country, beating us hard all the way. But one of them stayed behind as a spy; he was to follow later and report what steps were taken by the authorities to deal with the crime.

The hills were steep, my load heavy, and the journey interminable; soon I felt more dead than alive. However, I now decided to have recourse to the civil power and rescue myself from my dreadful predicament by appealing to the Emperor. It was already broad daylight when, as we passed through a large village where a fair was in progress, I tried to invoke the august name of Caesar before the multitude, in the native Greek tongue. I managed to shout 'O' loudly and distinctly, but that was all; I was unable to pronounce the word 'Caesar'. My discordant bray so annoyed the bandits that they whacked and poked at my miserable hide until it was hardly fit to serve as a sieve.

At last Jupiter generously offered me a chance to escape. After we had passed several farm buildings and large country houses I saw a charming little garden full of many different sorts of attractive flowers, among them budding roses still wet with the morning dew. I gasped for joy and quickened my pace, and had almost come up to the roses, my mouth watering hopefully, when at the last moment I thought of a much better plan. If I ceased to be an ass and became Lucius again, the bandits would be sure to kill me, either because they took me for a wizard or for fear that I might inform against them. For the present I must lay off roses and put up with my situation a little longer by chewing hay like the ass I was.

About midday under a scorching sun, we turned off the road and came to a hamlet where we stopped at a private house. Some old men came out. Any ass could have seen from the exchange of greetings and embraces and the long conversation which followed that these were friends of the bandits, who gave them some of the loot from a package on my back and whispered what must have been a warning that it was stolen goods. When we had all been unloaded, we were turned out to graze in the next paddock, but I would not feed there with my fellow-beasts, as I had not yet got accustomed to eating hay. So I had to find somewhere else to eat. Feeling half-starved I boldly jumped into a small vegetable patch behind the stable, where I filled my stomach with raw greens. When I had finished I silently invoked all the gods of Heaven and had a good look around me. There might happen to be a flowering rose-tree in one of the gardens near by, and this was such a secluded place, well away from the road and hidden by fruit-trees, and if I could find the antidote to my four-footedness and regain my upright posture, it was unlikely that anyone would witness the transformation. While I was excitedly weighing my chances of escape, I saw, a good distance off, a dip in the ground enclosed by a small plantation of ornamental trees, and against the variegated background of leaves I made out the bright red of roses. In my imagination, which was far from being that of a mere beast, I pictured the place as a grove of Venus and the Graces,[3] with the lovely colours of their royal flower glowing from a central shrine. Breathing a prayer to the Goddess Fortune,[4] I galloped off at such speed that I felt more like a fast-moving race-horse than an ass. But even with this remarkable turn of speed I could not out-distance the fate that dogged my heels; for when I reached the place it was not a dip in the ground after all, but a concealed stream with thickly wooded banks, and the roses were not nice tender roses, dripping with honey-dew and nectar, which grow out of rich lovely thorn-bushes. They were what country people call rose-laurels: cup-shaped, somewhat red blossoms, growing from a long-leaved bush resembling a laurel, which have no scent at all and are deadly poison to all cattle. Finding myself still entangled in bad luck I resolved, despairing of my life, to make a meal of these poisonous mock-roses.

As I walked hesitantly towards the bush, a young man who must have been the gardener ran angrily at me with a big stick. He beat me so hard in revenge for the damage I had done that he might have killed me if I had not had the sense to defend myself by raising my rump and letting out with my hind legs. I got my own back with a succession of such hard kicks that I left him lying injured on the slope of the hill. Then I bolted.

Unfortunately, his wife – at least, I suppose she was his wife – happened to be standing higher up on the same hillside and saw him lying below her half-dead. She rushed to his rescue, shrieking that an end should be made of me. All the neighbours, aroused by her lamentations, at once called their dogs and urged them furiously on to tear me to pieces.

It looked as if my last hour had come, because there were many of these dogs, huge mastiffs of the sort used for baiting bulls and bears. I took what seemed my last chance of survival: instead of running farther away, I doubled back to where we had lodged as fast as I could. The villagers called off their dogs, but had great difficulty in keeping them away from me. I was tied to a staple with a long leather strap and fiercely beaten again. That would certainly have been the end of me if I had not gorged myself on those raw greens: the blows raining on my narrowed stomach had the effect of squirting out its loose, undigested contents in my tormentors' faces. The stench was so disgusting that everyone ran out, but not before my back was shattered.

Not long afterwards, as evening began, the bandits loaded us up again, taking care to give me by far the heaviest load to carry, and led us out of the stable. I was exhausted by the long journey and the great weight on my back, my sides ached from the beatings and I could hardly walk because my hooves were so worn down. When we had come a good distance farther I began planning a new way of escape. We were following a road beside a gentle winding stream and I decided to fall down with my legs doubled under me and not to budge another inch, though the bandits beat me with sticks or even pricked me with their swords. Surely that would make them realize that I had been practically dead with weakness? Why shouldn't they grant me a discharge on the grounds of ill-health? I knew that they could not afford any delay and calculated that they would divide my load between the other animals leaving me there by way of further punishment as a prey for the wolves and vultures.

This splendid plan was thwarted by my luck. Milo's ass somehow guessed what I had in mind and forestalled me: he pretended to be completely worn out, fell sprawling on the road with all his load, and lay there as though dead. He made no attempt to rise in spite of whacks and sword-pricks, not even when the bandits made a concerted effort to haul him up by all four legs, both ears and the tail. Realizing that the case was hopeless they decided after a short discussion not to delay their flight a moment longer for the sake of a foundered ass. 'The brute is as good as dead,' they told one another. They divided his load between the horse and myself, hamstrung him with a sword, dragged him off the road and toppled him down from a great height, while he was still breathing, into the adjacent ravine.

The fate of my unlucky comrade scared me. I decided to play no more clever tricks but to show my masters that I was an honest and hard-working ass. Besides, they had been telling each other that we were quite near the cave where they lived and that their hard journey would soon be over.

One more hill, not a very steep one, and there at last we were at our destination. We were unloaded and all the treasures stowed safely away indoors. For want of water, I lay down and rolled in the dust to refresh myself.

Here the circumstances oblige me to give a close description of the cave and its immediate surroundings. This will be a test of my powers and at the same time allow you to judge whether or not I was an ass as regards my ability to size up a situation. To begin with the mountain, then. It was rugged and very high, a powerful natural fortress, covered with dark woods and cut by irregular bramble-choked gullies that ran obliquely across its slopes and were flanked by inaccessible cliffs. From near the peak a spring burst out and ran shining down the sides, breaking into a number of small streams that flooded the meadows below with what seemed like an enclosed sea of standing water. Above the cave, near the foot of the mountain, rose a tall tower, built of wattles fastened on a timber frame. The lower storey was extended on all four sides into a sheep-pen. In front of the door to the cave stretched a narrow, fenced-in footpath. You would certainly, I guarantee you, pronounce the place a den of thieves. There were no other buildings except a small thatched hut. Sentries, chosen by lot, were posted there every night.

>>>><<<<

THE BANDITS' CAVE

THE bandits tied us up with strong halters and one by one crept inside. They shouted unkindly at the bent old woman who by herself looked after all these young men and had charge of them. 'Here, you miserable, disgraceful old corpse, that even Hades is too disgusted to claim, are you just going to sit at home and play around doing nothing? Aren't you going to give us supper at this late hour, after all the dangerous work we've been doing, instead of merely swilling wine into your greedy belly day and night?'

This made the frightened old woman tremble, and she squeaked out: 'But everything's ready for you, my gallant and faithful masters! There's all sorts of meat stewing in the pots, very tasty too; and any amount of bread, and nice well-rinsed cups with lots of wine. What's more, I've heated you the water for your usual quick wash.'

After she had said this they all undressed and stood around a great roaring fire where they splashed themselves with hot water and afterwards rubbed themselves with hot oil before taking their places at a table heaped with every kind of food.

They had hardly settled down before another larger group of young men came in and took their wash in the same way. You could see at once that they were thieves too, because they brought in another haul of loot; gold and silver coin, plate, and silk and gold-embroidered robes. When they joined their comrades at table everyone drew lots as to who should wait on the rest. They ate and drank a very great deal! The meat was piled up in heaps, the loaves in large mounds, the wine cups were arranged in columns like an army on the march. They made a festive row, bawled songs and yelled tumultuous jokes. I was reminded of the way the half-animal Lapiths and half-human Centaurs[1] had behaved. At last the toughest bandit of them all began to make a speech.

'We stormed Milo's house at Hypata in fine style. It was a brave action, and it made us a fortune, and we didn't lose a man – in fact, we came back with four pairs of legs to the good, if that's worth mentioning. And as for your raids round the cities of Boeotia, what you brought in will never make up for the loss of your captain, Lamachus, who was a very brave fellow. Much too brave in fact, and that was his ruin. However, his noble memory will be honoured for ever, among famous kings and generals. But as for you doughty thieves, you just sneak around the baths and old women's hovels, like second-hand clothes-dealers, committing paltry, slavish burglaries.'

But one of the party that had come in later gave him an answer. 'When are you going to learn, you fool, that the bigger the house the easier it is to rob? Where there are plenty of slaves about, none of them ever thinks of saving his master's property before his own life. But people who live economically and by themselves not only keep their stuff pretty well hidden, but defend it fiercely at the risk of their lives, even if it isn't particularly valuable. Listen to our story and you'll find that I'm talking sense.

'As we went towards the Seven-gated Thebes we inquired who were the richest men in the district – you'll agree with me that the first rule of our profession is to find out where the money lies – and someone told us of a wealthy banker named Chryseros who made a great show of being a pauper for fear he might be called on to accept public office. He lived all alone and solitary in a small but strongly barred house, where he brooded in dirty rags over his bags of gold. We decided to pay Chryseros our first call and expected to find little difficulty in relieving him of his money; so many against one. As soon as it was dark we were ready outside his door but agreed that it was unsafe to lift off the door or remove it or smash it down because the noise would give the alarm to the entire neighbourhood and ruin us. So our noble captain Lamachus, confident of his proven courage, slipped his arm through the keyhole with the intention of pulling back the bolt. But that wretched biped Chryseros had heard us and was on the watch. He crept softly up to the door holding a big nail, and with a sudden sharp hammer-blow nailed our leader's hand to a door-panel. He left him writhing there like a criminal on the cross, rushed up to the roof of the filthy little house and shouted to his neighbours at the top of his voice: "Help, help! Fire, fire! Come quickly and help me put it out, before it spreads to your own houses!" He appealed to them all by name, and they rushed up in alarm terrified by the imminent danger.

'This put us in a dilemma, perilous as our situation was. We had to choose between abandoning our comrade or perishing with him. But we found an effective way out – with his consent. We hacked off our leader's arm at the shoulder and left the stump sticking through the hole. Then we bound up the stump tightly, swathed it with rags, for fear that the drops of blood might leave a trail, and rushed off with what was left of Lamachus. But while we hurried away from all the shouting full of anxiety because of the affection we felt for him, the terror our imminent peril inspired in us making us run as fast as we could, he was unable to keep up with us. Yet we could not leave him safely behind. He begged us to put him out of his misery and held us to the oath of mutual help which we had all sworn together by the right hand of Mars. He said that we couldn't leave a comrade behind to be tortured and gaoled and that his greatest happiness now would be to die, killed by us: for how long could a brave bandit survive the loss of a hand that he used for stealing and cutting throats? But however hard he pleaded he couldn't persuade any of us to such a deliberate murder – so he drew his sword with his left hand and, after kissing it repeatedly, plunged it with a powerful blow under his breast-bone.

'With reverent diligence we carefully wrapped our noble leader's body in a linen robe and consigned it to the sea,[2] and now our Lamachus lies in a watery grave. It was an end that matched his gallant life.

'We lost Alcimus too, a man of great enterprise, through another stroke of bad luck. He had broken into an old woman's cottage and got up to the attic bedroom where she was lying asleep; but instead of strangling her at once, as he ought to have done, he first decided to throw her stuff down through the window for us to collect. He cleared the whole room in workman-like fashion and then went up to the old woman's bed in which she was lying and pushed her out. He was about to throw down the coverlet after the other things when the wicked old creature clasped him by the knees and appealed to him: "O please, son, don't throw out my poor ragged little objects so that they can be got hold of by my rich neighbours, whose house this window looks out upon."

'This fooled Alcimus. He thought he had mistaken the window and instead of throwing the things into the street was really mistakenly throwing them into someone's property. So he went to the window and not realizing that he was in any danger leant out for a good look around, with a particular eye for the neighbours' house, to check her account of its wealth. While he was vigorously but rather unwisely engaged in this activity, the old bitch stole up behind him and gave him a sudden unexpected push – not a hard push, but he was off his balance at the time and down he went, head first. It was some little distance to the ground and he fell sideways on a big stone that lay near by, which smashed his ribs; he lay coughing up streams of blood. Before he died – and his torment did not last long – he managed to tell us what had happened. So we gave him the same burial as we had given Lamachus; yes, he was worthy of the honour.

'This double loss decided us against trying our luck in Thebes any longer. We trudged up to Plataea, the nearest town, and there we found everyone talking about a forthcoming gladiatorial show. Demochares, the nobleman who was to produce it, was as generous as he was rich; his entertainments were always on a scale worthy of his resources. It's no use trying to describe the lavish preparations made; I couldn't possibly do the man justice. At any rate he had got together a famous company of gladiators, hunters well known for their speed and criminals who were no longer free men and were being fattened up as food for the wild beasts. Then there were great timber structures on wheels, with towers and platforms and pictures painted on their sides, used as movable cages for the extraordinary collection of wild beasts that Demochares had got together. Many of these were specially imported from overseas; living graves for the criminals, but what handsome ones!

'But among all this expensive paraphernalia he had a particularly large pack of enormous bears, some of them trapped by himself on hunting expeditions, some bought from the dealers at great expense, others sent him by friends who competed for the honour of presenting him with such gifts. He looked after them carefully and at great expense. However, though his motive in making all these preparations was to please the public, they did not fail to attract jealous and hostile reactions. His bears began to pine and waste away, because of the heat and the long confinement and the lack of exercise, and then a sudden epidemic carried them off, one after another, until there was hardly a bear left alive. Soon the streets of Plataea were full of bears turned out to die, like so many stranded hulks, and then the common populace, forced by harsh poverty to cram their enfeebled bellies with any filthy offal that they could pick up for nothing, came flocking around to eat the banquets that were lying there.

'This inspired Eubulus[3] here, and myself, with a brilliant idea. We lugged one of the biggest bears along to our lodgings, as though we intended merely to carve it up for food; but what we did was to flay it, preserving all the claws carefully and leaving the head attached to the skin at the back. Then we scraped the inside of the skin with razors, sprinkled it with ash and hung it up to dry in the sun. While it was curing by the flames of a magnificent fire we gorged ourselves on bear-steaks and took an oath to stand by one another through thick and thin. The best man among us, which meant not the strongest but the bravest, would volunteer to put on the skin and pretend to be a bear; the rest of us would take him to Demochares' house, where he would easily be able to let us in through the door in the middle of the night.

'The ingenuity of the scheme brought several members of our courageous brotherhood forward for this cunning undertaking; however, Thrasyleon proved to be the man the band chose for the dangerous enterprise. He was perfectly calm as we stitched him into his bear-skin, which was now soft and pliable. We concealed the fine seams by brushing the coarse, shaggy hair over them and fitted his head into the opening of the bear's throat which we had cleaned out, leaving ventilation holes around the nostrils and eyes, so that he could breathe and see. Our brave leader looked just like an animal and we brought him a cheap cage into which he crawled at once — oh, he was a brave fellow, was Thrasyleon — and then everything was ready for our next act. This was to forge a letter in the name of Nicanor, a Thracian said to be one of Demochares' closest friends. We wrote that he was out on a hunting expedition and "dedicated the first fruits of the chase to his dear friend Demochares".

'It was late in the evening when we took the forged letter and the cage, with Thrasyleon inside, to Demochares. He was impressed by the huge size of the bear and delighted with Nicanor's generosity. The present was so opportune that he told his steward to count us out a reward of ten gold pieces, of which he had plenty. Meanwhile the whole household flocked around the cage crying: "Oh, isn't he a beauty? Isn't he huge?" But our Thrasyleon, to discourage their curiosity, cleverly started making sudden threatening rushes at the side of the cage, so that they kept well away.

'Demochares' friends all congratulated him: what good luck to be able to make up for the deaths of so many other animals, in part at least, by acquiring this splendid beast. Presently he ordered it to be led out, very carefully, into a nearby field. But I protested: "Excuse me, sir, this animal is tired after its long, hot journey. You must be careful about putting it among a quantity of creatures which, I hear, are not in the best of health. You ought to let it lie in some cool part of this house that catches the evening breeze; if possible, near a pool of water. You surely know that a bear always likes to lie in shady woods and moist caves and and beside pleasant waters?"

'He was impressed by my warning and, remembering his losses, agreed at once. "Put the cage anywhere you please," he said. Then I added: "We ourselves are perfectly prepared to stay here by the cage all night, to feed and water him at his usual time. He has suffered greatly from the heat and the uncomfortable journey." But Demochares said: "No, please do not trouble! Nearly everyone in my household has had plenty of experience of bears and knows all about feeding them."

'So we said goodbye and walked out. We went some little distance out of town until we came to a mausoleum in a lonely spot not far from the main road. We broke in and took the lids off some rotten old coffins – with the mouldering remains of corpses still inside – which would make convenient safes for the loot we hoped soon to bring back. Then we gathered, sword in hand, outside Demochares' gate, all set and ready for the attack; but waiting, as usual, for the dark, moonless part of the night when everyone is sunk in his first and deepest sleep.

'Thrasyleon played his part well. He waited for exactly the right moment before creeping out of his cage and killing all the house-guards, who were lying asleep near by. After this, he went on to stab and kill the porter, took the key off his body, opened the front door and let us in. Then he showed us the strong-room in the middle of the house, into which, on the evening before, he had noticed a large quantity of silver plate being stored away for the night. We broke it open by concerted force, and I told my comrades to carry off as much gold and silver as they could handle and hurriedly dump it at the mausoleum of our thoroughly reliable dead friends; then to come back at once for another load. I volunteered, in the common interest, to stay behind and keep guard at the gate until they returned. We thought that it would be a great help to have a bear running loose around the place: any member of the household who happened to wake up would need to be a bold fellow not to rush away and lock himself in the nearest room, shaking with terror, when he saw the huge beast lumbering about in the gloom.

'Our plan was working out smoothly when we had a piece of bad luck. While I was still anxiously waiting for my comrades to come back a slave happened to wake up – I suppose he heard a noise, as fate would have it. He tiptoed forward, and when he saw the bear roving freely about the house went back silently, roused the other slaves and told them what he had seen. The next minute they all came pouring out with torches, lanterns, candles, tapers and other lights. The whole place was lit up, and everyone was armed with a club, a spear or a drawn sword. They ran to guard all the exits of the court and then unkennelled the hunting dogs, with their huge ears and bristly hair, to pull Thrasyleon down. In the hubbub that followed I stole out with the idea of getting away. However, I stayed long enough to see him put up a wonderful fight against the dogs. It was as though he were struggling against Cerberus himself, with his grinning jaws. Although he knew he was doomed, he never forgot his honour, or the honour of our band, and acted his part in the most life-like way, first running off, then standing at bay, with many twistings and turnings of his body. At last he managed to burst out of the house. But he couldn't get clear away because all the dogs in the next lane – there was a large savage pack of them – joined in the pursuit.

'It was shocking and pitiful to see our Thrasyleon cornered by multitudes of maddened dogs, who fastened their teeth into various parts of his body and began pulling him to pieces. So I could stand his distress no longer: I rushed among the crowd and did all I could to rescue my good comrade by surreptitious means. I shouted to those who were leading the chase: "What a wicked shame to kill a beast like that! He's worth pots of money." But no one would listen to me, and suddenly up ran a big man with a levelled spear and thrust Thrasyleon right through the body. When all the others saw this, they overcame their fear and attacked him with their massed swords at close quarters. Upon my word, Thrasyleon died grandly! Though everything else was lost, he never lost heart and took whatever came to him. When another set of dogs' teeth met in his flesh or another sword sliced him, he just growled and bellowed in bear fashion so as not to betray us by shouting or yelling like a man. Yes, he met his fate unflinchingly. It was a glorious fight, and he'd struck such terror into the crowd that nobody laid a finger on him, although he was lying there on the ground. It was quite late in the morning before a butcher arrived who had more courage than his neighbours. He slit open the paunch and stripped our brave bandit of his bear-skin.

'That is how Thrasyleon died, but his glory has not died with him. After that, we packed up the loot that the faithful corpses had been guarding for us and hurried outside the boundaries of Plataea, continually reflecting that there is no loyalty among the living; and no wonder, since it has transferred itself to the ghosts and the dead out of hatred for our disloyalty. And so – tired out by our hard journey, burdened with our loads and with three of our comrades lost – here we are, and there's the loot.'

They filled gold cups with undiluted wine and poured it out as a libation for their dead companions. Then they sang hymns to the god Mars to appease him, lay down and went off to sleep.

*

The old woman gave us two beasts such a generous quantity of raw barley that my horse might have fancied himself the guest of honour at a banquet of the Salian College at Rome.[4] He had it all to himself because, though I liked barley, I had always eaten it properly pounded into a long-cooked mush or baked into bread. But I found the corner where the loaves left over by the rabble were stored and started munching ravenously. My jaws ached with hunger and seemed covered with cobwebs from long disuse.

Late that night the bandits woke up and left the cave; some were dressed up as ghosts, others wore ordinary clothes and carried swords. But not even the sleep that was stealing up on me could stop me from chewing on greedily, without a pause. While I was still Lucius I had been able to rise from table satisfied with a mere loaf or two, but now I had such a large belly to fill that I had nearly finished my third basketful of bread when dawn broke and discovered me still eating; then at last, with the shame of which even an ass is capable, I left my food – most reluctantly, I admit – and quenched my thirst at a neighbouring stream.

Soon the bandits returned, with very anxious and careworn faces. Despite their numbers and armed strength they brought back no loot at all, not so much as a ragged cloak; and only a single prisoner, a girl, Charite. To judge from her clothes, she belonged to one of the first families of the district and was so beautiful that though I was an ass, I swear that I lusted after her greatly. They brought her into the cave where, in her distress, she began to pull her hair out and tear her clothes. They did what they could to comfort her. 'We have no intention,' they assured her, 'either of hurting you or showing you any discourtesy. Be patient for a few days, if only as a kindness to us: you see, it was poverty that forced us to take up this profession and your parents, although close-fisted, are bound to hurry up with the ransom money. After all, you are their daughter and they are very rich.'

The girl's distress was not comforted by this babbling, and she laid her head between her knees and cried uncontrollably. They called the old woman and told her to console the girl as best she could, while they went off again on business.

The old woman could do nothing with her. She cried louder than ever, her breast heaving with sobs, until I too began to weep. She wailed: 'To think of losing everything! What a miserable fate for me! Such a lovely home and family and kind servants, and parents whom I love so much! To be kidnapped in this dreadful way and shut up like a slave in a rocky prison without any of the comforts which I have had all my life! Under constant threat of having my throat cut and in the power of these horrible bloodthirsty bandits! How can I possibly stop crying? How can I even stay alive?'

She went on lamenting in this strain, until depression, combined with a sore throat and weariness, made her stop; she closed her exhausted eyes and dozed off. Soon she awoke again and, like a madwoman, started beating her beautiful face and her breasts. The old woman begged her to explain this new outburst of sorrow, but she only groaned and said: 'No, there's no longer any doubt about it: I have no hope of escape. All I need now is a noose or a sword – or a precipice!'

The old woman grew increasingly angry. She put on a nastier expression and asked her what on earth she was crying about and why she had gone to sleep and suddenly woken up and started weeping unrestrainedly all over again. 'I suppose,' she said, 'you want to defraud my young men of their big ransom. But if you won't stop crying – and bandits aren't easily impressed by tears – I'll see that you get roasted alive.'

That frightened her. She seized the old woman's hand and kissed it: 'Take pity on me, mother, and give me a little comfort in my miserable situation, for the sake of human kindness. I don't believe compassion is altogether lacking in that venerable white head of yours. Listen to my sad story. I have an attractive cousin three years older than myself. We two have been inseparable since childhood – in fact, we once used to sleep in the same bed – and love each other dearly. He is a leading personage here, and the whole city has chosen him as a favourite son of the town. Finally by consent of our parents we offered our matrimonial vows and were to be joined in marriage: whereupon he went off to our wedding surrounded by his relatives and friends and sacrificed in the temples and public places. The whole house was decorated with laurel, and everyone was singing the bridal hymn. My mother, unhappy woman, had helped me into my wedding-dress and was hugging and kissing me and praying earnestly that I should be blessed with children when suddenly the bandits burst in with naked, menacing swords, just like gladiators. They made no attempt at killing or robbing anyone, but went straight for the room where I was, in a compact body. None of the household put up a fight or offered the least resistance, while the bandits snatched me, half-dead with fear, from my mother's arms. So the wedding came to a sudden end; it was like the ruined wedding of Attis or Protesilaus.[5] When I went to sleep just now I had a most horrible dream which brought all my misery back, worse than before. I dreamed that I was violently pulled out of my bridal bed, and out of the bedroom and out of the house, and carried off through a pathless desert, still calling the name of my miserable husband who had been cheated of my kisses. And in the dream he came after me, still drenched with scent and crowned with garlands, shouting to everyone to help him rescue his beautiful wife who had been stolen from him. This pressing pursuit made one of the bandits angry. He picked up a big stone and threw it at my poor young husband and killed him. Terrified by the dreadful sight I woke up from my horrible dream in a panic.'

The old woman sighed sympathetically. 'You must be cheerful, mistress,' she said, 'and stop worrying about dreams. The dreams that come in daylight are not to be trusted, everyone knows that, and even night-dreams often go by contraries. For example, to dream of weeping or being beaten or even having one's throat cut is good luck and usually means prosperous change, whereas to dream that one is laughing, stuffing oneself with sweets or making love is a sure sign of sadness or illness or some other misfortune. Now let me tell you a nice old wives' tale to make you feel better.'

>>>>><<<<<

CUPID AND PSYCHE (I)

'ONCE upon a time there lived a king and queen who had three very beautiful daughters. It was possible to find human words of praise for the elder two, but to express the breath-taking loveliness of the youngest, the like of which had never been seen before, was beyond all power of human speech. Every day thousands of her father's subjects came to gaze at her, foreigners too, and were so dumbfounded by the sight that they paid her the homage due to the Goddess Venus alone. They pressed their right thumbs and forefingers together, reverently raised them to their lips and blew kisses towards her. The news spread through neighbouring cities and countries that the goddess, born from the deep blue sea and nourished upon the froth of its foaming waves, had now come among the multitudes of mortal men and everyone was allowed to gaze at her; or else, that this time, the earth, not the sea, had been impregnated by a heavenly emanation and had borne a new Goddess of Love, all the more beautiful because she was still a virgin. The princess's fame was carried farther and farther to distant provinces and still more distant ones, and people made long pilgrimages over land and sea to witness the greatest wonder of their age. As a result, nobody took the trouble to visit Paphos or Cnidus or even Cythera to see the Goddess Venus.[1] Her rites were put off, her temples allowed to fall into ruins, her sacred couches trodden under foot, her festivals neglected, her statues left ungarlanded and her altars left bare and unswept, besmirched with cold ashes.

'Worship was accorded to the young woman instead and the mighty goddess was venerated in human form. When she went out on her morning walks, victims were offered in her honour, sacred feasts spread for her, flowers scattered in her path and rose garlands presented to her by an adoring crowd of suppliants who addressed her by all the titles that really belonged to the great Goddess of Love herself. This extraordinary transfer of divine honours to a mortal greatly angered the true Venus. Unable to suppress her feelings, she shook her head menacingly and said to herself: "Really now, so I, all the world's lovely Venus whom the philosophers call 'the Universal Mother' and the original source of the elements, am expected to share my sovereignty, am I, with a mortal girl! And to watch my name, which is registered in Heaven, being dragged through the dirty mud of Earth! Oh, yes, and I must be content, of course, with the reflected glory of worship paid to this girl, grateful for a share in the worship offered to her instead of to me – and allowing her, a mortal, to display her appearance as mine! It meant nothing, I suppose, when the shepherd Paris, whose just and honest verdict Jupiter himself confirmed, awarded me the prize of beauty over the heads of my two goddess rivals? No, I can't let this creature, whoever she may be, usurp my glory any longer. I'll very soon make her sorry about her good looks – they're against the rules."

'She at once called her winged son Cupid, that very wicked boy, with neither manners nor respect for the decencies, who spends his time running from building to building all night long with his torch and his arrows, breaking up everyone's marriage. Somehow he never gets punished for all the harm he does, though he never seems to do anything good in compensation. Venus knew that he was naturally bent on mischief, but she tempted him to still worse behaviour by bringing him to the city where the princess lived – her name was Psyche – and telling him of her rival beauty. Groaning with indignation she said: "I implore you, as you love your mother, to use your sweetly wounding arrows and the honeyed flame of your torch. You'll give your mother revenge in full, most secretly, against the impudent beauty of that girl. You'll see that the princess falls desperately in love with some perfect outcast of a man – someone who has lost rank, fortune, everything; someone who goes about in such complete degradation that nobody viler can be found in the whole world."

'After she had uttered these words she kissed him long and tenderly and then went to the nearby sea-shore, where she ran along the tops of the waves as they danced foaming towards her. At the touch of her rosy feet the deep sea suddenly calmed, and she had no sooner willed her servants from the waters to appear, than up they bobbed as though she had shouted their names. The Nereids were there, singing in unison, and Portunus, with his bristling bluish beard, and Salacia, with her bosom filled with fishes, and the little Palaemon riding on a dolphin.[2] After these came troops of Tritons swimming about in all directions, one blowing softly on his conch-shell, another protecting Venus from sunburn with a silken veil, a third holding a mirror before the eyes of his mistress, and a team of them, yoked two and two, harnessed to her car. When Venus proceeds to the ocean she's attended by quite an army of retainers.

'Meanwhile Psyche got no satisfaction at all from the honours paid her. Everyone stared at her, everyone praised her, but no commoner, no prince, no king even, dared to make love to her. All wondered at her beauty, but only as they might have wondered at an exquisite statue. Both her less beautiful elder sisters, whose reputation was not so great, had been courted by kings and successfully married to them, but Psyche remained single. She stayed at home feeling miserable and ill, and began to hate the beauty which everyone else adored.

'The poor father of this unfortunate daughter feared that the gods and heavenly powers might be angry and hostile, so he went to the ancient oracle of Apollo at Miletus and, after the usual prayers and sacrifices, asked where he was to find a husband for his daughter whom nobody wanted to marry. Apollo, though an Ionian Greek, chose, for the sake of this teller of a Milesian tale,[3] to deliver the following oracle in Latin verse:

> On some high mountain's craggy summit place
> The virgin, decked for deadly nuptial rites,
> Nor hope a son-in-law of mortal birth
> But a dire mischief, viperous and fierce,
> Who flies through aether and with fire and sword
> Tires and debilitates all things that are,
> Terrific to the powers that reign on high.
> Great Jupiter himself fears this winged pest
> And streams and Stygian shades his power abhor.

'The king, who until now had been a happy man, came back from the oracle feeling thoroughly depressed and told his queen what an unfavourable answer he had got. They spent a number of days weeping, mourning and lamenting. But the time for the grim fulfilment of the cruel oracle was now upon them.

'The hour came when a procession formed up for Psyche's dreadful wedding. The torches chosen were ones that burned low with a sooty, spluttering flame; instead of the happy wedding-march the flutes played a querulous Lydian lament;[4] the marriage-chant ended with funereal howls, and the poor bride wiped the tears from her eyes with her flame-coloured veil. Everyone turned out, groaning sympathetically at the calamity that had overtaken the royal house, and a day of public mourning was at once proclaimed. But there was no help for it: the divine commandment had to be obeyed. So when the ceremonies of this hateful wedding had been completed in deep grief, the entire city followed the tearful Psyche, a living corpse, in procession, escorting her not to her marriage but to her grave.

'Her parents, overcome by grief and horror, tried to delay the dreadful proceedings, but Psyche exhorted them: "Why torment your unhappy old age by prolonging your misery? Why weary your hearts – which I claim as my own rather than yours – with continual lamentations? Why spoil the two faces that I love best in the world with pointless tears? Why bruise your eyes – which are mine as well? Why pull out your white hairs and beat your breasts, which I so deeply revere? Now, too late, you at last see the reward that my beauty has earned you; the deadly curse of hateful jealousy for the extravagant honours paid me. When the people all over the world celebrated me as the New Venus and offered me sacrifices, then was the time for you to grieve and weep as though I were already dead; I see now, I see it clearly, that the one cause of all my misery is this use of the goddess's name. So lead me up the rock as Fate has decreed. I am looking forward to my lucky bridal night and my marvellous husband. Why should I hesitate? Why should I shrink from him, even if he has been born for the destruction of the whole world?"

'After uttering these words, she walked resolutely forward. The crowds followed her up to the rock at the top of the hill, where they left her. They returned to their homes with bowed heads, extinguishing the wedding-torches with their tears. Her broken-hearted parents shut themselves up in their palace and gave themselves up to unending darkness.

'Psyche was left alone weeping and trembling at the very top of the hill, until a friendly air of the gently breathing West Wind sprang up. It gradually swelled out her clothes until it lifted her off the ground and carried her slowly down into a deep valley at the front of the hill, where she found herself gently laid out on a bed of the softest turf, starred with flowers.

'And so Psyche, reclining comfortably in this soft and herbaceous place, upon a bed of dewy grass, began to feel rather more composed, and fell peacefully asleep. When she awoke, feeling thoroughly refreshed, she rose and walked calmly towards the great, tall trees of a nearby wood, through which a clear, crystalline stream was flowing. This stream led her to the heart of the wood where she came upon a royal palace, too wonderfully built to be the work of mortal man. You could see, as soon as you went in, that some god must be in residence at so pleasant and splendid a place.

'The ceiling, exquisitely carved in citrus wood and ivory, was supported by golden columns; the walls were sheeted with silver on which figures of many kinds of beast were embossed and seemed to be running towards you as you came in. To have created this masterpiece, with all those animals engraved in silver, was clearly the work of an exceptionally gifted man, or rather of some demi-god, or, truly, some god, and the pavement was a mosaic of all kinds of precious stones arranged to form pictures. How lucky, how very lucky anyone would be to have the chance of walking on a jewelled floor like that! And the other parts of the palace were just as beautiful and just as fabulously costly. The walls were faced with massive gold blocks which glittered so brightly with their own radiance that the house had a daylight of its own even when the sun refused to shine: every room and portico and doorway streamed with light and the other riches of the house were in keeping. Indeed, it seemed the sort of palace that Jupiter himself might have built as his earthly residence. Psyche was entranced. She went up to the entrance and after a time dared to cross the threshold. The beauty of what she saw lured her on; and every new sight added to her wonder and admiration. She came on splendid treasure chambers stuffed with unbelievable riches; every wonderful thing that anyone could possibly imagine was there. But what amazed her even more than the stupendous wealth of this treasury of ecumenical dimensions, was that no single chain, bar, lock or armed guard protected it.

'As she stood gazing in rapt delight, a disembodied voice suddenly spoke: "Do these treasures astonish you, lady? They are all yours.

Why not go to your bedroom now and rest your tired body. When you feel inclined for your bath, we, your maids, will be there to help you, and after you have refreshed yourself you will find a royal banquet ready for you."

'Psyche was grateful to the unknown Providence that was taking such good care of her and did as the disembodied voice suggested. First she relieved her weariness by a sleep and a bath, then straight away she noticed a semi-circular table, all laid for dinner, just for her. She sat down happily – and at once nectarous wines and appetizing dishes appeared by magic, not brought in by anyone but floating up to her of their own accord. She saw nobody at all but only heard words uttered on every side; the waiters were mere voices, and when someone came in and sang and someone else accompanied him on the lyre, she once again saw nothing. Then the music of a whole invisible choir came to her ears and she seemed to be in its midst, though none of the singers were to be seen.

'When these pleasures came to an end, and darkness called, Psyche went to bed; and at a late hour of the night she heard a gentle whispering near her. Being all alone, she feared for her virginity and trembled and quaked, and was all the more frightened by the prospect of something bad happening to her because she did not know what it might be. Then came her unknown husband and climbed into her bed, and made Psyche his wife.

'He left her hastily before daybreak, and at once voices were heard in the bedroom comforting her for the loss of her virginity.

'That is how things went on for quite a time until, as one might expect, the novelty of having invisible servants wore off and she settled down to what was a very enjoyable routine; despite her uncertain situation she could not feel lonely with so many voices about her.

'Meanwhile, her father and mother, as they grew old together, did nothing but weep and lament, and the news of what had happened spread far and wide until both her sisters heard all the details. In grief and sorrow they left their homes and hurried back earnestly to see and speak to their parents.

'On the night of their arrival Psyche's husband, whom she still knew only by touch and hearing and not by sight, warned her: "Lovely Psyche, darling wife, cruel fate menaces you with deadly danger. Guard against it vigilantly. Your elder sisters are alarmed at

72

the report of your death. They will soon be visiting that same rock you came to, in order to see if they can find any trace of you. If you happen to hear them mourning for you up there, you must not answer them, nor even look up to them; for that would cause me great unhappiness and bring utter ruin on yourself."

'Psyche promised to do as her husband asked; but when the darkness had vanished, and so had he, she spent the whole day in tears, complaining over and over again that not only was she a prisoner in this wonderful palace without a single human being to chat with, but her husband had now forbidden her to relieve the minds of her mourning sisters, or even to look at them. She spent the whole day weeping, and that night she went to bed without supper or bath or anything else to comfort her. Her husband came in earlier than usual, drew her to him, still weeping and expostulated with her: "O Psyche, what did you promise me? What may I – I who am your husband – expect you to do next? You have cried all day and all night, and even now when I hold you close to me, you go on crying. Very well, then, do as you like, follow your own disastrous fancies; but when you begin to wish you had listened to me, the harm will have been done."

'She pleaded earnestly with him, swearing she would die unless she were allowed to see her sisters and comfort them and have a talk with them. In the end he consented. He even said that she might give them as much gold and as many necklaces as she pleased; but he warned her with terrifying insistence not to be moved by her sisters' ruinous advice to try to discover what he looked like. If she did, her impious curiosity would mean the end of all her present happiness and she would never lie in his arms again.

'She thanked him for his kindness and was quite herself again. "No, no," she protested, "I'd rather die a hundred times over than lose my lovely marriage with you. I love you, I adore you desperately, whoever you are; even Cupid himself can't compare with you. So please, I beg you, grant me one more favour! Tell your servant, the West Wind, to carry my sisters down here in the same way that he carried me." She kissed him coaxingly, whispered love-words in his ear, wound her limbs closely around him and called him: "My honey, my own husband, soul of my soul!" Overcome by the power of her love he was forced to yield, however reluctantly, and promised to give her what she asked. But he vanished again before daybreak.

>>>>><<<<<

CUPID AND PSYCHE (II)

'Meanwhile Psyche's sisters inquired their way to the rock where she had been abandoned. Hurrying there they wept and beat their breasts until the cliffs re-echoed. "Psyche! Psyche!" they screamed. The shrill cry reached the valley far below and Psyche ran out of her palace in feverish anxiety, crying: "Why are you mourning for me? There's no need for that at all. Here am I, Psyche herself! Please, please stop that terrible noise and dry all those tears. In a moment you'll be able to embrace me, after all those lamentations for my fate."

'Then she called up the West Wind and gave him her husband's orders. He at once obliged with one of his gentle puffs and wafted them safely down to her. The three sisters embraced and kissed rapturously. Soon they were shedding tears of joy, not of sorrow. "Come in now," said Psyche, "come in with me to see my new home and relieve your sorrows with your sister Psyche." Then she showed them her treasure chambers and let them hear the voices of the big retinue of invisible slaves. She ordered a wonderful bath for them and feasted them splendidly at her magical table. But after they had filled themselves with all these divine delicacies they both felt miserably jealous – particularly the younger one, who was very inquisitive. She never stopped asking who owned all this fabulous wealth; and she pressed Psyche to tell her who and what sort of a man her husband was.

'Psyche was loyal to the promise she had made her husband and gave away nothing; but she made up a story for the occasion. He was a handsome young man, she said, a little downy beard just beginning to shadow his cheeks, and spent his time hunting in the neighbouring hills and valleys. But then, fearing that all this garrulity should make her contradict herself or cause her to make a slip and thus give away her secret, she loaded them both with goldwork and jewelled necklaces, then summoned the West Wind and asked him to fetch them away at once. He carried them up to the rock, but on their way back to the city the poison of envy began working again in these worthy sisters' hearts, and they exchanged animated comments.

'One of them said: "How blindly and cruelly and unjustly Fortune has treated us! Do *you* think it fair that we three sisters should be given such different destinies? You and I are the two eldest, yet we get exiled from our home and friends and married off to foreigners who treat us like slaves; while Psyche, the result of Mother's last feeble effort at child-bearing, is given all these riches and a god for a husband, and doesn't even know how to make proper use of her tremendous wealth. Sister, did you ever see such masses of glittering jewels? Why, the very floors were made of gems set in solid gold! If her husband is really as good-looking as she says, she is quite the luckiest woman in the whole world. The chances are that as he grows even fonder of her he will make her a goddess. And, my goodness, wasn't she behaving as if she were one already, with her proud looks and condescending airs? She's only a woman after all, yet she orders the winds about and is waited upon by invisible attendants. Whereas it's my wretched fate that my husband's older than Father, balder than a pumpkin and more puny than a little boy; and he locks up everything in the house with bolts and chains."

'"My husband," said the other sister, "is doubled up with sciatica, which prevents him from making love to me except on the rarest occasions, and his fingers are so crooked and knobbly with gout that I have to spend half my time massaging them. Look what a state my beautiful white hands are in from messing about with his stinking fomentations and disgusting salves and filthy plasters! I'm treated more like a surgeon's assistant than a wife. You're altogether too patient, my dear; in fact, to speak frankly, you're positively servile, the way you accept this state of affairs. Personally, I simply can't stand seeing her living in such undeserved style. Remember how haughtily she treated us, how she bragged of her wealth and how stingy with her presents she was. Then, the moment she got bored with our visit, she whistled up the wind and had us blown off the premises. But I'll be ashamed to call myself a woman, if I don't see that she gets toppled down from this lavish life she is leading. And if you feel as bitter as you ought to feel at the way she's insulted us both, what about joining forces and working out some plan for humbling her? Now, in the first place, I suggest that we show nobody, not even Father and Mother, these presents of hers, and let nobody know that she's still alive. It's bad enough to have seen her luck, and a lamentable sight it was, without having to bring the news home to our parents, and have it spread all over the place; and there's no pleasure in being rich unless people hear about it. Psyche must be made to realize that we're not her servants, but her elder sisters. We'll go back to our husbands and our shabby (but at least respectable) homes, and when we can finally think of an effective scheme let's see each other again here and humble her pride."

'The two evil sisters approved of this evil plan. They hid the valuable presents that Psyche had given them and each began scratching her face and tearing out her hair in pretended grief at having found no trace of their sister; which made the king and queen sadder than ever. Then they separated; each went back full of malicious rage to her own home, thinking of ways of ruining her innocent sister, even if it meant killing her.

'Meanwhile, Psyche's unseen husband gave her another warning. He asked her one night: "Do you realize that a storm is brewing? It will soon be on you and, unless you take the most careful precautions, it will sweep you away. These treacherous hags are scheming for your destruction; they will urge you to look at my face, though as I have often told you, once you see it, you lose me for ever. So if these hateful vampires, with their harmful designs, come to visit you again – and I know very well that they will – you must refuse to speak to them. Or, if this is too difficult for a girl as open-hearted and simple as yourself, you must at least take care not to answer any questions about your husband. For we have a family on the way: though you are still only a child, you will soon have a child of your own, which shall be born a god if you keep my secret, but a mortal if you divulge it."

'Psyche was exultant when she heard that she might have a god for a baby, and proud of this fine pledge of her love that was on the way, and of her exalted status as a mother. She began excitedly counting the months and days that must pass before it was born. But having never been pregnant before she was surprised that her belly should swell so large from such a diminutive beginning.

'The wicked sisters were now hurrying to Psyche's palace again, ruthless Furies breathing out the venom of snakes, and once more her husband, stopping briefly, gave her this warning: "Today is the fatal day. Your enemies are near. They have taken up their arms, struck camp, marshalled their forces and sounded the 'Charge'. They are enemies of your own sex and blood. They are your wicked sisters, rushing at you with drawn swords aimed at your throat. O darling Psyche, what dangers surround us! Have pity on yourself and on me. Keep my secret safe and so guard your husband and yourself and our unborn child from the destruction that threatens us. Refuse to see or hear those wicked women. They have forfeited the right to be called your sisters because of the deadly hate they bear you, which has shattered the blood-tie: they will come like Sirens and lean over the cliff, and make the rocks echo with their murderous voices."

'When she heard this Psyche, her voice broken with sobs, said: "Surely you can trust me? You have long since had convincing proof of my loyalty and my power of keeping a secret; and in the future you will once again approve of my steadfast behaviour. Only tell the West Wind to do his duty as before, and allow me to have a sight, at least, of my sisters; instead of seeing your own adored body, which you will not allow me to do. These fragrant curls dangling all round your head; these cheeks as tender and smooth as my own; this delightfully warm bosom; that face of yours that I shall only be able to know anything about by looking at our baby! So please be sweet and humour my craving – and make your Psyche happy, who loves you so much. I no longer feel so anxious to look at you, or so frightened of the darkness of the night, when I have you safe in my arms, light of my life!" Her voice and sweet caresses broke down her husband's resistance. He wiped her eyes dry with his hair, granted what she asked and as usual disappeared again before the day broke.

'The two sisters, their plot arranged, landed from their ship and, without even visiting their parents, hurried straight to the rock and with extraordinary daring leaped down from it without waiting for the breeze to belly out their robes. However, the West Wind was bound to obey its master's order, reluctant though he might be: he caught them in his robe as they fell and brought them to the ground.

'At once they rushed into the palace and embraced their victim with what she took for sisterly affection. Then, with cheerful laughter masking their treachery, they cried: "Why, Psyche, you're not nearly so slim as you used to be. You'll be a mother before very long. We're so delighted you're going to have a baby, and what a joy it'll be for the whole household. Oh, how we shall love to nurse your golden baby for you! If it takes after its parents, as it ought to, it will be a perfect little Cupid."

'By this pretended love they gradually wormed themselves into her confidence. Seeing that they were tired because of their journey, she invited them to sit down and rest while water was heated for them; and when they had taken their baths, she gave them spiced sausages and other marvellously tasty dishes, while an unseen harpist played for them at her orders, as well as an unseen flautist, and a choir sang the most ravishing songs. But even such honey-sweet music as that failed to soften the hard hearts of those wicked women. They insidiously brought the conversation round to her husband, asking her who he was and from where his family came.

'Psyche was very simple-minded and, forgetting what story she had told them before, invented a new one. She said that he was a middle-aged merchant from the next province, very rich, with slightly grizzled hair. Then breaking the conversation off short, she loaded them with valuable presents and sent them away in their windy carriage.

'As they returned home, borne aloft by the peaceful breath of Zephyrus, they held a discussion in these terms: "Now, what do you make of the monstrous lies she tells us? First the silly creature says that her husband is a very young man with a downy beard, and then she says that he's middle-aged with grizzled hair! Quick work, eh? You may depend upon it that the evil woman is either hiding something from us, or else she never sees what her husband looks like."

'"Whatever the truth may be, we must ruin her as soon as possible. But if she really has never seen her husband, then he must be a god, and her baby will be a god too. If that happens, which Heaven forbid, I'll hang myself at once. So now let us return to our parents and start telling some lies to suit our plans."

'In this state of excitement, they arrived and gave their father and mother an offhand greeting. Their disturbed feelings kept them awake all night, and in the morning the evil women hurried to the rock and floated down into the valley as usual with the help of the

West Wind. Rubbing their eyelids hard until they managed to squeeze out a few tears, they went to Psyche and said: "Oh, sister, ignorance is indeed bliss! There you sit quite happily, without the least suspicion of the terrible danger that threatens you, while we are in absolute anguish about it. You see, we watch over your interests indefatigably and are deeply upset by your misfortunes. For we are reliably informed, and since we share your sorrows and fortunes we have to tell you that the husband who comes secretly gliding into your bed at night is an enormous snake with many twisting coils, its neck bloodily swollen with deadly poison, its jaws gaping wide. Remember what Apollo's oracle said: that you were destined to marry a savage wild beast. Very many of the farmers who go hunting in the woods around this place have met him coming home at nightfall from his feeding ground and have seen him swimming across the river nearby. They all say that he won't pamper you with delicate meals much longer, but that when your nine months are nearly up he will eat you alive, when you have a tenderer morsel inside you. So you had better make up your mind whether you will come away and live with us – we are so eager to look after our beloved sister – or whether you prefer to stay here with this fiendish reptile until you finish up in his guts. Perhaps you're fascinated by living here alone with your voices all day and at night making secret and disgusting love to a poisonous snake. But at all events we have done what we could as dutiful sisters."

'Poor silly Psyche was aghast at the dreadful news. She lost all control of herself, trembled, turned deathly pale and, forgetting all the warnings her husband had given her and all her own promises, plunged headlong into the abyss of misfortune. She gasped out brokenly: "Dearest sisters, thank you for being so kind. I do believe that the people who told you this story were not making it up. The fact is I have never seen my husband's face and haven't the least idea where he comes from. I only hear him speaking to me at night in whispers, so tht I have to put up with a husband I know nothing about, who evidently hates the light of day. So I have every reason to suppose, as you do, that he must be some animal. Besides, he is always giving me frightful warnings about what will happen if I try to see what he looks like. So please, if you can advise your sister what to do in this dreadful situation, tell me at once; otherwise, all the trouble you have been kind enough to take will be wasted."

'The wicked women saw that Psyche's defences were down and her heart laid open to their attacks. They pressed their advantage: "Since we are so closely related," one of them said, "the thought of your danger makes us forget our own. We two have talked the matter over countless times and will show you how to save yourself. This is what you must do. Get hold of a very sharp carving knife, make it sharper still by stropping it on your palm, then hide it somewhere on your side of the bed. Also, get hold of a lamp, have it filled full of oil, trim the wick carefully, light it and hide it behind the bedroom tapestry. Do all this with the greatest secrecy and when he visits you as usual, wait until he is stretched out at full length, and you know by his deep breathing that he's fast asleep. Then slip out of bed with the knife in your hand and tiptoe barefooted to the place where you have hidden the lamp. Finally, with its light to assist you, perform your noble deed, plunge the knife down with all your strength at the nape of the serpent's poisonous neck and cut off its head. We promise to help you. The moment you have saved yourself by killing it, we shall come running in and help you to get away at once with all your treasure. After that, we'll marry you to a human being like yourself."

'When they saw that Psyche was now determined to follow their suggestion, they went quietly off, terrified to be anywhere near her when the catastrophe came; they were helped up to the rock by the West Wind, ran back to their ships as fast as they could and sailed off at once.

'Psyche was left alone, in so far as a woman haunted by hostile Furies can be called alone. Her mind was as restless as a stormy sea. When she first began making preparations for her crime, her resolve was firm; but presently she wavered and started worrying about all the different aspects of her calamity. She hurried, then she dawdled; at one moment she was bold and at another frightened; she felt nervous and then she got angry again. For, although she loathed the animal, she loved the husband it seemed to be. However, as evening drew on, she finally acted rapidly and prepared what was needed to do the dreadful deed.

'Night fell, and her husband came to bed, and after preliminary amorous skirmishes he fell fast asleep. Psyche was not naturally either very strong or very brave, but the cruel power of fate made a man of her. Holding the knife in a murderous grip, she uncovered the lamp and let its light shine on the bed.

'There lay the gentlest and sweetest of all wild creatures, Cupid himself, lying in all his beauty, and at the sight of him the flame of the lamp spurted joyfully up and the knife turned its edge for shame.

'When Psyche saw this wonderful sight she was terrified. She lost all control of her senses and, pale as death, fell trembling to her knees, where she tried to hide the knife by plunging it in her own heart. She would have succeeded, too, had the knife not shrunk from the crime and twisted itself out of her foolhardy hands. Faint and unnerved though she was, she began to feel better as she stared at Cupid's divine beauty: his golden hair, washed in ambrosia and still scented with it, curls straying over white neck and flushed cheeks and falling prettily entangled on either side of his head – hair so bright that it darkened the flame of the lamp. At his shoulders grew soft wings of the purest white and, though they were at rest, the tender down fringing the feathers quivered attractively all the time. The rest of his body was so smooth and beautiful that Venus could never have been ashamed to acknowledge him as her son. At the foot of the bed lay this great god's gracious weapons, his bow, quiver and arrows.

'Psyche's curiosity could be satisfied only by a close examination of her husband's weapons. She pulled an arrow out of the quiver and touched the point with the tip of her thumb to try its sharpness; but her hand was trembling and she pressed too hard. The skin was pierced and out came a drop or two of blood. So Psyche accidentally fell in love with Love. Burning with greater passion for Cupid even than before, she flung herself panting upon him, desperate with desire, and smothered him with sensual, open-mouthed kisses; her one fear now being that he would wake too soon.

'While she clung to him, utterly bewildered with delight, the lamp which she was still holding, whether from horrid treachery or destructive envy, or because it too longed to touch and kiss such a body, spurted a drop of scalding oil on the god's right shoulder. What a bold and impudent lamp, what a worthless servant of Love – for the first lamp was surely invented by some lover who wished to prolong the pleasures of the night – so to scorch the god of all fire! Cupid sprang up in pain and, seeing that the bonds of faith were shattered and in ruins, spread his wings and flew away from the kisses and embraces of his unhappy wife without a word; but not before Psyche had seized his right leg with both hands and clung to it. She looked very queer, carried up like that through the cloudy sky; but soon her strength failed her and she tumbled down to earth again.

'Cupid did not desert her as she lay on the ground, but alighted on the top of a cypress near by, where he stood reproaching her. "Oh, foolish Psyche, it was for your sake that I disobeyed the orders of my mother, Venus! She told me to inflame you with passion for some utterly worthless man, but I preferred to fly down from Heaven and become your lover myself. I know only too well that I acted thoughtlessly, and Cupid, the famous archer, wounds himself with one of his own arrows and marries a girl who mistakes him for a beast; she tries to chop off his head with a knife and darken the eyes that have loved her so greatly. This was the danger of which I warned you again and again, gently begging you to be on your guard. As for those fine sisters of yours who turned you against me and gave you such damnable advice, I'll very soon be avenged on them. But your punishment will simply be that I'll fly away from you." And when he had uttered those words he soared up into the air and was gone.

'Psyche lay motionless on the ground, following her husband with her eyes as far as she could and moaning bitterly. When the beat of his wings had carried him aloft clean out of her sight, she flung herself headlong into a river that flowed close by. But the kindly river, out of respect for the god and fearing for itself since even the waters do not escape his fiery attentions, washed her ashore and laid her on the bank, upon the flowery turf.

'Pan, the goat-legged country god, happened to be sitting near by, caressing the mountain nymph Echo[1] and teaching her to repeat all sorts of pretty songs. A flock of she-goats roamed around, browsing greedily on the grass. The goat-footed god was already aware, somehow or other, of Psyche's misfortune, so he gently beckoned to the desolate girl and did what he could to comfort her. "Pretty dear," he said soothingly. "Though I'm only a shepherd and very much of a countryman, I have picked up a good deal of experience in my long life. So if I am right in my conjecture – or my divination, as sensible people would call it – your unsteady and faltering walk, your pallor, your constant sighs and your sad eyes show that you're very much in love. Listen: make no further attempt at suicide by leaping from a precipice or performing any other fatal action. Stop crying and open your heart to Cupid, the greatest of us gods; he's a thoroughly spoilt young fellow whom you must humour by praying to him only in the gentlest, sweetest language."

'It is very lucky to be addressed by Pan, but Psyche made no reply. She merely did reverence to him as a god and went on. She trudged along the road for a while, until she happened to turn into a lane that led off it. Towards evening it brought her to a city of which she soon found out that the husband of one of her sisters was the king. She announced her arrival at the palace and was at once admitted.

'After an exchange of greetings and embraces, the queen asked Psyche why she had come. Psyche answered: "You remember your advice about that knife and the beast who pretended to be my husband, and lay with me, and was going to swallow me up voraciously in my misery? Well, I took it, but no sooner had I shone my lamp on the bed than I saw a marvellous sight: Venus' divine son, Cupid himself, lying there in tranquil sleep. The joy and relief were too great for me. I quite lost my head and didn't know how to satisfy my longing for him; but then, by a dreadful accident, a drop of burning oil from the lamp spurted on to his shoulder. The pain woke him at once. When he saw me holding the lamp and the knife, he shouted: 'How could you do me such a mischief? I divorce you; take your things away. I am going to marry your sister instead,' and he named you. Then he called for the West Wind, who blew me out of the palace and landed me here."

'Psyche had hardly finished her story before her sister, madly jealous of her and burning with lust, went to her husband and deceived him with a cunning tale, declaring that she had heard her parents were dead. Off she went and when at last she reached the rock, though another wind altogether was blowing, she shouted with misplaced confidence: "Here I come, Cupid, a woman worthy of your love. West Wind, convey your mistress!" Then she took a headlong leap; but she never reached the valley, either dead or alive, because the rocks cut her to pieces as she fell and scattered her flesh and guts all over the mountainside. So she got what she deserved and died, and the birds and beasts feasted on her remains.

'And it was not long before a second vengeance followed. For Psyche wandered on and on until she came to another city, where the other sister lived and took her in by the same deceitful story as she had told to her sister. She, too, was anxious to supplant her sister by making a criminal marriage, hurried to the rock and died in exactly the same way.'

>>>>><<<<<

CHAPTER IX

CUPID AND PSYCHE (III)

'PSYCHE continued on her travels through country after country, searching for Cupid; but he was lying in his mother's own room and groaning for pain because of his wound from the lamp. Meanwhile a white gull, of the sort that skims the surface of the sea flapping the waves with its wings, dived down into the water; there it met Venus, who was having a bathe and a swim, and brought her the news that her son Cupid was suffering from a severe and painful burn, from which it was doubtful whether he would recover. It told her, too, that every sort of scandal about Venus' family was going around. People were saying that her son had flown down to the mountain to have an affair with a whore, while she herself had gone off to swim in the sea: "The result is, they declare, that Pleasure, Grace and Wit have disappeared from the earth and everything there has become ugly, dull and slovenly. Nobody bothers any longer about his wife, his friends or his children; everything is in a state of disorder, and weddings are viewed with bitter distaste and regarded as disgusting."

'This talkative, meddlesome bird squawked into Venus' ears and succeeding in setting her against her son. She grew very angry and cried: "So my promising lad has taken a mistress, has he? Here, gull – you seem to be the only creature left with any true affection for me – tell me, do you know the name of the creature who was seduced my poor simple boy? Is she one of the Nymphs, or one of the Seasons,[1] or one of the Muses, or one of my own train of Graces?"

'The garrulous bird was very ready to talk. "Lady, I cannot say; but if I remember rightly the story is that your son has fallen desperately in love with a human named Psyche."

'Venus was absolutely furious. "What! With her, of all women? With Psyche, the usurper of my beauty, the rival of my glory? This is worse and worse. It was through me that he got to know the girl. Does the brat take me for a procuress?"

'Thus lamenting, she rose from the sea at once and hurried aloft to her golden room, where she found Cupid lying ill, as the gull had told her. As she entered she bawled out at the top of her voice: "Now *is* this decent behaviour? A fine credit you are to our divine family and a fine reputation you're building up for yourself. You trample your mother's orders underfoot as though she had no authority over you whatsoever, and instead of tormenting her enemy with a dishonourable passion, as you were ordered to do, you have the impudence to sleep with the girl yourself, at your age! To have someone I hate as my daughter-in-law! And I suppose you also think, you worthless, debauched, revolting boy, that you're the only child I'm going to have and that I'm past the age of child-bearing! Please understand that I'm quite capable of having another son, if I please, and a far better one than you. However, to make you feel the disgrace still more keenly, I think I'll legally adopt one of my slaves and hand over to him your wings, torch, bow and arrows, which you have been using in ways for which I never intended them. And I have every right to do that, because not one of them was supplied by your father. The fact is that you have been mischievous from your earliest years and always delighted in hurting people. You have often had the bad manners to shoot at your elders, and as for me, your mother, you rob me day after day, you matricidal wretch, and have constantly stuck me full of your arrows. You sneer at me and call me 'the widow', and show not the slightest respect for your brave, invincible stepfather; in fact, you do your best to annoy me by setting him after other women and making me jealous. But you'll soon be sorry that you played all those tricks; I warn you that this marriage of yours is going to leave a sour, bitter taste in your mouth."

'Then, to herself: "Everyone is laughing at me and I haven't the faintest idea what to do or where to go. How in the world am I to catch and cage the little viper? I suppose I'd better go for help to old Sobriety to whom I've always been so dreadfully rude for the sake of this spoilt son of mine. Must I really have anything to do with that dowdy, countrified woman? Well, revenge is sweet from whatever quarter it comes. Yes, I fear that she's the only person who can do anything for me. She'll give the little beast a thrashing; confiscate his quiver, blunt his arrows, tear the string off his bow and quench his torch. Worse than that, she'll shave off his hair, which I have often bound up with my own hands so that it glittered with gold, and clip those lovely wings of his which I once whitened with the dazzling milk of my own breast. When that's been done, I'll feel I've got my own back for the harm he's done me."

'After this declaration she rushed out of doors in a furious rage truly worthy of Venus and at once ran into Ceres and Juno,[2] who noticed how angry she looked and asked her why she was spoiling the beauty of her bright eyes with so sullen a frown. "Thank goodness I met you," she answered, "I needed you to calm me down. There is something you can do for me, if you'll be kind enough. Please make careful inquiries for the whereabouts of a runaway vagabond called Psyche – I'm sure you must have heard all about her and the family scandal she's caused by her affair with . . . with my unmentionable son."

'Of course they knew all about it, and tried to soothe her fury. "Lady," they said, "what terrible sin has he committed? Why try to thwart his pleasures and kill the girl with whom he's fallen in love? It is no crime, surely, to beam amiably at a pretty girl? You imagine that he's still only a boy because he carries his years so gracefully, but you simply must realize that he's a young man now. Have you forgotten his age? A mother and a woman of the world, ought you to persist in poking your nose into your son's pleasures and blame the handsome boy for those very sensual talents and erotic inclinations that he inherits directly from yourself? What god or man will have any patience with you, when you go about all the time waking sexual desire in people but at the same time try to repress similar feelings in your own son? Is it really your intention to close down the factory of woman's universal weakness?"

'The goddesses, in thus fulsomely defending Cupid, showed their fear of his arrows, even when he was not about. Venus, seeing that they refused to take a serious view of her wrongs, indignantly turned her back on them and hurried off again to the sea.

*

'Meanwhile, Psyche was restlessly wandering about day and night in search of her husband. However angry he might be, she hoped to make him relent either by coaxing him with wifely endearments or abasing herself in abject repentance. One day she noticed a temple on the top of a steep hill. She said to herself: "I wonder if my husband is there?" So she walked quickly towards the hill, her heart full of love and hope, and reached the temple with some difficulty, after climbing ridge after ridge. But when she arrived at the sacred couch she found it heaped with votive gifts of wheatsheaves, wheat-chaplets and ears of barley, also sickles and other harvest implements, but all scattered about untidily, as though flung down on a hot summer day by careless reapers.

'She began to sort all these things carefully, and arrange them in their proper places, feeling that she must behave respectfully towards every deity whose temple she happened to visit and implore the compassionate help of the whole heavenly family. The temple belonged to the generous Goddess Ceres, who found her busily and energetically at work and at once called out from afar: "Oh, you poor Psyche! Venus is furious and searching everywhere for you. She wants to be cruelly revenged and to punish you with all the strength of her divine power. I am surprised that you can spare the time to look after my affairs for me, or think of anything at all but your own safety."

'Psyche's hair streamed across the temple floor as she prostrated herself at Ceres' feet, which she wetted with her tears. She implored her protection: "I beseech you, Goddess – by your fruitful right hand, by the happy ceremony of harvest-home, by the secret contents of your baskets, by the winged dragons of your chariot, by the furrows of Sicily from which a cruel god once ravished your daughter Proserpine,[3] by the wheels of his chariot, by the earth that closed upon her, by her dark descent and gloomy wedding, by her happy torch-lit return to earth, and by the other mysteries which Eleusis, your Attic sanctuary, silently conceals – help me; oh, please, help your unhappy suppliant Psyche. Allow me, just for a few days, to hide myself under that stack of wheatsheaves, until the great goddess's rage has had time to cool down; or until I have somewhat recovered from my long and tiring troubles."

'Ceres answered: "Your tears and prayers go straight to my heart, and I would dearly love to help you; but I can't afford to offend my relative. She has been one of my best friends for ages and ages and really has a very good heart. You'd better leave this temple at once and think yourself lucky that I don't have you placed under arrest."

'Psyche went away, twice as sad as she had come: she had never expected such a rebuff. But soon she saw below her in the valley another beautifully constructed temple in the middle of a dark sacred grove. She feared to miss any chance, even a remote one, of putting things right for herself, so she went down to implore the protection of the deity of the place, whoever it might be. She saw various splendid offerings hanging from branches of the grove and from the temple door-posts; among them were garments embroidered with gold letters that spelt out the name of the goddess to whom all were dedicated, namely Juno, and recorded the favours which she had granted their donors.

'Psyche fell on her knees, wiped away her tears and, embracing the temple altar, still warm from a recent sacrifice, began to pray. "Sister and wife of great Jupiter! You may be residing in one of your ancient temples on Samos – the Samians boast that you were born on their island and uttered your infant cries there, and they brought you up. Or you may be visiting your happy city of Carthage on its high hill, where you are adored as a virgin travelling across Heaven in a lion-drawn chariot.[4] Or you may be watching over the famous walls of Argos, past which the river Inachus flows, where you are adored as the Queen of Heaven, the Thunderer's bride. Wherever you are, you whom the whole East venerates as Zygia the Goddess of Marriage, and the whole West as Lucina, Goddess of Childbirth, I appeal to you now as Juno the Protectress.[5] I beg you to watch over me in my overwhelming misfortune and rescue me from the dangers that threaten me. You see, Goddess, I am very tired and very frightened, and I know that you're always ready to help women who are about to have babies, if they get into any sort of trouble."

'Hearing Psyche's appeal, Juno appeared in all her august glory and said: "I should be only too pleased to help you, but I can't possibly go against the wishes of my daughter-in-law, Venus, whom I have always loved as though she were my own child. Besides, I am forbidden by the laws to harbour any fugitive slave-girl without her owner's consent."[6]

'Psyche was distressed by this second shipwreck of her hopes and felt quite unable to go on looking for her winged husband. She gave up all hope of safety and said to herself: "Where can I turn for help, now that even these powerful goddesses will do nothing for me but express their sympathy? Tangled as I am in all these snares, where can I go? Where is there a building, or any dark place, in which I can hide myself from the inescapable eyes of great Venus? The fact is, my dear Psyche, that you must borrow a little male courage, you must boldly renounce all idle hopes and make a voluntary surrender to your mistress. Late though it is, you must at least try to calm her rage by submissive behaviour. Besides, after this long search, you have quite a good chance of finding your husband at his mother's house."

'Psyche's decision to undertake this appeal was risky and even suicidal, but she prepared herself for it by considering what sort of appeal she ought to make to the goddess.

'Venus meanwhile gave up employing earthly means to find Psyche and returned to Heaven, where she ordered her chariot to be got ready. The fact that it had lost some of its gold – chiselled away to make a filigree decoration – made it more valuable, not less. It had been her husband the goldsmith Vulcan's wedding present to her. Four white doves from the flock in constant attendance on her flew happily forward and offered their rainbow-coloured necks to the jewelled harness and, when Venus mounted, drew the chariot along with enthusiasm. Behind, played a crowd of naughty sparrows and other little birds that sang very sweetly in announcement of the goddess's arrival.

'Now the clouds vanished, the sky opened and the high upper air received her joyfully. Her singing retinue were not in the least afraid of swooping eagles or greedy hawks, and she drove straight to the royal citadel of Jupiter, where she demanded the immediate services of Mercury, the Town-crier of Heaven, in a matter of great urgency. When Jupiter nodded his sapphire brow in assent, Venus was delighted; she retired from Heaven and gave Mercury, who was now accompanying her, careful instructions. "Brother from Arcadia,[7] you know that I, your sister, have never in my life undertaken any business at all without your assistance, and you know how long I have been unable to find my slave-girl who is in hiding. So the only solution is for you to make a public announcement offering a reward to the person who finds her. My orders must be carried out immediately. Her person must be accurately described so that nobody will be able to plead ignorance as an excuse for harbouring her."

'And as she spoke she handed him a document indicating Psyche's name and other particulars and immediately went home. Mercury did as he was told. He went from country to country crying out everywhere: "If any person can apprehend and seize the person of a king's runaway daughter, Venus' slave-girl, by name PSYCHE, or give any information that will lead to her discovery, let such a person go to Mercury, Town-crier of Heaven, in his temple behind the Circus column beside the temple of Murcia in Rome.[8] The reward offered is as follows: seven sweet kisses from the mouth of the said Venus herself and one delicious thrust of her honeyed tongue between his lips."

'A jealous competitive spirit naturally fired all mankind when they heard this reward announced, and it was this that, most of all, put an end to Psyche's hesitation. She was already near her mistress's gate when she was met by one of the household, named Habit, who screamed out at once at the top of her voice: "You wicked slave-girl, you! So you've discovered at last that you have a mistress, eh? But don't pretend, you brazen-faced thing, that you haven't heard of the huge trouble that you've caused us in our search for you. Well, I'm glad you've fallen into my hands, because you're safe here – safe inside the doors of Hell, and there won't be any delay in your punishment either, you obstinate creature." She seized Psyche's hair violently and dragged her into Venus' presence, though she came along willingly enough.

'When Venus saw her brought into her presence she burst into the hilarious laugh of a woman who is desperately angry. She shook her head and scratched her right ear. "So you condescend," she cried, "to pay your respects to your mother-in-law? Or perhaps you have come to visit your husband, hearing that he's dangerously ill from the burn you gave him? I promise you the sort of welcome that a good mother-in-law is bound to give her son's wife." She clapped her hands for her slaves, Anxiety and Grief, and when they ran up, gave Psyche over to them for punishment. Obeying their mistress's orders, they flogged her cruelly and tortured her in other ways besides, after which they brought her back to Venus' presence.

'Once more Venus yelled with laughter: "Just look at her!" she cried. "Look at the whore! That big belly of hers makes me feel quite sorry for her. By Heaven, it wrings my grandmotherly heart! How wonderful to be called a grandmother at my time of life! And to think that the son of this disgusting slave will be called Venus' own grandchild! No, but of course that is nonsense. A marriage between unequal partners, celebrated in the depth of the country without witnesses and lacking even the consent of the bride's father, can't possibly be recognized by law; your child will be a bastard, even if I permit you to bring it into the world.''

'With this, she flew at poor Psyche, tore her clothes to shreds, pulled out handfuls of her hair, then grabbed her by the shoulders and gave her head a violent shaking. Next she took wheat, barley, millet, lentils, beans and the seeds of poppy and vetch, and mixed them all together into a heap. ''You look such a dreadful sight, slave,'' she said, ''that the only way that you are ever likely to get a lover is by hard work. So now I'll test you myself, to find out what you can do. Do you see this pile of seeds all mixed together? Sort out the different kinds, stack them in separate heaps and do the job to my satisfaction before nightfall.'' When she had given this great heap of seeds to Psyche to deal with, she flew off to attend some wedding feast or other.

'Psyche made no attempt to set about the inextricable mass but sat gazing dumbly at it, until a very small ant, one of the country sort, realized the stupendous nature of her task. Pity for Psyche as wife of the mighty God of Love set it cursing the cruelty of her mother-in-law and scurrying about to round up every ant in the district. ''Take pity,'' she said, ''on this pretty girl, you busy children of the generous Earth. She's the wife of Love himself and her life is in great danger. Quick, quick, to the rescue!''

'They came rushing up as fast as their six legs would carry them, wave upon wave of ants, and began working furiously to sort the pile out, grain by grain. Soon they had arranged it all tidily in separate heaps and had run off again at once.

'Venus returned that evening, a little drunk, smelling of fragrant ointments and swathed in rose-wreaths. When she saw with what prodigious speed Psyche had finished the task, she said: ''You didn't do a hand's stroke yourself, you wicked thing. This is the work of someone whom you have made infatuated with you – though you'll be sorry for it.'' She threw her part of a coarse loaf and went to bed.

'Meanwhile she had confined Cupid to an isolated room in the depths of the house, partly to prevent him from playing his usual naughty tricks and so making his injury worse; partly to keep him away from his sweetheart. So the lovers spent a miserable night, unable to visit each other, although under the same roof.

'As soon as the Goddess of Dawn had set her team moving across the sky, Venus called Psyche and said: "Do you see the grove fringing the bank of that stream over there, with fruit bushes hanging low over the water? Shining golden sheep are wandering about in it, without a shepherd to look after them. I want you to go there and by some means or other fetch me a hank of their precious wool."

'Psyche rose willingly enough, but with no intention of obeying Venus' orders: she had made up her mind to throw herself in the stream and so end her sorrows. But a green reed, producer of sweet music, was blown upon by some divine breeze and uttered words of wisdom: "I know, Psyche, what dreadful sorrows you have suffered, but you must not pollute these sacred waters by a suicide. And, another thing, you must not go into the grove, to risk your life among those dangerous sheep, until the heat of the sun is past. It so infuriates the beasts that they kill any human being who ventures among them. Either they gore them with their sharp horns, or butt them to death with their stony foreheads, or bite them with their poisonous teeth. Wait until the afternoon wears to a close and the serene whispers of these waters lull them asleep. Hide meanwhile under that tall plane-tree which drinks the same water as I do, and as soon as the sheep calm down, go into the grove near by and gather the wisps of golden wool that you'll find sticking on every briar there."

'It was a simple, kindly reed, telling Psyche how to save herself, and she took its advice, which proved to be sound: that evening she was able to return to Venus with a whole lapful of the delicate golden wool. Yet even her performance of this second dangerous task did not satisfy the goddess, who frowned and told her with a cruel smile: "Someone has been helping you again, that's quite clear. But now I'll put your lofty courage and singular prudence to a still severer test. Do you see the summit of that high mountain over there? You'll find that a dark-coloured stream cascades down its precipitous sides into a gorge below and then floods the Stygian marshes and feeds the hoarse River of Cocytus.[9] Here is a little jar. Go off at once and bring it back to me brimful of ice-cold water fetched from the very middle of the stream at the point where it bursts out of the rock."

'She gave Psyche a jar of polished crystal and packed her off with renewed and even more menacing threats.

93

'Psyche started at once for the top of the mountain, thinking that there at least she would find a means of ending her wretched life. As she came up to the ridge of the hill she saw what a stupendously dangerous and difficult task had been set her. The dreadful waters of the river burst out from half-way up an enormously tall, steep, slippery precipice; cascaded down into a narrow conduit, which they had hollowed for themselves, and flowed unseen into the gorge below. On both sides of their outlet she saw fierce dragons crawling, never asleep, always on guard with unwinking eyes and stretching their long necks over the water. And the waters themselves seemed to have voices, which called out: "Be off! What are you doing? Take care! What are you at? Look out! Off with you! You'll die!"

'Psyche stood still as stone; the utter impossibility of her task was so overwhelming that she could no longer even relieve herself by tears – that last comfort. But the kind, sharp eyes of good Providence noticed when her innocent soul was in trouble, and Jupiter's royal bird, the rapacious eagle, suddenly sailed down to her with out-stretched wings. He gratefully remembered the ancient debt that he owed to Cupid for having helped him to carry the Phrygian cup-bearer to Jupiter,[10] and so, flying past Psyche's face, addressed her with these words: "Silly, inexperienced Psyche, how can you ever hope to steal one drop of this most sacred and terrifying stream? Surely you have heard that Jupiter himself fears the waters of Styx, and that just as human beings swear by the Blessed Gods, so they swear by the Sovereign Styx. But let me take that little jar." He quickly snatched it from her grasp and soared off on his strong wings, steering a zigzag course between the two rows of furious fangs and vibrating three-forked tongues. The stream was reluctant to give up its water and warned him to escape while he still could, but he explained that the Goddess Venus wanted the water and pretended that she had commissioned him to fetch it; a story which carried some weight with the stream. Psyche, accepting the brimful jar with delight, quickly returned with it to Venus, but still could not appease her fury. Instead, threatening even worse and grimmer acts of villainy, she said with a smile that seemed to spell the girl's ruin: "You must be a witch, a very clever, very wicked witch, else you could never have carried out my orders so diligently. But I have still one more task for you to perform, my dear girl. Take this box (and she gave it to her) and go down to the Underworld to the death-palace of Orcus. Hand it to Proserpine and ask her to send this box back to me with a little of her beauty in it, enough to last for at least one short day. Tell her that I have had to make such a drain on my own store, as a result of looking after my sick son, that I have none left. Then come back with the box at once, because I must rub its contents over me before I go to the theatre of the gods tonight."

'This seemed to Psyche the end of everything, since her orders were to go down to the Underworld of Tartarus. Psyche saw that she was undisguisedly being sent to her immediate death. She went at once to a high tower, deciding that her straightest and easiest way to the Underworld was to throw herself down from it. But the tower suddenly broke into human speech: "Poor child," it said, "do you really mean to commit suicide by jumping down from me? How rash of you to lose hope just before the end of your trials. Don't you realize that as soon as the breath is out of your body you will indeed go right to the depths of Tartarus, but that once you take that way there's no hope of return? Listen to me. The famous Greek city of Lacedaemon[11] is not far from here. Go there at once and ask to be directed to Taenarus,[12] which is rather an out-of-the-way place to find. Once you get there you'll find one of the ventilation holes of Dis. Open gates lead on to a pathless way which, once you have started along it, leads directly to the palace of Orcus. But take care not to go empty-handed through that place of darkness: carry with you pieces of barley bread soaked in honey water, one in each hand, and two coins in your mouth.

'"When you have gone a good way along that deadly road you'll meet a lame ass loaded with wood, and its lame driver will ask you to hand him some sticks which the ass has dropped. Pass him by in silence. Then you will soon reach the river of the dead, where the ferryman Charon will at once demand his fee before he takes you across in his patched boat among crowds of ghosts. It seems that avarice flourishes even among the dead, because Charon, the tax-gatherer of Pluto, does not do anything for nothing. (A poor man on the point of death is expected to have his passage-fee ready; but if he can't get hold of a coin, he isn't allowed to die.) Anyhow, give the filthy old man one of your coins, but let him take it from your mouth, with his own hand. While you are being ferried across the sluggish stream, the corpse of an old man will float by; he will raise a putrid hand and beg you to haul him into the boat. But you must be careful not to yield to any feeling of pity for him; that is forbidden. Once ashore, you will meet three old women some distance away from the bank. They will be weaving cloth and will ask you to help them. To touch the cloth is also forbidden. All these apparitions, and others like them, are snares set for you by Venus; her object is to make you let go one of the sops you are carrying, and you must understand that the loss of even one of them would be fatal – it would prevent your return to this world. They are for you to give to the huge, fierce, formidable hound with three massive heads, whose thunderous barking assails the dead; though they have no need to be frightened by him because he can do them no harm.

'"He keeps perpetual guard at the threshold of Proserpine's dark palace, the desolate abode of Pluto. Muzzle him with one of your sops and you'll find it easy to get past him into the presence of Proserpine herself. She'll give you a warm welcome, offer you a comfortable seat and have you brought a magnificent meal. But sit on the ground, ask for a piece of common bread and eat nothing else. Then deliver your message, and she'll give you what you came for.

'"As you go out, throw the dog the remaining sop to appease his savagery, then pay the greedy ferryman the remaining coin and, after crossing his river, go back by the way you came until you see once again the familiar constellations of Heaven. One last, important warning; be careful not to open or even look at the box you carry back; that hidden receptacle of divine beauty is not for you to explore."

'Such were the terms in which the prophetic tower offered its predictions. Psyche went at once to Taenarus where, armed with the coins and the two sops, she ran down the road to the Underworld. She passed in silence by the lame man with the ass, paid Charon the first coin, stopped her ears to the entreaties of the floating corpse, refused to be taken in by the appeal of the spinning women, pacified the dreadful dog with the first sop and entered Proserpine's palace. There she refused the comfortable chair and the tempting meal, sat humbly at Proserpine's feet, content with a crust of common bread, and finally delivered Venus' message. Psyche filled the box with the secret substance and went away; then she stopped the dog's barking with the second sop, paid Charon with the second coin and returned from the Underworld, feeling in far better health and spirits than while on her way down there and delighted to see the bright daylight again. Though she was in a hurry to complete her errand she allowed her curiosity to get the better of her. She said to herself: "I should be a fool to carry this divine beauty without borrowing a tiny touch of it for my own use: I must do everything possible to please my beautiful lover."

'Amid these reflections, she opened the box, but it contained no beauty nor anything else, so far as she saw; instead out crept a truly Stygian and deadly sleep which, as soon as the cover was taken off, immediately seized her and wrapped her in a dense cloud of drowsiness. She fell prostrate and lay there like a corpse, on the path, just where she had been standing.

'Cupid, now recovered from his injury and unable to bear Psyche's long absence a moment longer, flew out through the lofty window of the bedroom where he had been held prisoner. His wings invigorated by their long rest, he hurried to Psyche, carefully brushed away the cloud of sleep from her body and shut it up again in its box, then roused her with a harmless prick of an arrow. "Poor girl," he said, "your curiosity has once more nearly ruined you. Hurry now and complete the task which my mother set you; and I'll see to everything else." With these words he flew off, and she sprang up at once to deliver Proserpine's present.

'But Cupid, who had fallen more deeply in love with Psyche than ever and was alarmed by his mother's sudden respectability, returned to his old tricks. He flew at great speed to the very highest Heaven and flung himself as a suppliant at Jupiter's feet, where he pleaded his case. Jupiter pinched his cheeks and kissed his hand. Then he said: "My masterful child, you never pay me the respect which has been decreed me by the Council of Gods, and you're always shooting your arrows into my heart – the very seat of the laws that govern the elements and the constellations of the sky. Often you defile it with mortal love affairs, contrary to the laws, notably the Julian edict,[13] and the public peace, injuring my reputation and authority by involving me in sordid love intrigues and disagreeably transforming my serene appearance into that of serpent, fire, wild beast, bird or bull. Nevertheless, I can't forget how often I've nursed you on my knees and how soft-hearted I can be, so I'll do whatever you ask. But please realize that you must protect yourself against envious persons, and if any other girl of really outstanding beauty happens to be about on the earth today, remember the good turn I am doing you and get her to recompense me for it."

'After saying these words, he ordered Mercury to call a council of all the gods, with a penalty of ten thousand *sestertii* for non-appearance. Everyone was afraid to be fined such a sum, so the Celestial Theatre filled up at once, and Almighty Jupiter from his sublime throne read the following address:

> Right honourable gods and goddesses whose names are registered in the White Roll of the Muses, you all know the young man over there whom I have brought up from boyhood and to whose youthfully passionate nature I have thought it advisable to administer certain curbs. It is enough to remind you of the daily complaints that come in of his adulterous living and practising of every sort of vice. Well, we must stop the young rascal from doing anything of the sort again by fastening the fetters of marriage securely upon him. He has found and seduced a girl called Psyche, and so let him have her, hold her, possess her and enjoy her embraces from this time forth and for evermore.

'Then he turned to Venus: "My daughter, you have no occasion to be sad or ashamed that your rank and station in Heaven has been disgraced by your son's mortal match; for I'll see that the marriage is one between social equals, legitimate and in accordance with civil law." He ordered Mercury to fetch Psyche at once and escort her up to Heaven. When she arrived he took a cup of ambrosia and handed it to her. "Drink, Psyche, and become an immortal," he said. "Cupid will now never fly away from your arms, but will remain your husband for ever."

'Presently a great wedding feast was prepared. Cupid reclined in the place of honour with Psyche's head resting on his breast; Jupiter was placed next, with Juno and then all the other gods and goddesses in order. Jupiter was served with nectar, the wine of the gods, by the rustic boy, his personal cup-bearer; Bacchus attended to everyone else. Vulcan was the chef; the Seasons decorated the palace with red roses and other flowers; the Graces sprinkled balsam water; the Muses chanted harmoniously; Apollo sang to his own lyre; and fair Venus came forward and performed a fine step-dance in time to the music, while Satyrus and Paniscus[14] played on their pipes. And so Psyche was married to Cupid and in due time she bore him her child, a daughter whose name was Pleasure.'

★

That was the story the witless and drunken old woman told to the girl prisoner, and I, standing not far off, regretted that I had no pen or tablets to commit such a fine tale to writing.

CHAPTER X

>>>>><<<<<

DEFEAT OF THE BANDITS

THE bandits returned with a big haul of loot but evidently at the expense of heavy fighting, because some of the bravest of them were wounded. It was decided that these should have their wounds dressed and remain in the cave while the others went out again and fetched back some more loot which they had hidden in some cave. After hastily gobbling their dinner the unwounded men drove my horse and myself out into the road, beating us with sticks, and took us uphill and downhill by a roundabout way until towards evening we reached the other cave. We were very weary but they refused us a moment's rest: they loaded us up and hurried us back in such haste and with so many blows that they drove me into a boulder that was lying on the road and capsized me. Then blows fell thick and fast and I had difficulty in rising because I had badly grazed my off hind-leg and bruised the near hoof. A bandit shouted: 'How long are we going to waste fodder on this worn-out ass? Now he's gone lame as well.'

'Yes,' said another, 'he's brought us bad luck ever since we had him. Several of our brave comrades have been wounded and several more killed.'

Another agreed: 'Very well, as soon as he's carried this load back, which he seems most unwilling to do, I'll push him into the ravine as a nice present for the vultures.'

They were still pleasantly arguing over the best way of killing me when we reached home again, for fear had winged my hooves. They quickly unloaded us and without giving us food or water, or even troubling to kill me, they called their wounded comrades out and returned with them at once to the cache to make up, they said, for the time lost by my laziness.

The threat of death made me feel very uneasy. I said to myself:

'Lucius, why stand here tamely waiting for the last, fatal blow to fall? These bandits have decided to put you to death, a very cruel death too, and they'll find little difficulty in carrying out their threat. You see that ravine with the sharp rocks jutting out from its sides? When you're pushed over, those spikes will catch you and tear you to pieces before you ever reach the ground. The splendid magic that fascinated you so much has given you only the shape of an ass, and an ass's drudgery, not its thick hide; yours is as delicate as the skin of a horse-leech. Why not be a man in spirit at least and save yourself while you still have a chance? Now's the time to escape; all the bandits are away. Are you afraid of an old woman with one foot in the grave, whom you can finish off with one kick of your lame hoof?'

'But where on earth can I go?' I continued. 'Who will give me hospitality? No, that's a stupid question; only an ass could have asked it. What traveller wouldn't be glad to mount on the back of any stray beast he met and ride off on it?' Then straight away exerting all my strength, I snapped the leather thong by which I was tied and was off as fast as my legs could carry me.

The old woman had eyes like a hawk; she snatched up the end of the thong as I charged by and with a courage that surprised me in a creature of her age tried to lead me back to the cave. But the bandits had threatened to kill me, so I could hardly afford to pity her. I flung out my hind hooves and knocked her down, but even when sprawling on the ground she clung grimly to the thong, so that for a while I galloped along trailing her behind me. She yelled for someone to help, but that was wasting her breath. Nobody was about except Charite, who ran out of the cave when she heard the old woman's cries. It was a remarkable scene: little old Dirce hanging not on to a bull but on to an ass.[1] Charite rose to the occasion courageously. She wrenched the thong out of the old woman's grasp, coaxed me to slacken my pace, mounted nimbly on my back and urged me on again. My own desire to escape was now reinforced by my determination to rescue the girl, as well as by the whacks which she gave me. My four feet beat the ground like a racehorse's, and I tried to answer the sweet words of encouragement she gave me by braying. Sometimes I turned my neck, pretending to be scratching my flanks, and kissed her pretty feet.

She drew a deep breath and with an anxious upward glance began to pray: 'O Blessed Gods, please help me in this time of greatest danger. And you, cruel Fortune, stop being angry with me. Surely I have been tormented enough to appease you. And as for you, ass, if you bring me safely home to my parents and my marvellous husband, how grateful we'll all be, how we'll honour you! The best food in the world will be yours for the asking. To begin with, I'll comb out your mane and braid it with my own hands; then I'll arrange your forelocks beautifully and tease out and disentangle the matted hairs of your long unwashed tail. I'll hang you all over with golden plaques, until you twinkle like a starry sky, and I'll lead you in a triumphant procession with everyone applauding, and I'll bring you nuts and tit-bits every day in my silk apron. But don't run away with the idea that good food, perfect leisure and a long, happy life will be all the reward you get from me; I'll have a memorial set up at home, a painting depicting our flight, and I'll get some learned men to write the story out in a book for future generations to read: "How a maiden, a king's daughter, escaped from captivity on the back of an ass." It's not a very learned subject but you'll have your place in ancient mythology − I mean the stories of how Phrixus swam to safety on the back of a ram, and how Arion piloted a dolphin, and how Europa rode on the back of a swimming bull.[2] And if it's really true that Jupiter was that bellowing bull, why shouldn't my braying ass be some god, or perhaps a man in transformation?'

She chattered on, sometimes sighing anxiously, sometimes hopefully praying, until we came to a triple fork in the road where she tugged at my halter and did her best to make me take the righthand turning, which was her nearest way home. But I knew that this was the road that the bandits had taken when they went to recover what was left of the loot. I refused to do what she wanted and mentally expostulated with her: 'My poor girl, you're making very bad use of my services. What are you trying to do? Do you want to ride off to the other world? You'll bring both of us to our deaths, if you take that road.'

She insisted, I resisted, and while we were arguing the question like co-heirs in a law-suit about the division of landed property or, if you like, about a right of way, along came the bandits with the loot. The moon was full so they recognized us from some distance away and greeted us with shouts of ironical laughter. One of them cried:

'Whither away so fast by moonlight? Not afraid of ghosts and wandering spirits? What a good daughter you are, upon my word, stealing a visit like this to your parents. Well, it would be a shame to let you travel all alone, so we'll come with you as your escort and show you the way.' He caught hold of my bridle and turned me around, beating me mercilessly with a loaded stick. Naturally loath to face the death that threatened me as soon as I reached the cave again, I remembered my bad hoof and walked lame. But the man who was dragging me along uttered a jeer: 'So you stumble and stagger again, do you? Your rotten hooves are good for galloping but not for walking, I suppose? A moment ago you were flying along like Pegasus.'[3]

While joking in this amiable fashion they gave me another whack with the stick. When we came to the hedged enclosure outside the cave we found the old woman hanging by the neck from the branch of a tall cypress-tree. The bandits cut her down, dragged her along at the end of the rope and pitched her into the ravine. Then they chained up the girl and began ravenously eating the supper which the wretched old woman had cooked for them with posthumous industry. While gluttonously devouring their meal, they discussed how to avenge the insult we had done them. As might have been expected in a rowdy mob like this, all sorts of opinions were offered.

'Burn her alive!'

'Tie her up for the wild beasts to finish off.'

'What about crucifixion?'

'Torture her and flay her alive.'

At last one of them managed to calm the rest down and get them to allow him a hearing. In a mild and pleasant voice he said: 'Comrades, the rules of our company and our humaneness as individuals, and my own moderate nature, forbid us to inflict any punishment which exceeds the crime. Personally, I should be ashamed in the circumstances if we had to fall back on wild beasts, or the cross, or the stake, or any sudden death at all. So listen to my suggestion, and let the girl live – the sort of life that she deserves. This morning, you remember, you decided to kill the ass. He was always a lazy beast and a proper glutton, and now he has shammed lame and aided and abetted our prisoner's attempt at escape. I suggest that tomorrow, instead of throwing him into the ravine, you cut his throat, gut him and, since he has preferred the girl to us, sew her up naked in his belly. Leave only her head sticking out; the rest of her body can be tucked inside. Then expose this stuffed engrafted ass on a rock where the sun beats down hottest. Thus both of them will suffer all the punishments you have rightly awarded them. The ass will die, as he has long deserved to do; the girl will be mauled by wild beasts and her body gnawed by worms; she'll be scorched as though at the stake, when the hot sun begins to cook up the ass's carcase; and when the dogs and vultures finally get at her guts she'll fancy herself on the cross. Just count up all the miseries and torments she'll suffer. In the first place, she'll be left alive in the belly of a dead beast; in the second, her nostrils will soon be filled with a disgusting stench; in the third, she'll suffer desperately from hunger and thirst; lastly she'll not have the use of her hands to shorten her agonies by doing away with herself.'

The bandits agreed unanimously that this was the very thing. My long ears took in every word and I thought: 'O my poor body, tomorrow you'll be a corpse!'

When the night drew to a close and the whole world was lit up by the splendid chariot of the Sun, a man arrived at the cave and sat down exhausted at the entrance. I could see from the greeting they gave him that he belonged to the company. After recovering his breath he told his companions:

'It's all right about Milo's house; we have nothing to fear from the people of Hypata. You remember what my orders were after you'd robbed the place and started back here with the loot? I was to remain behind as a spy, mix with the crowd, pretend to be sad and angry at what had happened, watch what steps were taken to investigate the robbery and identify the robbers, then return to you with a detailed report. Here it is then. A man who calls himself Lucius − his real name is unknown − is accused by everyone in Hypata of having organized the robbery: "perfectly clear case, not mere guesswork," I was told.

'This Lucius had forged letters of introduction making him out to be a respectable person and used them to ingratiate himself with Milo, who invited him to stay at his house and treated him like one of the household. He spent some little time there, made up to the slave-girl, with whom he pretended to be in love, took careful stock of all the bolts and fastenings of the house and had a good look at the room where Milo stored his valuables. An important indication of his guilt, they told me, was that he had disappeared on the very night of the robbery and had not been seen since. They said it was easy enough for him to get clear away on his white horse, which disappeared with him. His groom, who was found in the house, was accused as accessory to the crime and his master's escape. The magistrates committed him to the town gaol and next day put him to the torture. They nearly killed him before they finished, and though he confessed nothing that incriminated his master, a deputation was sent to Lucius' province with orders to search him out and bring him to book.'

I groaned inwardly during this report, to compare my past with my present – that happy Lucius with this wretched doomed ass. It occurred to me that the old sages, versed in ancient doctrines, had pretended and pronounced that Fortune was eyeless because of the way she rewards the unworthy or the positively wicked. She never shows the least sense in selecting her favourites: indeed, she even prefers men from whom, if she had any eyes in her head, she would feel bound to recoil in disgust. Her worst fault is encouraging people to form opinions about us that are inconsistent with, and even plainly contradict, our true characters; so that the villain enjoys the reputation of the saint, and the completely innocent man gets the punishment earned by the wicked one. Take my case, for instance: she seemed to have done her very worst by changing me into an animal, a beast of burden, of the most ignoble sort, too. It was a misfortune that the most hardened criminal would consider a terrible one and deserving of his sincere sympathy; yet on the top of all, here I found myself accused not only of common housebreaking but of robbing my own beloved host – a far worse crime, amounting almost to parricide. I had not even been allowed to defend myself or utter a single word of denial. And now that the charge was made in my presence, I could not bear anyone to think that my silence implied acquiescence or a guilty conscience. I was tormented with a desire to speak, if it were only to say: 'No, I didn't do it!'

I roared out: 'No, no!' again and again but I found the rest impossible to pronounce though I made my loose lips quiver with the elocutory effort. So I went on with my 'No, no!'

'But why do I go on and complain of Fortune?' I asked myself. 'Could anything have been more shameless than making me a stable-mate and fellow-labourer with the horse that used to carry me and was my servant?' These reflections gave way to a more immediate one: namely that the robbers were about to sacrifice me and use my carcase as a sacrificial victim to Charite's ghost.[4] I looked at my belly again and again and seemed to have the unfortunate girl already sewn up inside me.

The person who had brought the news of my false accusation unstitched his clothes and took out a thousand gold pieces hidden in them which, he explained, he had robbed from different travellers whom he had met on his way home. He conscientiously put them into the common hoard. Then he asked anxiously after his comrades and when he was told that some of them, in fact all the bravest ones, had since been killed in one way or another, though all had died very gamely, he suggested that they should call a short truce in the war, leaving the roads in peace, and spend the time in a recruiting campaign. Some of the lads, he said, might have to be impressed and kept loyal by a sense of fear, some would be attracted by the prospect of loot and come forward as volunteers, others would be only too pleased to exchange a life of drudgery for membership of a company which exerted tyrannical power. He said he had come across a tall, powerfully built young beggar and told him that he ought to make better use of his hands than stretch them out for petty charity: why not help himself with them to gold? Lack of exercise was making him flabby, and it was a pity not to enjoy the advantages of health and strength while he still had them. After some argument the man had been persuaded to volunteer for service with the company.

The bandits all agreed to accept the new recruit, who seemed to have the right qualifications, and afterwards look out for others like him to bring the company up to full strength again.

So the spy went out and soon returned with the man. He was broadly built and a whole head taller than the biggest of the bandits, and though his beard was still mere down, he was incomparably the finest-looking man present. His powerful chest and muscular stomach seemed to be bursting through the seams of the patched rags which served him for clothes.

His greeting as he came in was: 'Good morning, you retainers of valiant God Mars. If you're as ready to accept me as I am to join your company, I'll be proud to be your comrade and serve with you. I'm not lacking in spirits and courage and always happier when blows are struck at me in battle than when gold coins are pressed into my palm. Others fear death; I despise it. Don't judge me by these rags. I'm neither a pauper nor a tramp, but the former captain of a powerful bandit company which plundered and terrorized the whole of Macedonia. Haemus of Thrace is my name – one that has made whole provinces tremble – and my father was Thero, an equally famous bandit. I was weaned on human blood, brought up on human blood, inherited my father's courage and followed in his footsteps. But in a short space of time I lost my entire band and all the huge treasures we had amassed. The god grew angry with me because I attacked one of the Emperor's chief officers, a former provincial governor with an annual salary of two hundred thousand *sestertii*, who had lost his appointment by bad luck.

'This officer, as I say, had an honourable career in the Imperial service and the Emperor himself thought highly of him. But he had jealous rivals who slandered him and got him sent into exile along with his wife, Plotina – a very loyal, decent woman, with a contempt for city life, who had borne her husband ten children and was now determined to follow him into banishment and share his misfortunes. She cut off her hair, tied strings of gold coin and her most valuable necklaces around her waist and put on man's clothes. The soldiers' drawn swords didn't frighten her and she took the greatest care of her husband; ran the same dangers, did all she could for him and behaved as courageously as the man she pretended to be. The worst part of the journey ended one evening when they sighted Zacynthus, where it was their destiny to stay for a time, and sailed into the Bay of Actium. There they disembarked, because they found the swell disagreeable, and spent the night in a seaside cottage.

'We had left Macedonia and happened to be roving around in that district, so we broke into the cottage and stripped it clean. But it was a close shave, because Plotina raised the alarm as soon as she heard the noise of the gate, running into the room where her husband was asleep and screaming at the top of her voice. She not only roused her armed escort and all her slaves, calling on each one by name, but also shouted to the people in the neighbouring cottages to come to her help. We should never have got off without loss if everyone hadn't panicked, and scrambled to a hiding-place.

'This wonderful woman – I won't apologize for calling her

wonderful because it's the truth — then returned to Rome and appealed to the Emperor. She made out so strong a case for her husband (to whom her loyalty was exceptional) that he consented not only to recall him from exile but to avenge the injuries he had suffered. In fact, he expressed the wish that Haemus' bandit company should cease to exist; and you know what authority Caesar's wishes carry. Troops were sent against us and chased us. The company was cut to pieces. But I managed to creep out from the very jaws of death. Dressed in a woman's gaily coloured dress, with full skirts, a cloth cap pulled over my head and my feet squeezed into a pair of those thin white shoes that women wear, and thus looking deceptively like a member of the inferior sex, I jumped on the back of an ass loaded with barley-sheaves and rode safely through the whole enemy battle-line. Nobody saw through my disguise because I was still beardless at the time and my cheeks were as smooth and pink as a boy's. Even after that I lived up to my father's reputation and my own, though I confess that the presence of those war-like drawn swords had made me a little nervous. Still disguised as a woman, I made single-handed raids on country-houses and even fortresses, and built up this small capital to help me along the road.'

He ripped open his rags and out tumbled two thousand gold pieces. 'Here,' he said, 'is my willing contribution to your company's funds — call it my dowry, if you like. And, if you'll accept me, I'm ready to captain your company and undertake in a short time to plate the walls of this rocky cave with pure gold.'

The bandits did not hesitate. They unanimously elected him captain and produced a tolerably elegant tunic for him to wear. He discarded his rags, put it on, and embraced each of his new comrades in turn. Then he took the place they had given him on the couch at the head of the table, where his election was celebrated with a supper and a grand drinking bout. The bandits told him about the girl and how she had tried to escape on my back and about the monstrous death sentence that they had passed on us. He asked where the girl was, and when they took him to her and he found her loaded with chains, he turned away with a contemptuous curl of his nostrils and said: 'Even if I dared quarrel with your decision, I'm not so stupid as to do that. All the same, I should be ashamed not to say anything that I feel would be useful, since I have made your interests mine, so please allow me to tell you frankly what I think; on the understanding, of course, that if you disagree your decision stands. My view is that wise bandits put profit before any other consideration whatsoever, even vengeance, which is a notoriously two-edged weapon. If you kill the girl by sewing her up in the ass's belly you may soothe your feelings, but there's no profit in it for anyone, whereas if you take her to some town or other and put her up for sale, a young girl like that ought to fetch a high price. I myself am acquainted with certain pimps, one of whom, I know, will pay you a really large sum for her and settle her in a suitably high-class brothel – from which she won't be likely to run away. And you'll have your revenge just the same; she certainly won't enjoy slaving in a brothel. Now, you're at perfect liberty to decide what to do, and I've offered you this advice merely because I think it will be to your advantage.'

He was arguing on behalf of the company's funds; but he was also pleading for us, so the tedious deliberations that followed were sheer torture to me. At last they willingly agreed to follow their new captain's advice and at once unchained the girl. Now, from the very moment that she saw this youth and heard him mention brothels and pimps, her spirits had begun to rise and her face was wreathed in smiles. I felt that this was really too much and almost turned misogynist then and there: to see a young girl, who pretended to be deeply in love with the man who was practically her husband and with whom she would have lived a most respectable life, suddenly entranced with the idea of working in a filthy brothel! The character of the whole female sex was on trial, and the judge was an ass!

The young captain said: 'I think we should invoke our comrade Mars about this selling of the girl and picking up recruits. So far as I can see we have neither a suitable victim for the sacrifice nor enough wine for a drinking party. I need ten men to come with me to the nearest town and fetch back for you a banquet fit for the Salian priests.'

He and ten other bandits went off, and were soon back with skins full of wine and a flock of sheep and goats. A large, shaggy old he-goat was chosen for sacrifice to Mars, our companion and comrade. Then a sumptuous supper was immediately prepared. 'You'll find that I take the lead not only in your raids but in your entertainments,' said the new captain. He went briskly to work and showed his versatility by first sweeping the floor and smoothing the couches, then cooking and seasoning the meat and finally serving it out to his comrades on handsome dishes, and filling and re-filling their large wine cups. Now and then he found time to visit the girl, on the pretext of fetching something that he needed from her end of the cave, and brought her food stolen from the table and cups of wine. She accepted them gladly, and once or twice when he wanted to kiss her she was only too pleased and kissed him quite affectionately in return. I was shocked. I said to myself: 'Have you forgotten your marriage, you supposedly chaste girl, and the man whom you loved and who loved you? Do you really prefer this stranger, a bloodthirsty bandit at that, to the man whom you were to marry with your parents' approval? Doesn't your conscience stab you, when you trample your love underfoot and behave like a whore in this robbers' den? Don't you realize that if the other bandits catch you out, you'll be right back with the ass and sentencing me to death a second time? Really, you're risking my skin as well as your own in playing that little game.'

However, my indignation cooled when I found that I did the girl an injustice; for I gathered from something he said in my hearing, not of course caring whether I heard it or not, since I might as well have been dead – something indirect but clear enough for any intelligent ass to understand – that the new captain was not really Haemus the famous bandit, but her bridegroom, Tlepolemus! What he said was this: 'Courage, dearest Charite, your enemies will all soon be your prisoners.' And I noticed that though he refrained from drinking much himself he continued to treat the bandits to more and more wine, undiluted now with water but well warmed, so that they were gradually falling into a drunken stupor. He may even – I suspect – have doctored their drink with some soporific drug. At last, when every single one of them lay dead drunk on the floor, Tlepolemus easily trussed them all up in turn with lengths of rope and lashed them together at his convenience; after which he mounted Charite on my back and made off homewards with her.

As soon as we came within sight of his town everyone flocked out expectantly. Charite's father, mother, relatives, dependants, child relations, slaves and all ran delightedly towards us and formed up in procession behind us, followed by crowds of men, women and children of every age. It was indeed a memorable spectacle: a virgin riding in triumph on an ass! As for myself, I rejoiced with my whole heart and decided to identify myself as closely as possible with the proceedings by pricking my ears, expanding my nostrils and braying strenuously; it was a thunderous noise I made. When we came into Charite's house she ran upstairs to her room, where her parents welcomed her lovingly, while Tlepolemus took me straight back to the cave. He had a large crowd of his fellow-townsmen with him and a train of baggage animals. I was quite ready to go because, curious as ever, I wanted to watch the robbers being taken prisoner. We found them still bound fast, with the bonds of wine as well as with cord, and the former were the more powerful. So Tlepolemus and his friends located and brought out all the gold and silver and other treasures and loaded us with it all, then rolled some of the bandits over a nearby precipice; they beheaded the rest with their own swords and left their corpses lying in the cave.

We returned in triumph, exulting in the completeness of our vengeance, and handed in the loot at the public treasury, after which the girl was married, in accordance with the law, to Tlepolemus who had got her back. Then my mistress called me her saviour and took every possible care of me. On her wedding-day she ordered my manger to be filled with barley to the brim, and gave me hay enough to satisfy a Bactrian camel.[5] But what sufficiently lurid curses could I heap on the head of Fotis, for having turned me into an ass rather than a hound, when I saw the dogs of the household gorged nearly to bursting on the meat left over, or stolen, from that lavish dinner?

The next morning, after a wonderful night, during which she had been initiated into Venus' lessons, the bride told her parents and husband how greatly indebted she was to me, and refused to change the subject until they promised to reward me with the highest possible honours. So they called a council of their wisest and most responsible friends to decide what form these honours should take. One suggested that I should be kept in a stable, excused all work and fed continuously on the best barley, beans and vetch; but another had more consideration for my love of liberty and suggested that I should run wild and have a good time in the meadows and father a set of fine mules for my mistress on her brood-mares that were pasturing there; and this was the decision that they finally adopted. So the bailiff of the stud-farm was sent for and I was handed over to him with careful injunctions about my good treatment. I trotted gaily off with him, delighted at the prospect of being at last free from packs and bundles and at liberty to run about the meadows until spring came with its new crop of blossoms, when somewhere or other I would find roses growing. It occurred to me that if my master and mistress showed me such gratitude while I was still an ass, they would probably show me even more once I was restored to human shape.

CHAPTER XI

>>>><<<<

AT THE FARMS

THE bailiff took me to a place a fair way out of the city, where I found that I was not to be given my liberty nor any of the other good things promised to me. On the contrary, his stingy and evil-minded wife harnessed me to a mill and made me grind corn for the family by the sweat of my poor hide, which she beat with a leafy branch. Not content with using me as her household drudge, she put me to grind corn for her neighbours as well, and so made money out of me. She even withheld the barley that I had been promised and forced me to go round and round all day milling it, then sold it to the neighbouring farmers; and towards evening, when I was tired out, she brought me supper of dirty, caked bran, full of grit.

This was bad enough, but Fortune cruelly exposed me to fresh trials – I suppose with the idea of allowing me to boast later on of 'distinguished conduct at home and in the field', as the phrase is. The bailiff had remembered his instructions, none too soon, and turned me loose for a while with the horses at pasture. Free at last, I frisked joyfully about and ambled up to the mares, reviewing them carefully to see which would be the most voluptuous to mount. But my hopes were utterly dashed when the stallions, who were in fine stud-condition from having been so long at grass and would in any case have been more than a match for a poor ass like myself, grew alarmed at the prospect of my tainting the purity of their stock. Disregarding the rules of Jupiter, God of Hospitality, they ran furiously at me and treated me like a hated rival. One reared up his huge forequarters and battered me with his hooves, another wheeled about and gave me a terrible kick with the full force of his hindquarters, a third let out a threatening whinny, laid back his ears and bit me all over with his sharp white teeth. I was reminded of the legend of that king of Thrace, a powerful tyrant who, in the cause of thrift, exposed his unfortunate guests to the rage of wild horses; he wanted to save barley by feeding the voracious creatures on human flesh.[1] Yes, the stallions gave me such a rough time that I would have given a great deal to find myself safely back at the corn-mill, going giddily round and round.

Fortune seemed insatiable; now she thought out a new torment for me. I was detailed by the bailiff to fetch down wood from the top of a high mountain and the boy he put in charge of me must have been the wickedest ever born. He not only tired me out by making me sweat up and down the mountain and wear out my hooves on the sharp stones, but beat me cruelly and persistently until my bones ached to the marrow. He always hit me on the same spot, the off haunch, until he made the hide fester and break; a great gaping hole, or trench, appeared in it and though the blood ran down he continued to plant his blows there. He used to pile such a huge load on my back that anyone would have thought it was intended for an elephant, rather than an ass. It was badly balanced too, and, whenever it tipped over on one side, he trimmed it by piling stones on the lighter side instead of moving some of the faggots across from the heavier one. Even these miseries of mine and immoderate burdens did not satisfy him; when we had to cross a stream he kept his boots dry by jumping on my back as if his weight were only a trifling addition to the dreadful load already piled on me. Then, if I happened to fall by the muddy waterside, on the slippery bank, instead of helping me, as he ought to have done – either by pulling me up by my halter or tail or by removing part of my load at least until I had regained my feet – this exemplary ass-boy did nothing at all, however weary I might be, but thrash the hair off my hide with a big stick, beginning with my head and ears and working towards my tail, until I was forced to stand up, as though under medical compulsion.

Another malicious trick that he used to play on me was to tie up a bunch of the sharpest and most poisonous thorns he could find and attach them to my tail; as I walked they swung against me and gave me almost unbearable torture. I was in a hideous dilemma; if I ran away to escape his beatings, I was pulled up short by the violent stabbing of the thorns, if I stood still to avoid the pain, his blows forced me mercilessly on once more. This detestable boy seemed to think of nothing else except how to kill me in one way or another, and used to swear that in the end he really would. Then something happened that provoked his beastly mind to still greater beastliness: which was that one day I lost my temper, lifted up my heels and kicked him to some purpose. His retaliation was terrible; he took me out into the road with a heavy load of coarse flax, securely corded to my back, then as we passed through a shepherds' village he stole a live coal from the kitchen outside a cottage and put it in the middle of the flax. A fire soon broke out in the dry stalks, and blazed up dangerously, scorching my whole back. I saw no way to avoid being burned to death. To stand still among the flames was impossible; but Fortune came to my rescue, if only to reserve me for greater dangers. I noticed a big, muddy puddle left over from the previous day's downpour, rushed towards it and rolled over. The flames were extinguished at once, and I got up again without my load and not seriously hurt. But the nasty, audacious boy threw the whole blame for his own wickedness on me; he told the shepherds that I had purposely stumbled against one of their cooking fires to set the flax ablaze. Then he asked laughing: 'How long are we going to waste fodder on this fiery creature?'

A few days later he thought out a scheme that was much more disagreeable still. He stopped at the first cottage he came to and sold the load of wood I was carrying; then he led me home with nothing on my back, saying that he couldn't control my vicious ways and that he refused ever again to take me up the mountain for wood. 'Do you see this lazy, slow-footed beast? A real ass, he is! Besides all his other dirty tricks, he's now frightening the life out of me with newly invented ones. Whenever he sees a good-looking woman coming along the road, or a nubile girl (or a delicate young boy, for that matter), he rushes madly at her, tossing off his load, saddle and all very often, and throws her down on the ground. Then he makes an unnatural assault on her panting lustfully and trying to force her to commit bestiality with him. He even puckers up his sinful mouth into a kiss and attacks her with disgusting bites. This could get us into all sorts of quarrels and fusses, and even criminal charges. Just now we met a respectable young woman in the road, and he scattered his load of wood all over the place and knocked her down on the dirty ground. He would have raped her in public, if she hadn't shrieked for help from between his hooves and been rescued by some passers-by. It would have been a hanging matter for me if the poor young woman had been smashed up and torn open and died of her injuries.'

He told several other lies of the same sort which offended me all the more because I had to keep silent. At last he worked the shepherds up into such excitement that they agreed I ought to be destroyed. One of them shouted: 'Yes, what about executing the promiscuous universal adulterer? He doesn't deserve to live. Hey, boy, cut off his head — then throw his guts to our dogs. But keep the meat, it will do for the workmen's supper. We can rub dust into his hide and take it back to the bailiff and easily pretend that the wolves got him.'

And straight away my pernicious accuser prepared to carry out the shepherd's sentence, exulting in my evil situation and remembering the kick I had given him. And, oh, how I regretted that it had not done the trick! He drew out his sword and sharpened it on a whetstone. But then another shepherd said: 'No, it would be a crime to kill so fine an ass and lose his services, just because he happens to be a bit frolicsome and randy. What's wrong with gelding him? That will cure him of his lust and make him sweet-tempered and perfectly safe to handle. He'll grow fat and better conditioned too. I've known a great many cattle in my day, not only sulky asses but fiery horses, which were perfect rogues until the cause was removed. Then they became as mild and tractable as you please — warranted quiet to ride or drive. So if you don't object, I'll first go to the market near by and then home to fetch my irons, bring them straight back here and castrate this fierce and disagreeable lecher of yours in next to no time. I undertake to return him to you as gentle a beast as any wether in my flock.'

When I saw that I had been snatched from the jaws of death only to suffer the worst imaginable punishment, I began to weep silently. With that back end of my body being removed, I might just as well be dead, I thought. Once more I contemplated suicide, either by starving myself to death or by throwing myself over some cliff; I was resolved that I would at least die unmutilated. But I had come to no decision by the next morning when the boy, who was determined to put an end to me, took me out again for my usual trudge up the mountain. He tied me to the branch of a huge oak and went off with his axe for a little distance to chop my load of wood. Suddenly a terrible she-bear popped her great head out of a nearby cave. The sight frightened me nearly out of my wits. I flung myself violently back on my haunches. The halter gave way, and I dashed off, not trusting to my hooves, but hurling myself bodily down the mountain slopes until I reached the plain at the foot; with no thought in my mind except how to escape from that frightful bear and from the still more frightful boy.

A traveller happened to be passing. He saw that I was a stray, caught me, jumped on my back and with the stick he was carrying whacked me along an obscure and unfamiliar lane. I carried him cheerfully in the hope of getting away from the cruel fate of gelding and cared little for his blows; I was used to blows by now. But Fortune, mischievous as ever, prevented me from escaping so easily and quickly caught me in a fresh trap; for the cattlemen who were out searching for a runaway cow happened to meet us. They caught me by my halter, which they recognized at once, and began to drag me off.

My rider resisted boldly. 'Why are you pulling me about in this rude way?' he asked. 'What are you attacking me for?'

'Why,' replied the cattlemen, 'do you really suppose we're treating you roughly, when you're stealing our ass? Tell us where you have hidden the body of the boy who was driving him. You killed him, didn't you?'

Then at once they knocked him down on the ground and kicked and punched him though he protested with oaths that he had seen nobody leading me. He said now that I had been straying and that he had caught me and ridden me off with the idea of restoring me to my owner and claiming a reward.

'How I wish,' he said, 'that I'd never set eyes on this ass! Or that he could speak and testify to my innocence. If he could tell you all he knows you'd be ashamed of the way you're treating me.'

The angry cattlemen paid no attention to his protests, but marched him along with a noose around his neck to the leafy mountain thickets where the boy had been chopping wood. He was nowhere to be found, but at last they came across his remains, scraps of human flesh strewn all over the place. I knew this was the bear's work and should certainly have said so, had I been able to speak; but all I could do was to rejoice in silence over my long-delayed revenge. They collected the pieces of his body and fitted them roughly together, and buried them then and there. As for my Bellerophon, they called him a bloody assassin, insisting that he had killed the boy and that they had caught him in the act of stealing me; tied him up and brought him back to their houses, intending to hand him over to the magistrates next day to receive his punishment. Then the boy's parents appeared and started wailing and groaning for the death of their son, and the noise was at its height when up came the shepherd who had promised to geld me.

But then someone told him: 'No, this wicked ass isn't responsible for today's tragedy; but come along tomorrow by all means and cut off not only his private parts but also his head. We'll be delighted to lend a hand.'

So disaster again was postponed until the next day and I felt grateful to the good boy whose death had won me a day's grace at least. But I was not allowed to spend even that short time in rest and gratitude. The boy's mother, in deep mourning, burst into my stable. She had been screaming and shrieking about her poor son's violent end, tearing out her white hair with both hands and sprinkling it with ash. Now she thumped her breast and howled: 'Look at him! Look at him, that heartless beast, that glutton, with his head stuck in the manger! Is it right that he should go on stuffing his guts with food and drink with never a thought for the awful fate that has overtaken his master? He cares nothing at all for an old woman like me. He even thinks that he'll pass for innocent and escape being punished for all his sins. Criminals are like that; however deeply their consciences may reproach them, they never expect to be caught. Now in the name of the blessed gods, you vilest of four-footed creatures – even if you could learn to talk, do you really think that you could persuade the biggest fool alive that you aren't responsible for the poor boy's murder? You could have fought for him with your teeth and hooves. You often used them to attack him; why couldn't you do the same in his defence? You should have galloped off with him on your back and saved him from that bandit's bloody hands. You shouldn't have thrown your rider – your fellow-servant, your master, your comrade, the kind friend who fed you. Don't you know that it's against all moral principle and a punishable offence, too, to desert anyone who's in danger of death? All right, you murderer, you shan't stand there much longer, gloating on my grief. I'll show you what reserves of strength people in grief can fall back on.' She untied her apron and used the strings to knot my legs together, each to each, as tightly as she could to prevent me from retaliating. Next she snatched up a great bar which she used to secure the stable door, and banged me with it until she had to let it drop in exhaustion. Then, complaining that her arms had got tired, she ran back into the house and took a burning faggot from the hearth to thrust between my thighs. I had only one means of escape: I squirted a volley of liquid excrement into her face and eyes, and drove her off, blinded and stinking, so that my life was finally saved. Otherwise I would have died, as an ass, by the stick, like Meleager at the hands of the maddened Althaea.[2]

*

About cockcrow, a slave employed by my mistress and former fellow-sufferer, Charite, arrived with the news of her death and of strange and terrible things that had happened to her family. 'Grooms, shepherds and herdsmen,' he said, 'our poor Charite has died in dreadful circumstances; but she did not go down to the Underworld without proper escort. I'll tell you the whole story from the beginning; it really deserves to be recorded by someone more gifted than I am, some great historian with a happy stylistic knack.

'In the next town from ours lived the well-born and wealthy Thrasyllus, a debauched young fellow who was always drinking and whoring in the public brothels. He was on terms of friendship with a company of bandits and sometimes even joined them in spilling human blood. Yes, that was the sort of man he was; and everyone knew it. When Charite was old enough to be married, Thrasyllus was one of her most persistent suitors and set his heart on winning her. But though he was outstanding among his rivals and brought her parents magnificent presents, he was turned down ignominiously because of his bad reputation. As you know, our master's daughter then married Tlepolemus, a very worthy young gentleman; but Thrasyllus, furious at having been rejected and more in love with Charite than ever, refused to abandon all hope of winning her, and waited for the opportunity of committing a bloody crime. He thought of nothing else, but it was some time before he had the chance of putting his plans into action. On the day that Tlepolemus had managed, by courage and cunning, to rescue the girl from those robbers' menacing swords, Thrasyllus was spokesman for a crowd of people who offered their congratulations. He said that he had come to express the joy of his fellow-townsmen that the young pair were safely re-united and their hope that the marriage would be blessed with children. He was welcomed to the house as a principal guest and shown the hospitality that his rank demanded; and he hid his wicked designs so cleverly that he passed for the most loyal of friends. There was much talk and conversation, and by dining and drinking with them he became an ever dearer friend – and, little by little, involuntarily, he lusted after Charite more and more ruinously. There's nothing so remarkable in that, because the fire of love burns small at first and gives out a pleasant warmth; but fan it with the wind of the loved one's presence and the flames shoot up and scorch you cruelly. Thrasyllus spent a long time wondering how to begin a secret love affair with our mistress. He found that too many eyes of those looking after her were on the watch to make adultery practicable; that even if she wanted to (though she did not), she knew nothing of the art of deceiving a husband; and that Tlepolemus and she were so deeply and increasingly devoted to each other that it would be impossible to separate them. But he was desperate to possess her and refused to regard the case as hopeless, despite these apparently insurmountable obstacles. You know that what looks difficult when one first falls in love after a time looks easy enough. Now note carefully the lengths to which his furious passion drove him.

'One day Tlepolemus rode out with Thrasyllus to hunt wild beasts – that is, if you can call a she-goat a wild beast – because Charite refused to let her husband hunt anything that was armed with tusks or horns. They ascended a thickly wooded hill and pedigree hounds were put in to dislodge the quarry. The well-trained pack fanned out at once and allowed no creature any chance to slip past them. For a time they followed the scent silently until at last the signal was given and then the noise broke out excitedly, making the whole wood ring. But it was no sort of she-goat, or timid doe, or hind, gentlest of all the beasts, that they had flushed out – but an enormous wild boar, the biggest ever seen, a brawny, thick-skinned, filthy beast with bristles rising along his hide and fiery eyes. Out he came like a thunderbolt, glaring menacingly and foaming at the mouth and gnashing his tusks. The leading hounds tried to get a grip on him but were torn open and tossed aside: then he broke the nets at his first rush and got clear away.

'We were unused to such dangerous boars, and, having no weapons or other means of defence, we scattered in panic and hid ourselves in thick bushes or behind trees. Here was Thrasyllus' chance for playing his treacherous trick. He said to Tlepolemus: "Why are we standing here and letting that wonderful beast escape? Is it just surprise? Or are we as frightened as those wretched slaves and go about trembling like a lot of women? Why not mount and go after him? You take a javelin; I'll take a spear."

'So they leapt on to their horses and galloped off in pursuit. But the boar was confident of his native strength. He wheeled round and stood glaring at them, with a horribly ferocious look, making up his mind which of them to charge first. Tlepolemus let fly his javelin, which lodged in the boar's back; but Thrasyllus, instead of following up this advantage, charged Tlepolemus' horse with his lance and hamstrung it. The horse sank in a pool of its own blood, rolled over and threw its master though it had no wish to do so. The boar attacked him at once, ripping off his clothes and wounding him in several places as he tried to rise. His good friend Thrasyllus, so far from feeling remorse for his criminal action, ran at Tlepolemus who was shouting for help and trying to protect his gored legs, and drove his lance into him. He aimed at the right thigh which was the safest place to choose, because the thrust would be indistinguishable, he knew, from a tusk-wound. Only then did he run the boar through, and killed him without difficulty.

'After the young man had been killed in this way, we all ran up out of our hiding-places. Thrasyllus was elated at the death of the man he loathed: but he disguised his feelings and taking his cue from us – we were all lamenting in deep and genuine grief – hugged and kissed his victim's corpse and played the part of mourner in realistic detail, except that he couldn't squeeze out a single tear.

'The news of Tlepolemus' death spread quickly and reached his own family first. The moment his unhappy bride heard about it she went frantic. She ran through the crowded streets of the town and across the fields like a Bacchant,[3] madly lamenting her husband's fate. Everyone she met turned and followed her with cries of sympathy, and soon the whole town was streaming after her to the scene of the murder. When she reached the spot she fell prostrate on his dead body and then and there all but gasped out the life that she had made one with his.

However, her friends succeeded in dragging her away and, greatly against her will, she remained alive.

'Then the corpse was carried to the tomb and the whole town formed the funeral procession. Thrasyllus was there. He wailed aloud, roared, beat his breast and even managed to weep; you see, the tears that he had been unable to force out in the first pretence of grief were now supplied by the joy of the occasion. He hid his true feelings with all sorts of affectionate phrases, pitifully calling on the dead man by name as "My friend, my dear old playmate, my comrade, my brother!" Every now and then he caught at Charite's hands to prevent her from beating her breast, and tried to blunt her distress with vibrating words of sympathy, quoting numerous historical instances of the uncertainty of fate. But of course this was only an excuse for laying his ostensibly friendly hands on the lady and titillating his odious lust.

'As soon as the funeral was over she tried to follow Tlepolemus to the grave. She did not care how, so she fixed on the easiest and least violent way, the one that comes closest to quiet sleep; that is to say, refusing to eat, neglecting herself, hiding herself away in a dark room and leaving the light of day for good and all. Thrasyllus would have none of this and, by pleading with her himself and then persuading her friends and relations and lastly her parents to plead in the same sense, forced her to refresh her poor body, now nearly wasted away by the ill-usage she had given it, with a bath and food. She would have refused even this but for the respect she felt for her parents and, though her looks were calmer now, they were still very sorrowful, and she went through the daily round of her life in inward torment. Day and night, longing for Tlepolemus ate at her heart; she ordered an image of the God Bacchus to be carved with his features, and paid it divine honours, but even this supposed consolation only added to her misery.

'The impatient Thrasyllus, true to his name,[4] couldn't bear to wait until the madness of her grief had gradually dulled into resignation, and her tears for her husband had stopped flowing. She was still at the stage of tearing her clothes and pulling out strands of her hair, when he began to discuss marriage with her; his indecent haste was almost a blurted confession of his unspeakable treachery. Charite was so shocked by his proposal, which came to her like a thunderclap, that she fell down in a faint, as though lightning-struck or blasted by the rays of some star. When she came to herself and remembered what had happened, she screamed aloud like an animal, but refrained from giving the villain his answer until she had time to consider carefully. Meanwhile the ghost of the miserably murdered Tlepolemus visited her chaste bed as she slept and displayed its ghastly blood-stained face. It said: "My own wife – nobody else will ever call you that, unless the bonds that united us have been severed by my terrible death, and my image is gradually dimming in your memory – ah, if this is so, marry again by all means, be happy, take any husband you please, but only not that traitor Thrasyllus. Have nothing to do with him: do not eat at the same table with him, do not even talk to him, let alone go to bed with him. His hands are stained with my blood; don't begin your marriage with a taint of murder. These gory wounds that you have bathed with your tears were not all of them made by the boar's tusks; it was the lance of the evil Thrasyllus that parted us." The ghost then explained in detail the crime that had been committed. When she had first gone to sleep the tears had been trickling down her beautiful cheeks, wetting the pillow; now, roused from this nightmare as though by the wrench of the rack, she broke again into a loud wail of grief, ripped her clothes apart and tore her pretty arms with furious nails.

'Well, at the time she told nobody about the nocturnal apparition and pretended to have no knowledge of the murder; but she decided in secret to punish the odious Thrasyllus before finally freeing herself from the intolerable burden of life. The detestable man came again to seek his ill-advised pleasures and, although she gently evaded these attentions, she dissembled with remarkable cleverness as his pressing talk and humble prayers went on and on. "Thrasyllus," she said, "you must remember that the face of my dear husband, who was like a brother to you, is still vivid in my mind; I seem to smell the cinnamon scent of his body; he is alive in my heart. It would be a kindness if you gave me time to lament his death in my misery, letting the remaining months of the year run out. You see, if we married too soon, that would damage my reputation and also be dangerous for you: my husband's ghost would have the right to feel resentful and might bring about your death."

'However, even this speech, with its promising implications, was not enough to check his greed and impatience. He began to needle her with indecent proposals and would not be refused. At last she pretended to give in and said: "At any rate, there's one thing upon which I must insist: that if we go to bed together, it must be in silence and secrecy, and nobody in this household must know anything about it, until the year has run its course."

'Her false promises completely deceived him. He agreed eagerly to the secret love affair, and in his delight he could hardly wait until darkness fell; nothing in the world mattered more to him now than possessing her.

'"Listen," she said, "you must come up to the door of my apartment about midnight, alone, well muffled up, then give a single low whistle and wait. My old nurse will be sitting just inside to let you in. She'll guide you through the darkness to my bedroom."

'How long the day seemed to Thrasyllus, who was greatly intrigued by this combination of mourning and secret passion! But the sun went down at last and he came to her apartment as she had instructed him and stumbled expectantly towards her bedroom. The old woman, who had been ordered by her mistress to treat him with obsequious politeness, noiselessly produced wine cups and a flagon of wine doctored with a sleeping draught. "You must please wait a little while," she said. "My mistress has been called to her father, who is ill." He suspected nothing, drank cup after cup and was soon fast asleep.

'As soon as he was lying helplessly on his back, the nurse ran for Charite, who came quickly in with a determined step and bent quivering with rage over him. "Look at him," she said, "look at him, my husband's faithful comrade, this bold hunter who thinks he's going to marry me! Look at his hand, the hand that shed my blood; look at his breast, in which so many stratagems were hatched to my ruin; look at his eyes, which I have been unfortunate enough to please. It seems he had some intuition of the fate prepared for him when he said that he was impatient for darkness to fall. Sleep soundly, sleep without fear! I have not come with a sword or a lance: do you think I would honour you with a death like my husband's? No, your eyes shall die in your living head, you will never see anything again except in your dreams. Oh, I'll make you envy Tlepolemus in his death! You shall never look at the sun again; you shall need a hand to guide you wherever you go. You shall never put your arms around Charite, nor enjoy any wedding. You shall experience neither the restfulness of death nor the pleasure of being alive, but wander like a lost ghost between the Underworld and the light of day. And you'll search for the hand that blinded you, but never know – this you'll find the hardest thing of all to bear – whom to accuse of the deed. For now I owe my noble husband's ghost a drink-offering of the blood that flows from your eyes. That will satisfy his vengeance.

'"But why do I allow you this short grace before the torture begins? Perhaps you are dreaming that you are in bed with me to your ruin. Come, it is time to wake from the darkness of sleep to a worse darkness; to lift up your blind face and know that I am avenged, to realize your misfortune and reckon up the full sum of your afflictions.

'"A chaste bride, am I? Your eyes charm me? How prettily the wedding torches have lit up your marriage-bed! The Furies shall be your bridesmaids: and your best man shall be Blindness, the keeper of your unquiet conscience for ever more."

'After this prophetic eloquence, she pulled a pin from her hair and plunged it again and again into Thrasyllus' eyes. Then, leaving him there to awake in pain and blindness from his drugged sleep, she caught up a naked sword that had been Tlepolemus' and rushed madly off with it through the town towards his tomb. We slaves streamed out after her, shouting for her to stop, because we were certain that she was about to perform some desperate act. We cried to one another: "She's mad, she's mad! Disarm her, for God's sake!" A great crowd of townspeople left their houses empty and joined us. But she stood by her dead husband's tomb and kept us off with the naked sword.

'We were all weeping and lamenting, but she reproved us. "This is not the time for tears or mourning. Why mourn when I have just done a great deed? I have avenged my husband's death; I have punished the man who destroyed our marriage, punished him as he deserved. Now I must find my way back with this sword to my Tlepolemus."

'She told us all about her husband's apparition, and how she had deceived Thrasyllus; then plunged the sword in beneath her right breast. She fell spouting blood, babbled a few incoherent words and died with courage worthy of a man. Then the relatives of the unfortunate Charite at once washed her corpse carefully and laid it in the same tomb as her husband, so the two are now reunited for all time.

'When the news of her death came to Thrasyllus he could think of no form of suicide dismal enough to atone for the catastrophe he had caused; his guilty heart told him that merely to die by the sword would be too clean a way out. So he asked to be carried to the tomb, where he stood crying repeatedly: "Here I am, ghosts whom I wronged! Here is a sacrificial victim for you." And with these words he carefully closed the doors of the tomb behind him, intending to die there of starvation and so yield up, voluntarily, his damned soul.'

>>>>><<<<<

WITH THE EFFEMINATE PRIESTS

SIGHS and tears from the listening countrymen greeted this tragic account of the calamity that had overtaken their master and mistress. But these were largely expressive of self-pity: they feared that when the estate changed hands it would be the worse for them. They all decided to run away. The bailiff, into whose charge I had been given with such careful orders to treat me well, stripped the house of everything valuable, loaded me and his other pack animals with the loot and left in a hurry. Women, children, cocks, hens, geese, kids and puppies – in short, whatever livestock could not keep the pace of the convoy – travelled on our backs. But, heavy as was my load, I did not mind in the least, so relieved I felt to escape the knife of that horrible gelder.

We crossed the rocky, wooded mountain and came down into the plain on the other side, and as the evening shadows lengthened on our road we reached a large and thriving town. Its inhabitants requested us not to continue our journey that night, or even the following morning, because the district was overrun by packs of enormous wolves, grown so fierce that they even turned highwaymen and pulled down travellers on the roads or stormed farmbuildings, showing as little respect for the occupants as for their defenceless flocks. We were warned that the road we wished to take was strewn with half-eaten corpses and clean-picked, white skeletons and that we ought to proceed with all possible caution, travelling only in broad daylight – the higher the sun, the milder the wolves – and in a compact body, not straggling along anyhow.

However, in their blind haste to shake off possible pursuers our rascally drivers disregarded this warning, loaded us up again without waiting for dawn, and drove us onward. Well aware of the danger, and not wanting to feel wolf-fangs in my rump, I worked my way into the middle of the herd of pack-animals. Everyone was surprised to see me outpace several horses, but this was due to my terror, not my natural fleetness of foot. It occurred to me that the famous Pegasus must have had a similar experience: the reason they called him 'the winged horse' was doubtless that he was so terrified of being bitten by the fire-breathing Chimaera[1] that he jumped right up to the sky.

The shepherds who led us had armed themselves as if for a pitched battle, with lances, spears, javelins and clubs. Some picked up stones from the rough road, a few carried sharp stakes, and most of them waved blazing torches to frighten the wolves away. It only needed trumpet music to give the impression that we were an army on the march. Whether because of our numbers and the great noise we raised, or because of the torches, we did not see a single wolf even in the distance; they may all have cleared off to some other district. But, although our fears had proved unjustified, we ran into much worse trouble, for when we reached a small village the inhabitants very naturally mistook us, because of our numbers, for a gang of bandits. They were in such alarm that they unchained a pack of large mastiffs which they kept as watch-dogs, very savage beasts, worse than any wolf or bear, and set them at us with the customary yells and shouts.

The mastiffs rushed forward and attacked us from all sides, mauling us indiscriminately and pulling several beasts and men to the ground. It was certainly a remarkable, though a very pitiable, sight: how they worked their way through the whole crowd of us, snapping and biting as they went, rounded up stampeding beasts, savaged men who stood their ground and mounted menacingly on the bodies of the fallen.

Worse followed. Posted on their roofs and on a small hill close by, the villagers pelted us with stones, until we could not decide which it was better to escape from: the dogs at close quarters or the stones from afar. A stone hit the head of a woman seated on my back, who began to scream and bellow for her husband. He ran to her and wiped the blood from her wound, shouting up at the houses: 'In the name of Heaven, why attack poor, hard-working travellers who have never harmed you? What loot can you be after? You don't live in dens like wild animals, or in caves like savages. Then why do you enjoy shedding innocent blood? Do you take us for bandits?'

Almost immediately the shower of stones ceased, the mastiffs were called off and one of the villagers shouted from his perch on the top of a cypress: 'All right. We aren't bandits, either. We've no desire to steal your goods. We're only trying to protect ourselves from an attack by you. Now you can go away without anxiety, in peace and quiet.'

So on we went, a good long way, some of us bitten, some bruised by stones, all of us more or less damaged, until we reached a wood with pleasant green glades and tall trees, where the bailiff called a halt for rest and refreshment. Our people threw themselves down on the ground until they felt rested, then they began to attend to their wounds, every man looking after himself, washing off the blood in a brook that ran through the wood, applying various remedies, then bandaging themselves; the bruises they sponged with water.

An old man appeared at the top of the hill with goats feeding around him that proclaimed him to be their herdsman. One of our people hailed him and asked whether he had any milk or fresh cheese for sale. He shook his head repeatedly before answering: 'How can you think of food or drink or anything else of the sort? Don't you know in what sort of a place you are?' And with these words he turned his back and went away with his goats.

His question and the abrupt way he left us alarmed our people. They all began wondering what was wrong with the place. But there was nobody to enlighten them until another old man appeared, a tall, bent old man, dragging his feet wearily towards us and leaning heavily on a stick. When he reached the glade where we had halted, he fell down on his knees, his eyes streaming with tears, embraced our people one after the other and groaned out: 'I appeal to you, as you hope to live strong and hearty until you reach my age, help a poor old man, who has lost his only comfort in life: save my little grandson from the jaws of death! He is a dear companion on my journeys. We were travelling along the road together when he heard a sparrow twittering on a hedge and tried to catch it. But he fell into a deep ditch hidden by rank undergrowth and is in mortal danger. I know by his constant cries for his grandfather that he is still alive, but as you see I am old and shaky and haven't the strength to pull him out. You strong young men could easily help me. Pity a poor unhappy old man! The child is the last survivor of my family.'

He tore at his white hair, and naturally we were all touched by his appeal. One of our company – the youngest, boldest and strongest of the whole group – the only one, too, who had escaped without a scratch from our one-sided battle, sprang up and asked where the boy was. The old man pointed at a clump of bushes a little way off and eagerly led him towards them. When we animals had grazed, and our drivers had finished eating and dressing their wounds, it was time to pack up and continue our journey. Loud cries were raised for the youth, who had been away a surprisingly long time, and when he did not reappear a friend was sent to warn him that we were on the move again. The friend returned almost at once, pale and trembling, with an extraordinary story: he had found the body of the young man lying on its back, half-eaten, with a monstrous snake coiled over it. The unhappy old man was nowhere to be seen.

So that was evidently what the man with the goats had meant: he had been warning us against the dreadful creature that haunted the glade. Our people hurried as fast as they could from the deserted and deadly place, whacking us hard with their sticks. The next stage of the journey was covered at high speed.

We spent that night at a village; I would like to tell you of an extraordinary deed of horror that took place there.

The previous farm-bailiff, who was married to a fellow-slave, had fallen in love with a free woman, not of his master's household, and made her his mistress. When his wife came to hear of it she was so vexed that she burned his account-books and all the contents of his store-room. Even this did not satisfy her determination to avenge the wrong done to her marriage: she tied one end of a rope around her neck and the other around the neck of the little child and, determined upon self-destruction, plunged into a well, dragging the poor child after her. Her death so shocked the owner of the farm that he seized the bailiff whose infidelity had provoked it and ordered him to be stripped naked, smeared all over with honey and bound fast to a rotten fig-tree which was swarming with ants inside and out. As soon as the ants smelt the honey they began running over him and with minute but innumerable and incessant bites gradually ate him up, flesh, guts and all. He survived the torture for some time, but in the end there was nothing left of him but his skeleton, picked clean; which we saw, shining white, still tied to the fig-tree.

The people who told us the story were still heavy-hearted about the bailiff, and we were glad to leave the unlucky place. We travelled all day over level country and that night reached a fine, handsome town which our weary people decided to make their home. It was a good place for eluding pursuers who came from some distance away, and also well stocked with grain. There the bailiff allowed us pack-animals three days to recover our condition, after which he led us out for sale.

The auctioneer shouted our prices at the top of his voice, and though all the horses and all my fellow-asses soon found prosperous-looking buyers I was passed over contemptuously. The rude way that people handled me and examined my teeth to see how old I was outraged me; one man poked his nasty, dirty fingers into my gums again and again until I caught his hand between my teeth and nearly bit it in two. This discouraged people from making an offer: they took me for a real rogue. Then the auctioneer, shouting till he almost cracked his throat, made all sorts of stupid jokes about me. 'What's the sense,' he cried, 'in asking you to bid for this dirty-coloured, hoofless old donkey, guaranteed lazy in everything but vice, with a hide like a sieve? What about making a present of the brute to anyone who won't mind wasting hay on him?' In this fashion the auctioneer made the bystanders roar with laughter.

But merciless Fortune, whom I had failed either to shake off or appease, however deeply I suffered, now again fastened her blind eyes upon me and, of course, found me a buyer whom she could depend upon to prolong my agonies. He was an old queen, nearly bald, with what greyish hair he still had left dangling in long curls on his neck: one of the scum that carry the image of the Syrian Goddess[2] along the roads from town to town to the accompaniment of cymbals and castanets. This creature was set on buying me and asked the auctioneer my history. The auctioneer joked: 'We got him from the Cappadocian slave-market; he's a fine strong fellow, too.'

'His age?'

'Five years, according to the astrologer who cast his nativity; but he may have more accurate information himself from the public registrar, if you care to press him on the point. No, sir, at the risk of falling foul of the Cornelian Law[3] by selling you a slave known to be a Roman citizen, I don't mind parting with him if you want to buy him. You'll find him a good worker, useful both on the road and in the home. Why not make an offer?'

The odious purchaser asked question after question, and finally: was I quiet to ride or drive?

'Quiet, is it?' said the auctioneer. 'This isn't an ass, it's gelded, so gentle that you can do anything you like with him. None of your biters and kickers, but the sort of animal that makes you ready to swear he's really a decent, honest man bound up in ass-hide. You can prove it easily. Lift up his tail, shove your nose in, and see how he takes it.'

The old rascal saw that he was being laughed at and lost his temper. 'You lunatic auctioneer!' he cried. 'You senseless lump of stinking meat! May the almighty and all-creative Syrian Goddess with the blessed Sabazius, and Bellona, and the Idaean Mother too, and Venus with her Adonis – and all the rest of them – knock out both your eyes!³ That will teach you to make stupid jokes at my expense. Do you think that I can trust my goddess to the back of any restive beast? Suppose he were to pitch her divine image to the ground? What would happen to poor me? I should have to run about with my hair all disarrayed in search of a doctor to attend to her bruises.'

When I heard these words I had a sudden impulse to rear up as though I were mad, so as to discourage him from buying me; but he forestalled me by making an offer of seventeen *denarii* and counting them out at once. The bailiff was as delighted as I was vexed; and glad to be rid of me. He picked up the coins and handed me over to my new master, straw halter and all.

My new master, whose name was Philebus, led me off to his lodgings. When he reached the door he called out: 'Look, girls, look! I have bought you a lovely new man-servant!' The 'girls' were a set of effeminate males who broke into falsetto screams and raucous giggles of joy, thinking that Philebus really meant what he said and that they would now have a fine time with me. When they discovered that I was an ass instead of a man (not that hind which took the place of a maiden),⁵ they began making nasty, sarcastic remarks: 'A man-servant for us? No, a husband for yourself, you mean! But you mustn't be greedy and eat up this pretty little creature all on your own, but must let us have a share of him now and then, because we *are* your little doves, aren't we?' Babbling on to each other in this manner, they took me and tied me to the manger.

Among them was one young man, with a massive physique, whom they had bought with money collected by begging. When they went out, leading the goddess in procession, he would walk in front playing the flute — he played extremely well — and at home they used him in all sorts of ways, especially in bed. When he saw me arrive he was delighted and heaped my manger with fodder. He cried out happily: 'Thank Heavens, you are here at last to help me with my terrible work. Long life to you! If only you can please your masters and give me a chance to recover my strength! I'm utterly worn out!'

His words set me worrying again about the miseries to come.

The next morning out they went, all dressed in different colours and looking absolutely hideous, their faces daubed with rouge and their eye-sockets painted to bring out the brightness of their eyes. They wore mitre-shaped hats, saffron-coloured vestments, silk surplices, girdles and yellow shoes. Some of them sported white tunics with an irregular criss-cross of narrow purple stripes. They covered the goddess with a silk mantle and set her on my back, the flute-player struck up, and they started brandishing enormous swords and maces, and leaping about like maniacs, with their arms bared to the shoulders.

After passing through several hamlets we reached a rich man's country-house where, raising a yell at the gate, they rushed frantically in and danced again to the accompaniment of the flute, as if they were mad. They would throw their heads forward so that their long hair fell down over their faces, then rotate them so rapidly that it wheeled around in a circle. Every now and then they would bite themselves savagely and as a climax cut their arms with the sharp knives that they carried. One of them let himself go more ecstatically than the rest. Heaving deep sighs from the very bottom of his lungs, as if filled with the spirit of the goddess, he pretended to go stark-mad. (A strange notion, this, that the presence of the gods, instead of doing men good, enfeebles or disorders their senses; but you will see how Providence eventually intervened to punish him.) He began by making a bogus confession of guilt, crying out in prophetic tones that he had in some way offended against the holy laws of his religion. Then he called on his own hands to inflict the necessary punishment and snatching up one of the whips that these half-men always carry, the sort with several long lashes of woollen yarn strung with sheep's knuckle-bones, gave himself a terrific flogging. The ground was slippery with the blood that oozed from the knife-cuts and the wounds made by the thongs, but he bore the pain with amazing fortitude. The sight made me uneasy. Suppose this foreign goddess might have a craving for ass's blood in her stomach, as some people have for ass's milk!

At last they grew tired, or thought that they had cut themselves about enough; so they stopped the business. The crowd that had gathered eagerly dropped money into the open pockets of their robes, and not only small change, but silver, too. They also gave them a barrel of wine, cheese, milk, barley for myself as the goddess's own beast. All this the greedy creatures stuffed into the bags that they had brought for the purpose, and I went off doubly laden: I was at once a walking temple and a walking larder.

They worked the whole district in this way until one day, after taking an unusually large collection in one of the towns, they decided to give themselves a really good time. First they got a plump ram from a farmer, by telling him some prophetic nonsense or other, and undertook to sacrifice it to appease the goddess's hunger. Then they got everything ready for the banquet, paid a visit to the public baths and came back with a hefty rustic, well-endowed in thighs and groin.

They had eaten only a few mouthfuls of the first course before, in front of the table itself, their unmentionable lusts propelled them savagely into the most filthy and indecent acts of unnatural lechery. They jumped up, crowded round their guest's couch, pushed him down on his back, pulled off his clothes and made such loathsome suggestions that I could stand it no longer. I tried to shout: 'O Romans, help!' But all that came out was 'O' in fine ringing tones that would have done credit to any ass alive.

The timing was unlucky, because a party of young men were out looking for an ass that had been stolen the night before, and going from inn to inn, searching the stables. One of them happened to hear me bray, and thinking that I might be the stolen beast, hidden somewhere inside the house, they rushed in unexpectedly and caught the creatures in the act of performing their filthy abominations. They roused the neighbourhood and told everyone about the disgusting scene, while ironically complimenting the priests on their truly religious chastity. The news ran from mouth to mouth, and everyone's feelings were outraged; the priests panicked, packed up every-thing and left the town hurriedly about midnight.

We covered a good deal of ground before dawn and when the sun was up found ourselves in a lonely spot, where the priests consulted together for a long time and finally decided to put an end to me. They lifted the goddess off my back and laid her on the ground, then took off my gear, tied me to a tree and flogged me with the knuckle-bone whip until I was nearly dead. One of them wanted to hamstring me with an axe in revenge for the scandal that I had spread about his shining chastity; but the others voted him down, not because they felt any mercy for me, but because if they killed me, where would they find another mount for the image that lay on the ground? So they loaded me up again and drove me forward, beating me with the flat of their swords until we reached a notable town. One of the leading citizens, a very religious-minded man who was especially devoted to the goddess, heard the tinkle of our cymbals, the banging of our tambourines and the soft Phrygian music.[6] He came out to meet us and devoutly offered to lodge the goddess in his spacious mansion. We all entered with her and he tried to win her favour by offering her the deepest possible veneration and the finest victims he could procure. But it was there that I ran into the gravest danger of my life.

One of our host's country tenants had presented him with a haunch of venison from a tall, plump stag; the cook carelessly hung it rather too low on the kitchen door, and a hound was able to pull it down and carry it off. When the cook discovered his loss, for which he had only himself to blame, he began to cry miserably. There seemed to be nothing he could do, and he was very much frightened about what would happen when his master called for his supper. He called his little son to him, kissed him a tender goodbye, picked up a rope and went off to hang himself. His devoted wife heard the dreadful news just in time. She wrenched the rope from his hands and asked him: 'My husband, has this trouble deprived you of your wits? Can't you see the door that Providence has kept open for your escape? If you still have any sense left after your awful discovery, use it and listen to me! Take this ass that was brought in to some lonely spot and cut its throat, carve off a haunch like the stag's, cook it carefully in a savoury sauce and serve it up to the master in place of the venison.'

The rogue of a cook, overjoyed at the prospect of saving his life at the price of mine, called his wife the cleverest woman in the world and began sharpening his kitchen knives for the butchery.

Time pressed. I could not afford to stay where I was and concoct a plan for saving myself. I decided to escape from the knife which I felt so close to my throat, by running away at once. I broke my halter and galloped off as fast as my legs would carry me, kicking out my heels as I went. I shot across the first portico and, without hesitating for a moment, dashed into the dining-room where the master of the house was banqueting with the priests on sacrificial meats. I knocked down a great part of the dinner-service and some of the tables, too, reducing them to chaos. He was greatly annoyed by this outrageous damage. 'Take away this frisky, savage brute,' he told one of his slaves. 'Shut him up in a safe place where he won't disturb the peace of my guests.' Rescued from the executioner by my own cleverness, I was glad indeed to be locked up securely in my cell.

But no one can prosper, however wise he may be, if Fortune should rule otherwise: no wise counsel or sage remedy can ever cancel or modify the fate predestined for him by Providence. My stratagem, which seemed to have saved me from immediate death, had landed me in another danger which nearly ruined me.

One of the house-slaves rushed terror-stricken into the supper-room, with the news that a mad dog had just entered the house through a back door which opened on a lane. First he had made a furious attack on the hounds, then broken into the stables to vent his rage on the animals, and lastly gone for the slaves as well. He had bitten Myrtilus the muleteer, Hephaestion the cook, Hypatarius the valet, Apollonius the house-physician and several other members of the staff who had tried to chase him away. Some of the animals on which he had inflicted his poisonous bites were already showing clear signs of rabies.

The news struck everyone present with dismay, and guessing from my wild behaviour that I had also become infected, they caught up whatever weapons lay at hand and began appealing to one another to avert their wholesale destruction. Really, it was they who were mad, not I. They would certainly have butchered me with the lances, spears and even axes which the slaves eagerly pushed into their hands, if I had not got wind of the sudden danger and fled before the storm. I rushed into the bedroom assigned to my masters. They shut and bolted the door after me and kept a guard all night outside, hoping that when morning came, instead of having to fight me, they would find me consumed by my pestilential madness, and dead. Well, there I was, free at last and all alone. I took full advantage of this blessed gift of Fortune: I lay down on the bed and enjoyed what I had missed for so long, a good sleep in human style.

It was broad daylight when I awoke. I jumped up, refreshed by the luxury of my bedroom, and heard those who had kept watch throughout the night discussing me outside. One of them was saying: 'The poor ass can't still be mad, surely? As the virus got worse it must have killed him.'

But being of various opinions they decided to peer at me through a crack in the door, and there they saw me standing at my ease, apparently quiet and well. They ventured to open the door and risk seeing whether I had become gentle or not. One of them, appointed by Heaven to be my saviour, suggested a simple way of discovering whether I were mad or not: to put a basin full of fresh water before me. If I drank it without hesitation, as usual, this would be a sure proof that I was in perfect health; but if I backed away in obvious terror, that would mean that I was still in the grip of rabies. The standard medical text-books, he said, all prescribed this test, and it was confirmed in practice.

They all agreed and at once fetched me a large basinful of fine clear water from the nearest fountain and placed it before me, not without hesitation. Feeling very thirsty, I went straight up to it, plunged my whole head in and drank every drop of water; which did me good in more ways than one. Then I stood still and allowed them to pat me, stroke my ears, lead me about by the halter and do anything else they pleased, to convince them that it was all a mistake: that I was a gentle beast and perfectly right in the head.

Next day, with these two great dangers behind me, I was loaded again with the goddess's trappings and we marched off to the sound of cymbals and castanets on our usual begging rounds. We passed through a few hamlets and military posts and came to a village said by the inhabitants to have been built on the ruins of a famous ancient city. We put up at the first inn we came to, where we heard a good story about one of the villagers, a poor man grossly deceived by his wife, and I should like you to hear it too.

This man depended for his livelihood on his small earnings as a blacksmith, and his wife had no property either but was famous for her sexual appetite. One morning early, as soon as he had gone off to work, an impudent lover of his wife's slipped into the house and was soon making love to her. The unsuspecting smith happened to return while they were still engaged in their erotic wrestling. Finding the door locked and barred, he praised his wife's chaste precautions! Then he whistled under the window, in his usual way, to announce his return. She was a resourceful woman and, disengaging her lover from a tight embrace, hid him in a big tub that stood in a corner of the room. It was dirty and rotten, but quite empty. Then she opened the door and began scolding: 'You lazy fellow, strolling back as usual with your hands wrapped in your cloak and nothing in your pockets! When are you going to start working for your living and bring us home something to eat? What about me, eh? Here I sit day and night at my spinning-wheel, working my fingers to the bone and earning only just enough to keep oil in the lamp in this hovel of ours. Oh, how much happier is our neighbour! Reeling with the food and drink she has been taking all day long, she can have as many lovers as she pleases.'

'Hey, what's all this?' cried the smith, his feelings injured. 'Though my boss has public business to do and has given us a holiday, don't imagine that I hadn't thought about our dinner: you see that useless old tub cluttering up our little place? I have just sold it to a man for five *denarii*. He'll be here soon to put down the money and carry it away. So lend me a hand, will you? I want to scrape it out and move it outside for him.'

The deceitful woman laughed rudely: 'What a husband I have, to be sure! And what a good nose he has for a bargain! He goes out and sells our tub for five *denarii*. I'm only a woman, but I have already sold it for seven without even setting foot outside the house.'

He was delighted by this larger offer. 'Who on earth gave you such a good price?'

'Hush, you idiot,' she said. 'He's still down inside the thing, having a good look to see whether it's sound.'

The lover took his cue from her at once. He bobbed up and said: 'I'll tell you what, ma'am, your tub is very old and seems to be cracked in scores of places.' Then he turned to the smith: 'I don't know who you are, little man, but I should be much obliged for a candle. I must scrape the inside and see whether it's the sort of article I need; unless you think money grows on apple-trees?'

So the excellent, brilliant smith lighted a candle without delay and said: 'No, no, brother, don't put yourself to so much trouble. You stand by while I give the tub a good clean-up for you.'

He peeled off his tunic, took the candle and began scraping away the old filth inside the rotten tub.

But the attractive young lover lifted up the smith's wife, laid her on the tub bottom upwards above her husband's head and drove into her in carefree fashion. Such was the trick she played on her husband, like the whore she was. With her head hanging back over the side of the tub she directed the work by pointing her finger at various spots in turn, showing that now this and now that had to be cleaned until both jobs were finished to her satisfaction. The smith was paid his seven *denarii*, but had to carry the tub on his own back to the lover's lodgings.

★

The pious priests stayed a few days at this place, where the public were very generous to them: in particular they made a good deal of money by professing to tell fortunes. Between them these pure priests composed an all-purpose oracle for the goddess to deliver by their mouths and used it to cheat a great many people who came to consult her on all sorts of questions.

It ran:

> Yoke the oxen, plough the land;
> High the golden grain will stand.

Suppose that a man came to ask the goddess whether he ought to marry. The answer was plain: he ought to take on the yoke of matrimony and raise a fine crop of children. Or suppose that he wanted to know whether he ought to buy land: the yoked oxen and the good harvests were quite to the point. Or suppose one sought divine advice about going on a journey: the oxen, the least restless of all beasts, were to be yoked and the golden grain spelt a prosperous return. Or suppose someone wanted to know whether or not he would fight a victorious battle, or successfully pursue a gang of bandits: the priests explained the oracle as meaning that he should put the necks of his enemies under the yoke and make a rich profit when the time came for the loot to be divided among the victors.

They certainly made a rich profit by this astute and dishonest way of foretelling the future. But one day they grew tired of answering these perpetual inquiries, and we went on again at nightfall and travelled all night. It was a worse journey by far than the one we had made before, because the road was full of deep holes and ruts, and covered in places with thick, very slippery mud. I had at last reached a firm stretch of country lane, exhausted and with my legs bruised by frequent falls, when a body of armed horsemen suddenly charged down on us. Reining in with difficulty, they rushed at Philebus and his companions, seized them by the throat and pummelled them with their fists, shouting that they were sacrilegious filth. Then they bound their hands and kept on demanding: 'Where's the golden cup that you dared to steal from the sacred couch of the Mother of the Gods with the excuse of conducting a solemn service there behind closed doors? You hoped to escape punishment for your sin, did you, by sneaking out of town before daylight?'

Presently one of the horsemen came up to me and, putting his hand into the lap of the goddess whom I was carrying, produced the lost cup and held it up for everyone to see. But even this glaring proof of theft caused these nasty creatures no embarrassment. They turned the whole affair into a joke by telling a lie. 'How unfair!' they cried. 'Isn't that just the sort of accident that would happen to honest men like ourselves? For the sake of one miserable little chalice, which the Mother of the Gods gave her sister the Syrian Goddess, we ministers of religion find ourselves threatened with death!'

However, for all their lies and frivolous excuses, they were marched back and immediately put into the town gaol. The cup and the sacred image I had carried were solemnly laid in the temple treasury, and next day I was led out and put up for auction again.

CHAPTER XIII

>>>>><<<<<

AT THE MILL-HOUSE

A BAKER from the next town bought me for seven *drachmae* more than Philebus had paid and, loading me up with a great deal of corn that he had just bought, took me by a rough road, all loose stones and tree roots, to his bakery.

A good many other beasts were kept there to turn his millstones all day and all night too, for they never stood still. He treated me with the consideration due to a new arrival by giving me a well-filled manger and a holiday; I suppose he did not want me to be discouraged by realizing at once the servitude that lay ahead. The joy of having nothing to do and plenty to eat did not last beyond the first day. The next morning I was harnessed to what seemed to me the largest mill of all, my eyes were blindfolded and I was put into a little circular track, along which I was supposed to go round and round without stopping. Not having yet taken leave of my wits I did not accept this discipline without protest, and though when I was a man I had often seen machines of this sort at work, I pretended complete ignorance of my duties and stood stock-still, as if dazed. I imagined that when they saw I was unfit for the mill they would put me to some other less exacting work, or even send me out to pasture. But my cleverness overreached itself. I was still blindfolded and not expecting any trouble, when several men with sticks came up, and at a given signal all shouted together and began whacking me. The sudden attack of noise startled me. Instead of stopping to think what I must do next, I heaved hard on my rush rope and started briskly along the track. All the men burst out laughing at my sudden change of behaviour.

When the day was nearly over and I was tired out, they un-harnessed me and let me retire to my manger. Although I was nearly fainting with hunger and weariness, and in great need of refreshment, fear and my old curiosity made me neglect the food they gave me – there was no lack of it – to observe the life at that detestable mill with a certain fascination. Ye gods, what miserable human beings were there! Their skins were seamed all over with the marks of old floggings, as you could easily see through the holes in their ragged shirts that shaded rather than covered their scarred backs; but some wore only loin-cloths. They had letters branded on their foreheads, and half-shaved heads and irons on their legs. Their complexions were frightfully yellow, their eyelids caked with the smoke of the baking ovens, their eyes so bleary and inflamed that they could hardly see out of them, and they were powdered like athletes in the arena, but with dirty flour, not sand.

As for my fellow-animals, what a string of worn-out old mules and feeble donkeys! How they drooped their heads over the piles of straw in their manger! Their necks were covered with running sores, they coughed ceaselessly and wheezed through their nostrils. Their chests were raw from the galling of the thongs, their ribs showed through their broken hides from the continual beating, and their hooves had broadened out hugely from the everlasting march round and round the mill. Age and the mange had coarsened their whole skins.

The dreadful condition of these poor beasts, whom I might soon be brought to resemble, so depressed me that I drooped my head like them and grieved for the degradation into which I had fallen since those far-off days when I was Lucius. My only consolation was the unique opportunity I had of observing all that was said and done around me; because nobody showed any reserve in my presence. Homer characterized the man whom he offered as an example of the highest wisdom and prudence as one who had 'visited many cities and come to know many different peoples'.[1] I am grateful now whenever I recall those days: my many adventures in ass-disguise enormously enlarged my experience, even if not my wisdom. It was at this mill that I picked up a particularly good story, which I hope will amuse you. Here it is.

The baker who had bought me was a decent and sober man. But his wife was the wickedest woman in all the world, and caused his bed and his home such grievous afflictions that I used often to groan in secret pity for him. There was no single vice which she did not possess: her heart was a regular cesspool into which every sort of filthy sewer emptied. She was malicious, cruel, spiteful, lecherous, drunken, selfish, obstinate, as mean in her petty thefts as she was wasteful in her filthy extravagances and an enemy of all that was honest and clean. She also professed perfect scorn for the Immortals and rejected all true religion in favour of a fantastic and blasphemous cult of an 'Only God'.[2] In his honour she practised various absurd ceremonies which gave her the excuse of getting drunk quite early in the day and playing the whore at all hours; most people, including her husband, were quite deceived by her.

Such was this woman, who persecuted me with amazing rancour. She used to call out from her bed before dawn, before she was up, ordering that I should be harnessed to the mill to grind. As soon as she had left her bedroom she made them give me an almighty beating under her personal supervision, and at breakfast time, when we were unharnessed, kept me from the manger until long after my companions had been fed and rested.

Her cruelty sharpened my natural curiosity about her goings-on. I knew that a young man was always visiting her bedroom, and I longed to catch a glimpse of his features; unfortunately, the blinkers that I wore for my work at the mill prevented this. But for them, I felt sure that I should have been able to catch the disgusting woman at her tricks. A depraved old hag acted as her confidante and go-between, and the two were inseparable. As soon as breakfast was over they would compete in their consumption of undiluted wine and, after this initial skirmish, they would plot and intrigue how to cheat and destroy the poor baker. Though I had never forgiven Fotis for her frightful blunder of transforming me into an ass instead of a bird, I had one compensation at least: that my long ears could pick up conversations at a great distance.

One day I heard the old woman warning her: 'It's your business, mistress, that you have chosen that lover of yours without consulting me. His feeble love-making falls so far short of your own sexuality that you suffer tortures. He's a born coward and your horrible distasteful husband's scowl frightens him out of his senses. Only compare him with young Philesitherus! Handsome, generous, strong and always to be relied on to trick the most suspicious husband. He deserves to enjoy the favours of every lady in the land; yes, if any man in all Greece is worthy to wear a gold crown it's Philesitherus – if only for the trick he played the other day on a jealous husband.

Listen to what happened and note the contrast between the two lovers.

'You know Barbarus, don't you? I mean the decurion,[3] nick-named "Scorpion" because of his nasty nature. Well, he married a beautiful girl of good family and now keeps her locked up in his house with every imaginable precaution.'

'Why, of course: I know Arete very well. We were at school together.'

'Then you know the entire tale of Philesitherus as well?'

'I haven't heard a word of it; so please, mother, tell me the whole story.' So at once the old woman, who was a great talker, began:

'Barbarus had to go on a journey, and he wanted to do everything possible to keep Arete faithful to him in his absence. So he sent for a slave of his called Myrmex, the most trustworthy member of his household, and secretly ordered him to keep an eye on her. "If anything goes wrong, Myrmex,' he said,' "if any man as much as touches her with the tip of his finger as he passes her in the street, I'll chain you up forever in a dungeon, and put you to a violent and horrible death."

'He confirmed this threat with such solemn oaths that Myrmex was terribly frightened and made up his mind to watch Arete with the utmost vigilance. Then Barbarus set out on his journey with his mind at rest, leaving Myrmex to keep a very close eye on his wife. Myrmex, on the other hand, was so nervous and so meticulous about obeying orders that he wouldn't let Arete out of the house. She sat all day spinning wool, and when she had to go out in the evening to the baths he went with her, clinging tight to a corner of her dress. But her beauty couldn't escape the amorous eyes of Philesitherus, who noted her impregnable virtue and the extra-ordinary precautions taken to guard it, and felt so excited that he was prepared to run any risk to win her. He summoned up all his resources to storm the determined defences of the house.

'He knew the frailty of human nature: he knew that gold can break down gates of steel. So catching Myrmex conveniently alone he confessed his love for Arete and implored him to find some way of easing his torment. "If I don't get what I want very soon," he swore, "I shall die. Besides, you have nothing to fear. All I have to do is to steal into the house by night, alone, and come out again almost at once."

'He reinforced his gentle pleas with a wedge that he reckoned would soon split this tough log wide open: he showed Myrmex a number of shining gold coins. "Of these thirty," he said, "twenty are for your mistress, ten for yourself."

'The unheard-of crime that was proposed so staggered Myrmex that he at once rushed away in terror. But he couldn't rid his mind of the glitter of the gold and, though he'd left it all behind and rushed home, he still seemed to have the beautiful coins sparkling before his eyes. The poor man was torn and convulsed by contradictory feelings: on one side loyalty, on the other profit; on one side torture, on the other delight. In the end desire for the gold prevailed over terror of death. His desire for the lovely money was not abated by geographical distance, but instead pestilential greed gnawed at him all night and, although his master's threats prompted him to remain at home, the gold beckoned him out of doors. So gulping down his shame, and putting an end to all hesitation, he delivered the message to his mistress.

'Being a woman wholly without principle, she sold her virtue for the filthy lucre without the least hesitation. Myrmex was so eager not merely to acquire but actually to handle the catastrophic money that he went joyfully to announce to Philesitherus that, owing to the mighty efforts of Myrmex, he was going to get what he wanted and immediately demanded the promised reward. And so Myrmex got ten gold pieces, when he had never even possessed copper money before.

'That night he brought Philesitherus muffled and disguised into Arete's bedroom, but about midnight, while the naked recruits in the service of Venus were just engaged in their preliminary combats, a loud knock sounded on the door: Barbarus had unexpectedly returned. When nobody came to let him in, he began shouting and pounding the door with a stone. The long delay made him more and more suspicious, and he threatened at the top of his voice to inflict horrible punishments on Myrmex. The suddenness of the disaster put Myrmex into a state of mortal terror, but he quavered back that he had hidden the key so carefully that he couldn't find it again in the dark.

The commotion gave Philesitherus the alarm: he dressed in a hurry and ran out of the room, forgetting his shoes in his confusion. Myrmex then put the key in the lock and admitted the bawling, swearing Barbarus, who hurried to Arete's bedroom while Philesitherus slipped out unnoticed, and Myrmex, when he had seen him safely out, locked the door behind him.

'Myrmex went back to bed in great relief. But Barbarus when he got up next morning found a strange pair of shoes under his bed and put two and two together. However, he didn't reveal his suspicions to Arete, or to any of the servants; he quietly picked up the shoes, slipped them into a fold of his clothing and ordered Myrmex's hands to be chained behind him. Then he strode towards the Forum, groaning with rage, his eyebrows drawn down in the grimmest sort of scowl and his face distorted with fury. He had sworn to himself to trace the adulterer by means of the shoes. Myrmex followed, heavily bound, and though he hadn't been caught red-handed in any crime his conscience tortured him. He wept and howled, trying to excite pity, though it did him no good.

'But now Philesitherus happened to come along and, though he had a pressing engagement elsewhere, the sight of the angry master and the terrified slave dismayed him, though he did not panic. It was a reminder of the slip he had made in his hurry. He guessed what had happened, but instead of losing his head he reacted with his usual presence of mind. Pushing the escort aside he rushed at Myrmex, shouting at the top of his voice and knocking his face about wildly with his fists – "You lying blackguard," he yelled, "I hope your master, and all the gods whose names you took in vain, will punish you as you deserve. I know you all right; it's you who walked off with my shoes at the baths. By God, you deserve to have those manacles left on your wrists until they wear out, in the darkest of dungeons." Barbarus was completely taken in. He turned around and went straight home, forgave Myrmex, handed him the slippers and ordered him to take them back to their rightful owner, from whom he had stolen them.'

The story was hardly done before the baker's wife broke in: 'Yes, indeed, Arete was a lucky woman to get a lover like that. Unfortunately, mine is such a coward that he trembles at every creak of the mill; even the blinkered face of that mangy ass over there scares him.'

'Never mind, I undertake to bring this smart, brisk, keen lover of yours along to you,' and with those words she left the bedroom, promising to return in the evening.

So she went off, and the baker's chaste wife prepared a supper grand enough for a priest's banquet, decanting expensive wine, cooking up a delicious meal of fresh meat and gravy and waiting for her lover's arrival as if for the advent of some god; luckily her husband had been invited to supper at the laundryman's, next door. When evening came I was unharnessed from the mill and allowed to go to my manger; it was splendid to be released from drudgery. Now that my blinkers were removed from my eyes, I could watch all that the wicked woman was doing.

Darkness gathered; the sun sank behind the Ocean[4] to give its light to the other side of the earth and presently the evil old woman brought the lover in by her side. He was only a boy, with no hair on his cheeks, but healthy-looking and very handsome. The baker's wife kissed him passionately again and again and sat him down to table. But he had just starting eating and drinking when the baker was heard returning hours before he was expected. 'Curse the man!' cried the devoted wife. 'I hope he breaks a leg.'

Her lover went pale with fright, but the bin into which she used to bolt the flour was not far off, and she shoved him under it. As the baker came in she concealed her wickedness with practised skill and asked her husband why he had come back so soon, leaving his dear friend's dinner so early.

'I could bear it no longer,' he broke in with a deep sigh. 'That dreadful wife of his! Heavens, I could never have believed it. She seemed so respectable, so well-behaved. I had to run away; I swear to you, by the image of Ceres over there, I could hardly believe the evidence of my own eyes.'

What he had said made his outrageous wife eager to know what had happened, and she went on importuning him until he described the disgraceful goings-on at his neighbour's house; quite unaware that there was anything wrong at his own.

'Well,' he said, 'you know that the laundryman is one of my oldest friends, and his wife has always seemed a very respectable woman, looked up to by the neighbourhood, and has managed her husband's affairs decently enough. But she fell in love with a man, and they began to have secret meetings, and tonight when the laundryman and I came back to supper from the baths, they had been making love. Startled and confused by our sudden arrival, she hid her lover in a high wicker cage, with cloths hung over it to bleach in the fumes of the sulphur fire inside. It seemed a safe enough place, so she came and sat down to supper with us without worrying. But the lover was forced to breathe in the suffocating sulphur fumes that enveloped him, the acrid and penetrating smell making him sneeze and sneeze. The laundryman, who was on his couch at the other side of the table from his wife, heard the first sneeze from immediately behind her. "Bless you, my dear!" he said, and, "bless you, bless you!" at the second and third sneeze. But the noise went on and on, and at last he began to take notice and suspect that something was wrong. He pushed the table aside, got up, turned the cage over, and there he found the youth panting for breath, nearly at his last gasp.

'He went mad with rage and shouted for a slave to fetch him his sword. He was on the point of cutting the poor wretch's throat, when I managed to restrain him, though with great difficulty. I pointed out that if left to himself, his rival would soon die from sulphur poisoning, without any harm coming to ourselves. My appeals failed to appease his rage. However, as he saw he must, he dragged the man out into the lane half-alive. Then I privately persuaded his wife to leave home at once and take refuge with friends until he had time to cool down slightly. He was so upset and furious that he'd probably kill her and himself, too. Well, I had had enough of my friend's supper so I got away, and here I am at home.'

The story was punctuated by exclamations of horror and curses from the baker's own impudent and wanton wife. She called her neighbour a shameless whore, a disgrace to her whole sex, a woman without a rag of decency left or any sense of what she owed her husband. 'Imagine her turning his house into a brothel!' she cried. 'A respectable married woman, too, behaving like a tart. Such women deserve to be burned alive.' Still, consciousness of her secret, sordid misbehaviour left her not altogether at her ease. She wanted to free her lover from his unhappy confinement as soon as she could and tried to make the baker go to bed early.

'No, wife,' said the baker. 'I missed my supper at the laundryman's and I'm hungry. Let's eat.'

She quickly but reluctantly served him up the supper that she had intended for quite another person. But I felt completely upset inside: first that criminal behaviour and now this horrible woman's persistence in her evil ways. I was anxious to find some way of helping my master by exposing her wickedness: for example by kicking the bin over and revealing her lover squatting underneath it like a tortoise.

'How scandalously she treats the poor man,' I thought. At this moment Providence came to my aid. It was our watering time and the lame old man who was in charge of all us animals came to drive us to the nearby pond. This gave me the chance I needed for paying her back. I noticed as I passed the bin that the boy's fingers were sticking out from underneath. I planted the edge of my hoof on them and squashed them flat. The pain was excruciating. He could not help crying aloud and pushing the bin over. And so the shameful woman was unmasked.

The baker did not seem particularly shocked by his discovery. He began mildly and quietly to reassure the boy, who was pale and trembling with fear, begging him not to be afraid. 'Don't take me for a barbarian or a savage,' he said. 'I don't intend to suffocate you with sulphur, in ferocious laundryman's style, and I won't invoke the severity of the Adultery Law against you, with its death penalty. You're much too pretty and attractive a boy for that. No, I'll go shares with my wife. I won't sue for a division of our property but we'll enjoy it in common. Without the slightest argument or dispute we'll all three share a single bed. My wife and I have never quarrelled about anything: we have been sensible enough to live together on such good terms that, as the wise men say, what pleases one of us has always pleased the other. But it's only justice that the wife should not have more authority than her husband.'

He went on joking quietly as he made the unwilling boy come along to the bedroom with him. Not to outrage his wife's modesty he locked her in another room, then climbed into bed with the boy and enjoyed a wonderful revenge for the wrong she had done him. The next morning at the first sign of dawn he called the two toughest of his slaves, who hoisted the boy up for him to thrash on the backside with a stick. 'Such a nice, sweet little boy, too!' he said. 'You ought to be ashamed of turning down lovers of your own age and going after free women and breaking up respectable matrimonial homes. You're getting yourself the name of an adulterer, at a very premature age.'

After this rebuke, and others like it, he gave him a further abundant whipping and chased him out of the house. So this most enterprising adulterer got away with his life, which was better luck than he had hoped for, but with sobs and cries for his white backside, which had suffered so much violation both by night and by day.

The baker divorced his wife by proxy soon afterwards. Naturally a very wicked woman, she was exasperated by this public affront, justified though it was, and turned back to her old tricks, indulging in the sort of practice that women like to engage in. She visited a witch, who had the reputation of being able to do whatever she liked with the help of charms and drugs, showered her with valuable presents and implored her either to make her husband relent towards her or, if that was impossible, to send some spectre of frightful power to drive the soul out of his body.

The witch, with her supernatural power, began with fairly mild experiments in her wicked art, trying to influence the heart of the aggrieved baker and return it to its usual affectionate feelings for his wife. But when she found herself unable to make any impression on it, she flew into a temper with the gods. She said that by treating her spells with contempt they were cheating her of the reward that had been promised her if she succeeded; so she threatened to kill the poor baker by setting on him the ghost of a woman who had died by violence.

(I hear some smart reader objecting: 'Look here, Lucius, you were an ass, tied up in the mill-house. How were you clever enough to find out the secrets of these women?' Read on, and you will soon see how I found out all about my master's death. I was an ass, I agree; but I still kept my human intelligence.)

About noon a hideous-looking woman suddenly entered the mill-house. She was dressed in dirty rags and displayed great grief; I took her for someone accused of a crime. She had a patched mourning mantle loosely thrown about her; her feet were naked; her thin face was the colour of boxwood under its coat of filth, and her grey hair, patched with white and daubed with dirty ashes, tumbled down over it. She took the baker gently by the hand and, pretending that she had something private to tell him, led him aside into the bedroom. She shut the door and they remained together for a long time.

When all the grain that he had given the men to grind had gone through the mill, and more was needed, they knocked at the bedroom door and called out to their master to give it to them. But when their loud and frequent cries elicited no answer, they knocked more loudly than before. The door had been carefully bolted inside, so suspecting that something serious had happened they decided to break it open. At last, with a concerted heave, they burst the hinges and broke into the room.

The woman was nowhere to be seen, but their master was dangling from a rafter with a rope around his neck. He was quite dead when they cut him down.

They raised the customary howl of mourning and all sobbed for grief; and when they had washed the body the funeral took place the same evening, a very large crowd gathering at the grave-side. The next morning the baker's daughter, who had recently married a man from a neighbouring village, came running to the mill-house with her hair disordered, weeping and beating her breast; no message about her stepmother's divorce and her father's suicide had yet reached her. But her father's pitiful ghost had appeared to her in the night, with the noose around his neck, telling her exactly all that had happened: the stepmother's wickedness and adultery and witchcraft, and how her enchantment had sent him down to the Underworld. After she had tormented herself for a long time the servants managed to quiet her, and eight days later, when the required sacrifices at the tomb had been completed, she auctioned all the slaves and furniture and animals – she was the sole heiress – and so, by the wanton luck of an unpredictable sale, that home disintegrated in all directions.

>>>>><<<<<

CHAPTER XIV

WITH THE GARDENER
AND THE SOLDIER

AMONG the bidders was a poor gardener to whom I was knocked down for the sum of fifty *drachmae*. That seemed to him a great deal of money, but he hoped to get it back by working hard and making me do the same. I must describe the life I led while in his service. He used to drive me to the nearest market every day with a load of green-stuff and after selling it to the dealers there would climb on my back and return to his garden. Then he dug his trenches or watered his plants or stooped over one job or another, while I rested contentedly. But then the circling year brought us from the vintage season of autumn, always a pleasant time, into the wintry sign of Capricorn with its frosts, torrential rains and nightly dews. My stable had no roof and was open to the skies, and I nearly died of cold, because my master could not afford to provide me, or himself even, with straw or the smallest covering. His only protection against the weather was the thatch of the small shed which served him for a home. Going to market I had no shoes to protect my hooves from the hard edges of the frozen ruts or projecting pieces of broken ice, and never had the breakfasts I was accustomed to. My master and I shared our meals, and very frugal they were: mainly nasty old lettuces that had run to seed and looked more like brooms, rotten, stinking and full of a bitter juice.

One moonless night a householder from the next village lost his way in the dark, got drenched to the skin and turned his exhausted horse into our garden. My master received him hospitably and made him as comfortable as possible, considering the badness of the weather and the poverty in which we lived; at least he managed to get some much needed sleep and showed his gratitude to his kind host by inviting my master to visit him, and promising him a present of grain, oil and a couple of wine-kegs. He jumped at the offer and, taking with him a sack and some empty leather bottles, rode me along to the farm, which was sixty stades[1] away.

The householder had gone ahead and on our arrival generously invited my master to join him in a good square meal. They were busily drinking and chatting together when a very startling thing happened. A hen ran cackling around the farmyard as though she badly wanted to lay an egg. The farmer saw her and said: 'You're a productive girl, who's fed us every day for quite a time, and now I see you're thinking of contributing something to our dinner ... Hey, boy!' he called to one of his slaves. 'Put the basket in the corner where she always lays.'

The boy fetched the basket but the hen refused to go into it. Instead, she ran up to her master and laid something at his feet. It was premature, and it was not an egg, but an ominous portent: a fully fledged chicken, with claws, eyes and complete, which immediately ran cheeping after its mother.

This was followed by another much more serious prodigy, which would rightly terrify anybody: the stone floor under the table seemed suddenly to split open and a gaping chasm appeared, filled with a fountain of blood, drops of which flew up and bespattered the table. While everyone sat staring in horror and dismay at this monstrous apparition, wondering what divine portent it indicated, a slave ran in from the cellar, to report that the wine, which had been racked-off some time before, was boiling in all the jars, as though a big fire had been lighted underneath. Next, a pack of weasels were seen outside the house, dragging a dead snake in their teeth. Finally, a small green frog jumped out of the sheep-dog's mouth, and an old ram that was standing close by leaped at the dog and severed its windpipe with a single bite. This sequence of wonders so dumbfounded the farmer and his household that they had no notion how they stood or what they ought to do, what they should do first and what afterwards, what more they could do and what less. Clearly, the anger of the gods must be averted with sacrifices, but with what sort of sacrifices and how many? They were all petrified by fear of some frightful thing that was going to happen.

At last another slave ran in with news of a great and terrible mishap that had befallen our host, the owner of several farms. He was the father of three sons, now grown up, well educated and highly respectable. They had long been friendly with a poor neighbour whose cottage stood near by, next to the estate of another young man who made very bad use of the power that his wealth and family connections gave him. He employed an army of retainers, kept the whole district under his thumb and had lately been treating his poor neighbour very high-handedly: slaughtering his sheep, driving off his oxen and trampling down his corn. Moreover, not content with thus devastating all the products of his neighbour's thrift, he was now trying to dispossess him of his land as well, by a fictitious claim that it fell wholly within the boundaries of his own estate.

The other man, a mild and inoffensive farmer, saw that he was being completely robbed by his rich, greedy neighbour and asked a number of his friends to help him determine what exactly were the limits of his family property; he told them that he hoped to keep enough of it at least to dig himself a grave. Among these friends were the three brothers, who saw that he was in great distress and determined to give him whatever help they could. But his demented neighbour, far from being persuaded or frightened by the arrival of so many of his fellow-citizens, refused to relinquish his thieving claims. At first he managed to keep a civil tongue in his head, but then, as they courteously expostulated with him and tried to soothe his vehement character with flattering words, he suddenly began to swear in the most solemn terms, by the lives of himself and all who were dear to him, that he cared not the slightest for the whole pack of mediators.

'Hey, slaves,' he shouted, 'take the fellow by the ears, haul him out of his cottage and deposit him somewhere far away, here and now.'

Everyone was scandalized, and one of the brothers spoke out at once, telling him that, rich though he was, his threats carried no weight. He was wasting his words: the law was so humane that even the poorest man could always get redress for the oppressions of the rich.

This retort was like oil to a lighted wick, or sulphur to a bonfire, or a Fury's whip to a guilty man: it roused him to a perfect frenzy of rage. 'They should all be hanged,' he yelled, 'and their laws too!' and ordered his men to let loose all the dogs on the estate, watch-dogs, sheep-dogs and all – bloodthirsty beasts, trained to worry the carcases of animals that had fallen dead in the fields and to fasten their teeth in the legs of passers-by and hold on tight.

And so, as soon as they heard the shepherds' signal, the maddened dogs rushed, barking horribly, at the poor man's supporters and began mauling them. They tried to escape but the dogs pursued them, and the faster they ran, the more furiously they were attacked. Amid this butchery of the terrified crowd, the youngest of the three brothers happened to stumble as he ran and stub his toes against a stone. Down he fell, and the dogs leaped on him and savaged him, ripping great pieces of flesh off his bones and making a horrible meal of them. The others heard his screams and turned back to his rescue, muffling their left arms with their cloaks and picking up stones to defend their brother and drive off the dogs. But nothing could be done. They could not curb the dogs' ferocity or frighten them or drive them away, so he was torn to pieces before their very eyes. His dying words called on them to take vengeance on the abominable rich man for the death of their younger brother.

With a complete disregard of the consequences they rushed at the rich man and pelted him with stones. But the bloodthirsty creature, who was not new to this kind of criminal activity, hurled a javelin at one of them and drove it through his body; yet, though it wounded him mortally, he did not fall. The point lodged in the earth on the other side and the greater part of the shaft followed it, leaving him writhing transfixed, with his body off the ground. Then a big, tall fellow, one of the murderer's retainers, let fly with a stone at the remaining brother from some way off, trying to put his right arm out of action. It grazed his fingers and glanced off, but everyone thought it had injured him seriously, which gave the quick-witted youth the chance of avenging his brothers. Pretending that his hand was disabled, he shouted at the villain: 'Very well, then, enjoy your destruction of our whole family, glut your vindictive heart with the blood of my two brothers and me! Enjoy your glorious triumph over your prostrate fellow-citizens. But remember this: that when you have thrown my poor friend out of his cottage, however far you push the boundaries of your estate, you'll always have neighbours of one sort or another. Meanwhile, by ill-luck a cursèd stone has left my hand hanging numb and powerless; otherwise I should certainly have used it to cut off your head.'

Exasperated by these words, the demented criminal drew his sword and rushed forward, intending to finish him off with a single blow. But he had picked a quarrel with a man as strong as himself.

His hand was caught in a powerful grip, the weapon seized from him, and he was struck with it again and again until the wicked spirit of that rich man was parted from his body.

The retainers came rushing to the rescue, but the victor was too quick for them. The sword, still dripping with his enemy's blood, served to cut his own throat.

★

This was the news that the portentous prodigies had foreshadowed for the unfortunate master of the house. Overwhelmed by all these misfortunes, the old man could not utter so much as a single word, nor even shed a silent tear. He picked up the knife with which he had just been cutting cheese and other parts of the dinner for his guests and, like his unhappy son, used it on his own throat. Then he fell face forward on the table and the stream of blood from his severed arteries washed away the prophetic stains that had fallen on it from the fountain under the floor.

My master, the gardener, condoled with everyone present on the sudden violent extinction of his host's family. He lamented the fate of the house, which had fallen into ruins in such a brief passage of time, and was deeply disappointed not to have got what he had hoped for. Tears had to take the place of dinner, and he repeatedly wrung his empty hands. Then he mounted on my back and rode home again by the same road we had taken.

It was an unlucky journey. We were stopped by a tall Roman soldier, a legionary (as his appearance and uniform made clear), who asked my master in haughty tones: 'Where are you riding that ass?' My master was still overcome with grief and, knowing no Latin, disregarded the question and rode on. His silence offended the soldier, who arrogantly struck him on the head with his vine-rod and hauled him off my back. The gardener meekly replied that he did not know the language and could not understand what he was saying. Whereupon the soldier demanded again, but this time in Greek: 'Where are you riding that ass?'

'To the nearest village.'

'Well, I need him. Our commanding officer's baggage has to be carried from the fort and the ass must join the other animals who're doing the job.' He caught hold of my halter and began leading me back along the road.

Wiping away the blood that trickled down his face from the cut made by the vine-rod, my master begged the soldier to treat him in a more courteous and considerate way. 'And if you do so,' he said, 'I'm sure that it will bring you good luck. Anyhow, this is a very lazy ass, and he has a nasty illness. It's as much as he can do to carry a few handfuls of green-stuff to market from my little garden: he's all blown at the finish. Load him up with a real burden and he won't be able to cope with it.'

But the soldier would not listen to a word of all this. When my master realized that he was resolved to steal me and that he had shifted his grip on the vine-rod and was about to bash in his head with the knobbed end, he took desperate action.

Pretending to clasp the soldier's knees in suppliant style he tackled him low, pulled both legs from under him, and brought him down with a crash on the back of his head. Then he jumped on him, hit him, pounded him all over – face, arms and ribs – first with his fists and elbows and then with a stone he grabbed from the road. Once he was down, the soldier could offer no resistance; all he could do was to gasp out threats of how, as soon as he was on his legs again, he would make mincemeat of my master with his sword.

This gave my master timely warning: he snatched the sword out of the scabbard, threw it as far away as he could and gave the soldier an even harder pounding than before. He lay on his back so bruised and wounded that he was incapable of rising and his only hope of escaping with his life was to sham dead. My master then retrieved the sword, mounted me again, and galloped me straight back to the village. Not caring to go home, for the time being at least, he rode me up to the house of a close friend of his, where he made a clean breast of what he had done to the soldier and implored his protection. 'Hide me and my ass somewhere safe for a couple of days until this trouble blows over, or they'll kill me.'

The shopkeeper at once undertook to help him for the sake of their old friendship. They tied my legs together and dragged me upstairs into the attic, but my master stayed in his friend's shop on the ground floor, where he climbed into a chest and pulled down the lid.

Meanwhile, as I heard later, the soldier tottered into the village like a man trying to walk off a drunken stupor, dazed with the pain of his injuries and leaning heavily on his rod. But, upset by his violent and feeble behaviour, he said nothing to any of the villagers, silently swallowing the disgrace instead. Presently he met some of his comrades and told them about the disastrous affair. They advised him to lie low for a while in the barracks. For, in addition to the humiliation he had suffered, he was afraid of being charged with violating his military oath because of the loss of his sword. However, he gave them full details of us and urged them to do everything possible to search us out and exact vengeance.

But a treacherous neighbour turned up, who revealed to the soldiers where we were hidden. So they went to the civil magistrate and told him that they had dropped a valuable silver cup on the road, the property of their commanding officer, and that a gardener had found it, refused to give it up and was now hiding in a neighbour's house. The magistrate noted the loss, and the officer's name, then came to the door of the shop, where he announced loudly that he had good reason to believe that we were concealed there and that if the owner failed to deliver my master to justice he might find himself sentenced to death.

However, the shopkeeper was not in the least frightened; but out of consideration for his friend's safety, and the promise he had made him, he replied that he knew nothing at all about us and that he had not even seen the gardener. But the soldiers, swearing by the Emperor's divinity, insisted that he was somewhere in that house and nowhere else. The magistrate then consented to make a close search of the premises, to find out how much truth there was in the shopkeeper's obstinate denial. He sent in the lictors and other local officials with an order to search the house from top to bottom; but they came out with the report that they could find neither ass nor man, either upstairs or down. The dispute grew hot on both sides, the soldiers with equal persistence swearing by all the gods that the lictors were telling lies.

I was an inquisitive and restless ass, and when I heard all this quarrelling and noise, I craned my neck a little way out of the attic window to discover what all the fuss was about. One of the soldiers happened to be looking up at the time. His eye was caught by the shadow of my head and ears that was thrown on the wall of the next house, and he called out to tell everyone. All the soldiers shouted, immediately set up a ladder, rushed upstairs to my hiding place and hauled me down. Then they made a thorough search of the shop itself, and when they opened the chest, there was the wretched gardener. They dragged him out for the magistrate's inspection, and he was taken to gaol on a capital charge.

The notion of my peering out of the window so tickled the soldiers that they joked about it a great deal; indeed, my peering out and casting a shadow have given rise to that well-known proverb.[2]

What became of my master, the gardener, next day, I have no notion, but the soldier who had been so well beaten for his extraordinary violence led me away from the manger where I had been tied up. There was nobody to prevent him. He took me to what I suppose was his billet, where he loaded me up and made quite a military figure of me. For I found myself carrying a twinkling helmet, a shield so highly polished that it could be seen from afar and a javelin with a remarkably long shaft. This careful arrangement, which made us look like an army, was not based on any military regulations but intended to overawe unfortunate passers-by. We went across a plain by a good road and finally came to a small town where we put up, not at an inn, but at the house of a municipal councillor. The soldier left me there in the care of a slave and reported at once to his superior officer, who was in charge of a thousand men.

>>>>><<<<<

AT THE COUNCILLOR'S HOUSE

A FEW days later, I recall, the place witnessed an appalling crime, which I record in this book so that you can learn about it. The master of the house had a son who had done very well at school and was, in fact, a paragon of all the virtues; he was just the sort of son you would like to have. His mother had died a long time previously and his father had married again, so that the other son, now twelve years old, was his half-brother. The new wife, whose looks were a good deal better than her character, gained a free hand in her husband's house; and whether she was naturally vicious, or whether it was fate, she fell in love with her stepson. Readers are warned that what follows is tragedy not comedy, and that they must change from the comic sock to the tragic buskin.[1]

Well, so long as Cupid was just a small boy and was only beginning to work on her, the woman found it easy to disguise her guilty blushes and say nothing about the affair. But when he grew up and began playing his mad tricks, setting her whole soul in a cruel blaze with his arrows of fire, she had to sham ill as the only possible means of hiding her torment. Now, everyone knows that the physical symptoms of love are not readily distinguishable from those of ordinary illness: for example, an unhealthy pallor, dull eyes, weakness of the knees, insomnia and fits of sighing which increase in intensity the longer the crisis is protracted. Her complaint might, in fact, have been fairly diagnosed as a fever but for her continual bursts of weeping. Alas for the ignorance of doctors! And what about her rapid pulse, her irregular temperature, the difficulty she seemed to have in breathing, her frequent tossing and turning in bed? Good God! The clever physicians might not know it, but anyone learned in Venus' amorous arts could have diagnosed what was wrong, seeing someone on fire, and yet the heat was not physical.

Her condition got worse and worse until she could bear the pain no longer and broke her silence by sending for her elder son, though she would have liked, if she could, not to have used the word 'son', which reminded her of her shame.

Obedient to the command of his ailing mother, he went to her bedroom at once, with anxiety puckering his forehead like an old man's. Since she was his father's wife and his brother's mother, he felt that he ought to go. Yet, though the effort of keeping silence so long had nearly killed her, she went aground on the sands of doubt and felt too deeply ashamed to use any of the conversational openings which she had carefully thought out for this embarrassing interview. Presently the unsuspecting young man asked her without any prompting and very respectfully what was really wrong with her.

Thus furnished, face to face, with her wicked opportunity, she burst into tears, hid her face in a corner of her dress and managed to sob out: 'You. It's you who are making me ill. And what's more you're the only remedy for my fever. I'll die unless you cure me. You looked into my eyes and set something inside me on fire. I'm being slowly burned to death. Don't let any silly scruples about your father's rights prevent you from taking pity on me: you'll be saving his wife from death. You can't blame me for loving you: you're a younger edition of your dear father. Come, we can be sure of being alone; it's a wonderful chance for you to enjoy yourself: "No crime discovered, no crime committed".'

The suddenness of this disastrous blow so confused him that, though he shuddered at the idea of committing such a crime, he thought it best not to upset her by too blunt a refusal. He played for safety by asking her to wait a little longer, meanwhile promising her, with abundant assurances, all she wanted. 'Cheer up', he urged, 'and recover your spirits and take care of your health. I'll soon find an opportunity to be with you, but we must wait until Father has gone out riding!' Then he left the disagreeable sight of his stepmother in a hurry. Realizing that the whole family could be ruined and that he must confide in someone really wise and sensible, he hurried at once to his old schoolmaster and explained what had happened.

The old man thought for a long time before telling him that the best advice he could give was to fly before the storm of fate by leaving home immediately. But meanwhile, his stepmother, who could not bear to wait even the shortest time, found a pretext for sending her husband off in a hurry to inspect one of his distant farms. No sooner was he out of the house than, in a state of frantic passion, she sent her stepson a message holding him to his word.

His loathing for her was so strong that he could not face a fresh interview. He sent back word excusing himself and when she twice repeated her demand made a different excuse on each occasion. She understood in the end that he had no intention of keeping his promise. At once her mood changed, and her wicked passion turned to even more extreme hatred. She called one of her slaves, who had formed part of her dowry, an evil man given over to every criminal practice, and disclosed all her guilty secrets to him. They decided that the best thing to do was to put an end to the stepson. She sent the scoundrel out at once to buy a poison that takes instant effect. When he came back with it she dissolved it in a cupful of wine which she put aside for the innocent stepson to drink, expecting fatal results.

While they were still discussing the best means of administering the poison, this wicked woman's own son happened to come home from school, ate his lunch, felt thirsty, found the cup of poisoned wine and, naturally not suspecting the secret plot, drank it down at a gulp. He fell dead to the ground. The slave whose task was to take him to and from school was horrified by the catastrophe and shouted at the top of his voice for the mother and the house-slaves. When it became known that the boy had just drunk a cup of wine, everyone immediately began to offer different accusations about the authorship of the terrible crime.

Stepmothers have a reputation for maliciousness which was perfectly justified in this case. She was by no means dismayed by the dreadful death of her own son, or by the guilt of being his murderess, or by the disaster to her house, or by the prospect of her husband's grief, or by the grimness of the funeral. All that occurred to her was a splendid opportunity for revenge, even at the cost of destroying her family. She sent a message at once to recall her husband with news of the disaster and, when he hurried home, she had the audacity to tell him that her son had been poisoned by his stepbrother. This was true in a sense: it was his brother's poison which had killed him. But her version was that the stepson had made immoral proposals to her and that when she had refused to listen he had retaliated by poisoning her son. She embroidered this terrible lie by saying that when she accused him of the murder he had drawn his sword and threatened to kill her, too, because she had discovered the crime.

The councillor was in a dreadful state. His younger son was awaiting burial; the elder brother was bound to be condemned to death for incest, fratricide and the attempted murder of his step-mother, and he could feel no pity for him either, but only hatred, when the wife whom he loved and trusted came weeping to him with this shocking story. After making arrangements for the child's funeral, the unhappy old man, with tears still running down his cheeks and ashes on his white hair, which he tore out by the handful, went straight to the market-place from the pyre. There, in a passion-ate address to the council members he did all he could to make them condemn his surviving son to death, pleading, sobbing and going so far as to embrace the councillors' knees.

They were moved to indignant sympathy, and so were the towns-people, who wished to waive the tedium of a trial, with the meticu-lous proofs given by the prosecution and the carefully planned circumlocution of the defence, and all shouted that he should be stoned to death, so that a crime against the public might be publicly avenged. However, the magistrates feared a danger to themselves and anticipated that such a concession might encourage mass rioting and the breakdown of law and order. They asked for the councillors' support (hoping to keep the people quiet) for their decision to hold a properly conducted trial, with witnesses called on both sides and carefully examined, and a verdict authoritatively delivered. 'No man,' they said, 'should be condemned without a hearing, as if this were a barbarous or tyrannical community; especially in such peace-ful times as the present. That would constitute a dreadful precedent.'

Their sound decision was accepted unanimously, and the town clerk was sent at once to convene a meeting of the council. The members were soon assembled, seated in order of rank and seniority. Then the town clerk summoned the prosecution to prepare their case, ordered the accused to be brought in and finally announced that, in conformity with Attic law and the procedure adopted by the Areopagus,[2] counsel on both sides must plead without preamble or any appeal to the emotions of the court. Since I was not present at the trial myself, but tied up to my manger, my story is necessarily derived at second hand from the conversation of various visitors to the stable; but I will be careful to record only what I found, after checking the accounts, to be the truth.

When both barristers had finished their pleas, the court ruled that they could not give their verdict in a case of such importance merely on circumstantial evidence and called the stepmother's slave, who was quoted as the only witness who knew all facts of the case. That gallows bird showed no nervousness when he stepped up to give his evidence: although it was a very serious case and the court was packed, he had no doubt about the verdict and no qualms induced by the crowded council or his guilty conscience. He made a long statement on oath, reaffirming all his lies with emphasis. His version was that the stepson, mortified by the repulse of his advances, had sent for him, requesting him to kill his brother so that he could avenge himself and promising a big reward if he kept his mouth shut; and when he refused, the stepson threatened him with death. Then he mixed the poison himself and passed it to the slave to give to his brother; and when he thought that the slave had not done the deed, but had kept the drink as evidence against him, he finally administered it to his brother with his own hand.

The witness was a good actor and when he had concluded his speech, with a convincing show of respectful agitation, the case was declared closed. None of the councillors was fair-minded enough to refrain from judging the stepson guilty and condemning him to be sewn up into the leather sack. Since all agreed, and were united in their verdict, it now remained, in accordance with ancient custom, to drop their ballots into a brass urn; if this registered a sentence of death the proceedings would be at an end and the condemned man would be handed over to the public executioner.

At the last moment, one single member of the council – an old doctor, widely respected and of unquestioned integrity – came forward and, putting one hand over the mouth of the urn to prevent anyone from dropping his ballot in prematurely, addressed the assembly.

'I am proud to think that I have never in all my life forfeited your good opinion and that I am not accounted the sort of man who would acquiesce in the judicial murder of an innocent man – or let you be deceived by the eloquent lies of a slave into breaking the oath you have all sworn, to deliver a truthful verdict. So I will not betray my own conscience or smother the reverence which I owe the gods by voting for the death sentence. Listen attentively and I will give you the true facts of the case.

'This slave, fit to be hanged, came to me two days ago and offered me two hundred gold pieces for a rapidly acting poison. He said he needed it for a friend suffering from an incurable disease who wanted to free himself by suicide from the misery of life. His story was glib but unconvincing, and I suspected foul play; so, though I gave him his packet, I was careful not to become a party to whatever crime he had in mind, by accepting immediate payment of the fee. I asked him to come with me to the goldsmith's on the following day, which was yesterday, to have the coins weighed in case any of them were counterfeit or of light weight. Meanwhile, at my request, he was to seal the string at the neck with his thumb-ring.

'All this he did, and sealed up the money, and when I heard in court just now that he was to be called as a witness, I hastily sent a slave back to my house to fetch the bag. Here it is. Will you show him the impression of his seal and ask him whether he acknowledges it? If it proves to be his, you will wonder how he dares accuse the prisoner of buying the poison which he bought himself.'

The scoundrel began to tremble violently, his face turned ashen and he burst into a cold sweat. Shifting his weight from one foot to another, he scratched various parts of his head, stammering out such wild nonsense that no reasonable person could possibly have believed him innocent. However, he presently recovered his self-composure, denied ever having visited the doctor and persistently accused him of lying. Not only was the doctor on oath to deliver a just verdict in this case but his truthfulness was now publicly assailed. He redoubled his efforts to bring the slave to book, and at last the magistrates ordered the court officials to seize the fellow's hand and compare the seal on his iron ring[3] with the wax impression on the bag. They corresponded exactly and the suspicions against him were confirmed.

He was then subjected to the tortures of the wheel and the rack (according to Greek custom) but showed remarkable toughness in persisting with his account, which beatings and the brazier likewise failed to shift. At last the doctor exclaimed: 'Upon my word, I refuse either to let the young man in the dock be punished by you for a crime of which he is not guilty, or to let this slave make fools of the Court and escape punishment for his wickedness. Allow me to give you clear proof of the truth of my statements. When this shameless rogue came to me for a deadly poison, I remembered that the art of medicine was invented for the saving, not the taking, of human life. But I feared that, if I refused to sell, he might go elsewhere for poison or commit the murder that he had in mind by some other means – a sword, for instance, or some other weapon. So what I gave him was not really a poison: it was a soporific called mandragora, which is of such powerful action that the trance it induces is practically indistinguishable from death. You need not be surprised that this slave has been prepared, in his desperation, to face those tortures, which seem comparatively light beside the death otherwise ordained for him by ancient custom. But if the boy really did take the drug I prepared with my own hands, then he must still be alive, though in a coma; as soon as the effect has worn off, he will wake up and will return to the light of day. But if he has really been murdered and is dead, then you will have to conduct a further investigation.'

This opinion of the old physician gained approval, and everyone set off rapidly for the pyre, on which the boy's body was lying; all the councillors and all the town's prominent figures and indeed the whole population congregated there with curiosity. Among them was the child's father, who lifted the coffin-lid himself, just as the child, coming out of his death-like trance, was trying to sit up. He hugged him close but, finding no words to express his joy and relief, carried him down for everyone to see, and presently brought him into Court still bound and swathed in his grave-clothes.

The wickedness of the slave and the still greater wickedness of the stepmother were finally exposed, and the truth was out. She was condemned to perpetual exile, he was hanged on the gallows; and, by a unanimous vote, the bag and its contents were presented to the good doctor as a reward for the coma which he had induced with such happy results. So divine Providence rewarded the deserving old man with great and wonderful fortune. A moment before he had believed himself childless; and now, suddenly, he was once more the father of two sons.

>>>>><<<<<

CHAPTER XVI

UNDER THE TRAINER

A SUDDEN change of fortune was awaiting me, too. The soldier who had commandeered me from the gardener was sent to Rome by his commander with despatches for the mighty Emperor. He sold me for eleven *denarii* to two brothers, kitchen-slaves to a wealthy and prominent personage. One was a confectioner, who made pastry and sweet cakes, and the other a cook, who specialized in the preparation of savoury sauces. The two men lived together, and drove me from place to place in order to carry the numerous utensils that their Lord needed while he was travelling abroad. I was accepted as a brother and companion and never had such a good time as with them. Every evening after their Lord had dined – and he always dined in grand style – my masters used to carry back the left-overs to our little room: one brought generous helpings of roast pork, chicken, fish and similar delicacies; the other brought bread, tarts, several kinds of pastry, long cakes and various honeyed sweetmeats. But when they had shut the door and gone off to the baths to refresh themselves, I used to cram myself with the splendid food the gods had graciously put at my disposal, not being such a fool, such a complete ass, as to turn it down in favour of the coarse hay in my manger.

For a long time I was wonderfully successful in my pilfering: my technique was to take only a little from each of the many dishes on the table, knowing that my masters would never suspect an ass of playing such tricks on them. But gradually I grew overconfident and ate whatever I fancied: in fact, I picked out the best dishes and licked them clean. My masters became distinctly suspicious and though even then it did not occur to them to fix their suspicions on me, they were determined to find out who was the daily thief. They now kept a jealous watch on the dishes and counted every one of them, each accusing the other of base theft.

Finally, all restraint was abandoned, and one of them addressed his comrade in these terms: 'Really is this fair or decent? Every day you have been stealing left-overs, always the best ones, too, selling them for your private profit and secretly increasing your savings,[1] and then expecting me to go halves with you in what's left. If you are tired of our business partnership let us dissolve it by all means but continue to live together affectionately like the brothers we are. Otherwise, the friction between us, because of our losses, will increase daily and end in a violent quarrel.'

'Good heavens!' retorted the other. 'How about that for determination? First you steal the stuff secretly and then, to forestall the complaints which I have been holding back patiently all this time – I was determined to put up with it as long as I could, rather than accuse my own brother of being a thief – you accuse me first! However, I'm glad that this question of the losses has come into the open; we can settle it somehow at last instead of smothering our feelings until they finally blaze up and destroy us . . . as happened in Eteocles' quarrel.'[2]

These exchanges ended only when each of them had taken a solemn oath that he had not been guilty of the slightest dishonesty or taken more than his fair share of the food. They agreed to form a united front and use every possible means to discover who was robbing them. 'It is out of the question, of course,' one of them said, 'that the ass, which was standing there by itself, could be the culprit. Asses don't like our sort of food.' Nor could they imagine that their room would be entered by flies as huge as the Harpies who carried away the dinner of Phineus.[3]

The welcome change in my diet from fodder to human food, plenty of it, too, had the effect of plumping me up, juicily softening my hide and giving my coat a handsome gleam. It was this physical comeliness that gave me away, because my masters realized that I was twice as stout as when they had bought me, though I was leaving my daily feed of hay untouched. So one day they pretended to go off to the baths as usual and locked the door behind them, but, before leaving, peeped in through a crack and watched me making short work of the delicacies left within my reach.

Forgetting all about their losses, they burst into a sudden roar of laughter at this extraordinary sight: the ass who was a gourmet! They called a number of other slaves to take turns at the crack and see what a remarkably greedy appetite a sluggish beast could display. Their laughter was so loud and prolonged that when their master happened to come by he wanted to know what the joke was. When he understood what was happening, he peeped through the crack and saw for himself.

He laughed until his stomach ached, then opened the door and observed me closely. When I realized that fortune was at last, somehow or other, smiling upon me, I went on eating quite at my ease, indeed even more relaxed than before. At last, fascinated by the novelty of the sight, he ordered me to be led to the dining-room – or rather he led me there himself. The table was already laid and he ordered every sort of food to be put in front of me, including dishes that had not yet been touched. Although feeling pretty full already, I was anxious to oblige him in any way I could and greedily ate everything he gave me.

As a test of my docility, they thought of all the things that an ass would be most likely to loathe and offered them to me. For instance, meat seasoned with asafoetida, fattened birds flavoured with pepper and some exotic sort of pickled fish. Meanwhile the whole room echoed with loud laughter.

At last a buffoon who was among those present asked: 'Now what about a drop of wine for our guest, eh?'

'Not at all a bad idea, you scoundrel,' our master answered. 'I dare say he wouldn't say no to a cup of honeyed wine – here, boy, give that gold cup a good rinsing and offer it to my guest! And tell him that I drink his very good health.'

Everyone awaited the result with intense curiosity. The huge cup was handed to me and, without pausing to consider whether it would be wise to drink, I screwed up my mouth and drained the cup at one gulp.

A storm of applause, and a general toast to my health. My enraptured host sent for his two slaves, my purchasers, and undertook to pay them four times the price they had given for me; after which he put me in the charge of a well-do-do freedman of his, to whom he was greatly attached, and begged him to treat me with all possible care. This freedman showed me tenderness and humanity and did his best to improve the good opinion that his master already had of him by teaching me to perform tricks for his amusement. First, he taught me how to recline at table, leaning on one elbow; next, how to wrestle and even how to dance on my hind legs; finally

– and this won me peculiar admiration – how to use sign language. I learned to nod my head as a sign of approval, and to toss it back as a sign of rejection, also to turn towards the wine-waiter when I was thirsty and show that I needed a drink by winking first one eye and then the other. I was a quick and docile pupil; which was not really very remarkable, because I could have performed all my tricks without any training at all. But I had been afraid of behaving like a human being without previous instruction; most people would have taken it as a portent of sinister events, and I should probably have found myself classed as a monster and a prodigy, beheaded and thrown out as a choice meal for the vultures.

The tale of my wonderful talents spread in all direction, so that my lord became famous on my account. People said: 'Think of it! He has an ass whom he treats like a friend and invites to dinner with him. That ass can wrestle, and actually dance, and understands what people say to him, and uses a language of signs!'

Here I must tell you, rather late in the day, who my lord was, and of what country. His name was Thiasus; he was born at Corinth, the capital of the province of Achaia, and having been successively raised to all the junior offices to which his rank and position entitled him he was now the quinquennial magistrate.[4] Since convention required him to live up to the dignity of this appointment by staging a public entertainment, he had undertaken to provide a three-day gladiatorial show in evidence of his open-handedness. He was now trying to please his fellow-citizens by buying up the finest wild animals and hiring the most famous gladiators in all Thessaly. Finally, having found all that he needed, he was on the point of returning to Corinth, but instead of riding in one of his own splendid gigs, some covered and some open, which formed the tail of his long retinue, or on a Thessalian horse, or one of the animals from Gaul, whose pedigree makes them exceptionally valuable, he preferred to mount lovingly on my back. I now sported gilt harness, gilt trappings, a dyed back-cloth, purple coverings, an embroidered belly-band and shrill tinkling bells. He used to talk to me in the kindest way, telling me for example how delighted he was to own a mount who was also a dinner companion. After a journey partly by land and partly by sea we arrived at Corinth, where a vast crowd poured out to greet us. I think, though, that more people were there to see me than to welcome Thiasus.

So many visitors wanted to watch my performances that he decided to make money out of me. He kept the stable doors shut and charged a high price for admittance. His daily takings were considerable.

Among these visitors was a rich and powerful lady. My various tricks enchanted her and she became deeply attracted by me, lusting after me to a remarkable extent. There was no way of curbing her insane desire, and she ardently awaited my embraces like some ass-obsessed Pasiphae.[5] So she bribed my keeper with a large sum of money to let her spend a night in my company. The rascal agreed, with no thought for anything but his own pocket.

When I had eaten and left my lord's dining-room, I found the lady waiting for me. She had been there some time already. Heavens, what magnificent preparations she had made! Four eunuchs had spread the floor with several plump feather-beds, covered them with a Tyrian purple cloth embroidered in gold and laid a heap of little pillows at the head end, of the downy sort used by women of voluptuous tastes. Then, not wishing to postpone their mistress's enjoyment by their presence, out they trooped, but left wax candles brightly burning to light up the nocturnal darkness.

She undressed at once, taking everything off, even the skimpy little garment fastened across her beautiful breasts, then stood close to the lamp and rubbed her body all over with oil of balsam from a pewter pot. She then did the same to mine, most generously, but concentrating mostly on my nose. After this she gave me a lingering kiss – not of the mercenary sort that one expects in a brothel, or from whores who beg for money which their clients refuse to provide – but a pure, sincere, really loving kiss. 'I love you,' she cried. 'You are all I want in this world. I could never live without you.' She added all the other pretty things that women say when they want to lead men on and to display their own passionate feelings. Then she took me by my head-band and laid me on the bed.

This seemed familiar enough to me – neither novel nor difficult. Besides, I had been continent for a long time, and now, with all this excellent wine inside me and fragrant scent all over me, I had worked up some excitement. All the same, I was very worried at the thought of mounting so lovely a woman with my massive legs and my hooves pressed against her tender milk-and-honey skin – her dewy red lips kissed by my huge mouth with its ugly rock-like teeth. Worst of all, how could any woman alive, though exuding lust from her very finger nails, take my huge genitals inside her? If I tore her apart – a noblewoman, too – my lord would use me in his promised entertainment as food for his wild beasts. But her burning eyes devoured mine, as she cooed sweetly at me between kisses and finally gasped: 'Ah, ah, I have you safe now, my little dove, my little birdie.' Then I realized how foolish my fears had been. She pressed me closer and closer to her and received every bit of me. Every time I pushed my buttocks backwards so as to spare her, she violently strained forward and clutching my back fastened herself to me more tightly than ever. Heavens, I could hardly believe that I possessed the capacity to satisfy her lust; I could see why the Minotaur's mother wanted a bull. She did not allow me to sleep a wink that night, but as soon as the revealing daylight entered the room she crept out, pleading with my keeper to spend another night with me for the same fee. He was willing enough to dispose of my sex-life in this way partly because she paid handsomely, partly because he wished to give Thiasus a novel peep-show.

The man went straight off to him and told the whole story of our lecheries. Thiasus rewarded him with a large tip, and decided to make a public show of me. But they could not allow that excellent mistress of mine to take part in the act, because of her high rank, and could not find any other volunteer, even for the most generous fee. In the end Thiasus did not have to pay anything: he got hold of a woman who had been sentenced to be thrown to the wild beasts. We were to be caged up together in the centre of the packed amphitheatre.[6]

*

I had already heard the woman's story, and I will tell it to you. Many years before this, the father of the little boy who afterwards became her husband had set out on a long journey, ordering his wife, who was expecting another baby, to kill it as soon as it was born, if it turned out to belong to the inferior sex. It was indeed a girl, born while her husband was away; not having the heart to obey his orders, she asked a neighbour to bring the child up for her and, on her husband's return, told him that a girl had been born and duly killed. When the girl grew up to marriageable age, the mother could not give her the dowry to which she was entitled by birth, or not without the father's knowledge; so she decided to take her son into the secret. For what if her brother, carried away by a youthful urge, should seduce his sister, without either of them knowing that that was what she was?

The brother, a good-natured man, felt obliged to obey his mother and behave as a kind brother should. He kept the secret dark and to all appearances what he did for his sister was merely an act of common charity: he gave her a home in his own house and let it be thought that she was a neighbour, both of whose parents were dead, whom he had decided to marry off to his best friend. He undertook to find her dowry himself.

This admirable, innocent arrangement somehow provoked Fortune to behave spitefully. The brother was already married to the woman whose story I am telling, and her bitter jealousy of the supposed orphan led her in the end to commit the series of crimes for which she was now condemned to be thrown to the wild beasts. She suspected her husband of having already made the girl his mistress and of intending to make her his wife. When suspicion turned to hate, she thought of a very cruel plan.

She would steal her husband's signet ring, go for a visit to their country house and from there send a slave to tell the girl that the husband wanted her to visit him there as soon as possible and without any escort. The slave who, though faithful to his mistress, was otherwise an absolute rogue, would show the girl the signet ring as a proof that the message was authentic.

The girl was anxious enough to obey her brother – for she knew now that he was her brother, as nobody else did – and the signet ring had the required effect. She hurried out all alone to the country house and there ran into the trap laid for her: she was set upon with fury, stripped naked and flogged till she was nearly dead. The poor girl was forced by the pain to reveal the secret. 'He's my brother, he's my brother,' she kept on sobbing: but she was wasting her words. In anger, at having been, as she supposed, deceived, the sister-in-law paid no attention to her, dismissing the story as an invention, and finally snatched up a blazing torch which she cruelly thrust between her thighs, so that she perished.

The brother and the friend whom the girl was to have married heard the news of her terrible death and arrived to fetch the corpse home for burial, each lamenting over it in his own way. The brother took the news especially hard, grieving not only for his sister's miserable death but because it was his wife who had caused it. He fell into such an anguish of mind that brain-fever set in and his temperature rose so high that nobody expected him to recover unless with the help of some very powerful remedy.

His wife, who had long since forfeited the right to be so called through her criminal action, then went to a doctor well known for his gross lack of principles – he could list the trophies of many deadly victories as the works of his own hands – offering him six hundred gold pieces for an instantaneous poison, so that she could purchase the death of her husband. When he consented, she came back and told him that he must drink a medicine known to eminent physicians as the 'sacred potion', the effect of which is to ease gastric pain and carry off bilious secretions. Really, of course, the potion mixed for him was sacred to Proserpine whose healing is death.

The whole family was present, and several friends and relatives as well, when the doctor came in with the potion, stirred it well in its cup, and offered it to the sick man. But the audacious woman decided to get rid of her accomplice in this new crime and at the same time save herself the expense of paying him. As the sick man was about to accept the cup, she restrained him. 'Doctor,' she said, 'I feel it my duty as a wife to insist on your having a good taste of this medicine yourself before giving it to my dear husband. I want to make certain that it contains no poison. I'm sure that so learned and so careful a man as you are won't be offended by my request. I make it only to demonstrate the dutiful, wifely solicitude I am obliged to feel for the health of my husband.'

The doctor was so surprised by this bloody-minded woman's outrageousness that on the spur of the moment he could think of no excuse for refusing. If he showed the least fear or hesitation everyone present would suspect him of poisoning the cup, so he was forced to take a good swig. The husband confidently followed his example and drank what was left.

That was all for the moment, and the doctor wanted to hurry home before it was too late for an antidote that would counteract the effects of the poison he had taken. The savage woman was bent on completing the infernal work she had begun and would not let him out of her sight. 'You must stay here until the potion has begun to work,' she said, 'and we can judge of its effect on my husband's health.' He begged repeatedly to be excused, but by the time she had agreed to let him go the poison was already playing havoc with his intestines. He managed to struggle home in excruciating pain and increasing faintness and had only just enough time before he died to tell his wife what had happened and ask her at least to collect the stipulated fee for the double poisoning. And that was the end of this celebrated doctor.

His young patient succumbed soon afterwards and the murderess wept long and deceitfully over the corpse. A few days later when the funeral rites at his tomb had been completed, the doctor's widow came and asked for her fee, pointing out that two murders had been provided at the price of one. The murderess remained true to character. In the friendliest tones and with a mendacious show of good faith she answered that of course she would pay the money immediately – if only she would give her a little more of the same mixture to complete the business she had begun.

The doctor's widow was taken in by these wicked deceits, declared that she would be delighted to oblige and, knowing that the murderess was a wealthy woman, tried to get into her good books by running home at once and fetching her the box of poisons. Once she had got hold of this abundant material for committing further crimes, she prepared to go in for murder on a large scale. She had a little daughter by the husband whom she had just killed and felt piqued that the child, as next-of-kin to her father, would inherit all his property. She longed to have it all herself, knowing that mothers, however criminal, always benefit from the reversion of legacies bequeathed to their children. In fact, she showed herself as dreadful a mother as she had been a wife: when she invited the doctor's widow to a meal and slipped the poison into the food she was about to eat, she also gave a dose to her own daughter. The child choked and died almost at once; but the doctor's widow, with the dreadful poison working in her intestines, at first felt doubts but then, when she found difficulty in breathing, realized what had happened. She rushed off to the home of the principal officer calling aloud for justice and declaring that she had some terrible crimes to reveal. A big crowd supported her, and the official, paying heed to her words, granted an immediate interview. She told him the whole story from beginning to end; then her head dizzied, her mouth closed convulsively, she ground her teeth and fell dead at his feet.

He was an experienced man and decided to allow no delays in bringing this poisonous serpent, guilty of so many crimes, to justice. He at once summoned the woman's bedroom servants and tortured the truth out of them. Doubtless the woman deserved a still worse fate than merely to be thrown to the wild beasts; still this was the most appropriate sentence that could be conceived.

>>>>><<<<<

THE GODDESS ISIS INTERVENES

THIS was the woman with whom it had been decided that I should enter into matrimonial relations in public. It was with extreme anguish that I waited for the day of the show. I was tempted to commit suicide rather than defile myself by intercourse with this criminal woman as a public spectacle.

But I had no fingers or palms: how could I draw a sword with the round stump of my hooves? Only one slender hope remained to console me in my miserable plight: spring was on its way and flowers would soon be bursting out all over the countryside, spreading a bright sheen of colour across the pastures. And in the gardens the imprisoned rose-buds would break out from their thorny stocks, and open, and exhale their delicate scents: they would make me the Lucius I was before.

The day of the triumphal spectacle came at last, and I was escorted towards the amphitheatre at the head of a long procession. During the first part of the performance, which was devoted to ballet, I was placed just outside the entrance, where I was glad to crop some tender young grass which I found growing there, raising my eyes curiously every now and then to watch the performance through the open gate.

A number of beautiful boys and girls in rich costumes were moving with dignity through the graceful mazes of the Greek Pyrrhic dance.[1] Sometimes different streams of dancers would weave in and out of the same circle; sometimes all would join hands and dance sideways across the stage, then separate into four wedge-shaped groups, which then dispersed.

Presently the trumpet blew, signalling that everyone should leave the stage, for these complicated dance-movements were at an end; the backdrops were removed, the curtains drawn apart, and the scene was set.

It displayed an artificial wooden mountain, supposed to represent Homer's famous Mount Ida, an imposing piece of stage-architecture, quite high, turfed all over and planted with scores of trees. The designer had contrived that a stream should break out at the top of the mountain and tumble down the side. A few she-goats were cropping the grass, and in came a young man, dressed in flowing Asiatic robes with a gold tiara on his head. He represented Paris, the Phrygian shepherd. Then a handsome boy came forward, naked except for a rich cloak, such as young men wear, over his left shoulder, and between the strands of his long yellow hair one could see two little golden wings; these wings, with the serpent-rod and the herald's wand that he carried, showed him to be Mercury. He came dancing towards Paris and after presenting him with a golden apple explained Jupiter's orders in sign language, then retired gracefully and disappeared from view. The next character to appear was Juno, played by a girl with very fine features, a white diadem on her head and a sceptre in her hand. Then a girl looking like Minerva[2] came running in, easily recognized by her shining helmet upon which a garland of olive-leaves was fastened; she was lifting a shield and brandishing a spear as if about to fight someone. She was followed by another girl of extraordinary beauty and such an ambrosial complexion that she could only be Venus – Venus before marriage. To show her perfect figure to fullest advantage she wore nothing at all except a thin silk robe, which inquisitive little winds kept blowing aside for an amorous peep at her lovely loins, or pressing tight against them so as to reveal their voluptuous contours. Two colours predominated: her body was dazzlingly white, to show that she had descended from Heaven, and her silk robe was blue to show that she would shortly return to her home in the sea.

Each of the girls who played the parts of these goddesses was escorted by attendants. Juno had two young actors with her, representing Castor and Pollux; on their heads were egg-shaped[3] helmets, shining with stars. The virgin Juno advanced calmly and unaffectedly towards Paris, to the sound of flute-music in the Ionian mode;[4] her short, confident nods were an assurance that if he judged her to be the most beautiful of the three she would make him Lord of all Asia.

The attendants of the girl whose arms and armour showed her to be Minerva were two young men, representing Terror and Fear, who danced before her with drawn swords, and a flute-player who

followed behind, playing a battle march in the D
deep drones contrasting with a shrill screeching sti
ecstasy, like the trumpet's call to battle. Minerva h
dance, tossing her head from side to side, her
daggers, and her quick, excited writhings promis
gave the verdict in her favour she would make h
tion, the bravest and most successful soldier alive.

Then in came Venus, smiling sweetly and greeted with a roar of
welcome by the audience. She advanced to the centre of the stage,
with a mass of happy little boys crowding around her, so chubby
and white-skinned that you might have taken them to be real Cupids
flown down from Heaven or in from the sea. They had little wings
and little arrows and all carried lighted torches as if they were
conducting their mistress to her wedding feast. In came a great
crowd of beautiful girls: on one side the graceful Graces, on the
other the lovely Seasons, who strewed the path before Venus with
bouquets and loose flowers, dancing elegantly and propitiating her,
as Queen of all Pleasures, with the foliage of spring.

Presently the flutes, with their many stops, broke into soft Lydian
airs. The audience was charmed, and even more so when Venus began
dancing to the music with slow, lingering steps and gentle swaying of
her hips and head, and hardly perceptible motions of her arms to match
the delicate modulations of the music. Her eyelids fluttered luxuriously
or opened wide to let fly passionate glances, so that at times she seemed
to be dancing with her eyes alone. As soon as she came before the judge
she promised with certain gestures that if she were preferred to her
rivals she would marry him to the most beautiful woman in the world,
her own human counterpart. Young Paris gladly handed her the
golden apple which he was holding, in token of her victory.

Well, why does it surprise you if the lowest of the low, the cattle
of the lawcourts, the vultures in togas, and every one of our judges,
sell their verdicts for money in our own day, when in the earliest
ages this simple shepherd, who had been appointed by Jupiter
himself to give judgement in a question between Heaven and Earth,
sold that first of all verdicts for a sexual inducement – which was to
prove the ruin of his entire family? Then came other precedents
among the noble Greeks, when the extremely wise and learned
Palamedes was condemned for treason by false insinuations,[6] and
Ulysses, who was only of moderate valour, was placed above the

ely valorous Ajax in respect of war-like bravery. And what
t that judgement given by the clever Athenian lawgivers, mas-
rs of every branch of knowledge, against Socrates whose wisdom
was commended by the Delphic oracle above that of all living
men?[7] Am I not right in saying that by the treachery and jealousy of
a wicked clique he was found guilty of corrupting young people –
though the truth was that his philosophy was directed towards
bridling and curbing their passions – and sentenced to die by drinking
the poisonous hemlock cup? This has left an indelible stain on the
reputation of his fellow-citizens, because even today the best philosophers, those who aspire to the highest form of human happiness,
regard his system as the most truly sacred of all and in their search
for the supreme happiness swear by his name.

But I can hear my readers protesting against this angry outburst
and thinking: 'Are we going to have to allow an ass to lecture us on
philosophy?' So I had better return to my story.

As I was saying, Paris gave his verdict. Then Juno and Minerva
retired from the scene in sorrow and rage, each of them gesticulating to
show her indignation at not having been awarded the prize. But Venus,
who was very pleased and happy, danced for delight, with the support
of all her attendants. Then a fountain of wine, mixed with saffron,
broke out from a concealed pipe at the mountain top, and its many jets
sprinkled the pasturing goats with a scented shower, so that their white
hair was stained a rich yellow. The scent filled the whole amphitheatre;
and then the stage machinery was set in motion, the earth opened and
the mountain disappeared from view.

After this, a soldier ran through the middle of the auditorium and
out of the theatre to fetch from the public prison, by popular
demand, the murderess who, though condemned (as I have already
explained) to be eaten by wild beasts, was destined first to become
my glorious bride. Our marriage bed, inlaid with fine Indian tortoise-
shell, was already in position, and provided with a well-stuffed
feather mattress and a colourful silk coverlet. I was not only appalled
by the shame of engaging in sexual intercourse in public, with this
criminal and degraded woman: I was in terror of death. It occurred
to me that when she and I were locked in an amorous embrace the
wild beast, appointed to eat her, would not be so naturally sagacious,
or so well trained, or so abstemious, as to tear her to pieces by my
side, sparing me as my innocence deserved.

While Thiasus was busy inside the cage putting the last touches to the bed, and the rest of his household staff were either admiring the voluptuousness of the scene or getting things ready for the hunting display which was to follow, I began to make plans. I had such a reputation for tameness and gentleness that nobody was keeping an eye on me. I edged towards the gate, which was quite near. Once outside I bolted off at top speed and went six miles at full gallop until I found myself at Cenchreae, a town belonging to the noble colony of Corinth, which is washed on one side by the Aegean Sea and on the other by the Saronic Gulf.

Cenchreae has a safe harbour and is always crowded with visitors, but I wanted to keep away from people. I went to a secluded part of the sea-coast and stretched my tired body upon the bosom of the sand, close to where the waves were breaking in spray. It was evening. The chariot of the sun was at the point of ending its day's course across the sky; so I too resigned myself to rest, and was presently overcome by a sweet, sound sleep.

*

At about the first watch of the night, I awoke in sudden terror and saw a dazzling full moon rising from the sea. I knew that it is at this secret hour that the Moon-goddess, sole sovereign of mankind, is possessed of her greatest power and majesty. She is the shining deity by whose divine influence not only all beasts, wild and tame, but all inanimate things as well, are invigorated; whose ebbs and flows control the rhythm of all bodies whatsoever, whether in the air, on earth, or below the sea. Of this I was well aware, and therefore resolved to address the august apparition of the goddess, since Destiny, it appeared, was now sated by all my great calamities and was offering me a hope of release, however belated.

Jumping up briskly and shaking off my drowsiness, I went down to the sea to purify myself by bathing in it. Seven times I dipped my head under the waves – seven, according to the divine Pythagoras, is a number that particularly suits all religious occasions[8] – and with joyful eagerness, though tears were running down my face, I offered this soundless prayer to the potent goddess:

'Blessed Queen of Heaven, whether you are pleased to be known as Ceres, the original harvest mother who in joy at the finding of your lost daughter Proserpine abolished the rude acorn diet of our forefathers, who makes her way across the soil of Eleusis; or whether as celestial Venus, now adored at sea-girt Paphos, who at the beginning of the world coupled the sexes in mutual love and so contrived that human beings should continue to propagate their kind for ever; or whether as the sister of Phoebus Apollo,[9] reliever, by your healing care, of the birth pangs of women, and now adored in the shrine of Ephesus; or whether as Proserpine, fearfully howling by night, whose triple face is potent against the malice of ghosts, keeping them imprisoned below earth; you who wander through many sacred groves and are propitiated with many different rites – you whose womanly light illumines the walls of every city, whose moist radiance nurses the happy seeds under the soil, you who offer your ever-changing illumination in accordance with the vicissitudes of the sun – I beseech you, by whatever name, in whatever aspect, with whatever ceremonies you deign to be invoked, have mercy on me in my extreme distress, restore my shattered fortune, grant me repose and peace after this long sequence of miseries. End my sufferings and perils, rid me of this hateful four-footed disguise, return me to my family, restore me to the Lucius I really am. But if I have offended some god of unappeasable cruelty, let me at least die, if I may not live as a man.'

When I had finished my prayer and poured out the full bitterness of my oppressed heart, sleep once more overcame me as I lay upon that same bed. I had scarcely closed my eyes before the apparition of a woman began to rise from the middle of the sea with so lovely a face that the gods themselves would have fallen down in adoration of it. First the head, then the whole shining body gradually emerged and stood before me poised on the surface of the waves. I will try to describe this transcendent vision, for though human speech is poor and limited, the goddess herself will perhaps inspire me with an eloquence rich enough to describe her.

Her long thick hair fell in tapering ringlets on her divine neck and was crowned with an intricate chaplet in which was woven every kind of flower. In the middle of her brow shone a round disc, like a mirror, or like the bright light of the moon, which told me who she was. Vipers curving upwards to left and right supported this disc, with ears of grain bristling beside them. Her many-coloured robe was of finest linen; part was glistening white, part crocus-yellow, part glowing red, and along the entire hem a woven bordure of flowers and fruit clung swaying in the breeze. But what struck my eye more than anything else was the deep black lustre of her mantle. She wore it slung across her body from the right hip to the left shoulder, where it was caught in a knot resembling the boss of a shield; but part of it hung in innumerable folds, the tasselled fringe quivering. It was embroidered with glittering stars on the hem and everywhere else, and in the middle beamed a full and fiery moon.

She carried a variety of objects. In her right hand she held a bronze rattle; its narrow rim was curved like a belt and a few little rods, which sang shrilly when she shook the handle, passed through it. A boat-shaped gold dish hung from her left hand, and along the upper surface of the handle writhed an asp with puffed throat and head raised ready to strike. On her fragrantly scented feet were slippers woven with palm leaves, the emblem of victory.

All the perfumes of Arabia floated into my nostrils as the heavenly voice of this great goddess deigned to address me: 'You see me here, Lucius, moved by your prayer. I am Nature, the universal Mother, mistress of all the elements, primordial child of time, sovereign of all things spiritual, Queen of the Dead, first also among the immortals, the single manifestation of all gods and goddesses that are. My nod governs the shining heights of Heaven, the wholesome sea-breezes, the lamentable silences of the world below. Though I am worshipped in many aspects, known by countless names and propitiated with all manner of different rites, yet the whole earth venerates me. The primeval Phrygians call me the Goddess of Pessinus, Mother of the Gods: the Athenians, sprung from their own soil, call me the Minerva of Cecrops' citadel; for the islanders of Cyprus I am Paphian Venus; for the archers of Crete I am Diana Dictynna; for the trilingual Sicilians,[10] Stygian Proserpine; and for the Eleusinians, their ancient Goddess Ceres.

'Some know me as Juno, some as Bellona, others as Hecate, others again as the Goddess of Rhamnus,[11] but both races of Ethiopians, whose lands the morning sun first shines upon, and the Egyptians, who excel in ancient learning and worship me with their appropriate ceremonies, call me by my true name, Queen Isis. I have come in pity of your plight; I have come to favour and aid you. Weep no more, lament no longer; the day of deliverance, shone over by my watchful light, is at hand.

'Listen attentively to my orders.

'The eternal laws of religion devote to my worship the day born from this night. Tomorrow my priests celebrate the new sailing season by dedicating a ship to me as the first-fruits of their navigation; for at this season the storms of winter lose their force, and the leaping waves of the sea subside. You must wait for this sacred ceremony, with a mind that is neither anxious for the future nor clouded with profane thoughts; and I shall order the priest to carry a garland of roses in my procession, tied to the rattle which he carries in his right hand. Do not hesitate, push the crowd aside, join the procession with confidence in my grace. Then come close up to the priest as if you wished to kiss his hand, pluck the roses with your mouth and you will immediately slough off the hide of what has always been for me the most hateful beast in the universe.[12]

'Above all, do not fear that any of my commands are hard to obey. For at this very moment, while I am with you here, I am also giving instructions to my priest, through a vision; and tomorrow, at my commandment, the dense crowds of people will make way for you. I promise you that in the joy and laughter of the ceremonies and the festival nobody will either view your ugly form with abhorrence or dare to put a sinister interpretation on your sudden return to human shape. Only remember, and keep these words of mine locked tight in your heart, that from now onwards until the very last day of your life you are dedicated to my service. It is only right that you should devote your whole life to the goddess who makes you a man again. Under my protection you will be happy and famous, and when at the allotted end of your life you descend to the land of ghosts, there too in the subterranean hemisphere you shall have frequent occasion to adore me. From the Elysian Fields you will see me, just as you see me now, as queen of the profound Stygian realm, shining through the darkness of Acheron. Further, if you are found to deserve my divine protection by careful obedience to the ordinances of my religion and by perfect chastity, you will become aware that I, and I alone, have power to prolong your life beyond the limits appointed by destiny.'

When the invincible goddess had finished her prophecy, she vanished away.

CHAPTER XVIII

>>>>><<<<<

THE ASS IS TRANSFORMED

I ROSE at once, wide awake, bathed in a sweat of joy and fear. Astonished at this clear manifestation of her powerful godhead, I splashed myself with sea water and carefully memorized her lofty orders. Soon a golden sun arose to rout the dark shadows of night, and at once the streets were filled with people walking along as if in a religious triumph. The whole world seemed filled with delight. The animals, the houses, even the weather itself reflected the universal joy and serenity, for a calm sunny morning had succeeded yesterday's frost, and the song-birds, assured that spring had come, were chirping their welcome to the Queen of the Stars, the Mother of the Seasons, the Mistress of the Universe. The trees, too – not only those fertile with fruits but those which, being barren, are grown for their shade – roused from their winter sleep by the warm breezes of the south and tasselled with green leaves, waved their branches with a pleasant rustling noise; and the crash and thunder of the surf was stilled, for the gales had blown themselves out, the dark clouds were gone and the sky shone with its own calm light.

Presently the vanguard of the grand procession came in view. It was composed of a number of people in splendid dress of their own choosing; a man wearing a soldier's sword-belt; another dressed as a huntsman, a thick cloak caught up to his waist with hunting knife and javelin; another who wore gilt sandals, a wig, silk dress and expensive jewellery and pretended to be a woman. Then a man with greaves, shield, helmet and sword, looking as though he had come out of a gladiators' school; a pretended magistrate with purple robe and rods of office; a philosopher with cloak, staff, woven shoes and goatee beard; a bird-catcher, carrying lime and a long reed; a fisherman with fish-hooks. And I also saw a tame she-bear, dressed like a woman, carried in a sedan chair; and an ape in a straw hat and a saffron-coloured cloak with a gold cup grasped in its paws – like the Phrygian shepherd Ganymede. Finally there was an ass with wings glued to its shoulders walking with an doddering old man; you would have laughed at that pair, supposed to be Pegasus and Bellerophon. These popular comedians kept running in and out of the crowd, and behind them came the special procession of the Saviour Goddess.

Women crowned joyfully with spring flowers pulled more flowers out of the folds of their beautiful white dresses and scattered them along the road. Next came women with polished mirrors tied to the backs of their heads, which gave all who followed them the illusion of coming to meet the goddess. Then a party of women with ivory combs in their hands whose gestures of arms and hands declared that they were to dress and adorn the goddess's royal hair, and another party who sprinkled the road with balsam and other precious perfumes; and behind these a mixed company of women and men who honoured the Daughter of the Heavenly Stars by carrying lamps, torches, wax-candles and so forth.

Next came musicians with sweetly harmonious pipes and flutes, followed by a party of carefully chosen boys in white ceremonial robes, singing a hymn in which a clever poet, by the favour of the Muses, had composed the prelude that explained the origin of the procession. The temple pipers of the great god Serapis[1] were there, too, playing their religious anthem on pipes with slanting mouth-pieces and tubes curving around their right ears; also a number of men crying out that room should be made for the goddess to pass. Then followed a great crowd of the goddess's initiates, men and women of all classes and every age, their pure white linen clothes shining brightly. The women wore their hair tied up in glossy coils under diaphanous head-dresses; the men's heads were completely shaven and gleaming, representing the great goddess's earthly stars, and they carried rattles of brass, silver and even gold, which kept up a shrill tinkling.

The leading ministers of the sacred rites, also clothed in white linen drawn tight across their chests and hanging down to their feet, carried emblems of the most powerful deities.[2] The first minister held a bright lamp, which was not at all like the lamps we use at night banquets; it was a golden boat-shaped affair with a tall tongue of flame mounting from a hole in the centre. The second priest held a sacrificial pot in each of his hands – the Latin name, *auxiliaria*, refers to the goddess's providence in helping her devotees. The third priest carried a miniature gold palm-tree with cleverly fashioned leaves, also the serpent wand of Mercury. The fourth carried the imperfectly executed model of a left hand with the fingers stretched out, which is an emblem of justice, because the left hand, with its natural slowness and lack of any craft or subtlety, seems more impartial than the right. He also held a golden vessel, rounded in the shape of a woman's breast, from the nipple of which a thin stream of milk fell to the ground. The fifth carried a winnowing-fan heaped up with sprigs made of gold. Then came another man, carrying a wine-jar.

Next in the procession followed those deities that deigned to walk on human feet. Here was the frightening messenger of the gods of Heaven, and of the gods of the dead: Anubis, lifting up his dog's head with a face black on one side, golden on the other, walking erect and holding his herald's wand in his left hand and in his right, a green palm-branch.[3] Behind, a man stepped along solemnly and happily, carrying on his shoulders the lofty statue of a standing cow, representing the goddess as the fruitful Mother of us all. Then along came a priest with a box containing the secret implements of her wonderful cult. Another fortunate priest had an ancient emblem of her godhead upon his robe: this was not made in the shape of any beast, wild or tame, or any bird or human being, but the exquisite beauty of its workmanship no less than the originality of its design called for admiration and awe. It was a symbol of the sublime and ineffable mysteries of the goddess, which are never to be divulged: a small vessel of burnished gold, upon which pictures in the Egyptian manner were cunningly engraved, with a rounded bottom, a long, low spout and widely projecting handle along which lay an asp, raising its head and displaying its scaly, wrinkled, puffed-out throat.

At last the moment had come when the blessing promised by the almighty goddess was to fall upon me. The priest in whom lay my hope of salvation approached, carrying the rattle and the garland in his right hand just as I had been promised – but it was more than a garland to me, it was a crown of victory over my cruel enemy Fortune, bestowed on me by the providence of the goddess after I had endured so many hardships and run through so many dangers! Though overcome with sudden joy, I refrained from galloping forward at once and disturbing the calm progress of the pageant by a brutal charge, but gently and politely wriggled my way through the crowd which gave way before me, clearly by the goddess's intervention. I saw that the priest had been warned what to expect in his vision of the previous night, but was none the less astounded that the fulfilment came so pat. He stood still and held out the rose garland to my mouth. I trembled and my heart pounded as I ate those roses with loving relish; and no sooner had I swallowed them than I found that the promise had been no deceit. My bestial features faded away, the rough hair fell from my body, my sagging paunch tightened, my hooves separated into feet and toes, my fore hooves now no longer served only for walking upon, but were restored, as hands, to human uses. My neck shrank, my face and head rounded, my great stony teeth shrank to their proper size, my long ears receded to their former shortness, and my tail, which had been my worst shame, vanished altogether.

A gasp of wonder went up, and the devotees, aware that the miracle corresponded with the vision of the great goddess, lifted their hands to Heaven and with one voice applauded the blessing which she had vouchsafed me: this swift restoration to my proper shape.

When I saw what had happened to me I stood rooted to the ground with astonishment and could not speak for a long while, my mind unable to cope with so great and sudden a joy. I could find no words good enough to thank the great goddess. But the priest, who had been informed by her of all my miseries, though himself taken aback by the remarkable miracle, made gestures ordering that I should be lent a linen garment to cover me; for as soon as I had shed my hateful ass's skin, I had done what any naked man would do – pressed my knees closely together and put both my hands down to screen my private parts. Someone quickly took off his upper robe and covered me with it, after which the priest gazed benignly and very courteously at me, wondering at my appearance.

'Lucius,' he said, 'you have endured and performed many labours and withstood the buffeting of all the winds of ill luck. Now at last you have put into the harbour of peace and stand before the altar of loving-kindness. Neither your birth and rank nor your excellent education sufficed to keep you from falling a slave to pleasure; youthful follies ran away with you. Your luckless curiosity earned you a sinister punishment. But blind Fortune, after tossing you maliciously about from peril to peril, has somehow, without thinking what she was doing, landed you here in religious felicity. Let her begone now and fume furiously elsewhere; let her find some other target for her cruel hands. She has no power to hurt those who devote their lives to the service of our goddess's majesty. What use was served by making you over to bandits, wild animals and slave-masters, by setting your feet on dangerous stony paths, by holding you in daily terror of death? Rest assured that you are now safe under the protection of the true Fortune, the Fortune that can see, whose clear light shines for all the gods that are. Rejoice now, as becomes a wearer of your white robe. Follow triumphantly in the train of the goddess who has delivered you. Let the irreligious see you and, seeing, let them acknowledge the error of their ways. Let them cry: "Look, there goes Lucius, rescued from his earlier miseries by the intervention of the great Isis, glorying in the defeat of his ill luck!" But to secure today's gains, you must enrol yourself in this holy Order, as a short time ago you pledged yourself to do, dedicating yourself to the service of our religion and voluntarily accepting the yoke of its ministry. For it is when you begin to serve the goddess that you will more truly enjoy the fruits of your freedom.'

When the noble priest, amid much laboured breathing, had ended his prophetic speech, I joined the throng of devotees and went forward with the procession, an object of curiosity to all Corinth. People pointed or jerked their heads at me and said: 'Look, there goes a man, restored to human shape by the power of the Almighty Goddess! Lucky, lucky man to have earned her compassion on account of his former innocence and good behaviour, and now to be reborn as it were, and immediately accepted into her most sacred service!' Their congratulations were long and loud.

Meanwhile the pageant moved slowly on, and we approached the sea-shore, at last reaching the very place where on the previous night I had lain down as an ass. There the divine emblems were arranged in due order and there with solemn prayers the chaste-lipped priest consecrated and dedicated to the goddess a beautifully built ship, with wonderful Egyptian pictorial signs painted over the entire hull; but first he carefully purified it with a lighted torch, an egg and sulphur. The sail was shining white linen, inscribed with the prayer for the goddess's protection of shipping during the new sailing season. The fir mast with its shining head rose aloft, the gilded stern was fashioned like a goose, and the entire ship was made of highly polished, glittering citron-wood. Then all present, both priesthood and laity, began zealously stowing aboard winnowing-fans heaped with spices and other votive offerings, and poured a milk-paste into the sea as a libation. When the ship was loaded with generous gifts and prayers for good fortune, they cut the anchor cables and she slipped across the bay with a serene breeze behind her that seemed to have sprung up for her sake alone. When she stood so far out to sea that we could no longer keep her in view, the men who had brought the sacred emblems then carried them away again and started happily back towards the temple, in the same orderly procession as before.

On our arrival at the shrine the priest and those who carried the oracular emblems were admitted into the goddess's sanctuary, along with others who had been earlier initiated into the sacred precinct, and restored the emblems to their proper places. Then one of them, whom everyone knew as the scribe, presided at the gate of the sanctuary over a meeting of the Shrine-bearers,[4] as this holy Order is called. He went up into a high pulpit and read out of a book blessings upon 'the mighty Emperor, and upon the Senate, and upon the Order of Knights,[5] and upon the whole people of Rome, and upon all sailors and all ships who owe obedience to our Empire'. Then he uttered, in the Greek tongue and ritual, the word *Ploeaphesia*, meaning that vessels were now permitted to sail, to which the people responded with a great cheer and dispersed happily to their homes, taking with them green boughs, leafy branches and garlands of flowers, but first kissing the feet of a silver statue of the goddess that stood on the temple steps. I, however, did not feel like moving a nail's breadth from the place, but stood with my eyes intently fixed on the image of the goddess and relived in memory all my past misfortunes.

Meanwhile, the news, which travels as swiftly as the flight of birds, had been carried forth concerning the provident goddess's wonderful goodness to me and my memorable good fortune, and had come to my own country. At once the members of my household, my servants and my close relatives forgot their sorrow and came hurrying in high spirits to welcome me back from the Under-world, as it were, and bring me all sorts of presents. I was as delighted to see them as they were to see me – I had despaired of ever doing so – and thanked them for what they had brought me: I was especially grateful to my servants for bringing me as much money and as many clothes as I needed.

I spoke to them all in turn, which was no more than my duty, telling them of troubles now past and of my happy prospects; then returned to what had become my greatest pleasure in life – contemplation of the goddess. I managed to obtain the use of a room in the temple precinct and took constant part in her services, which had hitherto been kept private. The brotherhood accepted me almost as one of themselves, a loyal devotee of the great goddess.

Not a single night did I pass, nor even doze off, without some new vision of her. She always ordered me to be initiated into her sacred mysteries, to which I had long been destined. I was anxious to obey, but religious awe held me back, because after making careful inquiries I found that the observances and obligations of chastity were hard and that an initiate has to be continuously on his guard against accidental hazards. Somehow or other, though the question was always with me, I delayed the decision which I was, in fact, rapidly reaching.

One night I dreamed that the priest came to me with his lap full of presents. When I asked: 'What have you there?' he answered: 'Something from Thessaly. Your slave Candidus has just arrived.' When I awoke, I puzzled over the dream for a long time, wondering what it meant, especially as I had never owned a slave of that name. However, I was convinced that whatever the exact significance of the portent, such an offering of gifts certainly foreshadowed something profitable to come. I waited for the opening of the temple in the morning, still in a state of anxious but hopeful expectation. The white curtains of the sanctuary were then drawn, and we adored the august face of the goddess. A priest went the round of the altars, performing the rites with solemn supplications and, cup in hand, poured libations of water drawn from a spring within the sanctuary. When the service was over the devotees saluted the breaking day with the hymn that they sing to announce that this first hour has come.

Then, behold, in came the slaves whom I had left behind at Hypata when Fotis had entangled me in my miserable strayings. They had evidently heard my tale and had brought me my horse, having recovered it after repeated changes of hand by identifying my brand on its haunch. Now I understood the cunning meaning of my dream: not only had the promise of gain been fulfilled, but I had received back my servant Candidus, namely my white horse.[6]

Thereafter I devoted my whole time to attendance on the goddess, encouraged by these tokens to hope for even greater marks of her favour, and my desire to enter the religious life increased. I frequently spoke of it to the priest, begging him to initiate me into the mysteries of the holy night. He was a grave man, remarkable for the strict observance of his religious duties, and checked my restlessness, as parents calm down children who are making unreasonable demands, but gently and kindly. He explained that the day on which someone might be initiated was always indicated by signs from the goddess herself, and that it was she who chose the officiating priest and announced how the incidental expenses of the ceremony were to be paid. In his view I ought to wait with attentive patience and avoid the two extremes of over-eagerness and obstinacy: being neither unresponsive when called nor importunate while awaiting my call. 'No single member of the brotherhood,' he said, 'has ever been so wrong-minded and sacrilegious, in fact so bent on his own destruction, as to partake of the mystery without direct orders from the goddess, and so commit a deadly offence. The rites of initiation approximate to a voluntary death and offer a salvation that remains precarious. So she usually chooses old men who feel that their end is fast approach- ing yet are capable of safely receiving her holy secrets; it is within the power of her divine providence to make them, in a sense, born again and restored to new and healthy life.'

He said, in fact, that I must be content to await definite orders, but agreed that I had been foreordained for the service of the goddess by clear marks of her favour. Meanwhile I must abstain from forbidden food, as the priests did, so that when the time came for me to partake of their most holy mysteries I could enter the sanctuary with unswerving steps.

I accepted his advice and learned to be patient, taking part in the daily services of the temple as calmly and quietly as I knew how, intent on pleasing the goddess. Nor did the saving kindness of the powerful deity deceive me, nor torment me with prolonged postponement. Soon after this she gave me proof of her grace by a midnight vision in which I was plainly told that the day for which I longed, the day on which my greatest wish would be granted, had come at last. I learned that she had ordered her principal priest, Mithras, whose destiny, she said, was linked with mine by planetary sympathy, to officiate at my initiation.

These orders and certain others given me at the same time so exhilarated me that I rose before dawn to tell the priest about them, and reached his door just as he was coming out. I greeted him and was about to beg him more earnestly than ever to allow me to be initiated, as a privilege that was now mine by right, when he spoke first. 'Lucius,' he said, 'how lucky, how blessed you are that the great goddess has graciously deigned to honour you in this way. There is no time to waste. The day for which you prayed so earnestly has dawned. The many-named goddess orders that you should be initiated in her most holy mysteries by my own hands.'

He took me by the hand and led me courteously to the doors of the vast temple, and when they had been opened in the usual solemn way and he had performed the morning sacrifice he went to the sanctuary and took out certain books written in characters unknown to me: some of them animal hieroglyphics, some of them ordinary letters protected against profane prying by having their tops and tails wreathed in knots or rounded like wheels or tangled together in spirals like vine tendrils. From these books he read me out instructions for providing such things as were necessary for my initiation.

I at once went to my friends and asked them to buy part of what I needed, sparing no expense: the rest I went to buy myself.

Then, saying it was the appropriate time, Mithras took me to the nearest baths, attended by a crowd of devotees. There, when I had enjoyed my ordinary bathe, he himself washed and purified me with water, according to the custom, offering up prayers for divine mercy. After this he brought me back to the temple and placed me at the very feet of the goddess.

It was now early afternoon. He gave me certain orders too holy to be spoken of and then commanded me in everyone's hearing to abstain from all but the plainest food for the ten succeeding days, to eat no meat and drink no wine.

I obeyed his instructions in all reverence, and at last the day came for taking my vows. As the sun went down and evening drew in, a crowd of priests came flocking to me from all directions, each one giving me congratulatory gifts, as the ancient custom is. Then, after all uninitiated persons had departed, I was robed in a new linen garment and the priest led me by the hand into the inner recesses of the sanctuary itself. It may well be, studious reader, that you are eager to know what was said and done there. If I were allowed to tell you, and you were allowed to be told, you would soon hear everything; but, as it is, my tongue would suffer for its indiscretion and your ears for their rash inquisitiveness.

However, not wishing to leave you, if you are religiously inclined, in a state of tortured suspense, listen to what I will now say and believe, because it is true. I approached the very gates of death and set one foot on Proserpine's threshold yet was permitted to return, borne through all the elements. At midnight I saw the sun shining as if it were noon: I entered the presence of the gods of the under-world and the gods of the upper world, stood near and worshipped them.

Now I have told you, and you have heard, though you must pretend not to know it. And I will continue, only telling what can be declared, without expiation, to the understanding of the profane.

The solemn rites ended at dawn and I emerged from the sanctuary wearing twelve different stoles, certainly a most sacred costume but one that there can be no harm in my mentioning. Many uninitiated people saw me wearing it when I was ordered to mount into the wooden pulpit which stood in the centre of the temple, immediately in front of the goddess's image. I was wearing a vestment of fine linen embroidered with flowers, and a precious cloak hung down from my shoulders to my ankles with sacred animals worked in colour on every part of it; for instance, Indian dragons and Hyper-borean griffins,[7] which are winged birds generated in the more distant parts of the world. The priests call this scarf an Olympian stole. I held a lighted torch in my right hand and wore a white palm-tree garland on my head, its leaves sticking out all round like rays of light.

The curtains were pulled aside and I was suddenly exposed to the gaze of the crowd, as when a statue is unveiled, dressed like the sun. Then I began to celebrate that most happy birthday of my religious life with a delightful banquet and merry party. Further rites and ceremonies were performed on the third day, including a sacred breakfast, and these ended the proceedings. However, I remained for some days longer in the temple, enjoying the ineffable pleasure of contemplating the goddess's statue, because I was bound to her by a debt of gratitude so large that I could never hope to pay it.

>>>>>><<<<<

CHAPTER XIX

AT THE BAR

At length the goddess advised me to return home. I had thanked her not so much as she deserved but as much as I could, and took time over my leave-taking, because I found it hard to wrench myself away from a place that I had come to love so dearly.

I fell prostrate at the goddess's feet, and washed them with my tears as I prayed to her in a voice choked with sobs which convulsed my speech: 'Holy and perpetual Saviour of Mankind, you whose bountiful grace nourishes the whole world; whose heart turns towards all those in sorrow and tribulation as a mother's to her children; you who take no rest by night, no rest by day, but are always at hand to succour the distressed by land and sea, dispersing the gales that beat upon them. Your hand alone can disentangle the hopelessly knotted skeins of fate, appease the tempests of Fortune and restrain the stars from harmful courses. The gods above adore you, the gods below do homage to you, you set the earth spinning, you give light to the sun, you govern the universe, you trample down the powers of Hell. At your voice the stars move, the seasons recur, the divinities rejoice, the elements obey. At your nod the winds blow, clouds drop wholesome rain, seeds quicken, buds swell. Birds that fly through the air, beasts that prowl on the mountain, serpents that lurk in the dust, all these tremble in awe of your majesty. My eloquence is unequal to praising you according to your deserts; my wealth to providing you with sacrificial victims; my voice to uttering all that I think of your majesty – no, not even if I had a thousand tongues in a thousand mouths and could speak for ever. Nevertheless, poor as I am, I will do as much as I can in my devotion to you; I will keep your divine countenance always before my eyes and the secret knowledge of your divinity locked deep in my heart.'

When I finished this prayer to the great goddess, I went to the priest Mithras, now my spiritual father, clung around his neck and kissed him again and again, begging him to forgive me for not being able to return his kindnesses as they deserved. After a lengthy rendering of thanks, at last I left him. I had decided to go straight home after my long absence. But a few days later the goddess warned me to pack up my things in a hurry and take ship for Rome. The wind blew fair throughout my voyage and I was soon at the Port of Augustus,[1] where I took a fast carriage and reached the Holy City on the evening of December 13th. Every day it was my greatest desire to offer devotion to the mighty divinity of Queen Isis, who under the name of Campensis – because of the site of her temple[2] – is greatly revered there. I was her assiduous worshipper, a stranger to her temple, but familiar to her religion.

The great sun had completed his course around the Zodiac when the kind goddess, who was still watching over me, visited me in a dream and warned me that I must be prepared for a new initiation and a new consecration. I could not make out what I was intended to do, what was supposed to happen. Surely I was fully initiated already? I pondered the question deeply and, in addition, consulted the devotees' council; when it occurred to me, with the force of a surprise, that so far I had been initiated only into the rites of the goddess, not yet into those of the great god and supreme Father of the Gods, the invincible Osiris.[3] Though their divine natures are linked and even united, there is certainly a great difference between the rites of initiation into their separate cults. I guessed that the great god needed me as a servant, and my guess was confirmed without delay. For that very next night I dreamed that a priest of Osiris clothed in white linen came to me bearing staffs intertwined with ivy and vine-shoots[4] and ivy garlands and certain other objects which I am not allowed to mention, and placed them among my household gods. He then sat down in my chair and told me to order a sumptuous religious banquet. I noticed that he walked with a limp, his left ankle being slightly crooked; which I took for a sign that would allow me to recognize him. The will of the gods had now been plainly expressed, and all ambiguities removed. I went off to the temple to pay my daily respects to the goddess, and no sooner had I finished than I looked closely at the priests to see whether any of them walked like him whom I had seen in my dream.

I recognized the man. He was one of the Shrine-bearers, and not only did he show the same lameness, but his height and general appearance corresponded exactly with my vision. It turned out that he was called Asinius Marcellus,[5] a name not irrelevant to my transformation. I went straight to him and found that he knew exactly what I was going to say, because he had been given instructions that matched mine. It seemed to him that the night before, while he was placing garlands on the statue of Osiris, he had been told by the god, who prophesies the futures of all individuals, that he was being sent a man of Madaurus[6] who, though poor, must minister at once to his ritual. The god added that under his divine care this man could achieve fame in a learned profession and that Asinius himself would be richly rewarded for his trouble.

This was how I was dedicated to the rites; unfortunately, much to my disappointment, I could not start work as yet because of lack of funds. The expenses of my voyage had eaten up my small capital, and life in Rome was far more expensive than in the provinces. To be baulked of my wishes by poverty distressed me; in the words of the proverb, I felt as though caught between the victim and the flint.[7] And yet since I was quite often urged on, which disturbed me greatly, and finally given outright orders, I had to sell the robe off my back and, though it was not a particularly good one, managed to scrape together just enough money. The god had said: 'If you wanted to pay for your pleasures would you hesitate for a moment before parting with your clothes? Then why, when about to engage in these great rites, do you hesitate to resign yourself to a poverty of which you will never need repent?'

I made all preparations, spent another ten days without eating meat and had my head completely shaved; after which I was honoured by admission to the nocturnal mysteries of the mighty god. I took part in his service with the confidence that my knowledge of the corresponding rites of Isis gave me. This consoled me for my enforced stay in a country that was not my own and at the same time enabled me to live less frugally: because, by a favourable set of circumstances, I made quite a decent living as a barrister, even though I had to plead in Latin.

Not long afterwards, I was granted yet another vision in which my instructions were to undergo a third initiation. I was surprised and perplexed, not being able to understand what this new and unexpected divine initiative signified and what still remained un-disclosed. 'Surely,' I thought, 'either the priests have given me a false revelation, or else they have held something back.' I confess that I even began to suspect them of cheating me. But while I was still puzzling over the question and driven nearly mad by worry, an apparition explained the case to me in a prophetic nocturnal dream. 'You have no reason,' he said, 'to be alarmed by your order to undergo still another initiation, or to suspect that something has been held back. On the contrary, you ought to be overjoyed at the repeated marks of divine favour shown you, and feel exultant at having been three times granted a favour that few receive even once. Rest assured that the number three will justly bring you everlasting happiness. You will see that the ritual in which you are going to be enrolled is a matter of the utmost necessity, when you consider that the equipment of the goddess, with which you were invested in the province, still remains in the temple there, so that you cannot wear that blessed habit to worship her in Rome on her feast days. Therefore if you wish to enjoy health, happiness and good fortune, treat the great gods as your counsellors and once more, joyfully submit to initiation.'

This holy vision convinced me that it would be to my advantage to obey. Without either neglecting or deferring the business on hand I went straight to the priest and reported my vision. Then I immedi-ately undertook the burden of fasting, this time voluntarily extending my abstinence beyond the ten days that were prescribed, and paid all the costs out of my own pocket, the scale being dictated by my religious zeal rather than by what was required.

I had no reason to repent of the trouble and expense, because by the bounty of the gods the fees that I earned in the courts were quite substantial. Finally, a few days later, the God Osiris, the most powerful of all gods, 'the highest among the greatest, the greatest among the highest, the ruler of the greatest', manifested himself to me in a dream, not disguised but addressing me in his own person, with his own divine mouth. He came to assure me that I was soon to become a famous barrister and that I must not fear the spiteful slanders to which the learning acquired by my difficult studies would expose me; also that he did not wish me to assist in his sacred rites in the company of all the others and had therefore chosen me not only as a member of his Order of Shrine-bearers but as one of his quinquennial councillors.[8]

Once more I shaved my head and happily fulfilled the duties of that ancient association, which was founded in the time of Sulla.[9] Making no attempt to disguise my baldness by wearing a wig or any other covering, I displayed it on all occasions.

THE END

>>>>><<<<<

NOTES

Introduction

1. e.g. Parthenius (who also wrote prose outlines of famous love stories); cf. Nicander, *Heteroioumena*.

2. See Pliny the Younger, *Letters*, II, 20, 1; Lucretius, *De rerum natura*, III, 12.

3. Noted at the appropriate points by P. Vallette in D. S. Robertson and P. Vallette (eds.), *Apulée: Les Métamorphoses*, Paris, 1940–46, 1972, 1985.

4. In his introduction Apuleius half-jokingly describes the book as *Graecanica* – 'adapted from the Greek'.

5. *Lucius, or the Ass* satirizes magicians, corrupt priests, unfaithful wives and gullible or bestial characters.

6. Photius 96b, 18 Bekker (Bibl. Cod. 129, P. Migne, [ed.], *Patrologie grecque*, vol. 330). Lucius of Patrae was the chief character, not the author (Photius).

7. It was strongly argued by B. E. Perry in *The Metamorphoses Ascribed to Lucius of Patrae: Its Content, Nature and Authorship*, Lancaster (Pennsylvania), 1920, and *The Ancient Romances*, Berkeley (California), 1967. Lucian's *True History* (*Vera Historia*; cf. 1.1) is an entertaining parody of the romance of adventure.

8. See A. Scobie, *Apuleius and Folklore*, London, 1983. It is not entirely clear how many of the known folk-tales are earlier or later than Apuleius. His story of Cupid and Psyche could be an adaptation of a work by the little known Aristofontes of Athens (see Fulgentius, *Mythographiae*, 3, 6), who might, however, have been later.

9. Aristides of Miletus (writing in Greek) and Sisenna (writing in Latin) were the most famous exponents (cf. Ovid, *Tristia*, 413f., 443f.). For an account of the low reputation of the Milesian tales see 'Clodius Albinus' in *Scriptores Historiae Augustae*, 12, 12.

10. The principal known Greek novels are by Chariton of Aphrodisias (who probably preceded Apuleius), Achilles Tatius, Heliodorus of Samosata, Longus of Lesbos, Xenophon of Ephesus. Fragments of the earlier *Ninus Romance* and *Joseph and Aseneth* (a Jewish story, see A. Momigliano, *Alien Wisdom*, Cambridge, 1975, pp. 117ff.) have also survived. All these works have been classified as 'ideal' novels, or romances (cf. T. Hägg, *The Novel in Antiquity*, Oxford, 1983, pp. 5ff.). There is a Penguin Classics edition of Longus, *Daphnis and Chloe*, 1956.

11. Translated for Penguin Classics by John Sullivan, 1965.

12. e.g. the *Iolaus* fragment, *Timouphis* and Lollianus' *Phoenicica*; cf. G.

Anderson, *Ancient Fiction*, London, 1984, pp. 152–9, and J. J. Winkler, 'The Novel', in M. Grant and R. Kitzinger (eds.), *The Civilization of the Ancient Mediterranean*, II, New York, 1988, p. 1569.

13. Apuleius' treatment of the bandits is mocking pseudo-epic, relevant in this modern epoch of self-heroizing terrorists.

14. e.g. the ass was the animal of Isis' divine enemy Typhon (Set).

15. G. Anderson, op. cit., stressed these origins – perhaps too much, though informatively.

16. Apuleian allegory is discussed by R. Heine, in B. L. Hijmans, jun., and R. Th. van der Paardt (eds.), *Aspects of Apuleius' Golden Ass*, Groningen, 1978, pp. 32ff. Psyche's pilgrimage is like Plato's pilgrimage of the soul in the *Phaedrus*. The Cupid and Psyche story was given a Jungian interpretation by E. Neumann, *Amor and Psyche: The Psychic Development of the Feminine*, London, 1956.

17. See J. G. Griffith in Hijmans and van der Paardt, op. cit., p. 141, and P. G. Walsh, *The Roman Novel*, Cambridge, 1970, pp. 188ff., on the Isis episode – which is such good evidence for her cult; cf. also Isidorus' *Hymn to Isis* (in J. Tatum, *Apuleius and the Golden Ass*, Ithaca (New York), 1979, pp. 183ff.) and 'Cyme Aretology' (Walsh, op. cit., pp. 252ff.). Apuleius infuses a strong autobiographical note here: he himself was initiated into many religious mysteries (*Apologia*, 55).

18. Fortune is also a dominant concept in Greek novels. Apuleius believed in the intermediate *daimones* – between gods and human beings in status (cf. *On the God of Socrates*, in J. Tatum, op. cit., p. 54) – of whom Cupid was one (cf. p. viii).

19. Middle Platonism was eclectic, and particularly motivated by a revulsion against scepticism. Apuleius called himself, and was called, 'Platonicus' (Saint Augustine, *City of God*, VIII, 12); his Platonism seems elementary, but may have been typical of the second-century sophistic world.

20. Saint Augustine, *City of God*, XVIII, 18. Lactantius (*c.* AD 240–320) had already believed Apuleius to be a diabolically inspired magician.

21. *Curiositas* was much discussed, cf. Plutarch, *Peri Polypragmosynes*, in which he argues that it should be diverted into intellectual enquiry; see P. G. Walsh, *Proceedings of the Classical Association*, lxxxiv, 1987, pp. 17ff., and the index of Hijmans and van der Paardt, op. cit., s.v.

22. On the structure of the work see A. Scobie, op. cit., pp. 43ff.

23. See note 20.

24. In Italy M. M. Boiardo's translation of the *Metamorphoses* was published posthumously in *c.* 1518.

25. The most famous work of art illustrating the story is Raphael's ceiling-painting in the Villa Farnesina, Rome.

26. All this makes the establishment of the correct text a problem; on its history

see D. S. Robertson in *Apulée: Les Métamorphoses* (op. cit.), pp. xxxviiiff. The *Florida* has quite a different style: calm, polished and stately.

27. Although Apuleius ironically described himself as half-Numidian and half-Gaetulian (*Apologia*, 23), the theory that this was an 'African' style is misguided. Africa (and especially Carthage) was in fact one of the Empire's principal Latin cultural centres (and the nursery of lawyers, Juvenal, *Satires*, VII, 148). Whether Latin, however, was Apuleius' *first* language, we cannot determine; that of his stepson Pudens was Punic.

28. Robert Graves, Introduction to Lucius Apuleius, *The Golden Ass*, Penguin Classics, Harmondsworth, 1988 (first published 1950), pp. 7–8.

29. Michael Grant, Introduction to Tacitus, *Annals of Imperial Rome*, Penguin Classics, revised edn 1989, p. 26.

30. W. Radice and B. Reynolds (eds.), *The Translator's Art: Essays in Honour of B. Radice*, Harmondsworth, 1987, p. 86.

31. cf. the comments of P. Vallette, *Apulée: Les Métamorphoses* (op. cit.), p. xxxvi, and J. Tatum, op. cit., p. 161.

32. Robert Graves, Introduction to Lucius Apuleius, *The Golden Ass*, op. cit., p. 8.

Apuleius' Address to the Reader

1. *Milesian story.* For the popular, scabrous 'Milesian tales', see the Introduction, section 3, p. xii.

2. *convention.* Apuleius writes, literally, of 'Egyptian papyrus inscribed with the sharpness [*argutia*] of a Nilotic reed'. There has been much speculation about what he is referring to, but there were Egyptian stories of metamorphoses, and the climax of the work is his initiation into the rites of the Egyptian goddess Isis; *argutia* also means cleverness.

3. *Quirites.* Roman citizens.

4. *a rider vaulting from one horse to another.* The *desultor*, in circus games.

I The Story of Aristomenes

1. *Plutarch ... Sextus.* Plutarch: the philosopher and biographer, from Chaeronea (born before AD 50, died after AD 120). Sextus: Platonist, teacher of the Emperors Marcus Aurelius (161–80) and Lucius Verus (161–9).

2. *Painted Porch.* The Stoa Poikile in the Market-place (Agora).

3. *God of Medicine.* Aesculapius (Asclepius).

4. *Ethiopians.* A distinction was made between eastern and western Ethiopian races.
   Antichthones. People of Sri Lanka; the name ('antipodes') suggests the inhabitants of another land-mass in the southern hemisphere, balancing our own.

5. *Corinth.* According to Euripides' *Medea*.

NOTES

6. *Endymion*. A beautiful young man, either a king of Elis or a Carian, loved by the Moon-goddess (the Roman Luna or the Greek Selene), who was identified with Diana (Artemis).

   Ganymede. A beautiful royal Trojan youth, carried off by an eagle to become Jupiter's catamite (from *Catamitus*, his Latin name) and cupbearer.

7. *island*. Calypso's mythical island, on which Ulysses (Odysseus) stayed for more than seven years in Homer's *Odyssey*, was Ogygia.

8. *Lamiae*. Witches believed to suck the blood of children.

II At Milo's House

1. *Hecale*. A goddess worshipped with Zeus Hecalos in the Athenian deme Hecale; said to have been an old woman who entertained King Theseus of Athens when he was on his way to fight the Marathon bull.

2. *drachmae*. The silver Roman *denarius* was equated with the Greek *drachma*; there were twenty-five to the gold *aureus*. *Nummus* stands for *sestertius*; there were four to the *denarius*.

3. *aedile*. Roman colonies and *municipia* were governed by two annually elected *duoviri* and two *aediles*, but here the term is used loosely, probably to translate the Greek *agoranomos*, inspector of markets.

4. *fish . . . pavement*. Apuleius was interested in different fish and wrote a treatise on them. The trampling of fish played a part in Egyptian religious ritual.

5. *people in feathered disguise*. A reference to mythological Procne and Philomela, who were turned into a nightingale and a swallow (or vice versa), and to Tereus, who was transformed into a hoopoe.

6. *goddess . . . about to bathe*. Actaeon came upon Diana (Artemis) as she was bathing with her nymphs on Mount Cithaeron.

7. *sea foam*. The Greeks derived the name of Aphrodite (Venus) from *aphros*, 'foam', with reference to her birth from the sea-foam.

8. *her own husband*. Vulcan (Hephaestus) was variously described as the lover or husband of Venus. Alternatively, Mars (Ares) was said to be her husband.

9. *God of Wine*. Bacchus or Liber (Dionysus in Greek).

10. *Lake of Avernus*. Lake Avernus in Campania was believed to be one of the entrances to the Underworld (the Greek Hades or the Roman Orcus).

11. *Sibyl*. Ten Sibyls, female prophets, were listed by the Roman scholar Varro, and a number of others were also named.

12. *Assyrian astrologer*. The Chaldaei (originally from Chaldaea, beside southern Babylonia and the Persian Gulf) cast horoscopes, and gave their name to all diviners.

13. *without official permission*. Wars were declared by the proclamation of the *fetialis*.

III The Story of Thelyphron

1. *province*. Thessaly belonged to the province of Achaia (Greece) from the time of Augustus, and then to the province of Macedonia from the Antonine period (second century AD).

2. *Lynceus*. The look-out man of the Argonauts.
   Argus. The hundred-eyed keeper of Io, after she was changed into a heifer by Jupiter.

3. *Aonian ... Pimpleia*. 'Aonian' is a poetic term for Boeotian; this 'proud young Aonian' refers to the mythological Pentheus of Thebes. Orpheus, here named after his birthplace or place of residence, Pi(m)pleia (Dium), a place or fountain in Pieria (Macedonia) sacred to the Muses, was said to have been torn to pieces by Thracian women.

4. *temples of Coptos ... the sacred rattle of Pharos*. These are probably references to the cult of Isis. The God Min at Coptos was her protector; she had a temple at Memphis; and the rattle of Pharos (an island off Alexandria) was her sacred *sistrum*.

5. *Laughter Day*. Some dismiss the Festival of Laughter (*Risus*) as a fiction, but it has been plausibly related to the authentic Festival of the Hilaria at Rome; and the Spartans, too, had a cult of laughter.

6. *Geryon*. Geryon, slain by Hercules (Heracles), was considered to have either three heads or the bodies of three men from the waist down (this is the version that Apuleius favours later).

IV The Festival of Laughter

1. *lictors*. The lictors were the attendants of Roman magistrates.
2. *clock*. The water-clock (*clepsydra*).
3. *Ajax*. Ajax, the son of Telamon, went mad and slaughtered cattle, believing that they were his enemies.
4. *Cerberus*. The three- (or fifty-) headed watchdog of Hades (Orcus).

V Lucius is Transformed

1. *Hospitable Jupiter*. Hospitalis ('hospitable') was one of the epithets for Jupiter.
2. *Epona*. The patron goddess of horses and stables.
3. *Graces*. The three Graces (*Gratiae* or *Charites*) were the daughters of Jupiter and Eurynome.
4. *Goddess Fortune*. Fortuna (Tyche), in both her good and evil aspects, plays an important part in this book, as in other ancient novels (p. xiii).

VI The Bandits' Cave

1. *Lapiths and . . . Centaurs.* The wedding banquet of Pirithous and Hippodamia was broken up by a brawl between the Lapiths and Centaurs.
2. *sea.* Characteristically, Apuleius does not care that the sea is a long way from Thebes.
3. *Eubulus.* 'Good counsellor'.
4. *a banquet of the Salian College at Rome.* An ancient Italian priestly brotherhood, which feasted after its ritual processions.
5. *Attis or Protesilaus.* The text is not specific about these allusions. Attis castrated himself on his wedding day, and the marriage of Laodamia and Protesilaus was interrupted when he was called away to fight at Troy.

VII Cupid and Psyche [I]

1. *Paphos . . . Cythera.* Paphos (Cyprus), Cnidus (Caria) and Cythera (an island off the Peloponnese) were famous centres of the worship of Venus (Aphrodite).
2. *Nereids . . . Palaemon.* The Nereids, the fifty daughters of Nereus, were sea-nymphs. Portunus, originally a god of doors (*portae*), was equated with Palaemon (Melicertes), who came to the aid of sailors. Salacia was a cult-partner of Neptune (Poseidon).
3. *Milesian tale.* See Introduction, section 3, p. xii. Robert Graves mistranslated this phrase as 'the true founder of Miletus'.
4. *Lydian lament.* The Lydian mode of music was plaintive, and considered lax and effeminate.

VIII Cupid and Psyche [II]

1. *Pan . . . Echo.* Pan, the son of Mercury, was native to Arcadia. Echo was a mountain nymph (Oread) whom he vainly loved.

IX Cupid and Psyche [III]

1. *Seasons.* The *Horae*, daughters of Justice (according to Hesiod), who roll aside the veil of clouds from the gate of Olympus (according to Homer).
2. *Ceres and Juno.* Ceres is the Greek Demeter, the Corn-goddess; Juno is the wife of Jupiter (the Greek Hera).
3. *Proserpine.* Proserpine or Proserpina (the Greek Persephone) was seized by Pluto (Hades) at Henna in Sicily.
4. *Carthage . . . chariot.* The Punic goddess Tanit (the Roman Dea Caelestis) was identified with Juno.

5. *Zygia . . . Protectress.* Psyche appeals to Juno in her three-fold aspect: Zygia (Goddess of Marriage), Lucina (of Childbirth) and Sospita (the Protectress).

6. *consent.* A joint rescript of Marcus Aurelius and Commodus ordained that property owners must give up slaves; so did the *Digest*, of which a chapter dealt with the subject.

7. *Arcadia.* Hermes (Mercury), the son of Maia, was said to have been born on Mount Cyllene in Arcadia.

8. *Rome.* The *metae Murciae* (in the Murcian valley) were the southern turning-posts of the Circus Maximus. Apuleius was evidently writing for a Roman public.

9. *hoarse River of Cocytus.* Cocytus is Greek for 'wailing'.

10. *Phrygian cup-bearer to Jupiter.* Ganymede (see above, ch. I, note 6).

11. *Lacedaemon.* Sparta.

12. *Taenarus.* Taenarus (Cape Matapan) was described by Virgil and Horace as an entrance to the Underworld (Orcus). Dis is Pluto.

13. *Julian edict.* Augustus' *Lex Julia de adulteriis coercendis* was passed in 17 BC, designed to check adultery.

14. *Satyrus and Paniscus.* Satyrus stands for the satyrs, woodland spirits in the form of men with some animal features. Paniscus, 'little Pan', was another deity.

X Defeat of the Bandits

1. *Dirce.* Dirce was killed by being tied by her hair to a wild bull in revenge for her similar cruelty to her rival Antiope.

2. *Phrixus . . . swimming.* A ram with a golden fleece saved Phrixus from death by carrying him across the Hellespont (Dardanelles). Arion, the great singer, was carried to Taenarus by a dolphin. Europa was taken to Crete on the back of a bull (Jupiter or his envoy).

3. *Pegasus.* A winged horse that was ridden by Bellerophon of Corinth and later carried thunderbolts for Jupiter.

4. *use my carcase . . . Charite's ghost.* It was believed that the ghost of a victim haunted its killer. Thus the robbers, by using Lucius' carcase to achieve Charite's death, are transferring the guilt of her death to him.

5. *Bactrian camel.* The two-humped 'Bactrian' camel came from central Asia, India and China.

XI At the Farms

1. *that king of Thrace . . . human flesh.* The capture of the man-eating horses of Diomedes, King of the Bistones in Thrace, was the eighth Labour of Hercules.

2. *Althaea . . . Meleager.* Enraged by her son Meleager's murder of his brothers, Althaea took the brand which the Fates had said was the key to his life and threw it into the fire, whereupon he died.

3. *Bacchant.* Maenad; devotee of Bacchus.

4. *Thrasyllus, true to his name.* Thrasyllus comes from the Greek *thrasus*, 'bold'.

XII With the Effeminate Priests

1. *the fire-breathing Chimaera.* A triple-bodied monster, killed by Bellerophon.

2. *Syrian Goddess.* Atargatis or Derceto of Hierapolis (Bambyce), consort of Hadad; often identified with Venus (Aphrodite). Her priests (better described, perhaps, as temple attendants or wandering mendicants) were generally self-castrated; Apuleius prefers to concentrate on their effeminacy.

3. *Cornelian law.* Unknown; maybe imaginary.

4. *Sabazius . . . eyes.* Sabazius was a Thraco–Phrygian god especially venerated in Phrygia and Lydia. Bellona was the Roman War-goddess. The Idaean Mother was Cybele, worshipped on Mount Ida in the Troad (north-western Asia Minor) or Crete. Adonis was a hero of Asian origin loved by Venus.

5. *hind which took the place of a maiden.* A reference to one of Euripides' two alternative versions of the story of Iphigenia, the daughter of Agamemnon, according to which, instead of being sacrificed at Aulis in Greece, so that the Greek fleet should be able to sail for Troy, she was transplanted to Tauris (the Crimea), a hind being miraculously substituted for her on the altar.

6. *Phrygian music.* A sober mode of music which Plato admitted to his ideal Republic but which Aristotle would not include in his educational system.

XIII At the Mill-House

1. *Homer characterized the man . . . peoples.* Ulysses (Odysseus); cf. Homer, *Odyssey*, I, 1–3.

2. *cult of an 'Only God'.* This has been widely interpreted as a criticism of Christianity, which it may well be, though it is also possible that Apuleius had Judaism in mind.

3. *decurion.* Town-councillor.

4. *Ocean.* Oceanus was the river that encompassed the earth.

XIV With the Gardener and the Soldier

1. *stades.* The Attic stade measured 194.3 yards and the Roman stade 185.

2. *that well-known proverb.* In the Greek original, apparently, the crowd saw the ass's head, and the author remarked that this was the origin of the well-known proverb 'from the peep of an ass' (referring to an ass that 'peeped'

into a shop-window and broke some pots, causing a lawsuit). But Apuleius makes the crowd only see the ass's shadow, so that he introduces a second proverb, quoted by Plato and Menander, about 'the shadow of an ass' (in which the driver of an ass refused to let a traveller who had hired the ass take his siesta in the animal's shadow, since had he had not paid for the shadow; they fought and both died).

XV At the Councillor's House

1. *tragic buskin*. The half-boot or high sock worn by actors in Greek tragedy.
2. *Areopagus*. The ancient State Council, and subsequently Homicide Court, in Athens.
3. *iron ring*. Slaves only had the right to wear an iron ring.

XVI Under the Trainer

1. *savings*. *Peculium* was the capital that slaves could save up, often with a view to buying their freedom.
2. *Eteocles*. Eteocles and Polynices were the two sons of Oedipus, who killed one another in their war to succeed him at Thebes.
3. *Phineus*. The soothsayer Phineus, blinded by the gods, had his food stolen or defiled by the Harpies, bird-like female monsters.
4. *quinquennial magistrate*. In every fifth year the *duoviri*, who were the principal officials in the Roman colonies and *municipia*, received the additional and more honorific title of *quinquennales*.
5. *Pasiphae*. Mother of the Minotaur.
6. *amphitheatre*. Although 'amphitheatre' is assumed, Apuleius does not specify, however, whether the show was to take place in an amphitheatre, theatre or a circus.

XVII The Goddess Isis Intervenes

1. *Pyrrhic dance*. A dance in armour; the term was applied to various kinds of performance.
2. *Minerva*. The Greek Pallas Athene.
3. *egg-shaped*. A reference to the egg of Leda, from which Pollux and Helen were born.
4. *Ionian mode*. Rejected by Plato as effeminate.
5. *Dorian mode*. Accepted by Plato as manly; the only musical mode included by Aristotle in his educational scheme.
6. *false insinuations*. Ulysses (Odysseus) had forged a letter from Priam, King of Troy, to Palamedes, arranging for him to betray the Greeks, and hid a

NOTES

sum of gold in his tent, upon which evidence Palamedes was condemned to death.

7. *Socrates ... living men.* The authenticity of this story about Socrates is sometimes doubted.

8. *Pythagoras ... occasions.* Pythagoras of Samos, who emigrated to Croton in c. 531 BC, to a large extent based his philosophical system on numbers.

9. *Sister of Phoebus Apollo.* Artemis (Diana).

10. *Goddess of Pessinus ... trilingual Sicilians.* Pessinus: temple city in Galatia, now Balhisar. Cecrops: the mythical first king of Athens. Dictynna: named after Mount Dicte in Crete, identified with various goddesses including Diana (Artemis) and Isis. Trilingual Sicilians: speaking Greek, Punic and Sicel.

11. *Hecate ... Goddess of Rhamnus.* Hecate: an Underworld goddess, worshipped at the cross-roads because these were believed to be haunted. Goddess of Rhamnus: Rhamnus was in Attica; this is also a title of the Goddess Nemesis.

12. *the most hateful beast in the universe.* The ass was one of various animals suggested as the prototype of the monstrous Egyptian demon-god Typhon-Set, who murdered Isis' partner, Osiris; Plutarch also seems to link the animal with Typhon.

XVIII The Ass is Transformed

1. *Serapis.* According to Tacitus and Plutarch, Serapis was brought to Egypt from Sinope by Ptolemy I.

2. *the most powerful deities.* Serapis and Isis.

3. *palm-branch.* Anubis was an Egyptian god of the dead, identified by the Greeks with Hermes-Mercury, the 'conductor of souls'.

4. *Shrine-bearers.* The Shrine-bearers (*pastophori*) were an order of Isiac priests who carried miniature temples in processions.

5. *Order of Knights.* The *equites*, an equestrian order.

6. *Candidus, namely my white horse.* The Latin for 'white' is *candidus*.

7. *Hyperborean griffins.* The Hyperboreans were a legendary race of Apollo-worshippers living in the far north; the griffin was a fabulous monster, part eagle and part lion.

XIX At the Bar

1. *Port of Augustus.* Portus Augusti, beside Ostia.

2. *site of her temple.* Isis was known as Campensis because her temple in Rome was in the Campus Martius (Field of Mars).

3. *Osiris.* Osiris, who reigned in the Underworld, was associated with Isis in the liturgical and ritual drama. He did not have a separate clergy in Rome.

4. *staffs intertwined with ivy and vine-shoots.* Bacchic staffs or *thyrsi.*
5. *Asinius Marcellus.* The name 'Asinius Marcellus' recalls *asinus,* ass.
6. *Madaurus.* By a slip (intentional?), Lucius is described as a man of Madaurus – Apuleius' home town – and no longer of Corinth (see Introduction, section 3, p. xv).
7. *flint.* The old sacrificial knife was made of stone.
8. *quinquennial councillors.* The temple functionaries (*quinquennales*) derived their titles from those of the administrators of Roman towns, with whom they may have been equated in rank (see ch. XVI, note 4).
9. *Sulla.* The dictator Lucius Cornelius Sulla, 82–79 BC.

>>>>><<<<<

SOME BOOKS

G. Anderson, *Ancient Fiction: The Novel in the Graeco-Roman World*, London, 1984.

G. Anderson, *Eros Sophistes: Ancient Novelists at Play*, Chico (California), 1982.

R. Beaton (ed.), *The Greek Novel AD 1–1985*, Bristol, 1988.

G. Day, *From Fiction to the Novel*, London, 1987.

D. Fehling, *Amor und Psyche*, Mainz, 1977.

G. F. Gianotti, *Romanzo e ideologia: studi sulle Metamorfosi di Apuleio*, Naples, 1986.

J. G. Griffiths, *The Isis Book*, Leiden, 1975.

T. Hägg, *Eros und Tyche: Der Roman in der antiken Welt*, Zabern, 1987.

T. Hägg, *The Novel in Antiquity*, Oxford, 1983.

E. H. Haight, *Apuleius and his Influence*, New York, 1927.

J. A. Hanson, *Apuleius: Metamorphoses* (Loeb edn), 2 vols., Cambridge (Massachusetts), 1989.

A. Heiserman, *The Novel Before the Novel: Essays and Discussions About the Beginnings of Prose Fiction in the West*, Chicago, 1977.

B. L. Hijmans, jun., and R. Th. van der Paardt (eds.), *Aspects of Apuleius' Golden Ass*, Groningen, 1978.

P. James, *Unity in Diversity: A Study of Apuleius' Metamorphoses with Particular Reference to the Narrator's Art of Transformation and the Metamorphosis Motif in the Tale of Cupid and Psyche*, Hildesheim, 1987.

D. Londey and C. Johanson, *The Logic of Apuleius*, Leiden, 1987.

B. E. Perry, *The Ancient Romances*, Berkeley (California), 1967.

L. C. Purser, *The Story of Cupid and Psyche as Related by Apuleius*, London, 1910, revised edn, New Rochelle (New York), 1983.

B. P. Reardon (ed.), *The Ancient Greek Novels*, Berkeley (California), 1989.

B. P. Reardon (ed.), *Erotica Antiqua*, Bangor, 1976.

D. S. Robertson and P. Vallette (eds.), *Apulée: Les Métamorphoses*, Paris, 1940–46, 1972, 1985.

C. C. Schlam, *Cupid and Psyche: Apuleius and the Monuments*, University Park (Pennsylvania), 1976.

A. Scobie, *Apuleius and Folklore*, London, 1983.

A. Scobie, *Aspects of the Ancient Romance and its Heritage*, Meisenheim am Glan, 1969.

J. Tatum, 'Apuleius', in T. J. Luce (ed.), *Ancient Writers: Greece and Rome*, II, New York, 1982.

J. Tatum, *Apuleius and the Golden Ass*, Ithaca (New York), 1979.

S. Trenkner, *The Greek Novella in the Classical Period*, Cambridge, 1958.

P. G. Walsh, 'Apuleius', in E. J. Kenney and W. V. Clausen (eds.), *Cambridge History of Classical Literature*, II, Cambridge, 1982.

P. G. Walsh, *The Roman Novel: The Satyricon of Petronius and the Metamorphoses of Apuleius*, Cambridge, 1970.

I. Watt, *The Rise of the Novel*, London, 1957.

J. J. Winkler, *Auctor and Actor: A Narratological Reading of Apuleius' Golden Ass*, Berkeley (California), 1985.

J. J. Winkler, 'The Novel', in M. Grant and R. Kitzinger (eds.), *The Civilization of the Ancient Mediterranean*, II, New York, 1988.

R. E. Witt, *Isis in the Graeco-Roman World*, London, 1971.

>>>><<<<<

INDEX

INDEX

READ MORE IN PENGUIN

In every corner of the world, on every subject under the sun, Penguin represents quality and variety – the very best in publishing today.

For complete information about books available from Penguin – including Puffins, Penguin Classics and Arkana – and how to order them, write to us at the appropriate address below. Please note that for copyright reasons the selection of books varies from country to country.

In the United Kingdom: Please write to *Dept. JC, Penguin Books Ltd, FREEPOST, West Drayton, Middlesex UB7 0BR*

If you have any difficulty in obtaining a title, please send your order with the correct money, plus ten per cent for postage and packaging, to *PO Box No. 11, West Drayton, Middlesex UB7 0BR*

In the United States: Please write to *Penguin USA Inc., 375 Hudson Street, New York, NY 10014*

In Canada: Please write to *Penguin Books Canada Ltd, 10 Alcorn Avenue, Suite 300, Toronto, Ontario M4V 3B2*

In Australia: Please write to *Penguin Books Australia Ltd, 487 Maroondah Highway, Ringwood, Victoria 3134*

In New Zealand: Please write to *Penguin Books (NZ) Ltd, 182–190 Wairau Road, Private Bag, Takapuna, Auckland 9*

In India: Please write to *Penguin Books India Pvt Ltd, 706 Eros Apartments, 56 Nehru Place, New Delhi 110 019*

In the Netherlands: Please write to *Penguin Books Netherlands B.V., Keizersgracht 231 NL–1016 DV Amsterdam*

In Germany: Please write to *Penguin Books Deutschland GmbH, Friedrichstrasse 10–12, W–6000 Frankfurt/Main 1*

In Spain: Please write to *Penguin Books S. A., C. San Bernardo 117–6° E–28015 Madrid*

In Italy: Please write to *Penguin Italia s.r.l., Via Felice Casati 20, I–20124 Milano*

In France: Please write to *Penguin France S. A., 17 rue Lejeune, F–31000 Toulouse*

In Japan: Please write to *Penguin Books Japan, Ishikiribashi Building, 2–5–4, Suido, Tokyo 112*

In Greece: Please write to *Penguin Hellas Ltd, Dimocritou 3, GR–106 71 Athens*

In South Africa: Please write to *Longman Penguin Southern Africa (Pty) Ltd, Private Bag X08, Bertsham 2013*

READ MORE IN PENGUIN

PENGUIN CLASSICS

Aeschylus	The Oresteian Trilogy (Agamemnon/The Choephori/The Eumenides)
	Prometheus Bound/The Suppliants/Seven Against Thebes/The Persians
Aesop	Fables
Ammianus Marcellinus	The Later Roman Empire (AD 353–378)
Apollonius of Rhodes	The Voyage of Argo
Apuleius	The Golden Ass
Aristophanes	The Knights/Peace/The Birds/The Assembly Women/Wealth
	Lysistrata/The Acharnians/The Clouds/ The Wasps/The Poet and the Women/The Frogs
Aristotle	The Athenian Constitution
	The Ethics
	The Politics
	De Anima
Arrian	The Campaigns of Alexander
Saint Augustine	City of God
	Confessions
Boethius	The Consolation of Philosophy
Caesar	The Civil War
	The Conquest of Gaul
Catullus	Poems
Cicero	The Murder Trials
	The Nature of the Gods
	On the Good Life
	Selected Letters
	Selected Political Speeches
	Selected Works
Euripides	Alcestis/Iphigenia in Tauris/Hippolytus
	The Bacchae/Ion/The Women of Troy/Helen
	Medea/Hecabe/Electra/Heracles
	Orestes/The Children of Heracles/ Andromache/The Suppliant Women/ The Phoenician Women/Iphigenia in Aulis

READ MORE IN PENGUIN

PENGUIN CLASSICS

Hesiod/Theognis	Theogony and Works and Days/Elegies
Hippocrates	Hippocratic Writings
Homer	The Iliad
	The Odyssey
Horace	Complete Odes and Epodes
Horace/Persius	Satires and Epistles
Juvenal	Sixteen Satires
Livy	The Early History of Rome
	Rome and Italy
	Rome and the Mediterranean
	The War with Hannibal
Lucretius	On the Nature of the Universe
Marcus Aurelius	Meditations
Martial	Epigrams
Ovid	The Erotic Poems
	The Metamorphoses
Pausanias	Guide to Greece (in two volumes)
Petronius/Seneca	The Satyricon/The Apocolocyntosis
Pindar	The Odes
Plato	Early Socratic Dialogues
	Gorgias
	The Last Days of Socrates (Euthyphro/ The Apology/Crito/Phaedo)
	The Laws
	Phaedrus and Letters VII and VIII
	Philebus
	Protagoras and Meno
	The Republic
	The Symposium
	Theaetetus
Plautus	The Pot of Gold/The Prisoners/ The Brothers Menaechmus/ The Swaggering Soldier/Pseudolus
	The Rope/Amphitryo/The Ghost/ A Three-Dollar Day

READ MORE IN PENGUIN

PENGUIN CLASSICS

Pliny	The Letters of the Younger Pliny
Plutarch	The Age of Alexander (Nine Greek Lives)
	The Fall of the Roman Republic (Six Lives)
	The Makers of Rome (Nine Lives)
	The Rise and Fall of Athens (Nine Greek Lives)
	On Sparta
Polybius	The Rise of the Roman Empire
Procopius	The Secret History
Propertius	The Poems
Quintus Curtius Rufus	The History of Alexander
Sallust	The Jugurthine War and The Conspiracy of Cataline
Seneca	Four Tragedies and Octavia
	Letters from a Stoic
Sophocles	Electra/Women of Trachis/Philoctetes/Ajax
	The Theban Plays (King Oedipus/Oedipus at Colonus/Antigone)
Suetonius	The Twelve Caesars
Tacitus	The Agricola and The Germania
	The Annals of Imperial Rome
	The Histories
Terence	The Comedies (The Girl from Andros/The Self-Tormentor/The Eunuch/Phormio/The Mother-in-Law/The Brothers)
Thucydides	The History of the Peloponnesian War
Tibullus	The Poems and The Tibullan Collection
Virgil	The Aeneid
	The Eclogues
	The Georgics
Xenophon	A History of My Times
	The Persian Expedition

READ MORE IN PENGUIN

PENGUIN CLASSICS

Honoré de Balzac	The Black Sheep
	The Chouans
	Cousin Bette
	Eugénie Grandet
	Lost Illusions
	Old Goriot
	Ursule Mirouet
Corneille	The Cid/Cinna/The Theatrical Illusion
Alphonse Daudet	Letters from My Windmill
René Descartes	Discourse on Method and Other Writings
Denis Diderot	Jacques the Fatalist
Gustave Flaubert	Madame Bovary
	Sentimental Education
	Three Tales
Marie de France	Lais
Jean Froissart	The Chronicles
Théophile Gautier	Mademoiselle de Maupin
Edmond and Jules de Goncourt	Germinie Lacerteux
La Fontaine	Selected Fables
Guy de Maupassant	Bel-Ami
	Pierre and Jean
	Selected Short Stories
	A Woman's Life

READ MORE IN PENGUIN

PENGUIN CLASSICS

Molière	The Misanthrope/The Sicilian/Tartuffe/A Doctor in Spite of Himself/The Imaginary Invalid
	The Miser/The Would-be Gentleman/That Scoundrel Scapin/Love's the Best Doctor/Don Juan
Michel de Montaigne	Essays
Marguerite de Navarre	The Heptameron
Blaise Pascal	Pensées
Marcel Proust	Against Saint-Beuve
Rabelais	The Histories of Gargantua and Pantagruel
Racine	Andromache/Britannicus/Berenice Iphigenia/Phaedra/Athaliah
Arthur Rimbaud	Collected Poems
Jean-Jacques Rousseau	The Confessions
	A Discourse on Equality
	The Social Contract
Jacques Saint-Pierre	Paul and Virginia
Madame de Sevigné	Selected Letters
Voltaire	Candide
	Philosophical Dictionary
Émile Zola	La Bête Humaine
	Germinal
	Nana
	Thérèse Raquin

READ MORE IN PENGUIN

PENGUIN CLASSICS

Pedro de Alarcón	The Three-Cornered Hat and Other Stories
Leopoldo Alas	La Regenta
Ludovico Ariosto	Orlando Furioso
Giovanni Boccaccio	The Decameron
Baldassar Castiglione	The Book of the Courtier
Benvenuto Cellini	Autobiography
Miguel de Cervantes	Don Quixote
	Exemplary Stories
Dante	The Divine Comedy (in 3 volumes)
	La Vita Nuova
Bernal Diaz	The Conquest of New Spain
Carlo Goldoni	Four Comedies (The Venetian Twins/The Artful Widow/Mirandolina/The Superior Residence)
Niccolò Machiavelli	The Discourses
	The Prince
Alessandro Manzoni	The Betrothed
Benito Pérez Galdós	Fortunata and Jacinta
Giorgio Vasari	Lives of the Artists (in 2 volumes)

and

Five Italian Renaissance Comedies (Machiavelli/**The Mandragola**; Ariosto/**Lena**; Aretino/**The Stablemaster**; Gl'Intronati/**The Deceived**; Guarini/**The Faithful Shepherd**)
The Jewish Poets of Spain
The Poem of the Cid
Two Spanish Picaresque Novels (Anon/**Lazarillo de Tormes**; de Quevedo/**The Swindler**)

READ MORE IN PENGUIN

PENGUIN CLASSICS

Bashō	The Narrow Road to the Deep North
	On Love and Barley
Cao Xuequin	The Story of the Stone *also known as* The
	Dream of the Red Chamber (in five volumes)
Confucius	The Analects
Khayyam	The Ruba'iyat of Omar Khayyam
Lao Tzu	Tao Te Ching
Li Po/Tu Fu	Li Po and Tu Fu
Sei Shōnagon	The Pillow Book of Sei Shōnagon
Wang Wei	Poems

ANTHOLOGIES AND ANONYMOUS WORKS

The Bhagavad Gita
Buddhist Scriptures
The Dhammapada
Hindu Myths
The Koran
New Songs from a Jade Terrace
The Rig Veda
Six Yuan Plays
Speaking of Śiva
Tales from the Thousand and One Nights
The Upanishads